CRYSTAL CAGED

AIR AWAKENS: VORTEX CHRONICLES

BOOK FIVE

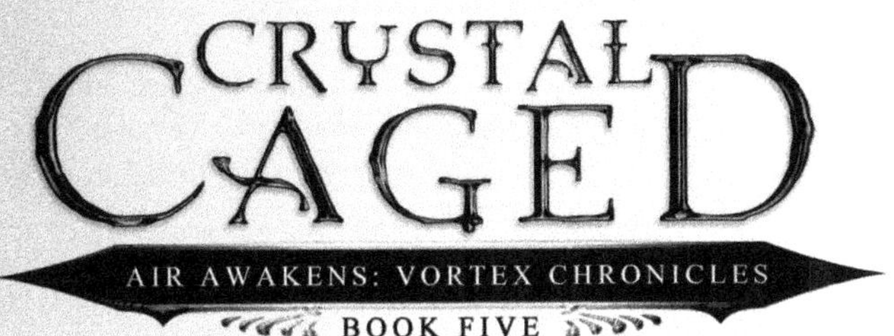

CRYSTAL CAGED
AIR AWAKENS: VORTEX CHRONICLES
BOOK FIVE

ELISE KOVA

Silver Wing Press

Published by Silver Wing Press
Copyright © 2020 by Elise Kova

Cover Artwork by Livia Prima
Editing by Rebecca Faith Editorial
Proofreading by Kate Anderson

eISBN: 978-1-949694-16-1
ISBN (paperback): 978-1-949694-17-8
ISBN (hardcover): 978-1-949694-18-5

Books in the Air Awakens Universe

AIR AWAKENS SERIES
Air Awakens
Fire Falling
Earth's End
Water's Wrath
Crystal Crowned

GOLDEN GUARD TRILOGY
The Crown's Dog
The Prince's Rogue
The Farmer's War

VORTEX CHRONICLES
Vortex Visions
Chosen Champion
Failed Future
Sovereign Sacrifice
Crystal Caged

A TRIAL OF SORCERERS
A Trial of Sorcerers

Also by Elise Kova

LOOM SAGA
The Alchemists of Loom
The Dragons of Nova
The Rebels of Gold

MARRIED TO MAGIC
A Deal with the Elf King

See all books and learn more at:
http://www.EliseKova.com

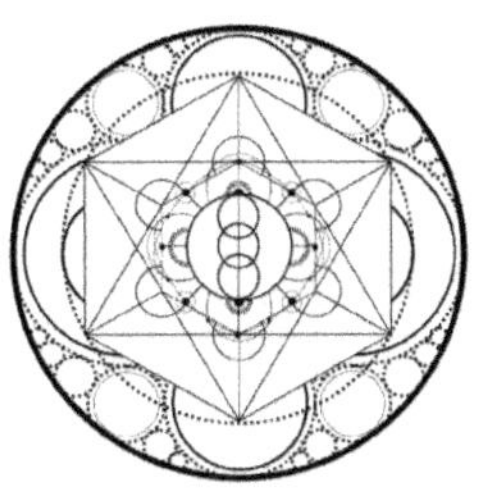

*for the Man
my muse, my light*

TABLE OF CONTENTS

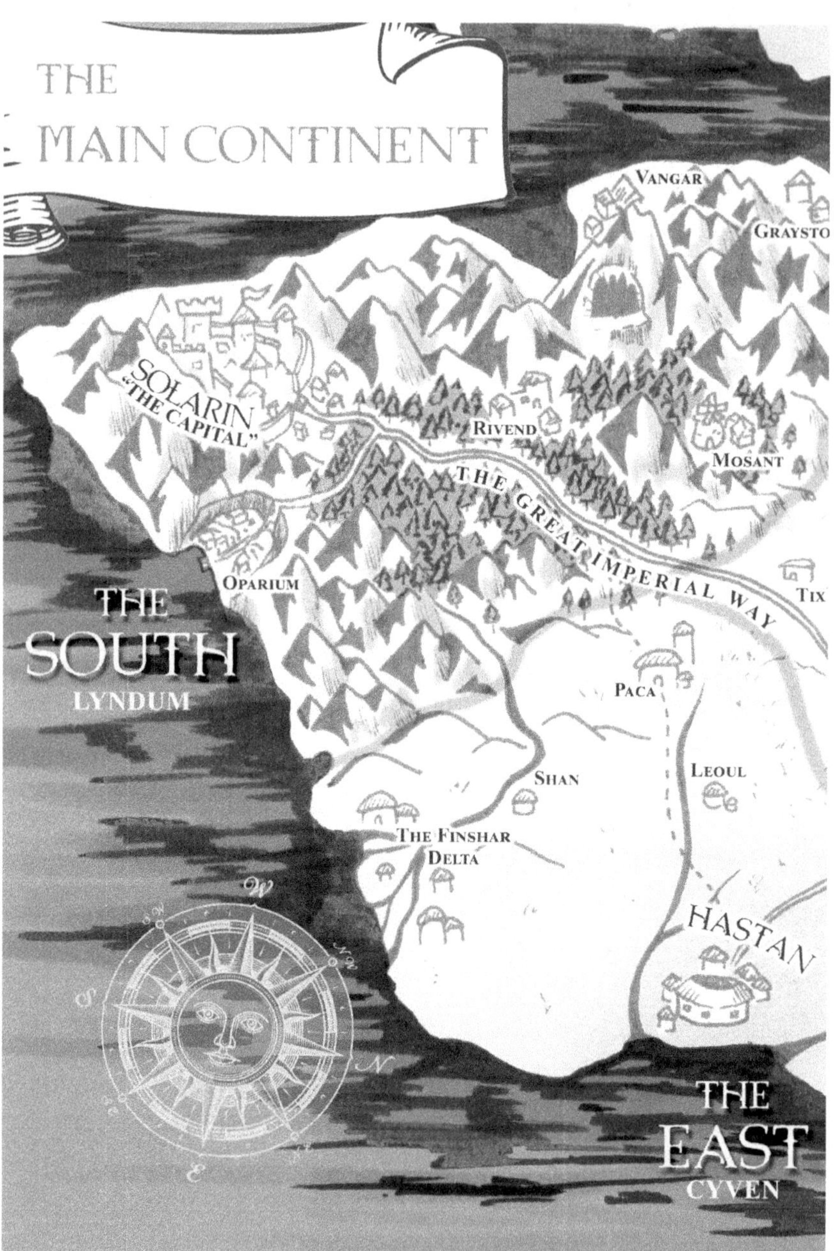

THE
MAIN CONTINENT
SOLARIN
"THE CAPITAL"
VANGAR
GRAYSTO
RIVEND
MOSANT
THE GREAT IMPERIAL WAY
TIX
OPARIUM
THE
SOUTH
LYNDUM
PACA
SHAN
LEOUL
THE FINSHAR
DELTA
HASTAN
THE
EAST
CYVEN

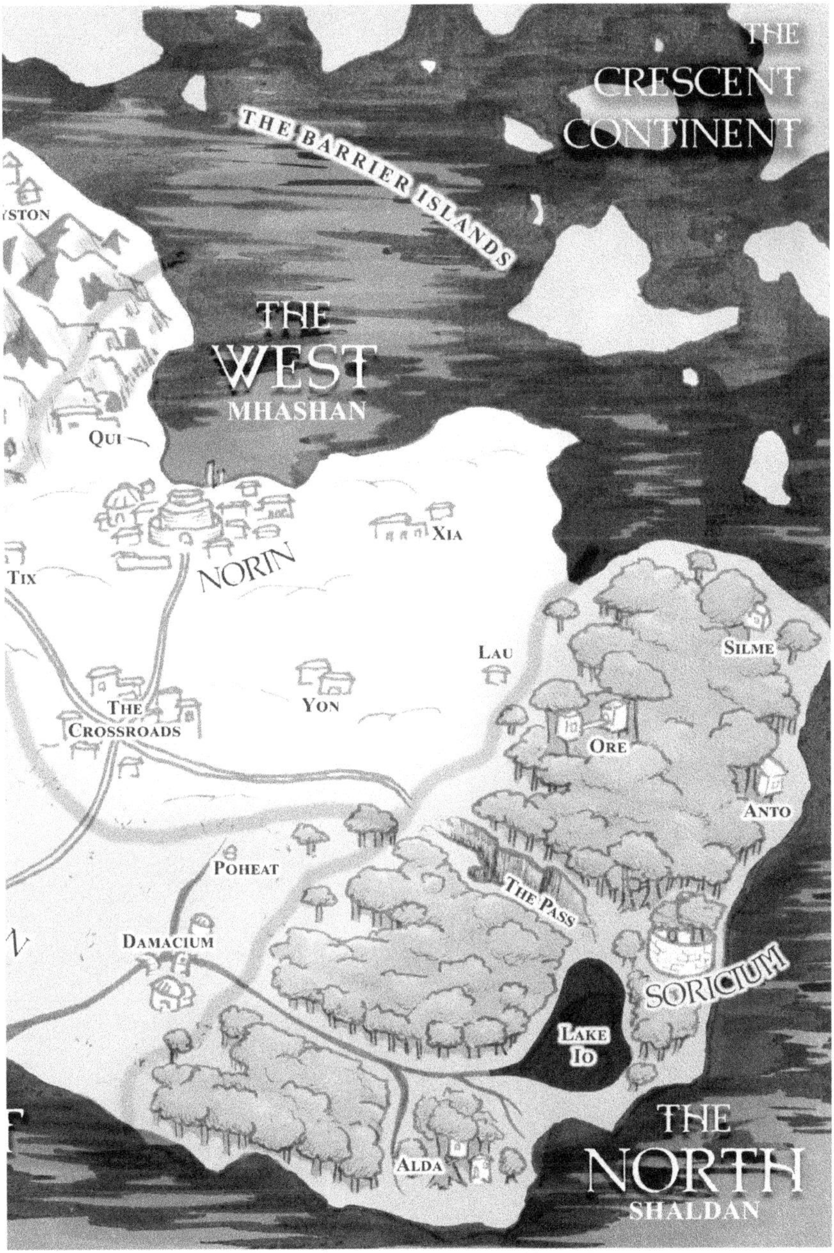

THE CRESCENT CONTINENT
THE BARRIER ISLANDS
THE WEST
MHASHAN
YSTON
QUI
TIX
NORIN
XIA
LAU
SILME
YON
ORE
THE CROSSROADS
ANTO
POHEAT
THE PASS
DAMACIUM
SORICIUM
LAKE IO
THE NORTH
SHALDAN
ALDA

N
DOLARIAN
DARK ISLE
BEAUTY'S BEND
TEETER ISLE
LITTLE BROTHER BAY
NORIN
MONLAN
GREATER ATOLL
SHATTERED INLET
VARGA
TWILIGHT FOREST
BELLAST
MAROON ATOLL
TORIS
DANT
MALLON
DIAMOND SANDS ISLES
THE SHATTERED ISLES
RISEN
MERU
WARICH
FARTH
ISLE OF FROST
LUTH
HOKOH
CASTAWAY ISLE

FOREWORD

Do you sometimes struggle to remember what's happening in a series from book to book? Do you find you forget names of people or places?

I know I do.

In an effort to help out any readers, like me, who want a bit of a refresher before starting the final book in the series, I put together a series summary on my website. **Head to this page to read a high-level synopsis of the events in the story so far:**

http://elisekova.com/vortex-chronicles-book-summaries/

This way you can relive all the major events of Air Awakens: Vortex Chronicles before starting the last book. I hope you find this helpful as much as I hope you enjoy the conclusion of Air Awakens: Vortex Chronicles! This has been a wild adventure and I've enjoyed every minute.

Your author,
Elise Kova

1

THE BLACK-BARKED PINE IN THE early morning almost reminded Vi of the Twilight Forest. Morning's first light glittered through specks of snow overflowing from too-heavy boughs down to shimmering snowdrifts. Vi paused to admire the beams of light, the snowdrifts, the crisp air, and the homey aroma of the fire that plumed smoke out of the chimney of the cabin behind her.

Each morning, she woke and was greeted by the quiet serenity of nature. For fourteen years, she had indulged in the bounty of this remote corner of the Solaris Empire. But it was all about to come to an end.

"I think that's it." Vi deposited the last of Deneya's work into the back of the cart attached to Prism—the massive warstrider previously owned by Princess Fiera.

"Did you get the quiver?" Deneya asked from where she was checking the saddle.

"I did, and the knife set." Vi scanned the items in the cart. It was a scant amount, but all of impressive make. At least, she was impressed. Vi had never suspected her elfin companion capable of such craftsmanship, but time and necessity had been the best teachers. While Vi worked on her magic, Deneya had kept her hands busy with leather and steel work.

Deneya rounded back, yanking on the woolen hat that Vi had knit for her two winters ago to hide her pointed ears, and assessed the load. "I think I'll fetch some decent coin for that set."

"I hope so. I'm tired of roots, pickled vegetables, and trying to cook frozen meat." Mosant was the nearest town, and they held their market once a month. Whenever Deneya went to market, she always came back with items that, a lifetime ago, Vi would've considered trivial. But now they were luxuries beyond compare.

"At least frozen meat doesn't go bad," Deneya said. In the summers, they had to either slowly smoke and dry their meat, or store it deep in the perpetually frozen caves of the mountains. "In a few months, when you're lamenting over meat gone foul because of the heat, I'll bet you'll be begging for next winter to arrive."

"Probably." Then again, Vi didn't expect to see next winter in this cabin.

Fourteen years they had lived in the woods at the far foot of the mountain that housed the Crystal Caverns. Fourteen years, and Vi still looked the same as she had when she'd first woken in this world. Save for the length of her hair. It was now down to her waist, usually woven into a simple, thick braid.

On the inside, however, Vi felt a world away from the young woman she'd been.

She'd learned to survive on her own, and how to go with and without. She'd learned how cold a night without shelter could be, what hunger really meant, what necessity could teach a person. She learned all the things a princess would've never been taught—all the things a princess would never have needed to know.

"I'll see what I can find for us," Deneya said, jolting Vi from her thoughts. "I have a trinket for the tavern owner. Maybe she'll spoil us with some roast hare again."

"We can only hope."

"You going up today?" Deneya's attention turned to the narrow path near their cabin that cut through the mountains.

"Of course." Vi touched the watch that never left her neck. It was tarnished and scratched, no longer the mirror surface Taavin had given her.

"Go on, then, while it's light and you can see the ice on the paths," Deneya encouraged.

"You should go, too. I don't want you traveling at night when the wolves are out." Deneya chuckled and Vi cracked a grin. They both knew the remark was more jest than worry.

"I am the wolf." Deneya's smile split into a wicked smirk. "More fresh meat."

"And more pelts." Vi stepped away as Deneya mounted Prism. "Safe travels."

"You as well. And good luck in there today!"

Before Vi could reply, Deneya clicked her tongue and Prism started his trudge through the snowy forest. The creaking of the cart covered any response she could've given. Not that Vi had any words worth saying.

Good luck in there. She needed more than luck. She needed results.

Their cabin was simple but well made. Deneya's brawn and knack for construction was a compliment to Vi's knowledge of architecture. It'd taken about a year to complete. But since then, they'd added onto it every summer. First it was the stables for their two large warstriders—Prism and Midsummer—and now their yearlings as well. The next year, before the summer rains, they'd replaced the initial thatching with wooden shingles of bark they'd sheared from trees. Another summer they'd laid wooden flooring inside. A different winter they cobbled the loveliest stones they could find over the hearth to make a mantle.

Inside there were two beds, a table, and two chairs. Vi walked over to the corner by her bed and lifted the sword that had been left behind in the Caverns years ago by the Knights of Jadar. She still wondered, from time to time, what the Knights said about that night. Did they recall it clearly? Or was the truth written and re-written through oral embellishments throughout time?

From their cabin, it took her about an hour and a half to walk up to the Crystal Caverns. She could do it in less time. But there wasn't a rush to anything these days. Time had continued its steady march as Vi worked in the shadows, determined to make the impossible happen.

Vi emerged from between cliffs and stepped into the light of the snowfield that coated the base of the mountain where the path up to the Crystal Caverns began. Tracks in the pristine white blanket weren't uncommon. There were a number of animals that continued to wander the mountainsides, even in the heart of winter. But these tracks were different, and fresh.

Someone was here.

Staying close to the rocky mountainside where there was less snow to show her footprints, Vi made her way to the tracks that led up toward the Crystal Caverns. She crouched beside the largest boulder she could find, wedging herself in a cranny.

"*Durroe watt radia*," she whispered. A glyph appeared around her wrist and magic shimmered at the edges of her vision. A cloak of invisibility settled on her shoulders and she prepared herself to wait.

After about an hour, she heard the whinny of a horse and the clop of hooves over the mountain path. Her muscles had long since seized and gone numb from the waiting. But Vi remained rigid, watching. Her time in the wild had taught her nothing if not patience.

The horse came into view. The broad-shouldered rider atop wore a hooded cloak of deep blue that covered almost all of his face. Vi leaned forward, as though that would help her sight penetrate the shadow the cowl cast.

He continued forward, oblivious to her, down the path he'd arrived from and eastward—the direction one would take to the Capital. Vi waited until he was long out of sight before releasing her magic and making haste up the pathway to the Crystal Caverns.

The moment she entered, Vi pushed magic out through her feet, the crystals illuminating in response to the arrival of the Champion. She searched, but nothing seemed out of place. "*Narro hath hoolo.*"

The words passed her lips easily. Glyphs shone above her bundled chest, hovering over where the watch was underneath. A man with deep plum hair, bright green eyes, and a crescent scar on his cheek stood before her.

He appeared from a slowly rotating glyph that unraveled to carve his outline from the thin air. But when the light faded, he remained. In this place, with the power of Yargen in the very air, he was more real than ever.

"Good morning," Taavin greeted her warmly, though the expression fell flat when his eyes settled on her. "What is it?"

"There was a man here." Vi continued to look around, running her fingertips over the crystals, feeling the magic stored within them and searching for some sign of trauma.

"What kind of man?" Taavin asked, tone grave.

"I couldn't see his face. He wore a simple woolen cloak of navy blue."

"From the Capital?"

"He headed back in that direction. But I can't say for sure." Vi's hand fell at her side. "I don't know what he did here. I can't feel anything different in the crystals."

"Then whatever he did, it wasn't anything significant."

"It worries me, though, seeing someone come to the Caverns."

The world had been quiet for the past fourteen years when it came to the Crystal Caverns. There had been a traveler only one other time—a Western man who arrived shortly after Fiera's death—likely in search of the sword or evidence of what had transpired. Since then, it had been quiet. The sort of quiet that Vi had allowed to lull her into a false sense of security.

"Based on previous timelines, people tend to become interested in this place again around now," Taavin said quietly, scanning the shimmering blue crystals.

"I know." She had made Taavin tell her of the different iterations of the world time and again, over and over, until she knew many by heart. Vi looked down at the sword clutched in her hands. "That means there isn't much time."

"You're close, and you know it." Taavin rested his hand heavily on her shoulder. Every time she summoned him here, Vi savored the slightest of touches for how real they felt. "Perhaps today's the day."

"Perhaps," Vi murmured.

Years ago, Raylynn, Zira's daughter, had asked Vi to make her a crystal weapon. Her answer then had been no. But if the girl were to ask today… Vi's answer would be different.

"I should get to work." She stepped away from him and Taavin assumed his position not far from her, leaning against a crystal. His tall form cut against the light with an agonizing handsomeness that still, even after all this time, stirred desire within her.

Her need for him didn't cool no matter how much she wanted it to. Seeing him like this would always be bittersweet. The truth of his nature was a barrier they'd never been able to surpass.

Focusing, Vi unsheathed the Sword of Jadar, set the scabbard aside, and held the hilt with both hands. She slowly lowered it and, when the very tip met the ground, a jolt of magic burst through the Caverns. The sword was made of crystals—the raw power of Yargen given physical form in the world—so its magic slotted in with the Caverns naturally.

Uncurling her fingers one by one, Vi pulled her hands away, holding them out. Magic arced like a cold, slow-burning fire between her palms and the weapon. She could feel it wrapped tightly around the backs of her fingers, trying to collapse in on itself and return to the sword. Vi twisted her wrists and lifted her hands upward. Her muscles strained, trembling, as though she were lifting a colossal weight.

But she made her mind calm and focused. She controlled this power—not the other way around. Turning her wrists inward once more, Vi felt the last dredges of power drain from the sword. The magic wrapped around her hands, but it almost felt as though it seeped into her. Making a cage with her fingers, she brought the magic together in a ball before her. It fought against her grasp, seeking freedom.

She continued to compress the magic, forcing it inward. The pale blue of raw magic became a blindingly bright light. Sweat dripped down her neck as she focused on condensing the magic.

Pop.

Blinking into the relative dimness, Vi stared at the crystal that hovered in an aura of seafoam blue between her hands. She had drawn the magic from the sword and condensed it down into a *new* crystal. She let out the breath she'd been holding. Vi hadn't dared breathe for the first part of the process.

Twisting her right hand so the crystal hovered just above her palm, Vi lifted her left.

Just as Fiera had done all those years ago, Vi tapped a nearby crystal jutting from the ground and beseeched the magic within. It came forth as she rotated her wrist with painstaking precision. *Come along now*, was her silent command. Magic spun out from the Caverns, condensing into glyphs with no meaning. Perhaps they were words, but neither Vi nor Taavin could read them. So if they had meaning, Yargen kept it hidden.

She poured the power into the crystal she held. The stone's glow intensified, but it didn't change shape or color. Yargen's magic defied time and space. An immense amount of power could be held in a vessel as large as the Crystal Caverns, or as small as the palm of her hand.

The lights in the Caverns began to dim and Vi slowed the rotation of her hand through the air, slowing the draw of power. Two tethers stretched out from the crystal floating above her palm—one to the Caverns and one to the sword.

"Keep going," Taavin commanded.

"What?" Here was where she usually stopped, allowing the magic to spill back into the dimming sword and Caverns.

"Just from the sword," he clarified. "Not the Caverns. Collect all the power from the sword and transfer it to the stone."

"But what if—"

"We do it all again, then."

Do it all again. He didn't mean today's practice. He meant the whole cycle of time they were trapped in.

"No," Vi whispered, mostly to herself. "We won't." This was to be their last time. She had vowed as much to herself, to the world, even if the world would never know it.

One way or another, this vortex would end.

Vi twisted her hand and severed the trembling thread of magic that connected the crystal in her palm to the sword, lifting it away. She watched as the last of the sword's power was extracted.

The weapon transformed into obsidian as the power drained. Once the last dredges were removed, it fell to the floor and shattered into pieces. The magic once held within the sword now hovered above her palm.

"Now, return the power to the Caverns," Taavin commanded.

Vi spun the crystal she'd made through the air, feeling the power unravel from it.

The magic didn't need much guidance from her to return to the crystals surrounding it. Yargen's magic naturally sought out its own. A phantom thread pulled through her. Magic that lingered on her palms was drawn away with the rest. All at once, the crystal hovering above her palm stopped spinning and fell. It had gone dark, just like the sword.

Vi stared at the obsidian around her feet, panting softly. She jerked her head upward. "The sword is gone."

"Make a new one."

"I've never made a sword."

"You just made crystal. You'll merely make it in a different shape this time." Taavin pushed away from the stone he'd been leaning against, his preternatural casualness belying the tension thrumming through Vi like the reverberations of a lightning bolt.

Vi turned back to the nearest crystal jutting from the floor. It was nearly twice the size of her. She rested both hands on the sides of the stone. She'd chosen this path; she could do this. Yargen's magic was around her, within her.

"Easy now, just as before," she whispered.

Magic shimmered underneath her fingertips in response.

Once more, Vi pulled power from the stone. It was easier this time. If working with the sword was like drawing from a pond of magic, this was an ocean. She had much more to work with and the magic sought her out eagerly.

Stepping back, Vi repeated the process and drew out the magic by spreading her hands. Yargen's raw essence shone brighter and brighter, the more she pulled. How much power had the sword held? She couldn't remember. But she doubted anyone but her and Taavin would be able to tell if the new Sword of Jadar was weaker than the last.

Bringing her hands together, Vi watched as the magic condensed once more into a crystal. This time, she kept flooding the stone with power. Glyphs she didn't recognize but inherently understood appeared within her mind: *grow, change, shape*. They were magic given form and tied to her will, forcing the stone to grow as she commanded. Crystals jutted out from that initial seed, becoming hilt and blade. In a blindingly bright minute, a new sword hovered in the air before her.

Taking the hilt in her hand, Vi pulled the blade from the magic forge in which she'd created it. The leftover power soaked back into the Caverns. Some lingered on the sword, flooding into her. As it sank into her bones, she felt a rush straight to the head.

Her thoughts spun dizzily until her attention settled on the weapon in her palm.

"It worked," Vi whispered in awe. A theory, inspired by a five-year-old, supported only by the existence of some black stone that had surrounded Vi after Yargen's magic had protected her once… she'd finally proved it right.

2

TWO ARMS CIRCLED HER waist. Vi dropped the sword, startled. A yelp became laughter that echoed off the soaring ceiling of the Caverns as Taavin leaned back and lifted her feet off the ground to spin her in place.

"Put me down!" Vi managed through bursts of laughter. Her sides hurt, though she didn't know if it was from his crushing grip or from laughing more than she had in what felt like years.

"You did it!" Taavin's voice bounced off every crystal as he spun her once more before setting her down. He grabbed her face with both hands and brought his lips to hers. Vi savored the feeling of his breath, hot on her cheeks, and the warmth of his palms, even if it was all over too quickly. "You did it."

"You helped a bit, along the way," she said breathlessly when they broke apart.

"Just a bit though." She couldn't tell if he was being sincere or if he realized he'd been a monumental part of her success. Perhaps he was playing along with her jest. He continued, "It's time for you to return yourself to the world and begin enacting this plan in earnest."

"I know." She'd known for years it was coming. But somehow part of her was still terrified. The truth was, she might never feel ready despite all her convictions. Perhaps that's how it was when the fate of the world hung in the balance. "Walk back with me?" Vi asked, sheathing the new sword and starting for the entrance to the Caverns. "Deneya will need to hear our next steps, too—and she's probably been back from Mosant for at least an hour."

"You could always summon me when you return?" Taavin asked, though his footsteps matched hers. "It's not as though you can't summon me there."

"I know." She had used *narro hath* at the cabin two years ago. That night, she and Deneya had returned from Mosant, where they'd found a bottle of the same spiced liquor they drank together in Norin. Taavin had laughed and reminisced with them. He'd regaled them with tales of Vi's former selves and worlds that were both similar and different.

But he couldn't partake in the festivities, not really. He couldn't drink with them. He couldn't take her to bed as Vi had discovered she'd wanted.

Vi had never allowed herself to summon him there again. The torture of seeing him, wanting him, but not having him, was something she couldn't regularly bear.

"Is it so much to ask to stroll with you?" she asked, pushing away the ache the thoughts left in her.

"I suppose not," he said with a soft chuckle.

They emerged into the sunlight and magic instantly shimmered around Taavin's shoulders. That magic was a reminder of what he really was. In the Caverns, he seemed like any other man. But he was consciousness tethered to a watch and held together by a goddess's words.

Even still, when he offered her his elbow, she took it and ignored the sensation of a thin barrier between them. She ignored that his feet didn't leave footprints in the snow. Vi pulled him close, and savored what already felt like one of the last peaceful moments they were going to have for a long time.

Someday soon... I'll make you real, Vi wanted to say, but the words remained a vow on her heart rather than lips.

She looked down at her hand, feeling the tingle of magic still underneath her fingers. Yargen had remade her body between worlds. The goddess's power was within her—it sought her out. It was the same power that allowed Vi to manipulate the crystals. She was determined to continue exploring the seemingly endless possibilities of the magic. What kind of last-chance-to-save-the-world Champion would she be if she didn't at least try to push the boundaries?

It took about an hour to walk back to the cabin. The late afternoon sun hung low in the sky. They didn't say much, though they didn't need to—just being together was enough.

Deneya was outside, just finishing covering their cart with a tarp to keep the snow off.

"About tim—*oh*, you're here too." Her eyes settled on Taavin. "Is that a good sign or a bad one?"

"I'll let you decide," he quipped in return.

"I had a breakthrough."

"Did you do it? Did you transfer the power in full?" Deneya set down her axe. Vi nodded. "By Yargen's flame, you actually did it!" The handle of the axe had barely fallen into the snow and Deneya was clapping Vi over the shoulders. "Well, this calls for a celebration. It's a good thing I got the roast hare."

"Thanks to Yargen for that." Vi's stomach growled as if on command.

"Come, tell me everything over food." Deneya headed right for the cabin door, holding it open for Taavin. What Vi considered a feast was already set out on the table.

"You set the table," she observed.

"And you say I never do anything nice for you."

"You let the food get cold is what you did." Vi grinned at Deneya as they sat across from each other. Taavin took his place at the foot of Vi's bed.

"Oh, I'm so sorry, *princess*. Let me save you from your portion." Deneya reached over to take her plate.

"I wouldn't do that if I were you. I'm armed." Vi brandished the knife that was set out by her fork.

"Not the mighty Champion and her terrifying, blunt-as-a-butterknife dagger." Deneya gasped. Vi gave a mock snarl, playfully jabbing the air in Deneya's direction until the woman let go of her plate. "Mercy, I'm unarmed."

"Perhaps I should level the playing field, then." Vi set down the knife, forgetting the food a moment, and untied the crystal sword from her hip. Deneya stopped laughing.

Vi drew the sword and held it out before her, parallel to the ground, at eye level. She focused on it, feeling the magic that collected together and gave the crystals shape. Vi tightened her grip, imagining her hold on the magic becoming greater in turn.

Change shape, she willed the crystals. Magic moved through the blade, invisible to anyone but her, and collected in the far tip of the sword. The blade thinned, transforming into a pole. The magic at the end jutted outward.

By the time the light faded, Vi was holding an axe of crystal.

"You've been making more progress than you've let on," Deneya said with quiet awe.

"You can hold it." Vi stretched her arm across the table.

"You're sure?"

"Yes."

Deneya took the weapon and twirled it once. She stood, swung it two times, and let out a low whistle. "I could cleave so many heads from shoulders with this."

Vi laughed.

"She's accomplished incredible things," Taavin said warmly. Vi glanced at him, the pride in his voice nearly making her blush.

"So, you can manipulate crystals however you please in addition to transferring power between them and the Caverns." Deneya turned back, passing her the axe. "It's what we were hoping for, isn't it?"

"Yes." Vi took the axe in both hands. She was silent a moment, intense focus overtaking her as she shifted the magic within the crystals once more. Like ice melting in sunlight, some of the crystals vanished, others jutted out, smoothed over, and the sword took shape once more.

"When the crystal weapons are taken to the Caverns, Vi will be there to transfer the power and—"

"The magic weapons won't actually be destroyed and the Caverns will remain intact," Deneya interrupted Taavin. "Then we'll combine the collective magic of the crystal weapons, the Caverns themselves, and what's trapped in the flame of Yargen in Risen to give a physical form to the Goddess herself. Then she'll duel Raspian in another battle of light and dark, yes, yes, I know."

"For a battle that the fate of the world hinges on, you make it sound boring," Taavin remarked.

"The fate of the world has been boring these past fourteen years," Deneya quipped without looking at him. She shoveled food into her mouth and Vi took the opportunity to do the same. "What I'm asking is… now that she can do this, what are our next steps?"

"We'll approach the weapons in order, based on Taavin's knowledge of past histories and stones in the river of fate," Vi mused aloud. "First is the sword. We know where the scythe is, so that won't be a problem."

"Glad getting to Meru is listed as 'not a problem'," Deneya muttered. Vi ignored her obvious disbelief and continued.

"The axe is safely hidden away in the North—or it should be."

"It's never been found before the War in the North." Taavin gave Vi a nod.

"That leaves the crown, then," Deneya said from behind her hand as she chewed. "Where do we think that one is?"

"Almost impossible to say. The crown is always so variable in its location." Taavin scowled. The crown was never a pleasant topic of conversation. It had the most variables and made them all nervous.

"For the time being, we work with the stones in the river. We try to vary the timeline as little as possible," Vi said calmly. "We'll go to the Capital and see Aldrik gets the sword so he can fulfill that stone in the river of fate: him bringing the sword to the Caverns."

"You're giving him the sword?" Deneya blinked in shock.

"Of course not," she said with a laugh. "I'm going to need you to make me a new one."

"*Me* make a new—" Deneya stopped herself, comprehension dawning on her face "—*oh*, I get it."

"And, honoring the stones in the river, will help ensure the birth of a new Champion," Taavin said with an approving nod.

The words grated her, but Vi didn't let it show. How were they supposed to look toward success if they were constantly planning for failure? For the time being, it wasn't a question she was ready to pose to him. They were on the same page, and the night was going beautifully.

She swallowed the uncomfortable thoughts with a hunk of rabbit and washed it down with a long drink.

"Then it's clear where we're headed next." She punctuated the statement by setting down her wooden cup heavily.

"Back to Norin?" Deneya said with a smirk, knowing full well what Vi was about to say.

"If you'd like." Vi played into the woman's jest. "But I'll be heading to the capital of the Solaris Empire."

"About time."

"About time?" Vi snorted. "Imagine how I feel… it's taken about thirty-two years and one rebuilding of the world for me to get to the home of my forefathers."

Solarin, the capital of the Solaris Empire, was nestled atop a twin-peaked mountain. At the very top of the city, stretching toward the taller of the two summits, was the Imperial Palace. It spilled downward into stone buildings with tiled roofs.

Even from the switch-back road leading up to the city, Vi could see the castle's golden-tipped spires and gigantic pennons forever fluttering in the mountain breezes.

"It's smaller than I imagined," Deneya said from the horse next to her, Midsummer. Vi rode Prism. Both women held lead ropes for the yearlings trailing close behind.

"Smaller, really?" From where Vi sat, it was massive. And they were still a good half hour down the mountain.

Deneya shrugged. "Nothing on the Dark Isle compares to Risen."

"You can't compare Solaris to Meru." Vi chuckled. They spoke of a world not too far from their own, yet the travelers around them continued on none the wiser. Anyone who overheard their conversation likely wouldn't believe or make sense of the remarks anyway.

They arrived at the main gate of the capital in good time. Their warstriders towered over most men and beasts; even their young offspring were the size of a regular horse. Rather than trying to fit in, Vi worked to stand out with her Western horses and dark hair.

"Excuse me, sir." They rode for one of the Imperial guards stationed by the gate.

"May I help you?"

"I'm looking to speak with the master of horse at the Imperial palace. We bring a gift for the young prince's fifteenth birthday and coming-of-age ceremony." Vi motioned to the yearlings and added the slightest hint of a Western accent to her words.

"That ceremony isn't for months yet."

"Horses take time to settle and train," she countered calmly.

"Head down the main road. It's hard to miss the castle entrance. You'll ask for Augus when you get to the stables," the guard answered dully.

"Thank you." Vi gave him a nod and they continued plodding along the main road of Solarin.

A sensation much like the first time she'd stepped foot on Meru overtook her. Icicles shone in the morning light hanging off undisturbed windowsills and gutters. Men leaned over balconies, taking drags off pipes that filled the air with sweet smoke. Music she didn't know lofted over the sounds of people talking.

This was the place where she should've lived… in another world.

The palace was built in layers up the mountainside. At its lowest point were long rows of stables that reminded Vi somewhat sadly of the castle in Norin. They were stopped by two guards at the gates.

"Business?" one of the men demanded.

"We're here to speak with Augus." Vi motioned to the all-black colt with a stripe of white on his forehead. "We have a gift for the prince."

"A moment." The guard ran into the stables and returned with a barrel-chested man who had a thick coating of golden hair over his forearms.

"I hear you've got something for the prince." The man pushed up his sleeves a little farther. "Well, bring him in, let me see the creature."

Argus led them into the stables, heading for an empty stall toward the back. Both women dismounted when they came to a stop. Vi untied the lead rope of the black yearling from her saddle, passing it to Argus. The stable master did a quick round of the horse and let out a low whistle. His eyes swept across the four mounts.

"Where'd you come across these lovely creatures?"

"My father was a horse trainer for the royal family." Vi thickened her Western accent slightly.

"Your father? Does he have a name?"

Vi wrung her hands, looking askance. "I shouldn't say."

"I can't rightly give the crown prince a gift that I can't verify."

"Clearly they're warstriders of good stock," Deneya huffed.

"Yes, I can see that, but the Emperor will insist."

"Then the Emperor is—"

"It's all right, Danya," Vi said hastily, interrupting the woman with the fake name they had agreed on. She looked over at the stable master, attempting to be the living embodiment of insecurity. "Between you and me?"

"Yes?" The man's eyebrows arched.

"My father was Ronaldo." There were a few events that Vi would never need Taavin's help recalling, and the night she escaped Norin with Fiera was one of them. The stablemaster in Norin had assumed she was taking Prism to Ronaldo for boarding, following the birth of the prince.

"Ronaldo… you can't be talking about *the* Ronaldo? Legendary breeder for warstriders?" Vi gave a meek nod. "I thought he only had two sons."

"I'm not…" Vi intentionally fumbled her words.

"Vivian was conceived on the wrong side of the sheets. Or barn, as it were," Deneya finished for her.

"Ronaldo, the dog." Augus shook his head. "Right, well, this all explains the apparent quality of the animals. You willing to part with the other yearling as well? Perhaps the whole family? I know the black one with the stripe is a gift for the prince. But I could pay you for the others."

Vi and Deneya exchanged a glance. They hadn't really discussed this. They'd managed to stretch the gold Vi had taken from Norin for years due to their own resourcefulness, with help from Deneya's profits selling her wares. But it couldn't hurt to have a little extra coin.

It also didn't hurt to have a swift getaway on good horses they didn't have to steal.

"I hadn't planned on it," Vi started slowly, hoping her hesitation read as a bastard daughter's love for tokens gifted from her father. "The other yearling we might be willing to part with." Vi looked at the creature. "But the parents…"

"The yearling is a start." Argus stroked his chin. "How long are you staying in the city? At least a year?"

"Hopefully longer than that. We wanted to find work," Deneya answered. "Perhaps establish a life here."

"You seem like an able-bodied young woman. I could put you to work here, in the stables. Even board these fine beasts at no extra cost to you."

"Really? That'd be great!" Deneya flashed him a bright smile.

"Excellent. And perhaps, if you're still here come summer… you'd let me breed these two again and sell me that foal too?" Argus showed the root of his kindness. "Warstriders of this caliber are hard to come by, and I would be remiss to let you go so easily."

He gave a genuine chuckle. The whole time the stable master had been stroking the mounts. Vi doubted he even realized that he'd gone through all of their bridals, checking them.

"Perhaps," Vi relented. Deneya had a job in the palace without too much effort. The longer the man thought they'd be useful to him, the better. "Thanks for offering my friend a job."

"No trouble. I could put you to work as well? Daughter of Ronaldo would be a welcome addition to my staff."

"Thank you, but I'm hoping to find a job that doesn't involve horses. I've mucked enough stables for one lifetime."

Argus chuckled at that. "Well, if you change your mind, come back. And you, Danya, I'll see you with the sun tomorrow."

"Of course." Deneya forced a smile so false that Vi had to struggle not to laugh at it.

"If you'll excuse us, we're meeting an acquaintance in the Imperial

Library."

"Is that right? Marc!" Argus called for the guard from earlier, who begrudgingly stepped over. "Take these two up to the library through the castle." He looked back to them. "Much faster than going through the city."

Vi and Deneya said their thanks and followed behind Marc into the palace of Solaris.

Gooseflesh covered her arms the moment they crossed the threshold and Vi let out a sigh of equal parts delight and awe. They went into a side hall that wound around the throne room and receiving area. Her breath hitched as they turned a corner, the room opening into a sitting area. Vi delicately lifted a hand, feeling the fitted stones of the wall.

She touched the masonry of the palace like she was greeting a long-lost friend.

Every twist and turn of the candle-lit halls thrilled her. Every stairwell that rounded back on itself, overlooking Solarin on each landing, sent shivers up her spine.

She knew this castle better than anywhere in the world, even though this was the first time she'd stepped foot in it. She knew the pathways that would head to the royal wing, guarded with a stunning gold gate. She knew the secret servants' halls her mother spoke of and that she'd delighted in finding on her maps.

She knew the moment they laid eyes on the library doors.

The heavy door glided over the plush carpet silently at the guard's slightest push. The smell of leather and parchment filled her nose. Vi's eyes settled on the gold-gilded cherry wood bookcases that lined up in rows down the center hallway of the library. She stared at the center circulation desk, and the ancient looking man behind it who didn't even so much as look up from what he was working on.

With a soft click, the doors behind them shut, and Vi was snapped back into reality.

"It's just as she said," Vi whispered. She was drawn to the books as if by a trance. Her hand closed around one of the metal sliding ladders that allowed people to reach the tops of the dizzyingly tall shelves.

"What is? Who?" Deneya asked.

"My mother." Vi ran her fingers along the spines. She looked ahead to the outer wall she knew was lined with windows. Her mother had spoken fondly of a particular window where she would always sit to read. Would Vi be able to tell which, even though Vhalla had yet to step foot in the castle in this world? Would she feel it in her marrow as keenly as she could feel Yargen's magic? "She always said she wanted to introduce me to her friends here."

"I doubt your mother's friends will show up for a few years yet." Deneya laced her fingers, placing them behind her head as Vi let out a soft laugh.

"Her friends weren't people… they were books."

"Books? Your mother sounds like a dull person."

Vi grinned at Deneya. "My mother's life was anything but. You'll see soon enough."

They reached the end of the bookshelf and Vi looked down the long line of windows. Each one had a seat carved out beneath its glass. Cerulean pillows turned them into comfortable reading nooks.

Vi couldn't tell which one had been, and would become, her mother's.

"So, now that we've met your mother's 'friends' and I somehow ended up with a job that will involve literal shit… it's your turn."

"Yes." Vi tore her eyes from the windows. "You wait here while I—"

"I'm not waiting with a bunch of books." Deneya's tone reminded Vi of the woman's disdain for reading. "I'm going to explore the city and begin to get a lay of the land."

"Where will I find you?"

"In the closest pub to this frosty library, I'd bet."

"Are you exploring the city or getting drunk?" Vi asked dryly.

"It's been a while since we had the comforts of a city." Deneya grinned.

"Keep your head about you and the gold in our pockets, please."

"I always have my head about me. And I have a *job*, remember? I'll be spending my coin how I please." Deneya stepped away with a wave and vanished among the rows of books.

Vi watched her for a moment before going in the opposite direction. She'd made it into the castle. Now it was time to break in to the Tower of Sorcerers.

3

T HERE WERE A FEW principles Uncle Jax had taught her since Vi was a little girl. Right at the top of the list was that the South hated sorcerers above all else.

Vi hadn't understood why when she was younger. She'd merely accepted it, as children do. But experience had taught her that the hatred went all the way back to the original, magic-less settlers of the Dark Isle, fleeing persecution on Meru. While that history had long been lost on the general public, it established Vi's expectation for her time here.

Starting with finding the Tower of Sorcerers.

The Tower was hidden in plain sight to prevent the servants and citizens of Solarin from being on edge all the time. There was a main entry accessible to the public, though even that was difficult to find. Vi knew where it was, of course. But she was closer to a back door. Sneaking in would have a far greater impact.

She stopped along one of the many hallways of the palace. She'd taken the long way to get here, savoring every step. No one stopped her. It was miraculous how far she could go when she walked with confidence.

Vi stood in front of a seemingly plain stone wall. On one of the stones was a symbol of two halves of a circle, broken apart and off-set from each other. It was a simplified version of the Broken Moon, the symbol of the Tower of Sorcerers.

Glancing around the hallway to make sure no errant servant would see her, Vi tapped the stone and watched her finger disappear within it. It was an illusion, carefully crafted and maintained by one of the Waterrunners in the Tower. She side-stepped through the wall with confidence, into a nearly pitch-black tunnel.

At the far end was a single flame bulb by an unassuming, unlocked door. The door led to a winding pathway that spiraled up higher and higher. Circular common areas were on her right, taking up the center of the tower. Doors to individuals' rooms were on her left. Flame bulbs lit the interior passage every several steps.

She passed by a group of people on her way up. They stopped talking, then quickly exchanged whispers and glances at the sight of her. But just like the servants she'd passed on the way here, no one made an attempt to speak with or stop her.

At the top of the tower was the office of the Minister of Sorcery. In her time, this room had been occupied by Fritznangle Chareem. This was where he would've greeted her and welcomed her as a new member of the Tower when she finally came home.

For a brief moment, Vi rested her fingertips on the door and closed her eyes, imagining that moment as she had so many years ago. Try as she might, she couldn't find the fantasy. Even opening her eyes and staring at the door, Vi had a hard time summoning what had been one of her more favorite daydreams.

The child who had dreamed them was long gone.

Vi gave a knock on the door and an unfamiliar voice responded, "Enter."

Letting herself in, Vi stepped into the generously sized office. The Minister of Sorcery sat at a desk, running a hand through his sand-colored hair. Books were crammed into shelves. A workstation bubbled with something sweet-smelling Vi couldn't place. She did a visual sweep of the room before her eyes met the bright blue ones of the Minister. His attention was focused solely on her.

"I don't know you." Egmun didn't mince words.

"Unfortunate for you, but easily remedied." Vi sat herself in one of the plush leather chairs that faced the desk. She tapped her fingers on the armrest, acting as though she was already somewhat impatient. "I'm here for a job."

"A job?"

"Yes."

His eyes narrowed. "You're not of the Tower."

"Not yet. Though I'm looking forward to being a part of it." Vi smiled sweetly at the face of the man whom she planned to play like a fiddle.

"Usually one would schedule a meeting with me, and I would meet them in the reception hall at the base of the Tower."

Vi couldn't tell if he was cross or impressed for the unorthodox way she'd gone about this. Egmun likely didn't know himself. "Yes, I thought this would be faster. Cut right to the chase."

"*How* did you get up the Tower without an escort? Someone must be stationed at the public entrance at all times to prevent wanderers like you." He tapped his fingers against each other; magic rose around him like a tide.

"I didn't use the public entrance."

"How did you get to a private one, then?"

"I have my ways." Vi tilted her head. "Wouldn't you like those ways to be under your employ?" He was curious. She'd tempted him with a nibble of knowledge. From here, she'd slowly feed him more in just the right amounts until he was eating from her hands.

"Do you enjoy avoiding questions?"

"Insofar as it suits me." Vi smirked.

"What's your name? Will you at least give me a direct answer for that?"

"Vivian."

"Vivian," he repeated. "And is there a family name to go along with that?"

She shook her head. "Just Vivian."

"I assume you have some kind of magic, otherwise you wouldn't be here looking for a job in the Tower of Sorcerers. Judging from your looks—you're a Firebearer?"

Vi lifted her hand and summoned flames around her palm. They snaked and wriggled between her fingers, illuminating the room in a red-orange glow. She extinguished them by balling her hand into a fist.

"Yes, well… I have enough Firebearers. Sorry to disappoint you." He pursed his lips together and looked back down at his desk. "If you excuse yourself without issue I will spare you the trouble of calling the guard for trespassing on the Tower uninvited." Vi didn't buy his dismissal for a moment. She'd bet anything that if she stood and walked off, he'd follow to see what secret passage was the Tower's weak spot.

"I never said I was here to offer you my skills as a Firebearer."

"You're still here?" Egmun glanced up at her.

"We both have something the other needs, and I think we should work together," Vi continued calmly, folding her hands over her lap. Egmun was now staring at her, saying everything with his eyes. Vi let the moment drag out. She was making a bold move, but the magnitude of her plans could hinge on little else. "I consider myself a researcher of crystals as well."

"I don't know what you're talking about."

"Of course you don't." Vi smiled and stood, walking over to one of the windows with purposeful strides as she spoke. She acted as though the office was her own. "Then I'll just talk *at* you for a moment, and let's see if anything sounds interesting to you…

"I grew up in the West reading about the power of crystals and hearing all the colorful stories that surround them. Stories of a power unlike any other. There was one thing, more than anything else, that entranced me—the Sword of Jadar."

"The sword is long gone." His whole attention was on her now.

"So they say… So I want people to believe." Vi glanced over her shoulder as the man jumped to his feet.

"You have it?" He was so hungry for the answer that he was nearly drooling over the question. Vi had been away from people for so long that she'd forgotten just how foolish power-hungry men could be.

"I do."

"Are you a Knight of Jadar?"

"If I was a Knight of Jadar, would I be offering the sword to a Southerner?" Vi arched her eyebrows. "The Knights seek the sword to bring back the might of Mhashan. They're old men yearning for a renaissance of their glory days because they can't handle that the world has changed." Vi allowed venom to seep into the words. "Mhashan is gone. And I don't want to use the crystals' power to bring back the past."

"Then what do you want?"

To save the world. "Must I want anything more than the pursuit of knowledge?"

The hard line of his brow softened at the question. She'd disarmed him. Just as Taavin had advised her, Egmun was a man who thirsted for knowledge above all else. Curiosity was an irresistible carrot for him that Vi now dangled at the end of a stick.

"Prove you have the sword," he finally demanded.

She clicked her tongue. "It doesn't work that way. Like I said, we each have something the other needs. It doesn't serve me to give you my bargaining chip without first getting something in return."

"The Sword of Jadar is quite the bargaining chip. What could I possibly offer you of equal value?"

"The crown prince."

"What do you need him for?"

"If you are as well-researched on the crystals as your reputation has led me to believe, then I assume you know about the barrier in the Caverns?"

"You mean the door?" he clarified. It didn't entirely confirm her suspicion that he was the dark-hooded man she'd seen at the Caverns, but it did support the theory.

"Yes, it leads to the heart of the Caverns, where the true power is. The sword can unlock that power, with the right ritual." The best lies were grounded in the slightest bit of truth. "But the barrier was formed by the late Empress Fiera."

"It's true then, the rumors of her death?" Vi nodded, wondering just what rumors had been flying about while she lived in the shadow of the Caverns. "Then, that means…"

"We need the crown prince to get to the true power. His magic is similar enough to his mother's. He'll be able to undo the barrier if we train him well enough with the crystals," Vi finished for him. She didn't actually know if Aldrik could undo the barrier alone or not. Fiera seemed to have an instinct for Lightspinning, despite all odds. Perhaps her son would as well. If not, Vi would be there to make sure there were no hiccups.

"*We?*" Egmun repeated, sounding somewhat offended.

"The sword is nothing if the door can't be opened. And opening the door is useless without the sword because you will not be able to access the heart of the Caverns without it." Vi crossed back over to him, perching herself on the edge of his desk. Placing her palm flat against its surface, ignoring the papers, Vi leaned toward the blue-eyed man. "Like I said, we need each other."

"How do I know I can trust you?"

"You don't. It'll have to be an act of faith on your end." Vi shrugged. "But if I were you… if I were a man of your talents and intellect, I wouldn't let an opportunity like this go. You don't have much to lose. Either I speak true, and the Sword of Jadar along with all the power in the Crystal Caverns could be *yours*," she whispered the words, letting them hang in the air. "Or I'm lying, and you can kill me for trespassing in the Tower of Sorcerers, or some other invented crime, whenever it suits you. I'm sure the Emperor will take your side over a random Westerner if it came to that."

Egmun considered this for a long minute.

"I do think I have an opening here at the Tower, for someone of your talents." Vi hummed as an invitation for him to keep talking. "Perhaps I could invite you to stay here as a personal assistant of mine? That way you're not troubled with the day-to-day, and your mind can be free to work on other projects."

"That would be wonderful." Vi leaned away and slid off the edge of the desk.

"Excellent. Now, regarding the sword—" he said eagerly.

"I'll show it to you when the time is right. Our deal is still fresh, minister, let it harden before we begin worrying about the next steps." Vi smiled. She needed to buy herself some time in the palace to search for the crown. The longer she could delay bringing Aldrik and the sword to the Caverns, the better. "In the meantime, I would like to get settled into my new quarters."

"Your… quarters?"

"Why, yes, I believe it's common for teachers and students of the Tower of Sorcerers to be given their own rooms?" Vi arched her eyebrows. Egmun pursed his lips, but didn't object. As long as she had the sword and knowledge to dangle before him, he would do her bidding.

"I fear the Tower is rather full at the moment."

"What a shame," Vi said, making it clear she really didn't have time for excuses with her tone alone.

"Though, I do have a room I think I could make do, if you're not too picky." He rummaged through his desk, producing an iron key. "This way, if you please."

The man led her out of his office and they wound even higher up the Tower.

"Beneath my office are the quarters I use," Egmun said. They stopped before an unmarked door, which Egmun unlocked before passing Vi the key. "This is an unused storeroom, which I will gladly appoint for your use."

Vi stepped into the chambers and waved her hand. Flames sparked to life in the braziers around the room. There wasn't much in it. Mostly empty shelves and cabinets lined the back wall. A few crates were piled up about the room and a doorway led to an attached bathroom.

"I think it was originally intended to be the minister's quarters. But I've never known a minister to use them since the lower chambers are much larger." Egmun shrugged. "Will this do?"

"Nicely."

"Excellent, I'll have Tower members start setting it up for you immediately. While they do, perhaps we can discuss our business further?"

"There is nothing more to discuss until you show me you can provide the prince."

"Tomorrow morning then," he said definitively. "Meet me in my office just before dawn, and you will meet Prince Aldrik."

"Most excellent." Vi smiled, as though the statement didn't curdle her stomach. She'd taken this young man's mother. Now, she'd lead him down a path that would result in extreme hardship.

"See you bright and early, Miss Vivian." Egmun spun on his heel and started down the Tower.

"I wouldn't miss it for the world."

DENEYA WAS TRUE TO her word. Vi found her in the second pub she checked with only the faintest flush to her cheeks. Her wits were still about her, and Vi filled her in on what had transpired with Egmun over a flagon of her own.

Night had fallen when she made her way back to the Tower. Vi strode with confidence up the main, spiraling walkway. The names engraved on silver nameplates and set on the doors to her left caught her eye.

She stopped, staring at one.

Friznangle Chareem.

Vi ran her fingers over the carefully engraved letters. Her other hand touched the watch around her neck lightly, remembering Fritz's original gift ages ago. How old was he now? Ten? Twelve? Vi didn't know. But this man was the one who had always given the watch to every new Vi. This was the current shade of the man who had given her Taavin a world ago.

She was still very much at the beginning of her journey. Yet Vi felt like she was catching a glimpse of the end.

Footsteps echoed up from below and Vi hastily stepped away from the door, starting up the tower once more. She kept her head down and her pace swift all the way back to her room, lighting the braziers once more on entry.

This time, the light didn't fall on a storeroom in disarray. Egmun hadn't lied about getting the Tower students to set up the room quickly. Where once there were crates, now a narrow bed stood beside a desk with a single chair. The shelves had also been emptied and dusted.

She locked the door behind her and uttered, *"Narro hath hoolo."*

Taavin appeared, inspecting the room as he usually did whenever she summoned him in a new place.

"You're in the Tower?"

Vi brought him up to speed. By the time she finished, she had completed several laps around the furniture and was now perched on the top of one of the low bookcases in front of the window.

"Then everything is going according to plan," Taavin said after a long stretch of silence.

Vi gave a nod. "This will give me enough time to look for the crown."

"And Egmun will be the one to take Aldrik to the Caverns to fulfill fate's needs, ensuring we continue toward the birth of the next Champion."

"Yes. I'll need to ask Deneya to continue working on the sword we'll illusion to fool Egmun. That way he doesn't get his hands on the actual crystal weapon." She went to pace, but Taavin grabbed her forearm. He pulled her a step closer to him, resting both hands on her shoulders.

"If everything is going well, why do you seem so restless?"

"It's hard to explain." Vi glanced askance. "I know what I'm doing. I know what the path I've chosen means: that people will suffer because of my actions. That instead of trying to stop that suffering, I will play into it, hoping it leads to success. And if we are successful, everything will have meaning."

"Or the world will be rebuilt and their suffering is lost."

"Yes, or that." Vi retrieved the unassuming, shimmering crystal that held all the power of the Sword of Jadar from the depths of an inner pocket on the long, threadbare coat she wore. She turned it over in her fingertips, watching the magic shift and swirl with each pass. The magic clung to her, begging her to absorb its power and use it to shape the world to her will. With a thought, she could make it grow into the sword if she so desired. "I was thinking about the weapons."

"All right?"

"When Yargen sealed Raspian away, she split herself into three—one part to the Caverns, one part to the staff of the Champion that would later become the crystal weapons, and one part to the flame of Risen."

"Yes?"

She could hear the confusion in his voice. This was something they'd been over countless times. Vi shook her head, trying to remain focused. A thought was taking shape.

"The flame in Risen… I keep thinking about it. When the world was rebuilt—when my body was rebuilt by Yargen's hand—it was because of the power stored in the flame. We unleashed it."

"Yes." This time, the word took on a heavier meaning. Taavin already knew what she had pieced together—she could hear it in his voice. Vi met his eyes, not allowing him to hide from her.

"You know what I'm about to say, don't you?"

"If my suspicions are correct."

"And you're so rarely wrong." It suddenly felt as though someone had punched her in the gut. She tensed every muscle and braced herself. "Tell me what happened to the other Vi's, after a new Champion was born? If I'm the ninety-third Vi, what happened to the ninety-second, after she failed at her mission?"

"She gave her power back to the flame."

"I'm a part of Yargen, now," Vi said softly. "My body isn't really my own." She'd known it wasn't from the first time she'd set foot in this world. She'd known it down in her marrow as keenly as she knew Yargen's magic was there. "If we succeed, my body will return to her as well."

"You don't know that." He took a step closer.

"How else could it happen?"

"How does she manage to both rewind time and begin a new

world? Even we don't fully understand the ways of the divine." Taavin rested his hand on the crystal, wrapping his fingers around hers. The motion was meant to take her hand. But the moment his fingers met the stone, he became that much more real. His touch was firmer, warmer. The faint glow that had emanated from him vanished entirely.

Vi twisted, careful to keep him as close as possible. Releasing the crystal into his palm, Vi ran her hands up his tunic and twirled her fingers in the hair at the nape of his neck. As long as the crystal touched him, he was as good as real.

She brushed her lips against his. Taavin ducked his head, leaning forward for another, longer kiss. She wanted to linger there forever, in ignorant bliss for him.

"Don't worry yourself so much about these things," he spoke against her mouth. "There is much that must come to pass before it's even a concern. Each event more unlikely than the last."

"Are you trying to make me ignore my responsibility as Champion?"

"At least for tonight," he said with a sultry note. Vi felt him grin against her mouth and it prompted her to mirror the action. Sometimes, there was simply too much to worry over.

Troubling herself with what would happen when all of Yargen's power was collected was pointless until she actually collected that power. First, she needed to worry about getting the crystal weapons and figuring out where the crown was hidden. But even before all that… she'd worry about the man before her.

She pushed him gently, allowing the back of his knees to meet the bed frame. Taavin sat heavily. The bed groaned under his weight—the ropes supporting the mattress tightened—and the sound jostled her from the trance his touch could put her under.

Vi blinked at him. His hands were on her hips as she straddled him, one still clutching the stone. Taavin looked up at her from underneath heavy lids lined with long lashes. His lips were already begging for hers again.

But all she could do was stare, running her fingertips down his cheek.

"What is it?" Taavin whispered.

"When you touch this, you're real. As real as you were in the Crystal Caverns," Vi mused gingerly. "I think if I linked your consciousness to the crystal, I wouldn't need to maintain *narro hath* and you would be here with me."

"Vi…" His free hand tapped at the watch around her neck. "I am always here for you. Isn't that enough?"

It should be. Some didn't get half as lucky. But she was needy. And there was some streak of selfish princess in her when it came to this man where Vi would never learn to leave well enough alone.

She wanted him. All of him.

"You are always enough." Vi kissed the tip of his nose lightly. "I just want all of you."

"You have all I am."

"I still want to try linking your form with the crystal," she persisted.

"You might have successfully managed the sword. But this is different. And the last thing you want to do is ruin the magic of the watch. Meddle with that incorrectly, and you really will lose me, along with your and your future selves' chances to save this world by benefiting from my collected memories."

"I know I can," she insisted. "Let me try."

"No, we must be cautious." A note of finality in his tone made Vi relent.

She sighed and pressed her forehead against his. "I want you like this." She wanted to feel warmth from him. To breathe in his scent. To feel his smooth skin and silky hair under her fingers.

"Do you think I don't want it?" He caught her lips again, planting a firm kiss as he pulled her closer to him and further away from the idea.

"I want to roll over and find you in the night. I want to come back and see you here, waiting to greet me," Vi whispered between short, sweet kisses.

Taavin leaned back, pulling her with him. He twisted, and Vi found herself beneath him. Their weight made the mattress sink further into the ropes as he continued to clutch the stone in his palm.

With *narro hath* he was real to her.

With the power of Yargen, he could be real to the world.

"I want to go about my day and run into you," he murmured, kissing her cheeks. "I want to catch your eyes from across a square, or a hall, or a library, and share a smile that only we would know. A smile to assure you that by night you will find your way into my arms once more." His lips moved down her neck and Vi let out a soft sigh.

I need you to give me a place to hide from the world when I need, Vi wanted to say. She had no reprieve, not really… not since she had fallen in love with him only to end his mortal form. The arms that had become her home were taken from her, just like everything else.

"It's a beautiful dream," Vi whispered.

"Indulge in that beautiful dream, tonight." Taavin brought his lips back to hers. Vi kissed him so firmly that when he pulled away, he was breathless. "Indulge in us, because that's all we have."

His words were like honey warmed in sunlight, bright, sweet, and oh so tempting. She found herself stuck in them as much as she was stuck in place, helpless beneath his wandering hands. It had been fourteen years since she had a room to herself, and the ground of the Crystal Caverns was far too cold and hard.

"I can't," Vi whispered.

"You can't?" He slowly pulled away and sat up on the bed.

"I need to start looking for some leads on the crown," Vi murmured, standing. She also had some research she wanted to do.

"Now?"

"No time like the present." Vi hooked his chin with her finger and pulled his lips to her for one more firm kiss. When they pulled apart, she gave him a beaming smile. "Perhaps I'll let you be the one to keep me up all night soon." Vi held out her hand expectantly.

"Don't tempt me." Taavin passed the stone back to her.

She leaned away and released her focus on *narro hath*. Taavin vanished.

With the stone in her pocket, Vi wandered down to the Tower library—a smaller and more private collection, separate from the Imperial Library. It was late, but she doubted she'd be able to sleep tonight. Her mind was far too full.

The library was dark and icy cold. Vi pushed her spark to burn beneath her skin, warming her as her breath fogged the air. There was a hearth on the far side of the circular room, but Vi didn't light it. She didn't want to draw attention from any other late-night wanderers.

A mote of fire appeared at her side, just enough to see by. The gold embossing on the spines that lined the shelves winked at her as Vi explored the library. She flipped the stone over and over in her pocket, her thoughts centering around it.

If she could manipulate the crystals to make weapons, she could manipulate them into the shape of a body. Crystals were Yargen's magic given physical form. Her presence in this world was proof of that. The body Yargen gave Vi between time, when the world was remade, was a result of Yargen's magic making a physical form.

Furthermore, if Taavin's consciousness could be anchored in a watch, it could be placed in a hypothetical body. It was all theory, yes. But she had facts to back up that theory.

Still, she knew no matter what she said, Taavin wasn't going to let her experiment… at least not until she could offer him some assurances that she would succeed.

Vi came to a stop by a back section of worn, tucked-away books. Most of the titles had flaked off their spines. Still, one volume caught her eye. She knew she should be looking for clues to the crown, but Vi couldn't stop herself. She hooked her finger on the book, sliding it from its place.

"The Windwalkers of the East," she murmured and flipped open the first page. It was a record, put together by none other than the current Imperial Librarian, Mohned Topperen. *Topperen.* The name was familiar to her—beyond the stories her mother told—but Vi couldn't place how or why.

The manuscript was an account of the Burning Times through interviews with one of the last surviving Windwalkers. Vi scanned the pages, which covered everything from magical theory to terrible experiments involving human sacrifice meant to unlock the true power of the crystals. Fiera had learned how to manipulate crystals by reading accounts from the Burning Times. Perhaps, if Vi did her own research, she could find something that would give her the additional evidence she needed to convince Taavin to let her experiment.

A pair of footsteps approached and Vi snuffed her flame on instinct. She hastily shut the book and returned it to the shelf. But she hadn't been fast enough.

"Who's there?" a male voice called into the darkness.

"*Durroe watt radia*," Vi whispered under her breath, stepping back against the wall.

"I'll give you one more chance. Show yourself."

Fire burst into life in the hearth. It cast long, shifting shadows on each of the bookcases. Vi could see its light shining through the tops of the books between the shelves from where she stood.

She saw the orange glow falling on a young man who needed no introduction. Her heart began to race.

Vi had wondered what she'd feel when she first laid eyes on Aldrik Solaris. The man who, in another world, had been her father. The man whose mother she'd taken from him.

There were too many emotions within her now to count, blending together into something impossible to name.

His dark hair went past his shoulders, unbound in a style Vi had never seen her father wear before. He was awkwardly tall, mostly legs and gangly arms—a body half grown and still trying to fill itself out. Vi recognized that phase. She'd been there herself.

This is not your father, Vi reminded herself. Yet her eyes, her heart, tried to tell her otherwise. The magic glyph around her wrist trembled with her hands.

He walked down the rows of shelves, searching. "I could've sworn…" Aldrik mumbled. Vi remained stone still, and the young prince eventually shook his head and rubbed his eyes. It was late, and he no doubt wrote off her faint light as a trick of his mind.

The prince set out purposefully for another section of the library. She watched him over the tops of the books. Every muscle was tense; she wouldn't have been able to move if she'd tried.

What is it you're looking for? Vi silently asked as Aldrik scanned the shelves with intent.

He slid a book from the shelf, his dark eyes almost meeting Vi's as she stared at him, entranced.

"Groundbreakers and their fortifications in Shaldan," he muttered to himself, scanning the first few pages. "Sky fortresses… impenetrable magic walls…" He stopped, eyes on a page. Aldrik snapped the book shut and started back down the row and out the library.

The fire in the hearth extinguished, leaving darkness in his wake.

Vi stepped out from her hiding place, listening carefully to the fading steps before relaxing her glyph.

"Groundbreakers, *hmm*?" Vi murmured. The prince was reading about the North when no one was looking. He was trying to hide his interest and Vi knew the reason why.

The Emperor was beginning to make moves against Shaldan.

And that meant she had less time than she thought to find out what happened to the crown of the first Solaris king, and get out of the capital.

5

"Ah, punctual I see," Egmun said as they met in the hallway outside his office door.

"I wouldn't want to be late after all you've promised me."

"What I promised, and will deliver." He ran a hand over the doorknob and the ice that blocked the lock withdrew into his fingertips. "Please, come in."

As they entered the office, the Minister went right for the cabinets in the back of the room. From the uppermost, he retrieved an unassuming box. Egmun set it on his desk reverently and Vi approached with apprehension. Engraved on it was Western writing, worn with time, and Vi knew what was inside before he opened the lid. The minister lifted a shimmering crystal from within.

"They're magnificent, no?"

"Where did you get those?" There were four more stones nestled against the plush velvet lining of the box.

"Western heirlooms." Egmun turned the crystal over in his fingers, the faint, blue light catching on the outline of his face and turning his pale hair to the same icy blue as his eyes. "They were a bit tricky to get my hands on, I admit. But I managed. The Knights of Jadar still claim I stole them." He chuckled. "I'm sure they'll claim I stole the sword, too, once it inevitably becomes known that it has returned to the world under my possession."

"I hope information about the sword doesn't get back to the Knights."

"Truth is like cupping water in your hands." Egmun glanced at her. "Impossible to keep to yourself for long."

"Well, either way, you don't seem like the sort of man who cares much for what others think." Vi leaned against his desk and plucked one of the smaller stones from the box. It shimmered brightly underneath her fingers, the magic calling out to her. Vi almost had to make a conscious effort not to absorb the frail power within. Vi suspected these crystals had been severed from the Caverns long ago, during the Burning Times and the reign of Jadar. She wondered if the Windwalkers she'd read about last night in the library were the last ones to have held these stones.

It didn't seem like enough power was collected in them that Vi needed to worry about their presence affecting her plans at all. She was trying to preserve Yargen's power, certainly. But Vi's plans hinged on the raw essence of the goddess, not tiny offshoots of magic from that essence.

"I've never seen a crystal have that reaction before." Egmun startled her from her thoughts.

"It's just a different way to draw out the magic. You use the flow from your own channel to pull it along." Vi pulled the lie out of thin air.

"I've never tried that before… or read anything about that." His eyes had an undeniably cautious glint.

"I picked it up in my readings in the West. This method is more similar to how the Windwalkers work with the stones."

"Not many tomes on the crystal magics still exist in the West. The Emperor took most of the writings with him when he returned south following the late Empress's death."

"What did you say about truth? Like holding water in your hands?"

Vi smiled thinly and returned the crystal to the box, hoping to end the conversation. Egmun placed his crystal back in the dip in the velvet.

"You said you weren't with the Knights of Jadar."

"I'm not," Vi insisted.

"Yet you have a fascination with the stones one would expect a Knight of Jadar to have. You have knowledge one would expect only a Knight to possess."

"Don't assume just because I am Western and appreciate the power of the crystals that I must also be a Knight of Jadar." Vi straightened away from the desk. "I don't assume that just because you are Southern and obsessed with items of great power that you are working on behalf of the Emperor to gain weapons for him to use against Shaldan." She let the words *unless you are* remain unsaid.

Egmun laughed from his belly. "Fair, fair." He shook his head, as though the notion had caused him great amusement. "Though I'm not working with the Emperor and have proof of that."

"Oh?"

"You'll see soon—" He was interrupted by a knock on the door. "There they are now." Egmun smiled in a most devious way. He passed her a folio on his way to the door. "Here, take this ledger and record what happens." Vi accepted it wordlessly, allowing the tides of fate to pull her along. "Good morning, my prince. Victor."

Victor. Vi recognized the name from her studies as a girl. She also recognized it from Taavin's tales of past iterations of their world. This man was always behind the ultimate destruction of the Crystal Caverns, usually involving the crown of the first Solaris King somehow.

He was the one whose name her mother cringed to speak, and her father scowled to hear. He had been the source of suffering in their lives. Vi could only wonder what he'd end up being to her now.

His eyes met hers as Victor entered the room with a relaxed gait. She kept her face passive save for the small smile that had worked its way onto her lips. In this world, she would be the one to find the crystal crown, not him.

"Good morning, Egmun."

Another voice stole Vi's attention. Her gaze shifted and Vi saw Aldrik clearly for the first time. His dark eyes settled on her and Aldrik froze in place.

"Who's she?"

"She's a recent graduate of the Academy of Arcane Arts in Norin," Egmun lied deftly.

"Does the Academy still accept students?" Aldrik asked, clearly unsure of the answer.

"Graduate? You don't look like you could be any older than I am." Victor rubbed the makings of a goatee on his chin, which was currently little more than a ghost of stubble.

"We all progress differently." Egmun said, going behind his desk. The two young men assumed their seats in the chairs opposite. Vi remained poised, her folio at the ready to take notes as instructed.

"Yes, not everyone is as slow as you, Victor," Aldrik said with a grin. He clearly intended the words to be mischievous, but even Vi could tell they struck a sensitive spot instead.

"And what is your name?" Victor asked her, pointedly ignoring the prince. He clearly had a well-established relationship with Aldrik, seeing as the prince let his doggedness slide.

"Vivian." Vi bowed her head. "It is an honor to be observing two of the Tower's most illustrious students."

"So you told her about us?" Aldrik lounged, looking between Vi and the box. "About everything?"

"She has a good handle of the situation herself." Egmun gave a nod. "Vivian is well studied on the matter of crystals." Just the word "crystals" felt like crossing a threshold from which there was no turning back. "She's my new research assistant."

"I thought you knew everything?" Aldrik quipped. He was the epitome of a young prince, from the way he draped himself across the chair to the way he said the first thing that flew into his mind without any concern or filter. Vi felt herself inwardly cringe in embarrassment on Aldrik's behalf... and her own. She was old and wise enough now to know that she had been much the same once. "Isn't that why we're bothering to learn from you?"

"We all have something more we can learn," Victor said firmly. "Now, don't embarrass yourself in front of our guest."

Aldrik glanced back at her, awareness of how he had sounded

appearing across his face. Vi held his eyes for a long moment—long enough that he was the one to break the stare.

Egmun slid the box across the desk and clicked it open. "Shall we begin?"

Vi watched with a mixture of curiosity and horror as the two young men picked up the stones. They each held them in their open palms and closed their eyes, an intense look of focus overtaking them. She twisted the quill between her fingers, eventually forcing herself to jot down a note. Writing after living in the woods for so long felt uncomfortable and awkward.

Perhaps it was just the situation that was uncomfortable.

"Good, join your power with the stone's. Try to connect your channel with it."

Egmun was stealing her words, though it did the young men little good. Vi kept her eyes on the crystals. They didn't change in the slightest.

"Let's start slow," Egmun continued.

Victor and Aldrik conjured ice and flame respectively, sometimes pitting their elements against each other, sometimes seeing how long they could sustain frost and blaze, and how intensely the magic could collect. Vi made some arbitrary scribbles, but mostly just gnawed on the end of the quill in thought. They weren't accomplishing much other than exposing themselves needlessly to the crystals for about half an hour in the name of seeing how crystals impacted their magic.

"That's enough for today. We don't want to risk your minds and bodies becoming corrupted from crystal taint." The minister finally stood, motioning to the box. "Please, return them."

"It feels strange... letting it go after you've had it." Aldrik curled and uncurled his fingers as if he were still imagining holding the stone.

"Strange how?" Vi asked.

"I forgot you were there." Aldrik blinked at her several times, as if he'd just returned to the plane of existence. Then, realizing he hadn't answered her question, continued, "You can feel it fueling your magic, making it stronger, sharper. When I hold it, I almost feel like I could make or do anything."

Victor was intensely focused on the box.

"And you, Victor?" Vi asked. "What do you feel?"

It took several seconds for him to shake his blank expression, for his eyes to regain clarity. The man pushed himself away from the chair, standing with a start. "I feel like I want more." With that, he abruptly left the office.

"Victor we haven't even—" Aldrik tried to call after him, but was met with a closing door. "What's gotten into him?"

"He's likely just jealous of your prowess," Egmun said.

"Well, he and I are on the same page. I want to practice more, too."

"I'm glad to hear that." Egmun returned the box to its hiding place. Vi's focus remained on the door. "But that's all we are going to work on today."

I want more. The words stuck with her. As soon as he'd said them, Victor had stormed off with purpose. A dangerous question crept into Vi's mind: *Had Victor already located the crown?*

Vi set down her notes and made her way out as Aldrik and Egmun spoke. Egmun gave her a questioning look. "Please excuse me, I just remembered an appointment I must attend," Vi said hastily and left the office.

She couldn't waste any time beginning her search, especially now that she knew Victor might already be ahead of her.

The Tower hallway was empty. She strode down the spiraling pathway, keeping her eyes peeled for Victor, but there was no sign of him. She'd waited too long to follow.

Cursing softly, Vi headed toward an unmarked door on the outer ring of the tower. Behind this door was a narrow path—a secret passage that connected the Tower of Sorcerers with the palace proper. Vi emerged into a servant's hall and, after orienting herself, started for the Imperial Library. She hadn't seen much that would be useful in the Tower Library, and the Imperial Library's collection was easily ten times the size.

On entering, she stepped hastily between shelves, easily avoiding the attention of any library staff without the need of flashes of Lightspinning. The last thing she wanted was someone asking too many questions about what she was doing.

"Histories… Histories…" Vi murmured to herself as she passed between the towering bookcases. Eventually, she made her way to a section dedicated to the histories of the Solaris Empire, organized by dates and rulers. The history of the Solaris Kingdom was tucked away in a corner of the tallest shelf, requiring her to climb one of the rolling ladders to reach.

Vi plucked the first book and skimmed the pages.

"Too long ago." She returned it and grabbed the next one. "The crown of Solaris was bestowed on the eldest son of the original Solaris. It was a boon given to him by the Mother, ordaining him to rule this land," Vi read aloud.

The words *boon given to him by the Mother* were underlined in mostly faded blue ink.

Vi flipped ahead a few pages. More words were underlined in the same pale ink.

… a powerful Waterrunner, the crown bestowed the Mother's blessing on him.

… then he crafted the first Solaris castle entirely of ice…

His son did not have magic. However, with the crown, he could inspire loyalty in those around him with powers unlike any other…

The book was littered with faint blue lines scribbled throughout. Some were dotted, some were double lined. A few passages were even circled. Vi furrowed her brow and ran her finger over a note at the end of the book. Scribbled in the corner on the back of the last page, it read:

One - Blue.

"One, blue," Vi read aloud. "What does that mean?" A frown crossed her lips. She didn't know what kind of notation system or code this person was using. But she did know one thing with confidence—someone else was tracking the history of the crown.

Vi just hoped it wasn't Victor.

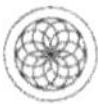

Vi's head jerked up as she was startled by a knock on the door—three fast raps, followed by two slower ones. Rubbing her bleary eyes, Vi glanced out the windows. The midnight oil was burning in the mostly dark city below and that meant she'd been at it for at least five hours straight.

Putting down the book she'd been combing through, Vi opened the door without hesitation. Only one person knocked that way.

She was met with the face of a Tower apprentice—a pale-skinned young woman with straw-colored hair.

"I wasn't expecting anyone," Vi said with a tired smile.

"Well, when you become a hermit for a few weeks, you run the risk of people seeking you out." The young woman's eyes darted down the Tower hall. "Now, let me in before someone sees I don't belong here."

"I doubt that would happen. For how secretive they are, the Tower doesn't seem like it has the best security." Vi stepped to the side to let Deneya enter, and she watched the illusion vanish from her shoulders.

"Can never be too careful." Deneya hoisted a folio in the air. "I found it."

"You did." Vi carefully grabbed the time-worn folio from Deneya's hands. She opened it on the table, pulling out the papers one by one.

"Don't get your hopes up. There's not much there about the theft of the royal treasure." Deneya leaned on the back of one of the chairs. "All the names have been redacted."

She wasn't wrong, of course. Four lone sheets of paper were all that remained recorded of the greatest heist in the history of the Solaris Empire.

"Why would they blot them out?"

"I have a theory. Here, look at this one." Deneya held up a sheet of paper. She pointed to one of the names that had been poorly inked away. The pen scribbles were hasty, and only covered half of the letters.

A—la

"Whose name does that look like to you?" Deneya asked with a grin.

"Adela." The ink in the books had been too faded to be recent. The person who made those notations to find the crown's location wasn't Victor. "She was the one searching for the crown and who ultimately stole it."

"That's my theory. Also why they blotted out all other references of her name."

"Men and their superstitions," Vi muttered. She remembered how just the whispered name "Adela" had been considered bad luck in Norin.

"My bet would be pride for this one. Losing your family's heirlooms and treasure is one thing… letting your father be murdered by that same thief and then having her slip through your grasp? Too much for a young, budding Emperor to handle."

"Do you know what happened to the rest of the records?"

"If there were more, they're long gone. It's a miracle I could find these."

"Thank you for your hard work." Vi paused her reading to look Deneya in the eye when she gave her thanks. Having another set of eyes on everything she was piecing together—another set of hands to double the work—was invaluable.

"I am in Lumeria's Order of Shadows." Deneya smiled gleefully. "Collecting information like this is my job. The Queen will be all too happy if it's also information on the bane of the seas."

"Adela," Vi whispered. She lifted another sheet of paper. "The thief fled to the coast. The treasure was never recovered." Setting down the paper, Vi quickly went to the shelves underneath the windows in the back of the room. Vi had grown tired of constantly going back and forth to the library, so she'd been ferrying books back and forth for weeks now in secret.

"You're amassing a little library," Deneya observed.

"I've had a lot of time to read lately," Vi murmured. She'd discovered reading to be different than she remembered—especially when it came to histories. She read both the black ink of the words *and* the white space between them. There were phantom memories within her; sections of her subconscious remembered past worlds and connected them in ways that should be impossible.

Likely, the memories weren't her own at all. They were Yargen's. But that was a truth Vi left in uncharted territory, for now. Taavin was right: they had enough to worry about.

"Here it is." Vi located the book she was looking for and crossed back to Deneya, handing it over.

"*The Imperial Summer Palace in Oparium.*" Deneya opened to the middle and was greeted by blueprints that were now familiar to Vi. "Architectural drawings?"

"Yes, I had to get into the Imperial archives for this one… Unlike my other stolen books, I'll need to return this soon. But for now, look at the foreword." Vi's mind was moving so fast her mouth could barely keep up. "The date, specifically."

"Construction began in 308." Deneya glanced up at her. Vi held out the paper she'd been reading. "The theft was in 307." Comprehension lit up Deneya's face.

"The theft of the Imperial jewels that dated back into antiquity was in 307. King Romulin Solaris was murdered the same year, leaving Tiberus Solaris to become King. Then, the man who was to declare himself Emperor the very next year decided to make his first act as a ruler building a summer home?"

"Young men are fickle creatures."

"You know Tiberus," Vi said seriously. "He wouldn't let Adela's transgressions go."

"Then what do you think it is?"

"The manor is a front for something, I'd bet."

"A front for what?"

"I don't know, but look." Vi took the book back from Deneya's hands and rested it on the table, flipping through. "These plans are incomplete… There are sections missing. Doors lead to nowhere and hallways crop up from nothing."

"How can you tell?" Deneya shifted, looking over her shoulder.

"I just can. See, here, there's—"

"I'm going to stop you there; I'm not going to understand anyway." Deneya laughed. "I trust you."

"I don't know how you can understand how to make leather and smithed goods, but claim you can't grasp architecture."

"We all have our strengths." Deneya held out her hands and shrugged with a small smile, but her expression turned serious once more. "So where does this leave us with the crown?"

"Adela successfully stole it, of that I'm confident." Just saying it aloud made Vi's toes curl with how *right* it felt. "She must have fled to Oparium. It's the largest port near Solarin."

"Makes sense for the most infamous pirate the world has ever seen. Tiberus followed her in pursuit and… built a house with incomplete architectural drawings?"

"I don't understand that bit either," Vi admitted. "But that's a mystery for another time. The first order of business is to make sure Adela actually got the treasure out of the palace. We have to rule that out with as much certainty as possible before we go chasing another lead." Vi doubted that Taavin would go with her on a gut feeling when it came to this. She needed more proof of her theories before they took action.

"If she didn't get it out of the palace, wouldn't someone have already found it?"

Vi glanced back at her collection of books—a wealth of history on the Solaris family. Theirs was a bloodline that ran all the way back to the eldest son of the Champion.

"No," Vi said. "This place is old, very old, and it's been built on time and again. Who knows what may be hiding in its depths?"

THE MOMENT DENEYA LEFT, Vi summoned Taavin. He barely had time to orient himself before she asked, "Do you know where Adela's room in the Tower of Sorcerers was?"

"Excuse me?" Two emerald eyes blinked at her in startled confusion.

"Adela's room, when she was a student of the Tower… do you know where it was?"

Focus crossed his face and Taavin shook his head. "A moment." He held out his arms and murmured the chant that connected him to all the knowledge of their past iterations. As the light faded from him, he shook his head again. "This isn't something you've asked me before. Why do you need to know about Adela?"

"I think she's the one who took the crown—well before the point at which the world is being rebuilt time and again. The crown's location has always been variable. Her stealing it may have been a stone in the river, but everything else about how she did it—"

"Changes," Taavin finished thoughtfully. "Adela would be an agent of chaos in the world."

"Exactly. I need to figure out if the crown left the palace or not." Vi filled him in on all her discoveries—the books, Deneya's records, her gut instinct. "If it's here, we have it. If I'm right, and it's not… then it's either in Oparium, or with Adela herself."

"Let's hope it's not the latter." Taavin sighed and raked a hand through his hair. "I'm sorry, I don't know where her room was."

"Do you know *anything* about her? Beyond the obvious? Any memories of her, no matter how insignificant, might be helpful."

"You seem desperate."

"I am." Vi folded her arms. "Victor might be ahead of me in the hunt for the crown. I'm not sure." She shook her head at the whole situation—at the mere thought of Victor getting his hands on the crown. In her world, when he had, he'd used the crystals' power to challenge the Solaris family in a bloody coup. He'd become known as the Mad King for his twisted ways, and any effort Vi could make to thwart or postpone his nefarious tendencies would be effort well spent.

"I see." A pained look crossed his features. "I'm sorry, Vi. I don't have much knowledge on Adela beyond what you likely already know."

"It's all right." Vi crossed to him and took both his hands in hers. She gripped them tightly. "The knowledge you've given me has already done so much. I can take care of this." Leaning forward, Vi placed a chaste kiss on his lips, quickly pulling away. Now was not the time for romance. Deneya's revelations had lit a fire in her. "I'll let you know what I find."

"Where are you—" She'd dismissed him before he could finish.

"Sorry," Vi murmured to the empty air and left her room. The night was young, and the iron of her mind was hot—ready to strike.

She wound about halfway down the Tower to a central room. Long tables stood empty, projects scattered about them, waiting for their Waterrunners to return in the morning. Around the outside of the room were narrow doors that led to private workshops.

Vi peered into the darkness, imagining Adela here. The woman was sixteen, or maybe just seventeen. She had the same icy blue eyes. Her hair was blonde, not white. She was younger, but as confident and arrogant as the Adela Vi knew. She sauntered around the Tower and this room like she owned the place.

This was the shade of the woman who had marked up Imperial Library books, if Vi's theory was right. She plotted the greatest theft in Solaris history right under the eyes of the royal guard and family. Adela had been so confident that no one would suspect her, she even left a paper trail.

"You wanted someone to find you, didn't you?" Vi whispered into the imaginary face of the young Adela. She could almost envision the teenager smirking back. Adela would want someone to piece together her brilliance.

What good was a history-making theft without leaving enough behind for the bards to spin tales of her infamy?

Vi's midsection tensed with a phantom pain and she suppressed a shiver, remembering where Adela had gouged her with an icicle. She hated the thought of playing into Adela's plans. But letting the crown slip through her fingers was not an option.

To the right of the door was a narrow bookshelf. Each of the books on it seemed to contain records of the projects and supplies used by Waterrunners within the Tower. Vi went right for the year 307.

Sure enough, a familiar pale blue ink was neatly scribbled next to various dates throughout the year. The Tower records had been exempted from the systematic expunging of Adela's identity. Likely, in part, because her name wasn't actually written anywhere.

Vi focused only on what she assumed to be Adela's entries.

A.L. — Storeroom duty.

A.L. — Borrowed seven tokens from the storeroom.

A.L. — Training grounds, Waterrunner combat.

A.L. — Storeroom duty.

A.L. — Waterrunner combat.

A.L. — Absent.

A.L. — Storeroom duty.

The combat made sense to Vi. Adela was frighteningly good in a fight. She'd bet the absence was a trip to Oparium to plan her getaway.

Perhaps that was when Adela had even purchased a ship.

"What was your obsession with the storeroom?" Vi murmured, replacing the book back on the shelf.

One by one, Vi opened each of the doors on the outer ring of the workshop. Black disks hung by each one, and every room was identical to the last. A single flame bulb hung over a center pedestal that had water in a shallow indent on top. Vi could only speculate as to the function of the rooms, but she was certain none of them was a storeroom.

Working to quell her frustration, Vi went to leave and it hit her. She froze, staring directly across the hall at an outer door marked *Waterrunner Supplies* rather than the name of an apprentice of the Tower.

"You arrogant pirate," Vi said with a small grin.

Luckily, the storeroom was unlocked. Inside were a few shelves on either side covered in all manner of baubles, books, quills, inkwells, and parchment. Vi closed the door behind her and brought a hand to the watch around her neck.

"*Narro hath hoolo.*"

Taavin appeared before her. "We're in… a closet?"

"A storeroom, more precisely. I think this was integral to Adela's plan."

"How so?"

Vi didn't appreciate his skeptical tone. But she didn't begrudge him it, either. "Perhaps she hid the crown here. Or maybe it leads to another secret passage. The palace is full of them."

"I'm surprised you don't know every last passage there is." Taavin folded his arms over his chest.

"I've been working on it." Vi gave him a mischievous grin. "I don't suppose you can use *uncose* to expose any hidden exits?"

"Not in this form, unfortunately." Taavin looked down at his palms and Vi barely resisted the urge to tell him that she would make him real. One way or another, someday soon, he would have a body and his magic once more.

"It's all right, help me look." Vi began scouring the shelf to the right of the door.

"I don't think we have to look very far."

"What?" Vi turned to find him pointing at a narrow strip of wood that ran the length of the wall, floor to ceiling, in the back corner. Cobwebs clung to it and Vi nearly coughed up a lung as she disturbed the dust to expose the wood to the light of her flame. The firelight clung to the carved shape of a trident, gouged deep. "Adela's symbol," she whispered. "How did you even see this?"

"Elfin eyes," he said with a grin.

Vi narrowed her gaze in his direction. "You just started in the right side of the room is all." She took a step back, pulling a heavy barrel away from the corner. She followed the strip of wood up, over, and back down, where a clean line ran behind one of the shelves. "I think it's a door."

"How do you figure?"

Rather than answering, Vi lifted her hand, pressing it to the wood. It went up in eager flames, turning to a pile of ash. Sure enough, hidden behind the wedge was a miniature handle mostly obscured by the shaded alcove.

"Like that."

"Why would Adela mark the entrance to her hideout?" Taavin asked as Vi gripped the handle, pushing her shoulder into the door.

"Two theories. One, she planned to come back here, or send someone else back here. Two, she wanted to be found by whoever was clever enough to follow her." Vi grunted and pushed harder. The stone door groaned on hinges that didn't want to open. "With any luck, we'll find the crown right—"

Vi paused as the door finally opened in full and she stared at the room beyond.

Dust had settled on every surface, from the mostly empty bookshelf to the cot. Vi's attention was drawn to the threadbare tapestry hanging by threads. A rudimentary trident was stitched on it.

"Was this her room?" Taavin asked, entering.

"No… she would've been given a Tower bedroom as an apprentice. This must've been her hideaway."

"She lived a double life even then. A bed as an apprentice… a bed as a pirate," Taavin murmured as Vi crossed to the bookcase.

Notebooks were still lined up on it.

She grabbed one off the top shelf, but it had nothing but notes on Waterrunner combat. Vi returned it as her eyes settled on another row of Adela's records. Each journal on the lower shelf had a different colored spine, and a number.

"One, blue." Vi took the first notebook. Within were scribbles in what was now an all-too-familiar ink. "Each of these notebooks corresponds to a book she'd read in the library." Vi flipped the pages. "There's a whole system here—circles, dots—these are the cyphers to all her markings."

Separately, Adela's notes didn't make any sense. They were jargon about ships, seafaring maps, and histories. But with the library books in tandem, Vi was getting a complete picture of how Adela had tracked the crown through the ages and planned her getaway.

"What does it say about the crown?"

"I don't know yet, other than she wanted it." Vi scanned the pages. "She knew it could give her great power. That seems to be enough for most mortals."

"Most… *mortals*?" Taavin repeated quietly. Vi tensed and looked up from the notebook. His emerald eyes searched hers with intense purpose.

"I'm not quite mortal, not anymore," Vi whispered. "We both know that."

"I've never heard you say it in such a way before though."

Don't look at me like that, she wanted to say. It was the same look he'd given her in those ruins a lifetime ago. A look that saw something in her she herself wasn't ready to see.

"Well, it's a good thing I'm not mortal." Vi closed the book and returned it to the shelf. "Otherwise I couldn't do what needs to be done."

She took another book off the shelf to avoid staring at him. This one wasn't a notebook, but a proper manuscript instead. It was all about the port of Oparium, the closest port to Lyndum, and how it had been built. There were underlined passages regarding the difficulties the builders had in constructing the town and port due to the craggy, cave-pocked rocks and cliffs surrounding it.

Scraps of papers caught her eye. Balancing the book in one hand, Vi unfolded the leaves. Rough sketches made up the lines on rudimentary maps of what appeared to be tunnels.

"What's that?" Taavin asked.

"Her heist." Vi held up one of the maps. "Adela found a room to store her information here in the palace. I'm sure she had another secret passage she used to escape, because if she was caught it would've been recorded in the guards' records. But since her name was blotted out, I can only believe that she—and the crown—at least made it to Oparium. I'd bet she used these tunnels when she was there to evade the encroaching Imperial guards." Vi put the map down, moving to hold up another when a slip of paper fluttered to the floor.

"What's that?" Taavin asked, crouching down. Vi mirrored the motion and picked up the note.

She recognized the script. *No*, she recognized a handwriting *very* similar—this writing looked just like her father's and was too close to be chance. Vi read the inscription aloud:

"My darling A.L.,
I know you've been fascinated lately on the histories of Oparium. I encountered these maps in the archives and thought of you. Consider it a gift.
Forever yours, T.S. "

"A.L. must be Adela Lagmir," Taavin said, looking up to her.

"I would assume." Vi returned the maps and the note to the book. The other ledgers could stay—they contained nothing more than notes and plans Vi already knew about. This book was coming back with her.

"Who do you think T.S. is? He seems fond of her."

"Isn't it obvious?" Vi started for the door. "Who else could take a book from the archives? Who else would Adela want to become close to?" A look of clarity overtook Taavin. "T.S. must be Tiberus Solaris."

"Your grandfather and Adela were… intimate?"

Vi cringed at the word. "I don't know about *my* grandfather. Though, it would explain why Adela hates and has always hated my family so profoundly, if he wronged her somehow…" All those years ago, when Vi had infiltrated a meeting of the Knights of Jadar, Twintle had said that Adela had reduced her rate to work against Solaris. The memory of the remark suddenly took on new meaning.

"Then she would want to get back at Solaris whenever possible."

They emerged back into the storeroom and Vi returned the barrel to where it had been. Hopefully, no one would notice the lack of wood or deep groove in the back corner. But, if they did, these were the sorts of things Adela's legends were made of. Vi could almost picture some Waterrunner gleefully telling his friends about the discovery.

"We need to get to Oparium and explore these caves." Vi tapped the book in her hands.

"Not until Aldrik goes to the Caverns with the sword." Taavin grabbed her shoulder and shook her gently. "We can't deviate from the stones in the river. A new Champion must be reborn."

"Taavin, we have the weapons in our grasp. Now is the time to act." Vi gripped his forearm, staring him in the eyes. "We can seize this opportunity and save our world."

"And if we fail, we have doomed it." His hold on her tightened. "You know what's at stake."

"Better than anyone."

"But not better than me." In his haunted eyes she could see every one of the ninety-three worlds he'd witnessed. "Aldrik must go to the Caverns. Give him your fake sword, if you must. But we will see the stones in the river honored. Yargen cannot just choose a new Champion from the masses and start the world over again. It must be the daughter of Vhalla and Aldrik Solaris, just as it was the first time. It's the only way to preserve this loop."

Vi swallowed once, twice; it took three times and a nod for the lump in her throat to finally go away. She knew what he said was true. In some deep and terrible way, she knew it to her core.

"All right," Vi whispered. "We do what we must here. And then to Oparium."

A FLURRY OF KNOCKS woke Vi with a start.

Adela's notebook fell from her chest and landed heavily in her lap. The maps were scattered around the bed. More knocking followed.

"Impatient…" she mumbled, cursing under her breath. Dawn was just breaking through the curtains of her room and after being up half the night, she'd planned to sleep in. "Just a moment!" Vi said, louder.

Swinging her legs off the side of the bed, she flung over the duvet to hide the books and parchment in its fold. Standing, Vi crossed to the door and grabbed the black jacket that hung on a peg next to it. She slung it over her shoulders, smoothed out her hair and clothing, and opened the door just as another set of knocks were about to begin.

Vi blinked grumpily at the blond man staring back at her.

"Victor, to what do I owe the pleasure?" Vi glanced around the hall. He appeared to be alone. "I don't believe we have lessons this morning." *And never this early*, she thought bitterly.

"Egmun has demanded to see you." Victor looked her up and down. Vi had no doubt done a poor job of hiding that she was still in her clothes from the day before—clothes she'd just been sleeping in. "Do you need a moment to put yourself together?"

Vi arched a single eyebrow and, rather than saying anything, strode out of her room like a princess. She locked the door behind her and returned the key to her pocket. Without waiting for him to lead, Vi descended toward Egmun's office.

"Are you his errand boy now?" Vi asked dryly.

"I'm his *most valued* assistant."

"I bet you are."

Victor paused in front of the door to the office of the Minister of Sorcery. A smirk spread across his lips. "I know I'm not up half the night, snooping through Tower storerooms and stealing Mother-knows-what."

Vi kept a sneer at bay, barely. She was too tired to deal with this petulant child. Vi took a step forward but Victor straightened. Even though she was higher on the slope of the hall, they were still eye to eye.

"Don't question what I do," Vi cautioned, "for it is far beyond the realm of what your mortal mind can comprehend."

"Mortal mind? Just who do you think you are?"

"I am the one who has seen the end, and will see the beginning of your destiny," she said ominously. It took everything in her not to have him flat on the ground, threatening him within an inch of his life. Only Taavin's abundance of caution, and Vi's fragile self-control, held her back. "Now get out of my sight."

"With pleasure." Victor didn't back down, right until the end. He took three steps backward and turned.

Vi watched him leave, firing curses at his back. Somehow, he knew she'd been in the storeroom. That made it only a matter of time until Victor found Adela's room. He was smart enough to piece it together, and all the pieces were secreted there.

The only thing that kept her from chasing after him was the knowledge that she had taken the key book on Oparium that contained Adela's maps. Additionally, the journals were useless without the library books also in Vi's possession. Trusting she was one step ahead, Vi knocked on the door to the minister's office.

"Enter," he said sharply. Vi did as he bid and found Egmun pacing the room. He stopped, spinning to face her, the moment the door closed. "I need to see it."

"You'd do well to not make demands of me in such a tone. I'm not one of your lapdogs." Vi was too tired to play along. He seemed genuinely taken aback.

"And you'd do well to not risk this shaky alliance we've formed. You need the prince, after all."

She didn't. Taavin did. But Vi was dutifully following his instructions still. Here she was, keeping the world on the rails, while Victor could be off hunting for the crown. Her lead on him slipped with every moment she wasted on Egmun.

"Bickering will get us nowhere." Vi pinched the bridge of her nose and sighed. "What have I done to earn such mistrust?"

"Nothing, and that's much the problem. I have given you everything these past weeks. I've given you food, shelter, access to the prince, even the ability to rummage through my Tower without an escort." Victor had run right to Egmun after tracking her last night. "And you've given me no indication other than your word that you have the sword at all."

Vi narrowed her eyes, though her displeasure was mostly directed inward. She'd been too focused on her movements and hadn't been accounting for the desires of others. The first night she'd seen Aldrik in the library, researching the North, came back to her.

"The Emperor is taking an interest in the Crystal Caverns, isn't he?" she said softly, so as not to speak over the pieces clicking together in her mind. Egmun's startled eyes said all she needed to know. The Emperor was interested in the Crystal Caverns because he wanted to go to war with the North and was looking for a secret weapon to bring with him. "You want to get there before he does."

Egmun was silent for a long moment. Then, "Yes."

"I'll show you the sword."

"You will?"

"Yes, but you must stay here and do not track me to its hiding place. I will know if you do."

"You really have it?" His voice was hurried and thin, as if he was afraid the truth was something that could break if he spoke too loudly.

"I always have."

Vi shut the door to the office firmly behind her and began down the halls. The spark had lit an inferno in her stomach, the likes of which she hadn't felt in some time. She wouldn't be surprised if steam was coming out of her ears.

She wanted to give chase down the hall and find Victor. She wanted to demand he tell her what he had seen of her movements, what books he had read, how close behind her he was. But that pursuit would have been futile.

Victor was a mortal, chained to fate, destined to heed the whims of two heartless gods. She couldn't concern herself with him any more than she concerned herself with the rats that ran through the sewers underneath her feet.

The walk to the stables did little to calm her. When Vi arrived, she could feel the sparks crackling around her knuckles. She scanned the mostly empty stalls, looking for a woman she recognized.

"You look like you're ready to murder someone," Deneya said, emerging and wiping her hands on a rag that she returned to a belt loop. "Don't think I've seen you like this since Norin. Welcome back."

"I need the sword you've been working on."

"It's not ready."

"It's going to have to be."

Deneya sighed and shrugged. "All right, follow me."

Vi followed her up a side stair that wound inside the outer wall of the palace surrounding the stables. Inside the wall was a series of doors that led to rooms for each of the stable hands, fitted with a bed, table, dresser, and a single window that overlooked the horses beyond.

"Here." Deneya lifted a short sword from behind her dresser, holding it out to Vi.

"It isn't long enough."

"He doesn't know that."

Vi pulled the sword from the scabbard. It was almost unnaturally light. The metal was nearly white from the alloys used.

"I was going to make a longer one. This was merely a first attempt. But it seems we ran out of time."

"You're right, he doesn't know the difference." Vi held out the sword before her, staring at the weapon intently. *"Durroe watt ivin."* Yellow glyphs, tinted with white, surrounded the sword. They sank into the weapon and painted it with new colors. Bright splashes of blue swirled against deeper shades, nearly purple. Sparks of magic drifted off the weapon. Vi gave it a swing, watching the illusion cling to the blade.

"It's more convincing than any other illusion I've seen here. I'm sure he'll buy it." Deneya laced her fingers and placed them behind her head. "But what's the rush?"

"He's suspicious of me." Vi sheathed the sword. Even though it could no longer be seen, her magic fed the illusion. "I need to give him something."

"Then I'll pray to Yargen it works."

Vi nodded. "Be ready to move, too. You might want to start gathering your things."

"So early? I thought we needed to see them to the Crystal Caverns?"

"We'll see. The crown isn't here; I think it's in Oparium."

"Then you know where all the weapons are."

"The crown's location is still just a hunch."

"And if your suspicion is right, you want to move to get the weapons all at once?" Vi nodded again. "I bet Taavin loves that."

"Yes, well..." Vi looked at the sword, promptly ignoring the remark. "I should be getting back to Victor."

Deneya stopped her from leaving by grabbing her wrist and locking eyes with Vi.

"Remember, Vi, he's only seen how you fail. Never how you succeed. You're the Champion, not him. You're the one who's going to show us all how this ends." Deneya continued to hold her gaze. Vi opened her mouth, but couldn't quite find words. So she shut it slowly, settling for a third dip of her chin. "I'm following *you* into this future, not him."

"Thank you." That was all Vi could think to say. It wasn't nearly enough, but it was everything she meant.

"You're welcome." Deneya released her and the woman's

lighthearted manner returned. "Now, off with you. Go quell the rage of a sorcerer who thinks he's powerful."

"With pleasure."

Sword in hand, Vi made her way back through the palace to the Tower of Sorcerers. The good thing about having spent years studying the architecture and maps of the Imperial Palace meant that if she didn't want to be seen, she didn't have to be. There was always a passage, and a passage deeper still, winding within walls and behind doors to get someone from where they were to where they needed to go.

Muffled voices indicated Egmun wasn't alone, but Vi knocked anyway. "Enter." And, for the second time in one day, she did.

Egmun was seated behind his desk, Victor across from him. The young man gave her a satisfied smirk. Vi ignored him completely.

"I have what you requested."

"Show me." Egmun's eyes never left the sword. But Vi's darted to Victor. "He knows of the crystal weapons."

"Very well." In a sweeping motion, Vi unsheathed the sword. It was whisper silent; the steel hardly reverberated underneath the illusion that remained solidly in place.

"There it is," Egmun breathed, drawn to his feet. "It's really there." He walked around his desk, as if he were approaching a sacred relic. Vi continued to hold out the sword as he approached, holding her breath, waiting. Egmun's fingers trembled as he reached upward. They came in contact with the illusion. Vi's magic held. "It doesn't feel the same as the other crystals."

"This much power wouldn't. It's far more refined, not wild like the stones you use. This has been honed."

"Yes, I read all about how Jadar honed the crystal with the blood and sacrifice of Windwalkers," Egmun said lightly, as if stating a passing fact about the lineage of Solaris and not the most heinous period of the Dark Isle's history. "Finally, after all this time, it's—"

"Minister." Victor stood, breaking the moment.

"What?" Egmun turned to glare at his young apprentice. But Victor wasn't deterred.

The young man reached out his hand. With one finger, he touched the hilt at the guard, running up along the blade. Victor's eyes narrowed. When he pulled his finger back, a line of red was cut into it.

"It doesn't feel like our crystals, Minister, because it's not." Victor leveled his gaze at Vi. She met it and kept her face passive.

"What are you talking about?" Egmun balked.

"Look closer," Victor practically snapped at the man. It seemed to jostle Egmun out of the power lust that had clouded his eyes. Now, he inspected the sword far more intently. "You're a Waterrunner too. You know illusions."

"What do you see?" Egmun asked.

"It's a subtle… shift. Only visible when you touch it. A good illusion, indeed. But not a perfect one. There is no such thing as a perfect illusion."

Vi watched as her hopes were crushed under the heel of Victor's boot. Egmun wrenched the weapon from her hand. He waved it around, watching it carefully. Then, Egmun began to laugh.

"Well done, Victor. You passed our test. You may go."

"Minis—"

"I said go!" Egmun barked. Victor dismissed himself, but not before giving Vi a rather satisfied side-eye. She had to hold herself back from reaching out and snapping his neck then and there. The world would be better for it. Of that, she was nearly certain. Once the door was closed, Egmun brandished the sword at her. "What is this?"

"The Sword of—"

"Lies!" he roared, slashing it through the air. "Lies, lies, lies." Egmun slammed the weapon into the side of his deck and Vi watched it leave a deep gouge. Sure enough, her illusion writhed as the weapon wriggled. He pointed it back at her, advancing. "You, you're a Firebearer. I saw it. You can summon flames."

Vi held up both hands in an effort to be non-threatening. But tiny fires illuminated each of her fingertips. Both to prove his point, and to show that she could fight back if she wanted.

"How are you doing this?" He stopped. "Unless… unless you have an associate. Someone working with you. Was that why you were in the Waterrunner storeroom?"

"No one is working with me," Vi insisted calmly. "The illusion is mine."

"Impossible."

Vi lowered her hands and with them, the illusion fell alongside her hopes.

"That's impossible," he repeated, looking between her and the now unveiled sword.

"It's not when you know how to use the power of the crystals. I *do* have the Sword of Jadar. But I will not show you until we are leaving for the Caverns with Prince Aldrik." Vi locked eyes with the man. "Consider this demonstration my proof of the sword."

"You—"

Vi wrenched open the door behind her and stopped him mid-sentence. "You will summon me when we are to leave for the Crystal Caverns and not a moment sooner."

Before he could answer, she slammed the door and retreated to her room, where the empty scabbard in her hand and the silence that surrounded her were solemn reminders of her failure.

8

VI PACED HER BEDROOM, looking out over the city of frost that glistened like fire in the light of the sun disappearing over the Western mountaintops. Solarin shone brighter than ever before, for every day brought them closer to the prince's coming-of-age ceremony. The relentless march of time continued against her, seeming faster and faster with each passing hour.

"We need to leave," Vi said to Taavin, worrying the crystal stone that contained the power of the Sword of Jadar between her fingers. "We should take the Sword and go, get the crown before Victor can, and put an end to this."

"We need to stay. Aldrik must go to the Crystal Caverns with the sword, otherwise we risk disrupting the flow of time so dramatically that a new Champion won't be born," Taavin said calmly, clearly trying to soothe her anxious energy. Vi bit her tongue. "You have already proved you can transfer the energy from the sword to the Caverns. All will be well. You'll preserve Yargen's essence."

Vi curled and uncurled her fingers over the crystal in her palm, feeling the magic move and stretch. Manipulating Yargen's power was becoming more and more instinctive by the day. The time she'd spent scouring the Tower and Imperial libraries for information on crystals, however little there was, seemed to help. It took a lot of reading between the lines, but there was knowledge there that enhanced her nightly practice.

"What if—" A knock on the door interrupted the thought, saving Vi from herself. It was three fast raps, followed by two slower ones. Vi opened the door to an illusioned Deneya.

"He's on the move," Deneya said as she entered, casting her magic aside with a flick of her wrist.

Several curse words lit across Vi's mind. But she kept her voice level. "What's happened?"

"Egmun went out this evening. He rarely goes by horse anywhere, so I followed." Deneya was still in her stable clothes, hay clinging to the rough wool covering her forearms. "He met with some Westerners down the mountain, at one of the last inns for travelers."

"Did you recognize these Westerners?"

Deneya shook her head. "But you know humans, they age so fast. I couldn't tell you for certain if they weren't boys the last time we were in the West."

"What did they discuss?"

"It was hard to hear from my hiding place. I had to remain inconspicuous so I stayed outside, underneath a window by the booth where they sat. But I know I heard mention of the Sword of Jadar." Vi let out the string of curse words this time and ran her hand through her hair. Deneya continued, "It seems you haven't given him enough. Egmun doesn't believe you have the sword."

"So he found the Knights of Jadar to make sure *they* don't have it." Vi's attempt at an illusion was costing them more than she could've imagined.

"And, in the process, let them know that *he* does," Deneya said grimly. "They attacked him on the spot, accusing him of somehow stealing it."

"And Egmun?"

"He's all right. Slipped out in the fray. Two Knights tried to follow him but their horses were spooked by a bear emerging from the woods."

"A bear?"

"Like this one." Deneya waved her hand and uttered, *"Durroe watt ivin."* A large grizzly bear materialized in the corner of the room, roaring soundlessly. She released the illusion as quickly as she made it. "It was more convincing when I had *curo* with it, for the roar."

"Thank you for helping Egmun out of there." Vi turned to Taavin with worried eyes. "What do you think?"

"I think your time is running short." He stood from where he'd perched on the low bookshelves by the window. "You can't risk getting caught off-guard and having the sword stolen by Knights intercepting you. Aldrik taking the sword to the Caverns is a stone in the river, as I've told you. The sword will find its way to him… one way or another. But if you want to transfer the power, we ought to be the ones to see both prince and weapon to the Caverns."

"I know." Vi chewed over her thoughts, which were unpleasant as a piece of raw fat. She looked down again at the stone in her hands. "I'll have to get him there tonight."

"How?" Deneya asked.

"I don't know yet, but I'll think of something." In one fluid motion of light and magic, there was the hilt of a sword in her hand where there had previously been none. It was shorter than the original Sword of Jadar, just the right size to fit in the scabbard Deneya had made.

"You've gotten better with the crystals," Deneya said, tilting her head to the side. Her eyes drifted to Taavin. "She been practicing when we're not looking?"

"She must've been," Taavin thoughtfully replied.

"No time to go over it now." Vi returned them to the matter at hand. "Deneya, ferry some items between here and the horses. We'll take Prism and Midsummer—get them tacked and ready."

"You want me to follow behind on the way to the Caverns?"

"No, get out ahead. Go to the cabin and stash our things there. I don't know what will happen, so I want you to be nimble and ready."

"All right, anything in particular you want me to ferry?"

Vi pointed the sword at two packs in the corner. "All my things are collected."

"You were ready to go?"

"I knew we'd have to move soon… I was just hoping it wouldn't be like this." She'd hoped to head right to Oparium and bypass the Caverns entirely. But there was no way to win Taavin over to that plan. "I need to go to Egmun."

Taavin grabbed her arm, stopping her. Vi swung to face the ethereal man. "Be careful," he said, far more tender than the moment deserved. "Remember, everything you're doing is a risk. And if you die now—" he touched the watch around her neck lightly "—if you don't get this to Vhalla when the time is right. There is no Champion reborn."

"*I know*, and I'll be careful." Vi was growing weary of Taavin's well-intentioned reminders. She'd been spoiled by fourteen years when he didn't feel the need to press the issue nearly every day.

"Your eyes say something different." His touch was feather-light, but Vi was as immobile as if he'd snared her.

"I'll be careful," she repeated, softer, gentler. Vi leaned forward and kissed him lightly on the lips, releasing her hold on *narro hath* before opening her eyes.

"It's a cruel existence," Deneya said faintly, looking at where Taavin had stood just moments before.

"It is for all of us, don't you think?" Vi shrugged and left before Deneya could answer.

She would take the sword and present it to Egmun now. It was only two weeks before the coming-of-age ceremony and Aldrik would be busy for at least one of those weeks. If she pressured Egmun hard enough, in the right ways, he'd spill about the incident with the Knights and from there—

"By the Mother." A gasp interrupted her frantic planning. Vi looked up. Egmun was there, staring up at her with a mixture of awe and, to her surprise, horror. "You look like Fiera reborn."

"So I've been told." Vi lifted the sword, pointing its tip at him. The subtle threat was intentional. "You wanted the sword. I want the prince. Tonight, let's put an end—"

"I had a meeting with the Knights of Jadar," he interrupted her a second time.

Vi lowered the weapon. She didn't even have to feign annoyance and irritation, just surprise. "You *what*?"

"I had my doubts," he began. "Perfectly rational… When we first met, you spoke of Fiera's death with confidence. My research shows that the only people there when she died were the Knights. Then, after the fake sword, after I thought you had help from a Waterrunner— conspirators… Well, what would you have thought in my position?"

He took a breath to continue, but it was Vi's turn to interrupt him. She stepped forward, lifted the sword once more, and put it under his chin.

"I would've known when I looked upon an entity greater than myself. I would've known not to question," Vi said, dangerously quiet. Even though he was held at sword point, Egmun didn't look the slightest bit scared. His eyes were wide with anticipation, thrill, and a shameful lust for the immense magic contained within the crystal. "Can you feel it? The power this sword holds? Does it make you shiver and shake and yearn for more?"

He swallowed, the lump in his neck nearly scraping against the sword point.

"There's more of this magic to be had, much more." Vi slowly lowered the weapon and his eyes followed. "We've wasted too much time. We go to the Caverns tonight."

"Tonight, there's no—"

"Let's step into your office." Vi glanced over her shoulder. Deneya would be coming down any moment with supplies to load before departing. She looked down the hall as well to avoid appearing suspicious. Egmun obliged her suggestion and Vi continued the moment the door was closed. "Soon Aldrik will be too focused on preparations for his coming-of-age ceremony. We should go now and break down the barrier. We can sort the rest later if needed. I can secure the prince. You go secure the horses necessary for our flight."

"*You* will secure the prince?" Egmun arched his eyebrows. "Don't you think I should?"

"I know where he is at this time of night." She'd run into him in the library more than once when she skulked around the Tower in the dead of night. Like Vi, he had a tendency to take books and not return them with any speed, so she hadn't put together a clear picture of everything the prince was researching so faithfully. "I know how to make him bend to our will.”

“If you're confident, then.” Egmun nodded, a satisfied smile spreading across his lips. “I'll meet you down at the stables.”

“Very good.” Vi sheathed the sword and emerged into the Tower hall once more. Just ahead, a Tower apprentice carried two bags slung over her shoulders.

Deneya. Good, she got out without suspicion.

Vi descended the spiraling walkway of the Tower. For a short stretch, Egmun's footsteps followed her. But he soon veered off, departing through one of the doors that connected Tower and palace. Vi continued on, straight for the library.

A man was seated by the lit hearth. Blessedly alone.

Aldrik's head bobbed as he fought off sleep. He didn't notice her approaching. His chin had met his chest when her feet came to a stop right before him.

Vi watched the boy for just a moment. He was fourteen, barely a man. A slip of a thing still in transition to the Emperor that would someday lead a united Solaris Empire. So much of the world's future rested on his shoulders. All Vi could do was guide him in the right direction. When it came down to it, the actions had to belong to him, and Vhalla, and all the other mortals confined to time.

“Wake up,” Vi said gently, kneeling down and shaking his shoulder lightly. “Your highness, wake up.”

“What?” He blinked sleep from his eyes. His tone became sharper as his eyes focused on her. “Vivian… Is this a dream?”

“No, it is not. Though you might wish it were come the dawn.” *More like a nightmare.* “I need you to listen to me, there's precious little time.” She couldn't keep Egmun waiting—he'd start to wonder. “Tonight, we must go to the Crystal Caverns.”

“The Crystal Caverns, why?”

“There is a barrier there, one only you and your magic can undo. It must be done, for the fate of this world… for the future of Solaris.” His eyes widened slightly as she spoke and Vi knew she'd struck the right chord. “Your father will bring the North to its knees with the power of the Caverns. But only you can unlock it.”

“Why now?”

"Because there are those who would move against you and your family." Vi lifted the sword. "*You* must be the one to act. Should this sword fall into the wrong hands, it will spell disaster for us all." Or at least another blasted revolution of the world. And Vi had vowed no more of those. This world would be it, the last time the vortex spun. "Before we go… there's something I wish to give you."

Vi pulled out the key to her Tower room from her pocket. "Minister Egmun allowed me use of the uppermost room in this Tower, but I fear I will not need it after tonight."

"Why?"

"Because that is how the wheel of fate turns," Vi said ominously. She wanted to seem mystical, too improbable to be real. "I have a feeling the room will prove useful to you."

Vi thrust the key in his hand, closing his fingers around it. Aldrik's hand wrapped around hers tightly, the key between them. He stared up at her with eyes so similar to Fiera's, similar to *hers*.

This man is not your father.

"Tell me what's really happening."

"I can't."

He ripped his hand away and stood, looking down at her. "You were insolent, right from the start. You're lucky you have such utility to Egmun and my family or I would've seen you thrown in the dungeon."

Vi lifted a hand to her chest and gave a small bow to hide her amusement. Her smirk would only make him more upset. "Thank you for not doing so."

"You said we must go." Aldrik shoved the key she'd given him into his pocket. "Carry on, then."

"Very well." She was on her feet as well, out the library, up, and across to one of the other doors that led to the palace. Aldrik faltered in the hall.

"The minister?"

"He will meet us at the stables." Vi held open the door for the prince. "Come along, now."

They walked in silence through the narrow hallway that connected the Tower to the palace. When they emerged, Aldrik immediately went for another side hall and Vi trusted him to lead them in the fastest way possible down to the stables. They passed a long stretch of windows that overlooked an inner courtyard. A lush garden flourished within—a greenhouse in the shape of a birdcage that Vi knew had been made to house Fiera's roses.

It was supposed to have been a gift from the Emperor—but it was a gift never seen by his bride.

The two emerged onto the dusty grounds of the stables. Two horses were out, tacked and waiting. Vi glanced around, seeing no sign of Deneya or their warstriders. She took a deep breath, ready to let out a sigh of relief. Everything was going according to plan.

A sharp pain seared through her abdomen. Vi's next breath emerged as a gurgle. The metallic taste of blood filled her throat.

She gawked, blood pouring from her mouth and down her chest. It mingled with the blood flowing around the point of a sword made of ice sticking out of her abdomen.

There was a sword of ice *sticking out of her abdomen*. Her first thoughts went to Adela. The bloody pirate queen had somehow found her after all these years. She'd known of Vi's hunt for the crown.

Yet another thing she'd missed.

Vi blinked several times, trying to force her eyes to focus around the pain. Aldrik's mouth was fixed in a soundless scream as he gaped at her. The presence of the boy was the only thing that didn't make Yargen's words of power come immediately.

The sword withdrew, and without its support, Vi fell limply to the ground.

“**M**-Minister, explain yourself,” Aldrik demanded, his voice shaking.

Egmun appeared in Vi’s field of vision. The sword of ice he’d been holding evaporated into mist. “She was a traitor to the crown. I was exploiting her for as long as she was useful.” Egmun led a blindfolded man with a rope, a gag suppressing his pleas for help. “Just like this one.”

“What’s going on?” Aldrik looked up at the minister with none of the ferocity his question held. “She told me we were heading to the Crystal Caverns, that people were acting against my family.”

“That is true.” Vi watched as Egmun rested his hand on the young man’s shoulder. She gritted her teeth to keep from saying anything. “They are called the Knights of Jadar; they’ve hated your family since well before you were born, and she was one of them.”

Aldrik looked to her and Vi pressed her eyes closed. Let him think she was a Knight of Jadar. Let her be branded as that—another nameless, faceless, unimportant traitor of the crown.

Let him think whatever he wanted but let them leave, because she'd bleed to death soon.

Her eyes opened as two hands slipped under her arms. Vi groaned as Egmun hoisted her, dragging her through the mud into an open stable.

"You thought you could have the power?" Egmun whispered into her ear. "You will *never* know the power of the Caverns. But I thank you for all you've done to help me get to it."

"And this man?" Aldrik asked, unaware of Egmun's sinister remarks. He held the bound man by the rope until Egmun returned.

"He is merely a run-of-the-mill criminal." Having discarded Vi's body like a piece of refuse, Egmun forced the bound man onto the saddle. "We will need him in the Caverns."

"For what?" Aldrik asked, following Egmun. He spared one glance back at her, though Vi could hardly make out his expression. Her head was swirling.

"I will tell you on the way." Egmun crossed over to where she'd dropped the sword. He hoisted it reverently—like it was the final piece of his plan falling into place as he slid it through a rope attached to his belt. "We must ride before dawn."

Vi closed her eyes, pressing her hands into the wound to try to stave the bleeding. Her whole body screamed in agony. She waited until she heard the rumble of horses departing the stables before she took a quivering breath.

"*Ha-hall-halleth…*" Her lips fumbled over the words. Yargen above, give her strength. "*Halleth,*" Vi started again, more determined than ever. She had to mend her torn flesh. She didn't care how gnarly the scar. If she didn't get on a horse now, everything would be forfeit. Red lightning cracked behind her eyes as she squeezed them shut, reminding her of what she fought for. Vi worked to dredge up strength as blood flowed freely from her. "*Halleth—*"

"*Halleth ruta sot.*" Light flared around Vi's body, illuminating the grime-coated walls of the horse stall. "*Halleth ruta sot,*" Deneya repeated.

Vi twisted, confirming that the voice wasn't a hallucination brought on by pain. The woman moved her hands over Vi's body. Glyphs soaked into Vi's torn flesh. She could feel her skin knitting underneath Deneya's skilled hands. "*Halleth ruta toff*," Deneya finished, pulling her hand away.

"What are you doing here?" Vi asked, rubbing the freshly mended skin of her stomach.

"By the light, woman, you just had a sword through you and you've not so much as a single tear on your cheek. Are you even human?"

"No." Vi sat upright. "It's hardly the worst I've endured. The prize for worst pain goes to my body being rebuilt between worlds," Vi said grimly as she pushed herself to her feet. There were aches and pains, but it was nothing *halleth maph* couldn't fix. "I thought I told you to leave."

"Well, aren't you glad I didn't?" Deneya walked out of the stable. "I was collecting my things from my room when I saw you."

"What about the horses? I didn't see them in their usual stalls."

"They're here." Deneya led her quickly down the long stretch of stables and out the main entrance to the castle. Sure enough, both horses were there, their reins looped lightly around a post at a tavern. "I hadn't put Midsummer back in since I followed Egmun. So all I did was take Prism out."

"Why aren't there guards posted?" Vi looked around, still making haste for the mounts.

"I'm sure there will be soon. Egmun sent them away. I didn't catch what he said, but they were sent running."

"Likely some lie about the Knights of Jadar attacking," Vi mumbled as she swung herself up onto the saddle. "That way he could argue my corpse was one of them."

"Things *really* didn't go well with the illusioned sword."

"I told you as much." Vi grimaced as she mounted. Deneya followed her lead. "Mistakes or no, this is all for nothing if they make it to the Caverns without us and destroy the sword. Let's go."

With a kick and call, Prism bounded down the main road of the city with Midsummer right behind. The glyph *halleth* was still around Vi's wrist, stinting any lingering pain. Her skin had been mended, but no glyph could return all the blood she'd lost. Her vision was blurry, and Vi felt faint.

"Look, there." Deneya pointed as they departed through the main gate of the city. "I think that's them."

Sure enough, on the switchback down the mountain, two other horses with three riders between them rode out through the night.

"Let's slow down. We don't want to give them room to be suspicious," Vi declared.

"Egmun thinks he killed you."

"Egmun will jump at his own shadow right now."

"Do you think he'll hurt Aldrik?" Deneya asked gravely.

"Not until Aldrik lowers the barrier." Vi cursed under her breath. "After that… Well, let's hope he doesn't try." She watched as the horses below turned, winding further down the mountain. "They'll take the direct path there, I'm sure of it. You and I will go the long way. Straight for the cabin and around the mountain from the other direction."

"Riding through the woods could take double the time."

"Perhaps for riders who don't know them as well as we do." Vi grinned wildly. Challenging fate itself required all the arrogance she could muster. "And for riders who don't have purebred warstriders."

"These beasts are getting pretty old." Deneya patted the neck of Midsummer.

"Hardly. Warstriders don't hit their prime until at least thirty years." Vi watched as the other two horses crossed into the tree line below before giving a light kick, spurring Prism into motion with her heels. It was a good thing warstriders could live till seventy. She'd been counting on it from the first moment she'd taken these horses.

The mounts didn't disappoint her. They expelled plumes of white from their noses into the brisk, late winter air. The wind pricked her face and made Vi feel more alert and awake despite the blood loss. Her heart raced and her watering eyes gained clarity somewhere between their turn into the forests and winding around the mountain near their cabin.

The horses began to slow as they emerged from the back path to the Caverns. Vi could see the outcropping of rock she'd hidden in months before, to watch Egmun ride off. She hurriedly dismounted and Deneya followed.

"Tie the horses out of sight," Vi whispered, knowing how voices could carry over rock and snow.

"I don't think they're far ahead." Deneya did as Vi instructed, pulling the horses into an alcove as Vi continued on. She could hear the rumble of hooves over the mountain pass, slowing as it became narrow and treacherous.

"They're not. We just have to stay out of sight." Vi leaned around the rocks, looking up the path. The swish of a horse's tail was barely visible.

"*Durroe watt radia,*" Deneya whispered, and Vi followed suit.

The chant was to conceal, a far easier task for something that wasn't moving. Whenever Vi glanced behind her, through the blurred and hazy edges of her vision, she could make out Deneya's form sliding over the rocks like running water distorting a riverbed. It wasn't perfect, but she suspected that the two men, in their haste, wouldn't look back long enough to notice.

Victor's keen eye for illusion wasn't here, thank Yargen.

They rounded the pathway and saw Egmun and Aldrik up ahead. Egmun was saying something to the young prince as he jerked the man he'd brought off the horse. Vi grimaced. She'd read about Jadar's attempts to use blood to open the Caverns. Apparently, that was something Egmun put stock in.

The three went into the Caverns with Vi and Deneya following closely behind.

Yargen's magic cast a blue aura on the fog that hung in the air. Egmun lifted a stone, dropping it to the floor. Vi used the distraction to slip into the Caverns. As was usually the case, the crystals illuminated at her presence. The magic greeted her with a familiar embrace, as if begging her to take the power that was here—to rejoin with it, once and for all.

Egmun smiled smugly at the light as he straightened.

I bet he thinks he did that, Vi thought bitterly.

"This way, your highness." Egmun led Aldrik through the main entry and into the antechamber with the confidence of a man who had walked among these crystals many times. Every few steps, he gave his prisoner a shove. The man attached to the rope carried on blindly, shivering in the dim light.

The poor sod had no idea where he was, or what awaited him.

Vi took a step forward to follow and Deneya grabbed her wrist. Their magics merged, and the woman was visible once more.

"What do you want me to do?" Deneya whispered to Vi, her voice no louder than the plops of water in the depths of the Caverns.

"Whatever you think needs to be done." Vi leveled her eyes with the elfin. "I trust you."

Deneya gave her a long, hard look and then a small nod. Vi stepped away, feeling her magic slip back into place around her. In the Caverns, Lightspinning was more of an art than a science. It was less about what words spoken and precise glyphs conjured, and more about intent.

Harnessing the true nature of Yargen's power was more like how she'd been initially taught magic: instinct. The more she worked with it, the more she understood it in a way that defied words, even the words of the goddess.

"Behind here," Egmun said, motioning to the crystal-covered doors at the top of a few steps, "is the heart of the Caverns. It is where the true power lies."

"Where we must go to help my father to victory," Aldrik murmured, repeating Vi's words from earlier.

Vi crept ever closer. The fingers on her right hand twitched, ready for magic, as her left hand remained balled in a fist, keeping her invisible.

"Just so." Egmun nodded. "You are the one who needs to undo this barrier. Only your great power can fell it."

"How do I do it?" Aldrik asked, looking up at the minister. He didn't seem to question for a second that he was the one destined for this greatness.

"Touch the crystals, and allow your magic to do the rest," Egmun answered cryptically. The man didn't know how to lower the barrier; Vi had never told him. And it didn't seem Fiera's instincts for the crystals had passed on to Aldrik. Lucky for them both, she was there. It wasn't how she imagined the sword meeting its end, but she had no other options.

Aldrik stepped forward, his hand held out rigidly as he ascended the stairs. Just once, he looked back over his shoulder and Vi froze, not wanting him to see the shift in her illusion. But the prince's eyes went to the minister. Egmun gave a nod, and Aldrik reached out to touch the thin layer of crystal covering the doors

"*Rohko*," Vi whispered, feeling the magic flare. *Rohko* was the word Fiera had uncovered in the crystals when she'd made the barrier. Vi could still sense the glyph holding the stones together.

Now, with that same word and her will, she'd see it dismantled.

The crystal glowed brightly in tandem with Vi's intensifying focus. Spiderweb cracks spread out from underneath Aldrik's hand and in a burst of light and sound, the stones came crashing down. Aldrik stumbled back, dazed. The minister stepped forward, catching the boy by the arm.

"*Kot sorre*," Deneya murmured from her side. *To push.*

"*Durroe watt ivin*," Vi whispered hastily. A flash of light hovered around Deneya's glyph, concealing it. The men were still blinking from the release of the barrier; Vi suspected they hadn't caught a glimpse of the true powers at work as the doors swung open.

"Wh-what's going on?" the blindfolded man had bitten through his gag. "Where am I?"

"Quiet, you," Egmun snarled, jerking the rope around his wrists so hard that the man tripped and fell in a heap.

"Was that necessary?" Aldrik said, still dazed, looking between the prisoner and Egmun.

"He is a criminal, the lowest of the low." Egmun wrenched Aldrik forward by the arm as the prisoner scrambled to find his feet once more. "Come, both of you. Destiny awaits."

You're not wrong about that, Vi thought grimly.

She'd practiced the transference of power from the weapon to the Caverns for fourteen years. After her breakthrough, her confidence and skill had increased at a shocking rate.

Yet a shiver still rattled her teeth.

It all came down to this. The sword Egmun held wasn't a decoy. She had one shot at seeing the sword's power returned to the Caverns. If Egmun's magic won over hers, if his clumsy attempts at manipulating Yargen's power bested her transference, the sword would be broken and irreparable damage done to the Caverns.

She would fail. And if she failed now, she failed the entire world.

Egmun led Aldrik and the prisoner into the depths of the Caverns. Vi could almost see Raspian's invisible hands reaching outward, seeking the world he was shut off from, yearning for release. Every vertebra in her spine vibrated in a resonance that screamed "no" the closer she drew to the final room in the Caverns, the place Raspian had been sealed away. Every sensation was deeper, heightened, worse than the first time she'd come to this place.

With a kick to the back of the man's legs, Egmun brought the prisoner to his knees in the center of the stone floor. Vi crept to the door, perching herself by a crystal at its side to remain hidden.

"Prince Aldrik." Egmun took a step toward the boy, who wore a mixture of fear and wonder. "Someday, you will be Emperor. Do you know what that means?"

"I-I do."

"So you know that justice will fall to you." Egmun took another step forward. "It was your mother's last request to your father to spare you these duties as long as possible."

Vi didn't recall Fiera ever making any such request. If anything, the duty-bound woman Vi had known would've wanted her son to grow up entrenched in politics, learning from them, and becoming cunning enough to stay alive.

"My mother?" Aldrik asked with such hope, Vi's heart ached.

The mother she'd taken from him. Had Fiera lived, perhaps Aldrik would've never sought out his father's attention to the point of resorting to crystals. But, had he not, he would've never come here, and the world would've been a failure.

Everything connected in ways that not even Vi could always see. Which was as thrilling as it was dangerous.

"But you will soon be a man, won't you?"

"I will."

"It is rather unfair, no? For your father to be treating you like a child?" *Ah*, so that was Egmun's game. Vi's nails dug into the crystal at her side. Egmun was using the young man's desire to prove himself against him. "Are you prepared to be the crown prince this realm needs?"

"I am." Even though it was positively frigid in the Caverns, sweat dotted Aldrik's brow.

"Then, my prince, for justice, for the strength of Solaris, for the future of your Empire, slay this man." Egmun dropped to a knee and freed the sword from where he'd tied it to his belt. He offered the crystal weapon to the prince.

"But…"

"This man has stolen from your family; it is a treasonous crime. He is not innocent."

"Should my father not—"

"I thought you were a man and a prince." Egmun's annoyance with Aldrik's hesitation was showing. Vi loathed herself for sympathizing with the wicked man. *Get it over with*, she wanted to scream. She wanted to know if her whole future was forfeit or not. "I did not take you as someone who shied from justice or power, Prince Aldrik." Egmun paused dramatically. "Why are you here?"

"For my father, to conquer the North."

"With this, all will bend to you." Egmun smiled encouragingly.

Aldrik took the sword and Vi's heart nearly lurched from her chest. Every hair on her body stood on end. *So… close.*

"M-my prince, m-mercy please. T-take my hand for m-my theft. Spare m-me," the man begged through sobs.

"Minister…" Aldrik hesitated. He'd never killed a man before, Vi realized then. A mere week before his coming-of-age ceremony, he would make his first kill.

"The guilty will say anything to you, my prince, to save their skin. This, too, is a lesson." Egmun stood and seemed to be holding his breath.

Aldrik unsheathed the sword and passed the scabbard to Egmun's eager palms.

"M-mercy," the man begged.

"*Kill him, Aldrik*," Egmun nearly shouted.

Aldrik set his jaw and hoisted the sword over his head. He paused with the blade stuck at the apex of his swing. Vi held her breath alongside the whole world.

He swung the weapon down.

Vi lifted her hand at the same time. Her other palm was flush against the crystal at her side. Magic sparked around the sword, almost like flames.

The strike was clumsy. The man groaned and gurgled, his pleas for help vanished. Aldrik raised the sword again, bringing it back down. Carnage splattered across the center of the room.

But Vi's focus remained on the blade.

She allowed the magic of the Caverns to combine with hers, to guide her as she mentally reached out to the weapon. Vi could feel another magic in the air. Egmun was trying to act on the crystals as well.

Pathetic, Vi thought snidely. This power was hers—hers to claim and hers to control.

The sword shone brighter, as though the power within was trying to burn through. Aldrik slashed twice more before the man lay limp on the ground. The sword clattered to the stone below.

That contact of sword to Caverns was all she needed.

Crystals flared around the perimeter of the room. Aldrik shielded his eyes. Egmun thrust out his arms, as if waiting for the power to sink into him.

One crystal connected to the next, and Vi wove her magic between them all. The stones inlaid on the floor illuminated and, for the first time, Vi understood what they were.

The light that shone between them connected to form a glyph. Setting her eyes on it filled her mind with a roar of sound. It was as if every person in the world screamed a single word in agony, a word so loud she could barely make it out.

Suladin—a glyph of sealing.

A word Vi didn't yet dare speak aloud.

Keeping her focus on the sword, Vi held out her right hand, reaching for it. The glyph around her left kept her invisible. The weapon was too far for her to touch, but through the bond of the Caverns, she could feel it.

Her fingers tightened around the magic of the sword, yanking it like a tether and sending the magic back into the Caverns. Power flowed into the stones around her. She felt it rush through her body, leaving her breathless and dizzy.

The glow of the crystals faded.

And the Sword of Jadar turned to obsidian, fractured, and dissolved into dust.

10

"WHAT?" EGMUN LOWERED HIS arms and spun as the light of the Caverns faded. "What did we do wrong?" he shouted to the ceiling above. The echo of his voice was the only reply.

"M-minister… I… I don't feel so well." Aldrik swayed. His eyes were still on the mangled body before him.

"She… it's her fault," Egmun seethed, ignorant to the boy. Vi almost felt proud that he was laying blame at her feet. "She knew what must be done and kept it from me and now—"

Aldrik interrupted Egmun's ravings by turning up the contents of his stomach. Egmun jumped back to avoid the vomit splattering on his shoes.

"We should go, you foolish boy."

"Foolish?" Aldrik looked up at the minister, as though in a daze.

"Your power was not enough," Egmun sneered. "And now your desire for power has opened the heart of the Caverns once more to any who would dare use it against your Empire."

"I only did as you asked!" Aldrik pleaded.

Vi's breath caught in her throat. This young man, this *child*, who stood stained with blood and bile, would one day become the rough-tongued, harsh man her father had always been rumored to be. It wasn't Fiera's death that had set her father on a torturous path of transformation. It was this moment.

Either way, it was her fault.

She tried to steel herself, but everything ached. The only thing she could tell herself was that this was all worth it. She would make it worth it. It didn't matter if he was aware of the vortex or not, this would be the last time Aldrik would suffer the loss of his innocence in such a brutal way.

Rumbling filled the Caverns, as though a mighty beast within was starting to wake. Vi looked around, as startled as the two men. The sound was followed by a burst of light that rose from the floor and flowed out the Caverns, rushing to the opening like a torrential river of magic.

"We must go," Egmun said grimly. "Before the crystal taint claims us." He grabbed Aldrik's arm and wrenched him from the room.

As the two sprinted out, Vi knelt down, dipping her fingers in the river of light. It felt like nothing. There was no power here, only air.

Vi lifted her eyes and released the glyph for *durroe watt radia*. She stepped out of the inner chamber and through the doors just in time to see Deneya emerging from where she'd wedged herself between two crystals. The two men were long gone.

"Think I need to keep this going?" Deneya held up her arm, a strip of golden magic rotating by her elbow.

"Maybe for a bit longer." Vi dragged her feet down the steps on the other side of the door, but she didn't quite make it to the bottom before she sat heavily. She still felt dizzy. Though Vi couldn't tell if the dizziness came from her earlier wound or the current of power still rushing through her. "Just until we're certain they're far enough away."

"*Durroe watt ivin*," Deneya murmured, flicking her other hand toward the entry. Vi saw a haze of light fill the air.

From Egmun and Aldrik's perspective, the beast that was the

Caverns had been woken with a roar, unfurled its tongue, and was letting out a sigh of pure magic.

"Clever." Vi appraised Deneya's handiwork.

"Thank you." As Deneya spoke the words, she tilted her head in a motion that said both, "don't worry about it" and, simultaneously, "I know I'm pretty great." Vi couldn't help but chuckle and shake her head. Deneya came over, glyphs still hovering around her forearms. She sat next to Vi. "I doubt we'll be seeing them back here anytime soon."

"They'll be back soon enough."

"Why?"

Vi sighed heavily, running a hand through her hair. Most of her braids had slipped out. "Because the river of fate moves forward, and the War of the Crystals Caverns is next."

"People fight over the Crystal Caverns?"

"Fight *against* the Caverns."

"How does one fight a cavern?"

"I wondered that myself, when I first learned of it." Vi thought back to her lessons with her tutors. The War of the Crystal Caverns had seemed like impossible lore. "In my world, the magic of the Crystal Caverns seeped out into the land and tainted the people and animals; they called it 'crystal taint.' The crystal taint disfigured man and beast, changing their minds and bodies into monsters.

"I think the taint comes from Raspian's power mingling with Yargen's in the crystals, once the glyph holding him back is weakened."

"Monsters, wonderful," Deneya murmured and looked back through the doors. "But we don't have to worry about any of this. You got the power out of the sword and into the Caverns, right?" Deneya leaned back and finally relaxed the glyphs. The illusion of magic faded and the air was still once more.

"I did…" Vi rested her elbows on her knees and folded her hands. She could almost hear Taavin.

Apparently, Deneya could, too. "Taavin is going to say there needs to be a war, isn't he?"

"I think so." In Vi's world, Vhalla's father had fought in the War of the Crystal Caverns. His valor in battle earned him a spot in the palace

guard—a post which he ultimately gave up for his daughter to become
a library apprentice. Which was an appointment that ultimately led to
her meet a certain crown prince.

"You have a plan for that?"

"I've an idea… but no reason to think it'll work."

"Lovely." Deneya pushed away from the stone, pacing once,
then stretching, as if unable to release all the nervous energy tensing
her muscles. "Well, this whole scheme of yours hinges on you doing
things that have never been done and have no reason to work."

"You have so much faith in me," Vi said dryly.

"I do." Deneya put her hands on her hips. "You know I have faith
in the fact that you seem to be able to accomplish anything with sheer
force of will." She shook her head and gave a look around the Caverns;
Deneya's gaze turned skyward before falling back to Vi. "Honestly, I've
always been rather shocked by this whole 'ninety-third try' business.
You've struck me as the sort of person who can move mountains with
nothing but an almost suicidal, ignorant determination."

"Thank you for saying so, I think." Vi grinned, an expression
Deneya returned in kind. Speaking of sheer force of will, Vi pulled
herself to her feet. There was still work to be done. "I intend for this to
be the last time, for all of us."

"As long as it's the last time because you succeed."

"Agreed." Vi rested her hand on a nearby crystal, feeling how the
magic within the Caverns had changed once more. It was just like
her first experimentation in transferring the sword. Now, she had to
take out that power and then some in an act that would make good on
another promise—one she'd silently made to herself, and to a man of
light, for nearly fifteen years. "Now, may I task you with heading back
to our cabin and starting a fire?"

"You may." Deneya adjusted her heavy winter coat before heading
out of the Caverns. "But I take it you won't be joining me just yet?"

"You know I still have some work to do here."

"Leave work to the morning; it's been an exhausting night,"
Deneya encouraged.

"No. I want this done before dawn. I suspect that once Egmun
and the prince arrive back at the Capital, it won't be long until the

Emperor finds out about what happened here. I want my business with the Caverns to be concluded before then."

"Concluded?" Deneya echoed skeptically.

Vi chuckled. "Concluded for at least a few decades."

"A few more decades of living in our cabin. Excuse my uncontrollable excitement."

"Maybe not in the cabin," Vi called to Deneya's retreating form. The woman paused, glancing back. "I think I'd rather go to the beach."

"The beach?" Deneya balked. Vi laughed at the expression, which proved the levity needed to break up the long night.

"I'll explain fully later."

"You'd better. I could use some warmth and sun again and couldn't bear it if you were merely teasing me." Deneya paused, almost at the entrance of the Caverns. "Be careful in here. Don't make me regret leaving you by yourself."

"I won't," Vi called back. With that minimal reassurance, Deneya left. "Right, then." Vi looked back into the heart of the Caverns, taking a slow breath.

She thought of summoning Taavin, but opted instead to remain silent and alone. Taavin would stop her, and Deneya's words had made her bold.

Vi went back up the stairs, through the doorway, and into the heart of the Crystal Caverns.

The magic was alive here. It welcomed her, surging through her veins. Vi held out her arms, inviting it to flow into her. This was Yargen's essence—the power that fueled the seal on Raspian, and the power that would challenge him once more.

Vi stared down at the stones embedded in the floor—the ones that formed the glyph that maintained the dark god's cage. She walked across them, her steps harmlessly connecting one to the next, until she reached the center of the room. Kneeling down, Vi rested her palms on one of the stones and closed her eyes.

She envisioned the Sword of Jadar. She dredged up memories of the scythe she'd held in another world. She recalled every last detail she could—how the objects felt under her hands, how much power they held.

"We'll start with that much," Vi said aloud, speaking to the crystals as though they were a sentient partner. For all Vi knew, they were. They held Yargen's essence after all; she couldn't rule out that they also held some of the goddess's consciousness. "Yargen, help me do this," she whispered. "I need him at my side."

Vi lifted her hands from the stone, drawing the magic in shimmering threads up with them. She twisted her left hand, palm to ceiling, and continued feeding magic from her right. Once enough power had collected in her upturned palm, Vi condensed it into a new crystal.

This would be the seed from which Taavin's new body would grow. She continued to string more magic from the Caverns into the stone, stopping when she'd reached the amount the Sword of Jadar had held.

Glancing to the heavens, Vi uttered one final silent plea to Yargen—*Let this work*—before continuing.

The crystals in the room flared and dimmed. Magic was drained from the stones along the outer ring of the room. It filled the crystals on the floor. They shone once more, the glyph they made barely visible in the beams of light reaching upward.

Siphoning this power, Vi felt something quiver between each draw off the Caverns.

Raspian could feel the weakening of power that confined him, she was sure. He could feel *her*. Just as keenly as she could feel him pressing, scraping, reaching, seeking a way out of his prison.

The phantom torment of red lightning cracking through her seared under her skin. She could feel the shadows of scars across her bones from where it had ravaged her body. Vi set her lips into a thin line and fought to keep her focus on her task.

"You'll be free enough to have your little finger escape," she said grimly to the dark god, not knowing if he could hear. "No more. No less."

The outermost stones on the floor began to dim against the brightness of the glowing stone in Vi's hand. It was a blue brighter than the sky, purer than the ancient ice of glaciers. It was bright enough to illuminate almost the whole of the Caverns and yet, looking into it didn't hurt. It felt… comfortable. Like staring into the eyes of an old friend.

With a flick of her wrist, Vi flattened her right hand and severed the connection with the Caverns. She could feel the remaining magic settling back into place, spread thinner, like water over a dry riverbed.

Sweat ran in rivulets down her neck and temples. Even in the chill of winter, holding the crystal, holding her focus, was extremely strenuous.

Vi placed the shining stone down gently before her. She ran her hands over it, murmuring, "*Kot sorre. Kot sidee.*"

Push and pull.

The magic was a tangible thing beneath her fingers. Vi manipulated it like a sculptor. She saw the crystal extend upward and downward. The stones smoothed and curved, taking on new shapes. Vertebrae appeared. Ribs stretched up from them. There were femurs that led to kneecaps, and ultimately toes. Collarbones sat beneath a strong jaw.

A skeleton of crystal was before her. The basis of her vessel. But it was nothing more than crystals in a new shape.

She wanted to lean back, sit on her heels, and catch her breath. But Vi couldn't allow herself to. Everything was fresh and new, waiting for the next layer of magic to be spun around it.

"*Halleth ruta sot. Halleth ruta toff.*" Halleth worked to create new flesh on an existing body. Why could it also not create new flesh for a new body?

A voice whispered in the back of her mind. The words were so faint that Vi couldn't decipher if it was instinct, or Yargen herself encouraging Vi in the right direction. "*Mysst ruta sot.*"

Mysst, to craft.

Ruta sot, inner flesh.

The words shouldn't have worked together. But here, in the Caverns, drawing on the raw power of Yargen, combined with Vi's unshakable determination, they did. It was as if she had the goddess's blessing to bend the words of the gods to her will.

For the first time, Vi truly made the words her own.

She was reminded of the moment she was rebuilt between worlds. The light intensified to the point that Vi could see nothing else. And from that light, substance took shape. The sensation of her veins unfurling like ribbons from a fresh heart was keen in her mind. Vi felt skin stretching across the form before her like a blanket, warm and safe.

When the light faded, she was left with the body of a man.

Reaching forward, she cupped the cheek of this lifeless body. It was still a vessel. There was no thought, no essence within. But Vi could see her plan taking shape. She could almost feel him there, and wondered if the warmth underneath her palm was the lingering magic in the air… or a fresh body seeking out life.

Vi gripped the watch with her left hand, white knuckled. With her right, she still caressed the man's face. Her eyes focused there.

Draw him out.

Lifting her hand off the watch as though it were a crystal, the magic of Yargen within followed her motions. She could see it in countless overlapping glyphs that hovered in the air. If she had to guess, there were ninety-three in total. Each one held the memories and essence of a different Taavin, including this one. They all combined together to compose the man she loved so dearly.

"*Narro hath loreth.*" Vi said the words to imprint a communication mark on the token—to first anchor Taavin's consciousness into this new vessel. On instinct, she repeated "*Hoolo, hoolo,*" over and over. *Stabilize, elongate, hold.* It was the first word Yargen had given her— the word that had truly brought Taavin to her.

Now, she would imprint that word, that glyph, over top of this body. Hold him there. Keep him within it. Let his consciousness be supported by the bedrock of her will and Yargen's magic.

"Come to me," Vi murmured as the magic sank into the flat plane of his chest. "Taavin, come to me. *Hoolo.*"

The body was still, unresponsive.

"*Kot sorre. Kot sidee.*" She would push and pull the air through his lungs and the blood through his heart. She saw his chest rise and fall with her words. But the moment she stopped, the body was lifeless once more.

"Taavin," Vi choked out. Exhaustion was knocking at her edges, cracking her resolve. "You can do this, Taavin," she pleaded, as though it wasn't all riding on her shoulders. "Yargen, please." Vi dropped her head to the man's bare chest, holding him as though he was already Taavin.

Vi took in a quivering breath. She could feel the magic seeping out of him. She could almost see the flesh turning gray and with it, her hopes dimming.

"*Narro hath hoolo*," Vi whispered. But what she really meant was, *wake up. Please, my love, wake up.*

There was a snap, like a tether breaking. Magic sizzled from the watch around her neck and she was thrown back. Her head hit one of the crystals embedded in the stone floor.

Everything went white and Vi blinked away stars with a groan. The sound echoed through the Caverns as she clutched her head, feeling for blood that thankfully wasn't there.

Twisting onto her side, her vision still hazy, Vi propped herself up onto her elbow.

There was another groan.

But this time the sound hadn't come from her.

11

Vi rubbed her eyes. Red lightning popped behind her eyelids and she snapped them open, looking around. The Caverns looked unchanged. But it felt as if the ground had been upturned, and the air had filled with invisible poison.

Her assessment of the environmental change passed when her gaze fell on a very naked man propping himself, his movements stiff.

"T-Taavin?" she asked weakly. For a terrible moment, she was overcome by fear that somehow everything had gone wrong, and she'd given a body to Raspian himself.

But the man brought his gaze to her, and she beheld the eyes that had never shone more brilliantly, set on an unscarred face. She knew it was him before he even spoke.

"Vi."

Her arm gave out, as though the sound of his voice reverberating through her took the last of her failing strength. Vi slipped back to the ground, but she didn't cry out. She laughed.

"Vi, are you all right?" Taavin rushed over, putting a hand on her shoulder.

"I'm fine—just tired." She made it a point to keep her eyes on his and not let them wander anywhere else. Especially further south than his collarbone. "Are *you* all right?"

"I've never felt better. I feel like—" He stopped short and looked down, taking in his full form for the first time. "I'm naked. And *cold*."

"Sorry." Vi laid back, staring up at the ceiling so he knew she wasn't taking advantage of the situation. "Making a physical vessel for you to occupy was a lot. I didn't figure out how to fashion clothing at the same time."

He gently rested a hand on her cheek. Taavin guided her eyes to his. Just the sight of him brought a noise of joy that was part hiccup and part laughter. An icy tear rolled down her temple.

Wordlessly, Taavin shifted, reached forward, and scooped her up. He sat and held her in his arms. *His arms*. They were sturdy, and stable, and warm. All things that made him distinctly real.

For the first time in over a decade, Vi was home.

She buried her face into the crook of his shoulder and breathed. He still smelled of warm summer days. Vi wasn't surprised. Yargen's magic lived in him now. He was made of the light itself.

"What did you do?" His voice was both stern and soothing.

"I made you a body."

"How?"

"I was inspired by how Yargen made a new body for me between worlds. I tried to mimic the process."

"Vi, that's impossible."

"Clearly not." She pulled away and looked to the doorway. Her unease only continued to heighten the longer they were in this center chamber of the Caverns. "I drew power from the Caverns, made your bones out of crystals, and wrapped muscle and flesh around them. You always said Yargen's magic was life," Vi explained hastily.

"I didn't mean like this," he murmured, kissing her temple lightly.

"Deneya wasn't wrong when she suspected I've been practicing. I have been, nightly, since getting to the capital. Transferring the power from the sword to the Caverns wasn't difficult. Neither was transferring the power from the Caverns to your body, or your consciousness from the watch to that body." She glossed over her moments of panic. He didn't need to know about that.

"We don't know what this means. You've never done this before. You could've risked my memories if you failed."

"What's done is done. And you're here now." Vi pulled away to look him in the eye. "I thought this through, Taavin. You want to ensure the world follows the path of the stones in the river. If the Caverns remain strong, there won't be a War of the Crystal Caverns. So—"

"So you stored the magic of the Sword of Jadar and some from the Caverns in me… to weaken the barrier on Raspian without actually harming or losing any of Yargen's power." He admired her with shining eyes. "You're brilliant. Reckless, but brilliant."

"Thank you." The War of the Crystal Caverns was a convenient excuse. Vi hadn't done this for the world. She'd done it for herself. She didn't know what pulling Taavin out of the watch would ultimately mean. But since this would be the last version of the world, Vi didn't worry too much about it. Not that she would say as much to him. "Maybe you'll start to trust my reckless ideas more."

"I likely should." She didn't miss the shiver that ripped through him as he spoke.

"We should go."

"We should," he agreed.

Yet they had a hard time moving. Standing would mean separating, at least for a little, and neither of them seemed to really want to do that at the moment. Vi could hold him until the day the world ended, now that she had him once more.

"Let's at least get out of this chamber." Vi rephrased her earlier statement, forcing them both into action. "We've lingered for too long."

"Yes, lets…" The way Taavin looked around and then scowled at the ground beneath them told Vi everything she needed to know: he felt the terrible aura that now hovered in the air of this place, too.

Vi pushed herself onto her feet and swayed a bit. She was only steady by sheer force of will.

Taavin rushed to her side, wrapping his arm around her waist. "I got you."

"I'm the one who's supposed to be helping you."

"You've helped me enough," he said as they hobbled down the stairs and into the antechamber.

"Here's good, set me down." Taavin did as instructed and Vi sat with a heavy sigh. She leaned back against a crystal, willing just a little bit more of Yargen's magic to seep into her and give her strength. With a thought, fire ignited around them in a semicircle, casting a warm glow over them.

"That's better."

"My horse is down at the foot of the mountain." Vi glanced toward the opening. "I have some clothes there. Nothing will fit you right. But it'll be *something* so we can get to the cabin. I just need another minute to regain my strength and then I'll make my way down."

"I don't want you trekking over that icy path in this state. I'll go."

Vi laughed at that. "You'll go? You'll freeze your bits off."

"I will not." He looked at her with a scowl.

"You will." She grinned in reply. "And I'd rather like those bits to stay attached." She'd meant it as a jest. But the words were softened by sincerity. Her cheeks were warm, and not because of the fire.

"Would you?" he murmured, his face close to hers.

"I would," Vi whispered. "I've dreamed of this moment for years."

"Really, *this* moment?" He arched a single dark eyebrow. "This moment where I'm naked in a cavern, a stone's throw from Raspian's tomb, holed up to escape the elements and figuring out how not to freeze to death?"

"Goodness, I forgot how annoying you can be in person."

"No, you didn't. You could just send me away when you wanted."

"And now I can't."

"And now you can't," he echoed tenderly. Taavin reached up, tucking a strand of hair behind her ear. His fingers lingered. They ran down her cheek, along her jawline, to her ear and back around the nape of her neck. His fingertips pressed into her and Vi tilted her head forward and up on command.

Their lips met.

Soft, was the first thought that ran through her mind. He was so soft. The thin barrier of magic between them was gone.

He was here. And he was hers.

Vi shifted, pressing forward until their sides were flush. He wrapped his arms around her while her fingertips spread across the unbroken, unblemished plane of his chest.

"My scars are gone," Taavin whispered huskily.

"They are. Mine disappeared too when my body was remade in this world." Part of her already missed every nook and cranny of his old body. "All the more reason for me to explore and discover this new form you're in."

His hand grabbed hers as it grazed over the raised muscles of his abdomen. Taavin swallowed hard and locked his eyes with hers. "Yes."

"Yes, *but*?"

"Not here." He glanced over her flames and toward the open door. "Not so close to *him*."

Vi let out a groan of discontent. Taavin wasn't wrong. But she wanted him to be. She wanted to object to his postponement of this inevitable and most delicious moment between them.

She pried herself away.

"Where are you going?"

"To get my horse." Vi stepped through the flames.

"Are you sure you can—"

"You stay there and stay warm so you don't get frostbite and ruin that body I just made. I'll be fine. If anything was going to motivate me… this was it." She gave him a wink, and marched out of the Caverns with purpose.

Vi practically flew down the mountainside. Her heart was pounding and her magic was thin. She could feel every ache in her tired body. It had been a long night, and the first makings of a gray winter dawn were on the sky by the time she mounted Prism.

She raced back up the mountain and rode Prism into the entry of the Caverns, his hooves echoing off every surface. Vi ignored the sensation of Raspian, now as clear as Yargen's essence, permeating the entirety of the Caverns. She dismounted and rummaged through the clothing she'd packed. Luckily, unlike the last time she'd ridden out from a capital city, she was far more prepared for winter.

"Come on over." Vi relaxed her magic and the flames vanished.

Taavin appeared in the archway of the antechamber, clutching himself and bracing against the winter winds that blew in through the cave mouth. Vi held out a pair of oversized trousers—one of the few things she'd lounged in, the brief moments she had time for lounging—and then a woolen knit shirt that should have enough give to fit his taller, broader body.

"This is comical," Taavin chuckled. It was a deep and rumbling sound, resonating within her more than anything else he'd ever said or done.

"I could never look at you and see anything but perfection."

"You're just trying to sweet talk me," he said as she threw one of her older cloaks over his shoulders. All she needed to do was keep him warm enough to get back to the cabin. Tomorrow she could ride to Mosant and find better-fitting clothes for him.

"I am. Is it working?"

"Yes." He caught her lips before she could pull away, his hands wrapping around hers.

"Good." She stepped away, a slight sway and twirl to her step. "Now, let's go home."

She mounted first, he swung up behind her. Judging from how tightly he clutched her, Taavin didn't have much experience riding horses. She'd take it easy on him if she wasn't so worried about him catching a chill on the way back to the cabin. And if her lower stomach hadn't become something molten hot at the sight of him.

They left the weakened Caverns behind and rode into the hours just before dawn. Clouds were gathering in the southern skies with what looked like the last blizzard of the season on the horizon. There were worse fates than being snowed in for a while, Vi supposed.

Smoke drifted into the gray sky from the chimney of the modest cabin. The windows splashed golden streaks across the snow. Midsummer was in the stable and it looked like Deneya had even found dry hay from their stores.

"Yargen bless, it's *cold*." Taavin's teeth chattered. "Or is it just my senses being heightened in this new body after not feeling the world for so long?"

"Both, likely." Vi and Taavin dismounted and she led Prism into the simple stable attached to the cabin. Trudging in the same line of snow as Deneya, she opened the door without preamble.

"How did it—" Deneya sat up from her bed, freezing the second her eyes landed on Taavin. She narrowed them slightly and tilted her head. "He…"

"I made him a body."

"You… made him… a body."

"I haven't seen you this flummoxed since we first met." Vi laughed lightly. She hadn't laughed so much in months—years. Things were finally going her way. After years of practice and waiting and praying, things had gone right.

"People don't make bodies."

"Women do it all the time."

"Firstly, babies don't count for what we're talking about here. Secondly, they don't count because you made an adult man's body out of thin air. Thirdly, do not dodge the topic." Deneya stood, walking over to Taavin. She poked his shoulder lightly. "You seem a lot more real than you used to."

"It's an adjustment for me, too." Taavin had a relaxed smile on his face, as though he'd just eaten a full meal. "I apologize that my presence might make things tighter for a while. You only have two beds here and—"

"You can share mine," Vi interrupted without hesitation. Both of them seemed surprised, though Vi didn't know why. It seemed like a perfectly reasonable solution to her. Perhaps neither expected her to be so brazen about it.

Despite what her body looked like, Vi wasn't a blushing young woman anymore.

"Right, well…" A knowing smirk played on Deneya's lips. She looked Taavin up and down. "Those clothes clearly don't fit you."

"They're mine," Vi said. "I was planning on going to Mosant tomorrow to buy some new ones."

"How about I go now?" Deneya promptly grabbed a satchel off the peg by the door and shoved a few coins into it.

"You don't have to. I can—"

"I really don't mind going." Deneya shook her head and gave Vi a pointed look. "It's only an hour into town. I can ride leisurely, maybe grab a hot meal. I should be back by noon."

Oh. A smile slipped across Vi's cheeks. She understood now. And respected Deneya all the more for it. The woman was a true friend.

"Right, then, you should get off your feet. You look dead tired." Deneya started for the door, pausing before she opened it. "Have a good, ah, *rest*." She left with a wink and not a word more.

They were alone. Taavin and Vi stared at each other as the sounds of Deneya's horse rumbled away. It didn't sound like a leisurely pace. But Vi had every reason to believe the woman would slow as soon as she was out of ear- and eye-shot of the cabin.

"Does she always leave just before dawn to head into town?" Taavin asked.

"Can't say she's ever done it before."

"So I should take this to mean she cares deeply about me and my new wardrobe?" He wore a smug, knowing grin. The look suited him. It'd look even better if it was the only thing he was wearing.

"I can't speak for Deneya… But I can speak for myself." Vi crossed the distance between them and rested her hands on his hips. "I think I care deeply for you."

"Care deeply?" He arched his eyebrows. "Vi Solaris, I think you *love* me."

"A bold claim, sir."

"I'm pretty confident it's true."

She kissed the smirk off his lips, then trailed her fingers up his body. They caught on the hem of the sweater she'd given him and pulled upward. She'd seen him fully naked. No matter how much modesty she'd tried to offer him, it was impossible not to have noticed the naked man standing before her.

Vi saw no point in hesitating now.

She wanted him. She'd wanted him for years. She'd yearned to run her fingers up his stomach and chest and twirl them in his hair, to the point of dreaming about it for days on end.

Taavin broke away from her mouth and trailed sweet kisses down her jaw and neck. His palms mirrored the movements of her own. They ran up her chest, fingers quivering with hesitation.

"Touch me, for the love of every god, Taavin, touch me," Vi groaned.

He obliged. His hands found their way up her shirt. The man's touch was searing hot—hotter than the glorious heat melting her from the inside out.

Her clothes were on the floor and the mattress sagged beneath her. It reminded her of their first night in the Tower. Kissing him then, holding him as he held the crystal. Now, the crystal was in him, and he was with her. No limits. No holding back.

Vi gasped as he explored with his mouth and hands. Her breathing hitched as he found a particular spot and Taavin caught a moan with his mouth. It fed his already eager movements, quickening them.

When he pulled away he was as breathless as she was. "I love you," he murmured.

"I love you," Vi whispered in reply. The firelight was generous to his sharp curves, casting stunning shadows over his body as it hovered above her. She tightened her grasp on him as he shifted. The distance between them diminished to nothing. "I will never let you go again."

"Please don't." He pressed himself against her, holding her tightly.

"I will save this world. And when it's over, it will just be us." It was a dangerous promise. Even if she could manage to save the world this time, she didn't know where it would leave them in the end. Yargen's magic was within him—in her—power that Vi knew they'd eventually need to return to see the goddess ready to take on Raspian.

Taavin sighed softly.

Pressing her eyes closed, Vi pushed the thoughts from her mind and bit his shoulder gently. She'd focus only on tonight and this release she'd been yearning and waiting for.

Delicious frustration built within her. She wanted him to move. She wanted him to be still. She wanted to sleep in his arms and do nothing. She wanted to do *everything* with him and to him.

"Let's not talk about the world." He pulled away, kissing up her cheek to rub the tip of his nose against hers. "Let's just focus on our world tonight. Right here, right now."

She nodded eagerly. And, as if he'd been waiting for that permission, Taavin moved, kissing her as he did.

Vi allowed her mind to go blank. For a few hours, she would burn hotter than the fire in the hearth, the spark within her, or the magic that remade the world.

12

The War of the Crystal Caverns started with trumpets and the echoes of military horses clomping through the mountain pathways and valleys. It was just over a week since Aldrik and Egmun had left the Caverns, and the start of the war signified that it was time for Vi and Deneya—and Taavin—to leave their cabin behind once more.

As they passed alongside the military party, heading in the opposite direction, Vi reflected on her lessons from years ago.

The Solaris army would march to the Caverns and become transformed into monsters. They would blame it on the crystals, never knowing the real culprit was Raspian. The untainted portion of Solaris's army would battle against the twisted version of itself for just over a year. Then, none would return to the Caverns for years to come.

In Vi's time, the next man to head to the Caverns and seek their power was Victor. He would use the Cavern's strength—Raspian's strength—to stage a bloody coup. He was the man she was working to stay one step ahead of. That meant she had to leave the War of the Crystal Caverns behind her, in the hands of fate.

Vi's focus was on the crown of the first King Solaris. They followed Adela's path and headed south to Oparium in search of the crown.

The port town was nestled in a valley in the mountains east of Solarin. The coast of Lyndum was mostly cliffs, making this cramped valley the only place to construct a larger port. It was nothing compared to Norin, and barely a slip for dinghies compared to Risen. But it was the best port the early Kingdom of Lyndum had, and it was where Vi suspected Adela had escaped to after fleeing with the crown treasure of Solaris.

When she'd first laid eyes on the city, months ago now, Vi had been optimistic. The crown was either hidden here, or with Adela herself. She'd either find it, or narrow down its location with confidence once more.

Now, all Vi felt was frustration.

"Months, we've been here for *months*, and not a single lead on QA or the treasure," Vi muttered. Southerners were even more superstitious about Adela than Westerners. Deneya had made the mistake of mentioning her name once, and their information gathering was near-instantly stinted. Now, the pirate queen was always "QA"— even when they were in the very back of what had become their favorite place to escape their shared hovel, The Cock and Crow brewery.

"It's not like someone's just going to come up to us and say, 'You know, you look like people in search of an infamous pirate treasure. Why not follow me and I'll show you where it is?'" Deneya quipped.

"It'd be nice if they did… or gave us *some* kind of lead." Vi sank her chin into her palm, looking out over the brewery. It was as lively as it ever was, and haunted by the same faces. "Nothing changes here."

"People are enjoying themselves after the end of a war." Taavin stretched, leaning back in the booth beside her. "They don't want excitement right now. They want stability and comfort."

"A shorter lifespan really does give some perspective." Vi envied them, in a way, for their ability to carry on dancing, laughing, and joking, ignorant to the world's imminent demise.

"I'd argue the opposite." Deneya took a long sip of her brew. "They can only focus on one existential threat at a time. Once that's settled, the world is all right."

"They can only do that because there are people like us to worry about all the others," Taavin murmured.

Vi brought her attention back to the ale slowly growing warm in its flagon. She took a sip and refocused herself.

"What's our goal tomorrow?" Vi produced the worn book, still filled with the maps Tiberus had gifted Adela years ago. Vi had added onto those maps over the past months. "I'd propose we head north through the tunnels."

"Seems as good as any idea." Taavin pointed at one of the winding tunnels. "You mean this one?"

"I was thinking so."

"Might as well keep crossing them off one by one." Deneya took a long drink. "Eventually, we'll go through them all." The woman met Vi's eyes. "What if the crown isn't—"

The door to the tavern opened and a rowdy bunch came singing in, interrupting Deneya. A noisy crowd wasn't particularly uncommon. What made Vi turn her head was the language they were singing in.

The throaty tones of Mhashanese filled the tavern as they finished the last refrain and devolved into laughter. They continued to carry on, heading straight for the bar. The leader among them, a man with dark, spiked hair, ordered from the young woman behind the counter.

"A round of your finest for my crew."

"Comin' right up." Maleese wasn't bothered. Even though she couldn't be much older than seventeen, the young woman was accustomed to bawdy sailors running amok in her bar. She'd clearly grown up among salt-crusted, curse-spitting men and women. "Not often we see Westerners in here," she said on behalf of every patron in the bar who was carefully regarding the newcomers.

"We're not Westerners," the man said. Vi knew that voice. How did she know that voice? She fought to place it, shifting in her seat.

"I hear it too," Deneya whispered over the top of her ale.

"Hear what?" Taavin leaned closer to say.

"The voice is familiar, but I can't place it… I want to see the man's face."

"What are you, then?" Maleese set four flagons heavily on the bar and went back to filling four more from the tapped keg. "Look

Western to me."

"We're Mhashanese," the man said proudly. A notable distinction to make.

"*Oy*, Violet," Maleese called over to Vi. It was the name she was going by now. "You *Mhashanese* too? Have I had it wrong this whole time?"

The man at the bar turned his head. Vi locked eyes with him.

He was older now, resembling more and more of his father by the day. The father Vi had killed with two words.

Hello, Luke, Vi thought darkly.

"You can call me whatever you like, as long as you keep the ale coming," Vi said with a wink. A few of the other patrons gave her an approving nod or cheer in agreement.

Luke took his drink off the bar and walked over. He had a relaxed smile—more of an arrogant grin.

"*Fiarum evantes*," he said to the table.

"*Kotun in nox*," Vi replied deftly.

He paused, staring at her for a long minute. "Do I know you?"

"I don't know how you would." Vi shrugged.

"You look like a woman I once knew. But by now she would be…" He trailed off, and then shook his head, as if dismissing the notion. Luke had become a middle-aged man, and Vi still looked eighteen. Even if he recognized her perfectly, he clearly doubted his eyes. The man continued speaking in Mhashanese; knowing him, it was likely some kind of test. "Not common to see Westerners in the land of gold hair and snow fields."

"Could say the same to you," Vi replied in the old Western tongue. Even though she knew her pronunciation and grammar were flawless, thanks to Yargen's magic, it still felt odd to pronounce the words once more. "What brings you here, brother?"

"We're starting a sailing route between here and Norin. Regular runs on fast ships." He swept his eyes across the table; Deneya and Taavin both gave nods. They had begun inking Taavin's hair to make it black. With the deep tan of his skin, he looked the part as much as Deneya. "I don't think we'll have much room for passengers. But for the right price, I could liberate you from this icy prison."

Vi chuckled. "Perhaps we should take him up on it?"

"I miss the desert sun." Deneya sighed longingly.

"I'm afraid we don't have much in the way of money." Vi turned back to Luke. The son of the maritime minister in the West. A loyalist of the Knights of Jadar still, no doubt. In the face of an old enemy, Vi saw an interesting opportunity. She lowered her voice and leaned forward, speaking conspiratorially. "Not a lot of opportunities for us here."

"I've no doubt." He muttered something she couldn't make out, but it ended with "Southerners" in a nasty tone.

"Perhaps… we could work for passage?"

"I have all the crew I need."

"One of us can do the work of two men without tiring," Deneya boasted.

Taavin remained silent. His expression was passive at a glance. But she could see the questions in his eyes. *What are you doing?* he silently asked.

He'd just have to trust in her. It was a skill Vi was still teaching him.

"Is that so?" Luke hummed at Deneya. "I believe it of you. But these two…"

"We're stronger than we look," Vi insisted. "Give us a chance. You won't regret adding additional red-blooded Westerners to your crew." *Red-blooded Westerners*—she'd heard the Knights of Jadar using the term and hoped it struck a chord.

"I'll be the judge of that. But consider me intrigued. Plus, I'm always happy to help out my kin." Luke held out his flagon and Vi knocked hers against it before they both drank. "Come to the docks tomorrow. We'll put you through the wringer. If you can keep up, I'm sure I can find a position for you three."

"Thank you, sir…" Vi paused.

"Lord," he corrected. "Lord Twintle."

"Lord Twintle." Vi gasped, then bowed her head low. "Forgive our impropriety." Taavin and Deneya followed her motions. No matter how much time passed, Vi was certain a Twintle would always appreciate people prostrating before him.

"You know of me?"

"Oh yes," she said eagerly. "Who of Mhashan's blood doesn't know of the illustrious Twintle family? You stood up for the old ways when very few would. Or so I've heard…"

"Luke! Are you going to spend the whole night over there?" A burly man lumbered over, throwing his arm amount Luke's shoulders. "Your crew would like a drink with their benefactor."

"Yes, Cole, I'll be over." Luke looked back to them, pointedly at Vi. "And I look forward to seeing you three bright and early at the *Lady Black*."

The two men went over to the pack of Westerners, talking as they left. Vi saw Cole glance back on more than one occasion. She busied herself with her flagon as she stole glances from the corners of her eyes. She didn't remember a man named Cole the last time she'd been in the West.

But that had been nearly twenty years ago, which was plenty of time for Luke to find new allies. Especially now that he was the new Lord Twintle.

"Want to tell us what that was about?" Deneya asked in hushed tones. The Westerners were no longer paying them any mind.

"And why we're trying to get on a ship with *Twintle* of all people." Even though Taavin couldn't have recognized the man by face, he recognized him by name.

"To find an enemy, we have to go were enemies lurk," Vi whispered back. "Twintle is up to something. If he's coming to Lyndum willingly, I'd stake my life that whatever he's up to is big, and intended to work against Solaris. He and the rest of the Knights have had decades to lick their wounds from the blows they were dealt at the fall of Mhashan, and my cutting their ranks in the Caverns. They're emboldened again, and their coffers are fat."

"You think they might be planning something with QA."

"I can't be certain, but they've done it before. Why not go to her again?"

"And your rationale is there's only one way for us to be certain—to get on his ship," Deneya continued.

"Yes. Either Adela didn't manage to get the treasure off the Dark

Isle and it's here somewhere, or she took it, and it's on the *Stormfrost*. If it's the latter, the Knights might be our best way to get to her."

"Clever, I'll give you that." Deneya grinned and stood, sliding out from the bench of their booth.

Vi and Taavin followed. They slipped out the main door and into the cool night with only a glance from Twintle. It was the last weeks of summer, and the chill of autumn was already beginning to settle on the world.

Taavin linked his arm with Vi's, allowing Deneya to walk ahead. He lowered his voice. "Are you sure about this?"

"Do you have a better idea?"

"I don't like the notion of working with the Knights."

"Trust me, I'm not a fan of it either."

They arrived at the single-room hovel they'd been staying in near the market. Most nights, Vi longed for something better. But it was a roof over their heads and they didn't have much in the way of gold or silver—some pilfered treasure Vi had stolen from the palace before they left, Deneya's meager wages from working in the stables, and whatever coin Deneya's craftsmanship brought in.

In the back corners of the room were three pallets. Two were pushed together, the third on the opposite side. They went about their business, readying for bed with habitual precision before crawling under their respective blankets.

"Think the beds on the ship will be better than this?" Deneya asked the darkness.

"There will be bunks or hammocks, if it's anything like the other vessels I've been on," Vi answered, twisting both her body and her words as she dodged the heart of the question.

Taavin slotted into place behind her, one arm stretched out underneath her pillow. The other wrapped around her waist and tugged lightly, bringing her close.

"A hammock sounds nice. Fewer bugs probably." Deneya yawned. "I bet it sways with the rocking of the ship. Lull us to sleep like babes."

Vi laughed. "The first time I was on a ship, I was nothing like a babe. More like a drunkard, vomiting everywhere."

"It can't be that bad. The ride over from Risen was easy enough."

"Risen," Taavin murmured sleepily in her ear. Warmth flooded her at the sound of his voice so close, at the feeling of his body flush behind her. Vi savored every precious sensation. She'd been taking them for granted since he'd gained his body. "If we get all the weapons—" he yawned "—we'll need to go to Risen and get the flame, to get Yargen's essence within it."

"I know." Vi had been accounting for it from the start. She kept track of where Yargen's essence was stored: the flame, the Caverns, the three remaining crystal weapons, Taavin, and herself. Every night, Vi reminded herself of the count. Because the question of what would happen to her and Taavin when the time to summon Yargen came always circled back into the front of her mind. "One step at a time. First we have to find the crown."

"And get all the other weapons."

Thoughts of Risen brought her mind in another direction. "Deneya."

"*Argh*, I was just about to fall asleep. What?" she said with a flair of drama.

"You were not about to fall asleep." Vi grinned. "What does Lumeria think has happened to you?" It had been over ten years since Vi had last heard of Deneya checking in with the queen.

"I told her when we last spoke that business here would keep me from giving updates to her regularly. I'm sure it'll take about fifty years of silence before she starts to wonder."

"Makes sense," Vi muttered, her lids becoming heavy.

It didn't even occur to her that she had just found the idea of someone checking in once every fifty years reasonable. Fifty years would've been half of her lifespan once. Now, it was little more than a moment.

With every day that passed, she drew closer to the end of the world and further from the world she'd known… and the woman she'd been.

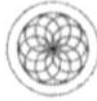

Vi woke up before her friend and lover.

Taavin's breathing was slow and easy. The sunlight from underneath the crack of the door was already bright enough to see by.

Vi twisted in Taavin's arms. He sighed softly in his sleep and tightened his embrace slightly.

She ran her fingertips from the point of his ear down his cheek. His eyes fluttered open at the touch.

"Sorry to wake you," Vi whispered, soft enough that Deneya wouldn't hear.

"Waking next to you is nothing to be sorry about." He blinked the morning's haze from his eyes. "How did you sleep?"

"Wonderfully."

He must've seen something on her face. "Is everything all right?"

"I hope so," Vi started cautiously.

"What is it?"

"I'm going alone this morning."

His brow furrowed. "All three of us are going—" She silenced him with a finger across his lips.

"Listen… I don't know what 'wringer' Luke will put us through to see if we can keep up with his crew. But even if somehow you two can hide your ears for the test… you'll never be able to conceal them long-term on the vessel. All it will take is one gust of sea breeze to take off your caps or bandannas, and then everyone will see them."

"We can illusion them."

"Those same sea breezes will make your hair wild. You won't be able to predict its movements with an illusion."

"We'll illusion the whole head of hair, then," he countered.

"And you don't think that would ever look suspicious?"

"Dark Isle dwellers don't understand what our ears mean. We could say it's a birth deformity."

"One you both share?" Vi arched her eyebrows.

"We'll say we're siblings."

"Even though you look nothing alike?" Vi barely refrained from rolling her eyes.

"We both have black hair."

"*I* have black hair, Taavin. You have bottles of ink."

"There are bottles of ink in Norin as well. We can keep up the deception," he insisted.

"I need you both here." Tired of arguing, she got to the heart of the matter. "You need to keep exploring the tunnels and caves to look for the treasure. This way, we can divide our efforts: I'll go and ensure Adela doesn't have the crown while you two remain here to look."

"You have no guarantee they're working with Adela."

"And you have no guarantee they aren't." Just when she was on the verge of exasperation, he cracked a grin and pulled her closer. There wasn't a bit of space between them and she was left breathless as Taavin leaned in and placed a gentle kiss on her lips.

"I understand, and I know." He sighed. "I'm not going to fight you further."

"Really?" Vi asked skeptically.

"If I tried, I think I would lose."

"You would, because I'm right about this."

"And I know it." Taavin kissed her lightly once more. No matter how much time passed, the act still sent sparks up her arms that were their own, unique type of magic. He pulled away and murmured, "I still don't want to let you go."

"If it's any consolation, I don't want to leave your side. But whenever I'm docked here, I'll be with you."

"And the weeks or months when you're sailing to and from Norin?"

"I'll yearn for you—for where I am home." Were she able, she'd hide from the world and spend forever in his arms. Taavin's embrace was one of the few places she still felt fully herself. She was Vi, here, nothing more or less. "Hopefully, I can gain some kind of lead on Adela early and I'll return to you quickly."

"Or maybe we'll find something and call you home."

Vi nodded and heard Deneya begin to stir. Before the woman was up and about, Vi leaned in for one more kiss—for one last, longing second when they were entwined. Then she pulled away.

There was work to do.

Deneya was understandably frustrated by the notion of not getting to go on the ship and prove her prowess. But she ultimately agreed with Vi that it would be for the best.

Then, with just a pack to her name once more, Vi emerged into the early morning.

She made her way through the narrow streets and alleyways of the compact city down to the docks. Vi instantly knew which ship was the *Lady Black*. It bore Twintle's family crest on an oversized sail.

"And what'll you be wanting?" A gruff sailor sitting at the end of the gangplank stopped her as she approached.

"I'm here to see Lord Twintle," Vi said in Mhashanese, hoping to earn some favors with the man.

"You really think the Lord sleeps on a ship when he has the comforts of port?" *So much for winning him over.*

"Then I'd like to speak with the man named Cole."

"That's cap, captain, or Captain Dower to you," the sailor corrected.

"May I please see Captain Dower?"

The sailor stared her down for several long seconds, spit something he'd been chewing into the strip of water between the boat and the dock, and finally pushed away from the pylon he'd been leaning on. "All right, green gills, come along. You'd best hope it's something good to be troubling the captain this early."

Vi followed him onto the main deck of a narrow ship. She was instantly reminded of the *Dawn Skipper*. The *Lady Black* was a little larger, designed to carry more cargo, but both vessels had clearly been designed with speed in mind.

"You wait here," the sailor ordered, disappearing into the captain's quarters at the stern for a minute before reemerging with the man Vi recognized from the night before as Cole—Captain Cole Dower, she now gathered. "This is the one looking for you, sir."

"Thank you." Cole dismissed the man and looked Vi up and down. "You had two others with you last night."

"They decided the high seas are a bit too intimidating for them."

"So the scrawniest came instead." Cole shook his head and turned away. "Go home, girl."

"No." Vi stood firm. But the man didn't so much as glance over his shoulder. When he continued toward his cabin, Vi had no choice but to scamper after him. "I said I would not leave."

"Well, there's no room for you here." Cole opened the door and disappeared into his cabin, leaving Vi standing on deck, a bit dazed.

This was a test. Her trial period had begun and they were going to see how determined she really was.

Vi did a quick scan of the deck and then started toward a man who was pulling out a bucket and mop. The ship was fairly quiet in port. But that didn't mean there weren't chores that needed doing.

"Give me those."

"Who are you?" the man asked, but he was already handing her the mop.

"Your new crew mate," Vi declared, hoping she'd be right by the end of the day. "When I'm done with this, what can I do next?"

The man gave her a long list. After she finished swabbing the deck, Vi coiled rope and sanded a portion of the wall underneath one of the windows in the crew's quarters. She worked without question or comment other than, "What's next?" or "What else can I do?" until the sun hung low in the sky. The narrow opening to the cargo hold kept catching her eye, but Vi ignored it, for now.

If there was one thing she'd learned, it was how to be patient.

"I thought I told you to go home."

"I'm almost done with this for the day," Vi replied, not even looking back to confirm what she already knew from the voice alone: Captain Dower had come to check in on her.

"I have no pay or berth for you. Go home."

"I don't have a home, sir," Vi said. The feeling of Taavin's arms, closing tightly around her, filled her mind. He was the only home she had.

"Is that supposed to illicit sympathy from me?"

"No," Vi answered, dipping her brush into the heavy paint and caking it onto the wall she'd spent the better part of the afternoon sanding down. "I'm merely stating facts."

"Then my facts remain as well: I have no room for you. Now, off my boat," he growled.

Vi calmly finished the section she was working on, returned the brush to the bucket, went to where she'd originally collected the paint from, closed the bucket, and dropped the brush in a soaking basin. When she emerged on deck with Cole, she noticed more than a few eyes on her. A group of sailors who were drinking on the quarterdeck went silent. Vi strode down the gangplank and settled herself on the pylon opposite the guard.

"Get going, girl," Dower called down.

Vi wondered briefly how old Dower was. Thirty? Forty, perhaps? They might be nearly the same age, and here he was, calling her "girl."

"You told me to get off your boat, sir. I am off of it. You said nothing about the docks and don't control them."

"Suit yourself," he grumbled and disappeared.

That night, Vi slept on the docks in a twilight haze. She was ever aware of the heavy footfalls along the creaking wood, always listening for a threat. When dawn came, she unfolded her cold, damp body and ascended the gangplank to begin her work once more.

Once more, Captain Dower told her he had no room and no pay for her.

Once more, Vi slept on the docks.

It took a week.

Twintle suddenly appeared on the boat without warning, looking quite smug. He didn't so much as spare her a glance as he went right for Dower. Vi hoped that Taavin and Deneya had been keeping an eye on the man while he was in town.

The call to cast off was made soon after.

Dower said nothing about having no space for her as they readied to set sail.

THE PASSAGE FROM OPARIUM to Norin took about four weeks, round trip, depending on weather. They usually stayed in Oparium for two weeks when docked, and in Norin for a month or two.

In total, the trip to and from Oparium usually took about two and a half months.

Vi had done that trip four and a half times when things finally got interesting. They were docked in Norin when a woman with a scar over her left eye boarded late in the night. Vi had seen the woman on the docks when she was off the boat with the other sailors in search of a drink or card game. But she'd never had much of a reason to pay attention to her. That was… until now.

"I'm here to speak with Cole."

"Not often a Southerner comes knocking in Norin." Vi folded her arms over her chest. She'd worked her way up through the ranks swiftly and deliberately, to be one of Cole's agents. He trusted her to not let just anyone onboard the ship.

"Twintle sent me." The woman tucked her hand into her coat and produced a folded letter sealed with the same symbol emblazoned on the sail.

"Well, then, don't keep the captain waiting with your lordly business." Vi pushed away from the dock pylon and led the woman up the gangplank.

A Southerner… what would have Twintle working with a Southerner? Whatever it was, Vi was certain it wasn't good. But perhaps, hopefully, this marked the start of a lead that would bring her to Adela.

Whatever the woman and Cole spoke about was short. She was strolling back down the gangplank with the same smug smile in only ten minutes. Vi worried the chain around her neck and wished, not for the first time in Norin, that she could still summon Taavin.

A few hours later, when the decks had long since quieted, a red-cloaked figure emerged from the night's haze. Vi shifted off her perch, instantly alert.

"*Fiarum evantes*," Luke said, just as he had all those months ago.

"*Kotun in nox*," Vi replied, eying the red cape around his shoulders. Did the Knights of Jadar still meet in that warehouse? She'd cased it a few times without success, but perhaps she should do so again.

He started up the gangplank, but stopped only a few steps up and faced her once more. "You were that girl we liberated from the South. What was your name?"

"Violet," Vi said.

"That's right. You were the one who knew of my family." Luke paused, hands folded behind his back. He looked more and more like his father as his hair began to salt. "How did you put it? That my kin, 'protected the old ways'?"

"It's what I was always taught growing up here in Norin. And it's made working for you an honor, sir."

"Is that so?" He stepped forward, looking her up and down in the dim light of the docks. "How old are you, Violet?"

"Twenty, sir." She looked like she could be twenty, right? The longer Vi was alive, the harder it was to feel any age.

"You were a toddler when this city fell, then."

"But I grew up with the stories. They were vivid enough that, even as a girl, I felt like I had been in those battles."

"You remind me of a woman I knew, then," he said, his voice going soft with memory. Vi smiled innocently. He'd said as much in Oparium.

"Who?" *Let's see if you can remember this time.*

"I can't recall." Twintle shook his head. Couldn't? Or didn't want to? Vi didn't ask. "But more importantly, I have a proposition for you."

"Oh?" This was the most Twintle had spoken to her in the past year. They'd otherwise had only brief, polite interactions.

"I'm going to expand the business ventures of this vessel. We'll need an *adaptable* crew. One that is loyal above all else. Dower only has good things to say about you and your work ethic. I've never seen you fraternizing with the wrong crowd."

"I'm flattered you've taken such an interest in me."

"It's one of my duties to see that the young men and women of the West are both protected and raised with our ideals. You do share our ideals, don't you?" Vi nodded. "Good. Then perhaps I could put in a word with Dower and you will remain one of the crew."

"I'd be honored." Vi didn't like the idea that she was at risk of getting kicked off the ship. It would make returning to Oparium difficult, at the very least. She watched Twintle start up the gangplank once more. Vi stepped forward before she could think better of it, stopping him with a soft, "Sir?"

"Yes?" He turned, his expression one of surprise.

"In the stories of the old West my parents told me… red-hooded knights were always the saviors." Vi motioned to the cape he now wore. "This made me remember those words."

"I see." He had a knowing smile.

"If such knights existed, it would be my life's goal to serve them." Vi stopped herself there. If she said too much, she'd risk suspicion.

"That is most good to know." Luke bowed his head and Vi mirrored the motion. He disappeared up the gangplank and onto the ship.

The next morning, the whole crew was brought on deck. Dower walked the line of them, looking each up and down.

"For many of you, this is your last day of service to Lord Twintle and the *Lady Black*." Murmurs rippled through the assembled crew. "Many of you have been top-notch sailors the likes of which any captain would be lucky to have. I've communicated this to the Lord and he will be offering you a generous severance and a glowing recommendation for any future captains you wish to sail under."

"If we're such good sailors, why is he letting us go?" one of them asked.

"Because Lord Twintle is having the *Lady Black* take on a new directive that requires a specialized crew," Dower answered lightly. *Nothing to worry about here; don't read too closely into this*, Vi mentally filled in the blanks for him. "Now, please step forward if I call your name…"

"Louis." That was Cole's first mate. Expected.

"Joyce." The woman was a Western Waterrunner, but that was all Vi knew about her.

"Violet." Vi stepped forward, relieved to be included. If she stood with Louis, she stood with the group that was staying.

"You three will remain. The rest of you can go."

"A-All of us, cap?" the man from earlier stuttered in shock.

"Yes, you're dismissed." At Cole's final command, the crew of the *Lady Black* trudged belowdecks to gather their things. Vi stood a little straighter as he addressed them once more. She was still the newest of the lot and the one with the weakest relationship with Cole. "Louis, wait for me in my cabin; we need to go over what we'll be looking for in our new hires. Joyce, see to the crew below and escort them off if need be."

"Make sure there's no trouble, you mean." She had a wicked glint in her eye.

"Behave," Cole cautioned her before turning to Vi. "You, join me on the quarterdeck."

Vi did as she was told. Anticipation built with each step toward the back of the vessel. Cole went straight to the railing, glancing over his shoulder to make sure no one was around. When he spoke, he didn't look at her.

"You're here on the direct order of Twintle. If it were up to me, you'd be leaving with the rest of them."

"Thank you for that," Vi said, somewhat dryly. She folded her arms and leaned against the railing, looking in the opposite direction. "Or should I say to pass on my thanks to Lord Twintle?"

"Don't get me wrong, you're a fine sailor, Violet. But this is going to require loyalty—something you haven't really been tested on."

"What is?" She wanted him to say it outright, whatever *it* was. Vi was more than ready to know if all of this following Twintle was actually going to lead to information on Adela and the crown, or not.

"Know I won't hesitate to gut you and tip you over the railing should you betray us."

"Noted. Now tell me what we're doing."

"We need to make some special deliveries into the South. Henrietta—you met her last night—is going to help us with that." The Southerner with the scar over her eye.

"What kind of deliveries?"

"You don't need to know that."

"Are we still docking in Oparium?"

"Yes."

"Will Henrietta be part of our crew?"

"In a matter of speaking. We'll pick up some new crew members that are specially trained for this work." Vi opened her mouth for another inquiry but Cole interrupted her. "That's all you need to know for now. Do as you're told. Keep your head down and your mouth shut." Vi physically shut her mouth on the recommendation. "Good. We set sail with our new crew tomorrow."

Vi watched Cole descend to the main deck amid the steady flow of departing sailors. Twintle was clearly up to something. The question was... what? And, more importantly, was Henrietta working for Adela?

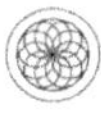

Every time Vi laid eyes on Oparium, her heart fluttered to the point of breathlessness. She'd made five runs now with the *Lady Black*, working with Henrietta and her crew.

Henrietta turned out to be the captain of a small smuggling operation that was now under Twintle's employ. A day before the *Lady*

Black reached Oparium, they'd drop anchor in the sheltered cliffs of the southern mountains and meet up with Henrietta and her crew. Vi and the rest would connect the two vessels by a few precarious planks and carefully offload heavy crates of Western rubies onto Henrietta's boat.

Henrietta would then sneak the crates of rubies into the South through some secret dock to avoid taxes and questions raised about where they were going. Judging from the rumors Taavin and Deneya had heard, Henrietta was using Waterrunners to illusion her ship to look like the *Stormfrost*. No one in town wanted to investigate a ghostly-looking vessel that might belong to the infamous Adela.

But where the rubies came from, what the money from their sales was going toward, who was buying them, and whether Henrietta was actually in league with Adela were all things Vi had yet to find out. Despite having so many unanswered questions, every time she returned to Oparium, she did so with optimism… and excitement.

Taavin, Taavin, Taavin, every pulse whispered. Vi paused at the deck rail, watching the city come into focus through the early morning fog. She knew he'd be waiting at the docks for her. Sometimes Deneya was there, sometimes not.

But as the ship neared port, Vi knew immediately that something was wrong. A host of city soldiers were lined up, waiting where the *Lady Black* usually tied off her ropes. Vi, along with the rest of the crew, regarded each other skeptically. No one said anything until Cole was on deck, staring down at the portmaster and the head of the city guard.

"What's the meaning of this?" Cole asked.

"Your ship is temporarily embargoed," the head of the guard announced.

"Under what cause?"

"We have reason to believe you're not accurately representing your goods," the portmaster said meekly.

Cole scoffed. "Your men inspect our goods every time."

"This time the city guard will do it," the head guard said, taking control of the situation once more. "No one on or off the ship until my men have time to go through every box and bag in your hull."

"Be my guest. I'll lower the gangplank now."

"Unfortunately, I can't spare you the men now." The head guard smirked.

He couldn't spare the men? But he had a whole score of them lined up for their arrival. *Typical power play.*

"When do you think you can spare them?" Cole ground out.

"We'll see." Yes, the city guard was toying with them, no doubt ensuring that they would be punished regardless of whether or not they were found guilty.

She swept her eyes over the docks, looking for Taavin, as the head guard appointed someone to watch their ship day and night. Taavin and Deneya likely knew what was going on, and the real meaning behind this holdup. She just had to get to them.

Vi waited until nightfall. There wasn't much to do on the ship, and it was hard to slip away from the crew unnoticed. She made the excuse of a trip to the latrine. When she was there, she uttered *"durroe watt radia,"* then slipped out the next time a sailor opened the latrine door.

She'd been practicing her Lightspinning. Vi couldn't shake the feeling since making a body for Taavin that she had been given permission to challenge the conventions of how the magic worked. Nothing seemed impossible anymore—not even moving while invisible, without any kind of distortion. It still wasn't perfect. But with more power, perhaps it could be.

Perhaps with the scythe…

Padding lightly on the main deck, Vi headed for a spot she'd identified earlier, where the crates stacked on the docks were high enough for her to jump. She listened to the creaking of the ship, memorizing the patterns the waves made. During one loud groan of the vessel, when no one was looking, Vi jumped off. She left a rope right at the deck's edge that she could push down with *kot sorre* later to get back aboard.

"Durroe watt ivin," she whispered quickly, replacing one glyph for another. Vi slipped into the second skin of a Southerner, and made her way through the city to the one-room abode Deneya and Taavin still occupied.

Vi didn't even bother knocking.

"What the—"

"It's me." Vi closed the door, relaxing her illusion.

"See, told you she'd make it." Deneya gave Taavin a look of triumph. "And you were worried."

"We were just discussing how we'd break you out," Taavin said, standing. He crossed over to her and, without hesitation, enveloped her in his arms. "I was worried I wouldn't get to see you this time."

"If the world itself being rebuilt couldn't keep me from you, nothing will." Vi held him tightly and sneaked in a kiss before they broke apart. "But what's going on in the city? They've finally decided to investigate all the pirate talk?"

"The rumors of Adela have gotten worse," Deneya said. "Henrietta is getting bold or sloppy, but sightings of her vessel have increased and it's roused all kinds of suspicion."

"Too bad it's not actually Adela," Vi muttered.

"First time I've ever heard someone say that." Deneya snorted with amusement. "Any confirmation if Henrietta is actually working for Adela?"

Vi shook her head. "Though I'm beginning to wonder if her ability to masquerade her ship as the *Stormfrost* without Adela coming to put an end to it is proof enough."

"Adela could be on the other side of the world. She might not even know."

"There have been some other developments since you were last here," Taavin said. "Notably, the prince has come to town and things seem to be escalating swiftly with his presence."

"Again? He came last summer and nothing changed." Vi didn't need to ask which prince. According to all rumors, Aldrik had grown to be a harsh man, shaped by the cards Vi had dealt him with her own hands. Only Baldair left the capital with any regularity.

"There's been a murder on the royal estate during one of his infamous parties," Deneya picked up the explanation. "He's now looking into the Adela rumors as a result."

"What made him link the murder to Adela? Or Henrietta?"

"According to talk on the town, the murdered woman had the mark of Adela carved into her dead body," Deneya said grimly.

"Henrietta's getting greedy," Vi muttered. All good things had to come to an end, especially when those good things involved smugglers teaming up with traitors. Despite what was claimed, there was never honor among thieves. "Do you think Henrietta has a lead on Adela's treasure?"

"I don't see how she couldn't. She's been docking in the Caverns and using their tunnels for over a year."

Vi folded her arms, a scowl on her lips. She'd hated the feeling of stagnancy for years. It was becoming harder and harder not to just rush in and smoke out the smuggling rats with her own flames.

"I take it you still haven't made much progress investigating the tunnels with them there?"

"We've had to be cautious," Taavin said grimly. "We don't want to disrupt fate too much."

Vi barely resisted screaming.

"But we did find something," Deneya said hastily, as if sensing her agitation.

"What?" Vi asked eagerly.

"It'll likely be easier if we showed you."

They each donned an illusion, stepping into the skin of a Southerner so as not to stand out. The three traveled down the winding staircases that descended to a rocky beach not far from the port. From there, they went north, until the beach was nothing more than a narrow line of rocks where the waves ended. Soon, there wasn't a path anymore, and large boulders blocked their progression. The stone was slick with sea spray and it made the going slow.

Eventually, they came to a narrow pebble beach, and Deneya took the lead. The cliffs had completely hidden the town from view. Vi followed along to a point where the sea flowed in to a giant cavern.

"We've seen a ship go in and out of here—judging from your description, and those of the other sailors in town, likely Henrietta's."

"You couldn't investigate the caves anymore, so you investigated the cliffs," Vi said aloud as it dawned on her. "That's brilliant."

"This isn't even the most interesting bit." Taavin stopped at the water's edge. "We'll get wet from here on."

They swam across the deep channel—definitely deep enough for

Henrietta's smuggling vessel—to the rocky beach on the other side. From there, they continued walking, climbing, and scrambling across boulders and cliff faces that had long ago fallen into the sea. There were a few other channels they had to swim across, and just when Vi was about to suggest they just *tell* her rather than show her whatever it was they were bringing her to, the roar of water could be heard.

"What's that?"

"What we want to show you." Deneya walked ahead this time.

"About a month ago, we came across this." Taavin pointed.

They stopped at another opening in the cliffs. Water roared out of the mouth of a cave in giant splashes, foaming with white, and racing to the sea. All of the other openings had water flowing *in* from the ocean. But this one was like a giant spigot someone had long forgotten to turn off.

"Some kind of spring, or waterfall created by mountain run-off?"

"We thought that too since the water is icy and fresh," Deneya said.

"But look closer." Taavin pointed to something wedged between the rocks just under the water's surface. It was a speck of gold, shining in the moonlight.

Vi crossed over and knelt down. Reaching into the chilly water, she retrieved a coin from where it had been stuck for what appeared to be a long time, judging by its worn surface. Vi flipped it over in her fingers, summoning a mote of flame to see by. On the side of the coin that had not been blasted by water for years, an imprint was still legible.

"Solaris," she murmured. But this was not a coin used by the Solaris *Empire*. "The Kingdom of Solaris." Vi stood. Now that she knew what to look for, dozens more flashes of gold illuminated the night. "Then this means…" She turned her gaze back toward the sheer rocks. Vi could think of only one way ancient treasure would be collecting here—Adela's stolen gold was somewhere close. The treasure, and the crystal crown, had never left the Dark Isle. "We should go into the caves tonight."

"I wanted to when we found it a month ago. He wanted to wait for you." Deneya gave Taavin a look. Vi's attention went to the man as well.

"You didn't need to do that."

"You are the Champion. It is your right to find and protect the crystal weapons." The sentiment was sweet, even if it made Vi tremble with agitation.

"Then we go now."

"Henrietta's crew will be docked in the caves. It's not safe to go through them now. We could risk altering something in the flow of fate that would result in a new Champion not being born."

"*I* am the flow of fate!" The words burst from her with a ferocity Vi didn't know she possessed. Taavin and Deneya both gaped at her. Vi pushed slick strands of hair from her face, fighting to compose herself. "We are trying to stop the world from ending. This is it; this is our chance. We get the crown now—we know where it is. Even if we change things, we will have all we need to stop the world from ending. All of the other crystal weapons are waiting for us. A new Champion doesn't need to be reborn."

"And if you fail?" Taavin stepped forward.

"I won't."

"If you do?" he repeated. "Are you ready to condemn every man and woman on this earth to death? Are you prepared to know that *you* alone were responsible for the end of light and life? Are you ready to usher in an age of darkness from where there is no return?"

"Taavin, that's enough," Deneya said gently. But Taavin didn't back down. He continued to lock eyes with her in an outright challenge.

"I won't fail," she repeated, though her voice was weaker than it had been a moment before.

"Guarantee me you won't," Taavin demanded. Vi was silent. It was a promise she couldn't make. "Guarantee it!" His voice echoed off the cliffs, briefly overpowering the waves.

Another shout of frustration struggled to rise from her throat. All Vi let escape was a meek, "I can't."

"Then we do as I say." Taavin put his back to her and stalked away.

Vi glared at his back, her eyes burning with frustrated tears. *What was the point?* She wanted to ask. What was the point of any of it if they weren't willing to take risks?

Clearly, she didn't have an answer. She fell into step behind him, and didn't speak another word about the crown.

VI SHOULD BE EXHAUSTED. After being up half the night and sneaking back onto the *Lady Black*, she'd only managed a few hours of shuteye. But she was up and tending to her duties, more alert than ever.

Her spat with Taavin was still mostly unresolved. At least, it felt unresolved. They hadn't spoken for the rest of the night.

Vi finished swabbing the deck and looked out to the cliffs. The crown was there. It had to be. She took a deep breath. One more week, and the *Lady Black* would leave without her. She would go get the crown, and then… *What?*

Her path forward seemed murky and uncertain. Taavin was the only person in the world who could shake her like this.

"Drop the rope ladder!" the guard on the deck called up, distracting her from her thoughts.

Another of her shipmates looked at her and Vi gave him a nod, a non-verbal, *I got this.* Hopefully this would be the head of the city guard here to make his check. He would find out that everything matched up, since the *Lady Black*'s illegal cargo had been offloaded days ago.

She crossed over to the railing, adjusting her braids to look over at who was coming to call. All the air in the world vanished.

Three men stared up at her: the young prince Baldair, Erion Le'Dan, and a familiar set of dark eyes that Vi would have known anywhere. She knew them as well as her father's because another version of this man, in a lost world, had been like her father. Tears stung her eyes as emotions bubbled up that Vi couldn't contain.

Jax.

"Don't just gawk, girl. This is an Imperial prince who's waiting on you," the guard scolded, jostling Vi from her shock. She knelt down and tossed the rope ladder over the side of the ship.

Vi rushed over to Cole's cabin. "Prince Baldair is here," she said hastily.

"What the—oh, by the Mother's love," he grumbled. "All right you lot, all hands on deck," Cole commanded. The crew lined up in their usual places for greeting Twintle.

Vi fidgeted as the three men tipped over the railing, landing on the deck with small bounces. She forced herself to stay still, pushing her emotions away.

"They sent a prince to inspect my goods?" Cole tilted his head to the side.

"It should be an honor to have the attention of an Imperial prince," Erion retorted. Even though Vi had only met his father briefly in Norin, she could see so much of Richard Le'Dan in him. But his blue eyes were that of a Southerner. She'd told Richard he'd learn to love the South. It looked like she'd been right.

"Oh, I'm *honored*. I just don't want to waste your time." Cole chuckled and spread out his arms. "I'm Captain Dower, and it's a pleasure to meet you, Prince Baldair. Let's settle this matter behind us. My cabin is this way. I'll let you review my logs and written inventory, complete with signatures all the way from Norin."

"My prince," Erion started as Cole was leading them to the cabin. "May I propose we go with the good captain while Jax goes directly to the hold? We can check at the same time."

"Good suggestion," Cole said, knowing he had nothing to hide.

"I leave it to you." Baldair passed the papers he was holding to Jax.

"Jax?" Cole stroked his scruff thoughtfully. "Unique name, that. I heard of a man named Jax a few years back. Did something monstrous, somehow didn't lose his head, and became a dog of the crown instead."

Vi bit the inside of her cheek. She saw the flash of hurt in Jax's eyes at the horrible brand he couldn't escape, not even in the South. Yet he grinned, pushing the pain away and pulling a mask in place.

This was certainly the start of the man she'd known as her uncle. But he was rougher, less polished and confident.

"You caught me! Though you're a little late, as the crown got me first."

"This matter has long been decided and need not to be discussed further," Baldair said with a firm tone.

"I don't know if I want such a man—"

"If Jax isn't endeared to you, you only have yourself to blame," the prince said sharply. Vi barely resisted cheering. "I trust Jax to do the right thing more than any other guard in this city."

Jax took the last of the papers from the prince and asked, "Where's this cargo hold?"

"Louis, you show him," Cole said, starting for his cabin.

Vi struggled to resist the urge to do it herself. But she had no reason to insist she be the one to show him. Violet didn't know this man.

So she was left standing uncomfortably as Louis led Jax below decks to the dark cargo-hold.

She milled about the deck as she waited, using the time to think. If the prince cleared the ship, she could get off. The ship would offload and be out of port. Then—

A conversation disrupted her thoughts.

"Fallen lord, how dare he step foot on this ship."

"Henrietta wants us to teach the royal and his lackeys a lesson for poking their noble noses into our business. They've been rooting around where they don't belong since they got to Oparium and hosted that little soirée of theirs."

Someone *shh*-ed. "Don't say her name so loudly."

"They're going to find out if they keep investigating."

Vi strolled over to the railing to get closer to the whisperers without looking suspicious.

"Stay calm and don't act rashly."

"Twintle doesn't pay us enough for this."

The conversation was between some of Henrietta's crew and Dower's. Usually, a few of Henrietta's crew stayed with the ship after they traded off the rubies. They were there to make sure that everything went according to plan—that was all the explanation Vi ever got.

Movement distracted her. She saw Joyce walking down into the hold. Vi pushed away from the railing as magic rippled the air. The last thing Vi saw was dagger of ice in the woman's hand.

At the same time, Dower's door opened.

The next few seconds unfolded as the world slowed to a fraction of its speed. Magic ignited below deck while Joyce retreated above. Vi lifted her hands and blocked the woman's path with fire. Joyce had gone rogue.

Vi's fire melted away with a hiss of steam as water pushed against it. A trident made of ice appeared in Joyce's hand and she lunged. Vi clamped her mouth shut so Lightspinning didn't escape.

She could go for the rest of her life without ever seeing an ice trident again. Joyce dropped her other hand, spreading ice across the deck, slowing the rest of them as she launched herself over the railing.

"Stop her!" Jax shouted as he emerged from below, alight with fire. He threw himself over the railing in hot pursuit of Joyce.

Vi followed on instinct.

They pushed through the crowds on the docks, already dissolving into panic. Vi watched Joyce cut down any who stood in her way. Behind her, Vi could hear Erion and Baldair shouting, but she worked to keep up with Jax. Instinct told her to do so above all else.

They rounded market streets, not far from the hovel. Joyce headed down a side alley and Vi was just close enough to see Jax disappear through an illusion in a cliff-side. Sprinting over, Vi ran her hands along the surface of the wall; sure enough, they sank through a misty illusion concealing a narrow passage.

She plunged through.

"Stop and I might make this painless for you," Jax's voice echoed ahead. Vi pushed her feet harder as magic erupted.

The narrow passage opened up into a cavern that had an interior cliff with a sheer drop down to the sea. It was no doubt one of the openings she'd seen the night before, with Taavin and Deneya. White hot flames assaulted Joyce as she levied a volley of ice spears with a wave her hand. Jax lifted his arms on instinct. Vi did the same, bringing a thin veil of flames to cover them both.

"What're you doing here?" He blinked at her.

"Helping you!" Vi shouted back. "I'll keep her pinned, you kill her!"

With a scream, Jax lunged forward for Joyce, fire alight. He missed his target. Vi watched him twist and Joyce caught his leg, ice coating his foot.

He certainly wasn't the skilled combatant he'd been in Vi's time— at least, not yet.

"You never should've chased me." Joyce looked to her with a snarl. Then turned to Jax. "You shouldn't have gone asking about Adela Lagmir."

Joyce pushed Jax away and his arms pinwheeled. Vi caught him, helping right him, but let go just as quickly to lunge for Joyce with flames alight.

The Waterrunner parried her blow for blow. Vi had spent decades learning and perfecting her Lightspinning. Her Firebearing had improved naturally with her combat instincts, but she wasn't nearly as good with it.

If only she could use her chants.

"I'm not letting you go," Vi growled, throwing a ball of fire.

"Petulant child."

Jax was all flaming hands and feet as he rejoined the battle. He was more of a liability than a help in such close proximity. Vi found herself dodging his attacks as frequently as she was avoiding Joyce's.

The awkward dance distracted her and Jax reached out, searing a spear of ice that was meant for her. Vi's breath hitched. He'd overextended and left himself exposed. Joyce impaled him to the hilt on an icy weapon and Vi bit back a cry of agony on Jax's behalf.

This could still be salvaged. If she let his consciousness fade due to blood loss then she could use her Lightspinning to finish off Joyce and heal him. Assuming Jax didn't die in the gamble.

"What a noble soldier," Joyce sneered as Jax coughed blood. "You shouldn't have gone looking for the pirate queen if you didn't want to find her." Joyce pushed him away and Jax staggered backward.

Vi stepped forward. Joyce levied a spear of ice against her. Vi melted it and uttered, "*Juth calt.*"

Two simple words, and Joyce was dead with a flash of light. *Now, for Jax.* Vi was just in time to see him stumble back into the open air beyond the cliff. Gravity mercilessly pulled the dying man down into the dark waters below.

"Jax!" Vi screamed, lunging into that void as well. She would not let him die.

Saltwater went straight up her nose and Vi surfaced, sputtering and looking around frantically for Jax. The tide was heading out—her first lucky break. They wouldn't be pushed deeper into the Caverns.

A lifeless body rolled over in the currents, dipping below the surface.

"Yargen above, don't you dare die on me," Vi snarled. Looking behind her, she said a quick "*Kot sorre.*" The glyph pushed on the water, giving them forward momentum.

As she tumbled in the waves she made, Vi reached for Jax. Dark waters, swirling with blood, surrounded her. Sand crunched beneath her feet as she found footing. Her elbows scraped against pebbles and rocks.

Her arms closed around the man and she pulled him to her. Vi tipped her head back, surfacing for air, clutching onto him for dear life. She gasped as they beached on one of the rocky shores she'd walked with Taavin and Deneya only a night before.

The wound was bad. Jax was coated in blood. But his heartbeat was weak and fluttering under her fingers. Water gurgled up from his throat as his lungs struggled to inflate.

Vi closed her eyes, dipping her chin down as she laid her hands over his chest. She could feel the man's shaky breaths, his struggling body, his quivering magic, his fleeting life. She could see it all as clearly as she'd seen Taavin's body, inside and out, when she'd made it.

"*Halleth ruta sot,*" she whispered. Glyphs illuminated her hands. She opened her eyes, both seeing and feeling his skin mending.

"*Halleth ruta toff,*" Vi continued. She moved deliberately, as if guided by an unseen teacher. Light and skin merged, weaving together and becoming one. Vi gave herself to instinct and her body moved as though it were no longer her own.

It was afternoon when she finally finished the job. Vi looked up at the young man. She reminded herself for the dozenth time in a few hours that this was not her Jax.

But… she would look after him to honor the memory of the Jax she'd known. He had spent the latter half of his life looking after her. Even if this Jax had nothing to do with the man who had made that sacrifice, Vi would look after him. She would repay that favor as best she could.

Vi twisted and sat with a sigh. She wiped the salt water that mixed with sweat from her eyes—certainly, these were not tears from emotions she didn't have names for—and looked out to sea. Jax slumbered at her side, breathing steadily; Vi would wait for him to wake naturally. She'd monitor him. And when he was ready, they would take on Henrietta's crew together.

A sigh at her side had Vi stopping the tune she'd been humming. She didn't know where she'd heard the song, or where it came from. Phantom memories that didn't quite feel like her own paraded through her head as she'd sat watching the waves, thoughts and visions that scattered like rats as Jax stirred.

"The Mother did not want you yet," Vi said faintly. Perhaps that was what had allowed her to pull him back from the edge of death— Yargen's blessing. At the edges of her vision she could see him turning to look at her.

"You're the sailor," he said slowly. Vi nodded in reply. "You saved me?" She merely nodded again. Not going into too much detail was for the best. "Where are we?"

"I don't know exactly." Though Vi had a very good suspicion. "We got dumped out here after you fell off the ledge and I went in after you."

Jax finally sat and Vi paid careful attention to his movements. Luckily, nothing seemed out of sorts. She watched as he inspected the holes in his clothing, pressing on newly mended flesh.

"How long was I out for?"

"A few hours."

"How did you heal me?"

Vi fought a smirk at that question. "Magic," she answered coyly. He stared at her, disbelieving, and Vi laughed. He'd never understand Lightspinning, and she wouldn't tell him. "Fine, fine, I had a salve on me. So you're doubly lucky I was here," she lied.

"*Why* did you save me?"

Her insides knotted at that question. He was so shocked someone would, and clearly confused as to her motives.

"Should I not have?" Vi leaned against the cliff at her back. Jax just shrugged and silence passed between them. They should get moving; things in town were no doubt escalating quickly. But she stayed where she was, saying gently, "I know who you are."

More panic across his eyes.

"I know you are Jax Wendyll, the man they call the 'Fallen Lord' in Norin," she said. She'd been in and out of the port for years now, she'd heard the stories. But she'd mostly ignored them. She knew the type of person Jax was in any world. "I know that, three years ago, you were tried for the murder of the Zower family, including the young Lady Zower to whom you were engaged.

"I know you were conscripted to the crown for your seemingly heinous crime."

"My crime was heinous," he retorted.

"It *seems* it."

"What would you know?" he snapped. "Who are you anyway?"

For one brief moment, Vi was back with Fiera on her birthing bed. She thought of telling him he had been like a father to her in another place and time. "Just a traveler," Vi said simply. He snorted.

"You're not 'just' a traveler."

"Perhaps not 'just.'" Vi grinned. He was astute. More than he realized. "But I have traveled from far away to investigate this Adela Lagmir impostor and her treasure." It was technically true. Just not in the way he'd interpret it.

"So you've heard of it, too?"

Vi nodded—that was one way to put it. "They've been running a criminal ring for over a year in the coves further south of here. Ships dock and unload cargo… some legal that they're avoiding tariffs on, others not so much. The coves are all connected, as you know. It's a maze, but that's how the real Adela gave the Emperor the slip about thirty-five years ago."

"Along with her treasure," Jax bitterly lamented.

"I wouldn't be so sure about that. Just because you haven't found the treasure doesn't mean it isn't here."

"What do you know?" His skepticism and self-doubt were becoming less jarring and more tiring by the moment.

"Help me take out this pirate queen impostor, and I'll tell you what I know about the treasure. I want to be the one to find it." She could imagine Taavin's face when he heard what she was doing. But *she* wasn't the one going rogue and finding the treasure. She was just following along with the prince and his merry band to make sure they didn't find it first. She was allowing fate to play out and give her the opportunity to get the crown.

If she lied to herself enough, perhaps even she'd believe it.

"Fortunate for me, that's an easy deal to make." A rush of relief overcame her and Vi beamed from ear to ear. "I would've done it anyway," he added, as though trying to somehow make it seem like the whole thing was, at least in part, his idea.

"I suspected we were aligned when I saw you chasing after her." Vi stood, dusting the sand and stones off her clothes. She had what she wanted, Jax was healed—no point in lingering. "Your little investigation into the treasure and soirée with the prince helped fluster the ring into making a mistake that has led me right to them."

"And now you're planning on going after her?"

"Will you help me?" Vi didn't understand the question—she

thought the matter settled.

Jax sighed and pulled himself up to his feet as well. Vi regarded him with a careful eye, making sure her healing was as good as she thought. He didn't even stagger. "You're lucky we happen to be aligned."

"I think you were the lucky one." Vi smiled thinly. He would've died had she not been here. Taavin had never mentioned anything about Jax dying, and finding a time to ask when they were more at peace with each other was now high on Vi's list. Not that it mattered now. But she needed to make sure he wasn't keeping potential futures from her to spare her heartache.

He certainly hadn't with Fiera.

"Thank you," he said sincerely.

Vi waved away the notion and started along the beach. "I scouted an entrance up here. It's a bit of a climb, but if we fall heading for it, we fall into the water."

"What's your name?"

The question struck her harder than she'd expected. *You know me*, her heart wanted to scream. But her mind knew better. She searched his expression. There was no familiarity there.

She was no one to him.

Even after all this time, this new world could still cut deeply, and it would hurt more with every year that passed as the people here grew more and more to look like those she once loved.

"It's not important," Vi finally said.

"I must have something to call you."

"I've gone by many names. You pick." *Vi, pick Vi out of everything in the world*, her heart asked as she began to walk again.

"Fine, I shall call you," he paused and Vi's heart pounded, "Nox."

Vi chuckled. How dare she, after all this time, have hoped for anything else.

"Very well, if that's the name you choose."

"One more thing."

"What?" Vi stopped just as she'd been about to start climbing.

"You never told me why you saved me. If you were here to kill the Adela impostor and put an end to this criminal ring, why throw away the chance you had on saving me? Even if I could help, you had your quarry."

"Who said I threw away my chance? The woman we chased was not the leader."

"That's still not answering my question." And curse him for seeing so.

"Because all men are worthy of saving." Vi saw him open his mouth, no doubt with an objection. She cut him off at the pass. "Even—no, *especially* you, Jax."

His lips parted in shock and Vi turned away, beginning to climb. If she looked at him a moment longer, she would tell him there had been a young princess, long ago, who still thought of him like a father.

15

"So, how are we going to find them?" he asked as they headed deeper into the darkness of the caves.

"Patience." Vi shrugged as if she didn't know where they were going. Vi knew exactly where they needed to go to find Henrietta and her crew. If she led Jax there, perhaps she could encourage him to continue searching for the treasure. And if she *happened* to be there when he found it, she wouldn't have gone against her word to Taavin.

"And what if we get lost in here?"

"Then I suppose it's a good thing we're both people who've lived colorful lives. We'll have a lot to talk about while we wait to die." Vi gave a smirk over her shoulder. They weren't dying here.

"This, coming from the woman who wouldn't even tell me her name," he muttered.

"Well, maybe if we're on the brink of death, I'll tell you everything. Though, it'd take more lifetimes than we have."

"You love playing the mysterious card, don't you?"

"I am what I am." Vi shrugged. She didn't always know what that was anymore. "Quiet now. The ship docks in an inner cove to the south of town. I'm trying to listen for the workmen."

They continued into the darkness, winding through the dripping caves by the light of her flame. The sounds of people talking grew and Vi stopped, turning in place to stop him as well.

"I don't know where this is going to put us out." She feigned ignorance. He'd be suspicious if she knew too much. "We should stay low, make for good hiding the second we see it," she whispered in his ear. Jax nodded as she pulled away and followed her into a crouched position.

Vi waved away her mote of flame as its light merged with the ambient light of the cave beyond. She stopped for a moment, allowing her eyes to adjust, only to find Jax staring back at her.

"Do you want a 'we might be about to die' kiss?"

Vi fought the urge to burst out laughing with the competing urge to vomit at the suggestion. "This is not the place where you die," she whispered, cutting through his levity. "But this is the place where you will kill again." Vi grabbed his hand tightly. "You have to fight. You must fight for yourself, fight to live." *Not just now, but through all the years to come.*

Jax opened his mouth to speak and Vi silenced him with a finger. In him, she still saw the Jax who had raised her. But now she was the adult and he was the child in some ways.

"Just be quiet, and take the advice of a friend, Jax." Vi moved again before he could say anything else.

The cavern narrowed to a chute and they crawled forward side by side. It opened into a large room, though their vision was obscured by boxes and crates. Vi recognized them as the same boxes she'd helped unload from the *Lady Black* days ago.

"… their bodies recovered." Vi recognized Henrietta's voice. "None of you are to rest until their bloated corpses are here on a spike to warn the next captain who even thinks of challenging us." So Dower would take the fall for Vi running after Joyce.

"Henrietta, they've surely been lost to the sea." That was the voice of the woman who'd been on the *Lady Black,* murmuring dissent before Joyce attacked.

"Silence! It was your incompetence that got us into this mess. I'll hear none of it."

"Henrietta is their leader," Vi whispered to Jax. "You'll know her by the scar over her right eye. Go for her first." She'd never seen Henrietta in action, but suspected the woman was lethal. Anyone bold enough to use Adela's name had to be.

Vi took a deep breath, steadying her hands. They trembled in excitement, anticipation. It had been years since she'd felt like she'd accomplished anything, and now everything was happening all at once.

She emerged from the narrow opening into a bowl-shaped cavern. Vi rushed over to a larger crate and scoped out the six talking. Jax joined her shortly after. At least he was keeping up. Though, judging from his expression, only barely.

Vi took his hand once more. Fire licked from her fingers to his, as though she could give him her strength. His breathing slowed and he nodded. Vi faced forward, ready to—

"Drop the boxes," a booming voice shouted. Vi heard a groan from Jax. "You are under arrest by the will of the crown for smuggling, theft, murder… and many other horrible things."

She'd always heard her father was "silver-tongued." Clearly, that was a trait he'd inherited from Fiera. Because his brother was sorely lacking in eloquence.

Henrietta laughed. "Kill him."

Vi didn't waste a second longer, launching herself at the six smugglers. She'd told Jax to go for Henrietta. If he could handle that, she'd take on the other five.

Fire erupted around her hands as Vi swung, shooting a tendril of flame at one of the men still focused on Baldair and Erion. He screamed as the fire consumed him, though the sound was cut short as the fire was doused. Vi dodged backward, narrowly missing a spear of ice thrown.

She side-stepped, dodging another spear, and swept her foot across the ground. A wall of flame sheared off. The burnt man fumbled with his sword, determined to fight until his last breath. The woman shielded herself with a wall of ice that promptly became steam. Vi went for her—she was the more troublesome one.

With a flash of flame into the veil of steam, Vi stunned her, closing the gap. She grabbed for the sword the man was fumbling with, drawing it from the scabbard. Vi sliced his throat and swung for the Waterrunner. The woman had recovered, but her attention was elsewhere as she now engaged Erion Le'Dan.

The Waterrunner sunk a blade of ice into Erion's side. Vi crossed the distance with a lunge and threw out her magic. "*Juth starys*," Vi hissed under her breath—she wasn't taking chances on the smuggler countering her attack. The woman erupted into white-hot flames.

"Up with you!" Vi shouted at Erion. He blinked, startled. The lot of them were young men, fresh to bloodshed. She'd have to keep pushing them, especially knowing what trials their futures held.

Jax needed her help next and Vi launched herself back into the fray. She moved around him, preempting his motions; she knew his openings and could cover his vulnerabilities now that she'd fought with him once before.

Among the four of them, they dispatched Henrietta and her crew easily. Vi surveyed the room, making sure no others were about to spring toward them, as Jax went to his comrades.

"Erion, you got one on your hip."

"It's not that bad," Erion said bravely and pressed his hands into the wound.

"Nox, do you have any more potion?" Jax asked her. Vi shook her head. Lightspinning wasn't an option now.

"I'll burn it to stanch the bleeding." Jax leaned forward, flames licking around his fingers.

"Nox? From the *Lady Black*? The sailor who chased the smuggler?"

"She saved me."

"And the rest of you," Vi added as she adjusted her braids. This didn't seem like a group that valued girlish modesty, so Vi wouldn't play that card. She slipped into second skins easier than pairs of leggings. "I was told you were a noble fool, but that truly exceeded my every expectation."

Baldair, the golden prince, the playboy prince, the head of the

Golden Guard—his reputation preceded him even after his young death in Vi's world. Though, seeing him now, at sixteen, it was hard to imagine him as any of those things. All he looked like to Vi was a spitting image of Tiberus.

"Jax, I didn't realize you were now in the business of babysitting lost, sassy children." Baldair laughed, his words lacking bite.

"I think I'm the babysitter," Vi mumbled as she began searching the crates.

"What're you looking for?" he asked.

"It's not here, either." Vi sighed. She should be happy that Henrietta hadn't found the treasure. But that meant the hard work was still ahead of them.

"You still haven't told me what we're looking for."

"Adela Lagmir stole the crown of Lyndum and fled with the other wealth of the last king." Vi straightened, placing her hands on her hips. "When the Emperor—your father, Baldair—chased her down the coast, she fled, giving all the impression that she'd taken the treasure with her. But I *know* it's still here."

"How are you so sure she left it?" Jax asked. "You said, if I helped you, you'd give me information on the treasure."

"I overheard them talking when we were docked in the port here to unload stolen goods," Vi lied. "They said someone was searching the caves and found 'it.' I assumed 'it' must mean the treasure. What else?"

"I think you're right." Baldair reached down, grabbing a wad of folded papers from his boot. "And we just so happen to have the map."

"You do?" Vi couldn't believe it. "Someone made a map to the treasure?" Someone who was very stupid to write such a thing down.

"Renalee had apparently been searching for the treasure for some time."

"Well, show me," Vi demanded, not bothering to ask who Renalee was.

"The city guard is coming; we can ask them for help." The young prince hesitated.

"I'm not interested in waiting." Vi tried to wave the idea away casually. Involving the city guard was a terrible idea—that was a whole lot of variables Vi didn't want to deal with. "Besides, it would mean more people can get their hands on it. Don't you want to be the only one to touch it, to hold it? Think of what the history books will say about 'he who finally rested his hands upon the lost treasure of Adela.'" What did young men want more than glory? Vi was betting on very little.

"It's *my* family's treasure. If anyone gets to hold it, it'll be me."

"I think I deserve this," Vi said with a roll of her eyes. "Especially after I helped you."

"Lay out the papers, Baldair." Erion was the one with sense in the group. Vi could tell that much. "I'm sure there's more than enough treasure to go around."

"Now you want a cut too?"

"I agree with the lady; I think we've all earned it," Erion said to the prince coyly. "What better way to end the summer than actually finding some long-lost pirate treasure? We've already hunted a ghost, stopped a murderer, and caught smugglers red-handed. We earned it."

"I agree. At this point, it's basically our divine right," Jax chimed in.

Vi snorted. *Divine right*—they had no idea.

Baldair relented with a chuckle, laying out the papers. He connected different curving lines stretching across multiple sheets to form a map, and Vi's mind was already committing each to memory. Some of the tunnels she knew from exploring herself, or seeing the maps of Deneya and Taavin's explorations. But other tunnels were paths they'd yet to go down. Dead ends and switchbacks were already recorded. The hard work was complete.

"All right," she declared once the map was solidly in place. She didn't need a moment more with it. "Let's go." The other three looked at her with surprise but fell into step.

They made their way through the tunnels, Vi dragging a dagger she'd lifted from one of the dead pirates along the wall to mark the way in case she returned with Taavin and Deneya.

There was some brief debate when they met a fork in the road. Ultimately they went right—something about a woman wearing an earring contributing to the decision.

At the end of the path was a dead end. Though wind howled through it. The four set to feeling out the walls, eventually finding an illusioned tunnel.

On the other side was another cavernous space, large enough to fit two of the *Lady Black* side by side. The platform they stood on was just wide enough to stand comfortably without fear of falling. Beneath them, at the bottom of a sheer drop, was a swirling whirlpool. White caps battered the rocks, and the churning waters made it impossible to tell its depth. Though Vi knew, somewhere beneath it all, was a short tunnel that cut through the cliff and let the water rush out to sea.

Stretching from the middle of the room was a column. Nestled at the top was a block of ice that had a mountain of treasure frozen within. That treasure was further protected by the column's distance from all the walls, the sheer drop, and the deadly water below.

Vi looked from water to ice to treasure as the men spoke.

"So then who made the ice?" Baldair was saying. "It's still frozen solid, so it must have been recent."

Vi doubted that. "Adela," she chimed in.

"I thought Adela was dead," Erion said cautiously.

"Just because she hasn't been seen in a few decades doesn't mean she's dead." Vi shrugged. It was the best tip she could give them on Adela, and she hoped to Yargen they listened. "And she seems to be as greedy as ever."

Adela never got the treasure out, so she froze it in place to prevent anyone else from getting to it as if to say "see but don't touch." It seemed like a very Adela thing to do.

"It doesn't matter who's making the ice—made the ice—if we can't even get to it," Baldair said. "We have no Waterrunners in our party to cross the gap."

"Should we go back to town and look for one?" Erion thought aloud.

"I don't think we need to," Vi said, her mind working swiftly to avoid bringing more people into the situation. "Adela was a smart woman—or it seems." Vi was loathe to pay Adela a compliment, but intellect didn't play favorites between good and evil. "She wanted to keep the treasure from anyone else, but it wouldn't be impossible to believe that at some point, she might need to send someone who was not a Waterrunner to fetch it. Maybe she would've made it more difficult for them… but there has to be a path."

"Or Adela was a murderous madwoman who wanted to keep her prize only to herself and send anyone who attempted to claim it to a watery grave," Erion said grimly. Vi hated that a part of her agreed that it was possible.

"No… I don't think so…" Vi looked up to the ceiling that was mostly cast in shadow. The only chutes of light were coming from three-fourths of the way up on the walls around one side of the room—the side that faced the beach where she'd found the coin, she hoped. "We merely have to see past another illusion."

A dark line of shadow caught her eye and Vi lifted her hand, sending a burst of fire up to the ceiling.

"Look there." She pointed to the line she saw, the firelight illuminating it. "I would bet that's wide enough to shimmy around."

"How did you even see that?" Baldair murmured.

Vi focused solely on moving forward. She was so close now, and all she wanted to do was get to that treasure.

"There are cut hand- and foot-holds here." Vi gripped a narrow outcropping of stone. "Had to be some reason why someone wasted the time. I would bet that behind that pillar is a bridge of some sort, connecting it to the far wall. We just can't see it from here, and Adela knew this would be the only entrance."

Jax boldly followed behind her as she began to climb.

"Jax, wait, what're you doing?" Baldair stole Vi's words from behind her lips.

"Someone is going to go over, right? We're not really going to get this far and just wait for a Waterrunner, are we? We all know I make the most sense. It's not like my life really matters, not like yours or Erion's."

"Your life most certainly matters," Erion blurted, warming Vi's heart. "If you are reckless here, I will pull you from the Father's halls myself."

"You're our brother," Baldair said, joining Erion's cause. "And I don't want to see you die here."

"Is that an order, my prince?" Jax asked in an almost timid tone that nearly betrayed all the brokenness she'd seen in his eyes.

"It is," Baldair affirmed. "Stay alive, Jax."

Vi continued her climb so she wouldn't be caught staring at the unorthodox little family—the start of the illustrious Golden Guard. Jax's feet scraped the stone behind her as they shimmied across the narrow ledge that rounded the room. Vi glanced at him from time to time, wondering if she could, somehow, convince him to turn back. But it would be suspicious if she pushed too hard. So Vi said nothing and prayed his balance was good enough to stay on the path.

Finally, on the other side of the cavern, they descended onto a narrow ledge that had a wooden bridge connecting it with the column in the center of the room.

"Do you think it's safe?" Jax asked.

"We came this far. Are you really going to turn back now?" Vi hoped he'd say yes, but knew from his determined expression, he wouldn't. "I'll go first."

"Wait—"

"What?" She stopped, one foot on the bridge.

"Be careful." He eased away.

Vi gave him a faint smile. "Worrying about little ol' me?"

"Have you looked at this bridge?" He grinned and pressed himself against the wall, putting as much distance as he could between them.

"It's all I'm going to look at," she muttered, shuffling her weight onto the planks of wood.

The bridge held as Vi walked, arms outstretched for balance. She crossed without the boards even creaking. Vi went immediately to the ice, taking a deep breath and whispering *"Juth starys"* before Jax could cross.

The fire burned underneath her right palm, outstretched to the ice. Vi lifted her left hand, summoning tendrils of flame to hide the glyph that spun there. The ice was certainly Adela's magic and it would need more than the splintered elemental affinities of the Dark Isle to bring it down.

Motion caught her eye. Jax was at her side, hands lifted as well, fire burning from them. She kept her gaze forward, focused, digging into Yargen's power and pushing it outward. She begged for the magic that lived in her to seek out its own and find the crown hidden underneath this frosty tomb.

Her hands were nearly on the crown after years of searching. The thought made her almost dizzy.

A monumental crack in the ice was accompanied by a rumbling roar that echoed against the cavern walls. Vi pushed harder. Steam filled the Caverns as the magic that gave the ice shape gave way beneath their joint efforts.

She saw Jax slump, panting. Vi launched herself forward into the haze.

The gold was so cold it nearly burned her fingers. Vi pushed through it, scattering coins across the scant platform, discarding them into the waters below. She knew the water was moving fast enough to carry the coins—at least some of them—out. There was enough gold here to buy a ship, and she needed the wealth far more than any of these young men did.

"What're you doing?" Erion shouted.

"S-Stop!" Baldair bellowed. "That belongs to the crown."

Vi ignored them, taking bags of gold, ripping them open, and tossing them over. It rained coins and jewels into the raging waters. She'd secure as much gold as she could for her, Taavin, and Deneya. In the process, she'd find the crown.

"Nox, stop!" Jax reached for her and Vi swung. He dodged backward and Vi grabbed for another bag.

Where was the crown? Yargen above! The damn thing must be here. Her mind raced as panic began to fill her. What if the past years of searching were for nothing? If the crown wasn't here, then where was it? Did Adela have it, after all?

Had she already failed? Had Victor beaten her here and this was his ruse, not Adela's? The thought nearly made her scream. It would be too much to bear.

"Jax, stop her!"

Jax kicked at Baldair's command and Vi dodged. She tumbled, rolled, and righted herself.

"Don't touch it!" she yelled. She needed him to wait a moment, just one moment to—

"What're you doing? Tell us, we can help you!" Jax pleaded.

As if you could.

Vi's eyes landed on the last, plump bag that'd been hidden at the bottom of all the other treasure. She lunged for it and Jax stepped on her hand. Vi pulled away with a hiss and grabbed a bunch of coins, throwing them at his face. When he was distracted, she grabbed the final satchel.

If she could get it all in the water, she could search through it later. The crown must be in this bag. It would be in her possession and this whole infernal vortex would be put to an end once and for all. If she got the crown here and now, she could get the scythe, and the axe, and then—

A hand grabbed the bag as she began to hurl it forward.

"No!" The word burst from her like fire, hot, singeing, painful.

The canvas ripped and its contents exploded. Vi twisted, off-balance. She stepped hastily, trying to recover. Her eyes landed on the gold-plated crown that now sat lonely on the mostly empty column of stone. Yargen's magic called out to her longingly.

Vi's arm rose. It was there, so close—she'd almost had it.

Her vision shifted. Jax was reaching for her—he was still going to try to save her. Even after she'd knowingly begun to try to push him away. The tiniest smile crossed her lips as Vi tipped backward.

Jax's compassion was the only thing she could find joy in, given her failure. Cursing herself and her arrogant greed as she fell, Vi took a deep breath right before she plunged into the icy water below, and allowed the currents to carry her out to the sea.

16

VI ROLLED ON THE stone and sand for the second time in the span of a day. Gold coins clanked and scraped against the rocks around her. Treasure glittered across the beach in the early morning light.

Dragging herself far enough out of the icy water that she could breathe without sputtering, Vi brought the spark under her skin. The water evaporated in shimmering waves of heat. She gulped in air by heaving lungful, staring up at the bloody sky. Spending years on boats and ships had turned her into a strong swimmer—strong enough to navigate the currents through the short passage out to the beach beyond.

She waited until her breathing slowed and her chest stopped burning, murmuring curses on the exhales. Failure felt like a noru on her chest, keeping her pinned. The crown had slipped through her fingers and who knew what the young men would do with it now.

Eventually, Vi pried herself up, left the gold behind for now, and began the long walk back to the hovel.

She didn't even knock on arrival, allowing herself in. The room was empty and Vi helped herself to the bed, inhaling the familiar scent of the blankets as she collapsed and fell into a dreamless, exhausted, sleep.

"Vi," Taavin said, shaking her shoulder. "Vi," he repeated. She cracked open her eyes. "Oh thank Yargen."

"You worried us," Deneya said from over his shoulder.

"Sorry, things happened quickly." Vi sat and Taavin helped her up. His fingers laced around hers as Vi rubbed her eyes with her other hand.

"You're being reckless again," he murmured.

"I had no choice." Vi shook her head, her hand falling. "The prince and his group were going after the crown. I was trying to get to it before they did. I knew once it was found, taking it would be nearly impossible."

"We know they found the treasure." Deneya sat on her bed across from them. "The whole town is abuzz with it."

"That was fast."

"Word moves fast when it comes to ghostly prizes." Deneya grinned. "What happened?"

"Jax, Erion, and Baldair showed up at the *Lady Black…*" Vi started, telling them the events of the past day that had ultimately led to her failure. "… but I didn't manage to get the crown."

"So they have it, then," Taavin said faintly.

"I can only assume."

"Years…" Deneya trailed off, staring at nothing. But she didn't have to finish her sentence; they all felt the shared sentiment. They'd spent years hunting for the crown. Now, all that time meant nothing.

"They had a map. Someone else was searching the caves," Vi said.

"We had no idea." Taavin shook his head. "But perhaps all will be well. In all other worlds, the crown has come to light after the War in the North began, at the earliest. We can find out what they did with it later."

"In all other times, we hadn't been meddling as much with the crystal weapons." Vi folded her arms.

"What if we steal it back?" Deneya said, suddenly eager once more. "You studied the Imperial estate here. You know the manor.

You just said there were secret tunnels connecting to it—hence why the blueprints you showed me ages ago were so strange. We could sneak in."

"We could," Vi said uncertainly. Deneya was right, Vi knew the manor. And now that she'd seen the prince's map, she knew how the caves connected to it. "But I think they'll have tighter security now that they have the lost treasure—or at least a small portion of it."

"Nothing we can't handle."

"I appreciate your confidence," Vi chuckled softly.

"We can't take it." Taavin put the notion to rest. "You're right, we've been meddling. If the crown goes completely missing at this point, it's impossible to say what would happen. We can't risk the birth of a new Champion."

"I grow weary of your obsession with Vhalla Yarl's womb," Deneya shot the curt remark at Taavin.

"He's right though," Vi said. "If it went missing now, they'd hunt for it."

"They didn't care to hunt for it for decades," Deneya countered.

"But now they know it exists. They'll know someone stole it. Getting the crown only worked so long as its location was a mystery."

"We can handle them if they come after us; it wouldn't be the first time we've fallen off the pages of history." Deneya was making it difficult for Vi to think rationally. All she wanted to do was go after the crown *right now*. But rushing in with Jax hadn't yielded results.

Patience, she reminded herself. Time and again, patience was the best way forward.

"What if I made another crown and you illusioned it again?" Deneya suggested.

"No," Vi said immediately and firmly. "That didn't work last time." She rubbed her midsection, remembering the price she'd paid for it. "If Victor sees it—"

"And we have every reason to believe he will," Taavin interjected, "if past worlds are any indication of how Victor might act now."

"Victor will see right through any illusion."

"How did he see through it the first time?" Deneya asked.

"A shift in the light," Vi said, recalling that fateful encounter.

"Well, you're more powerful now. I think—"

"Wait," Vi whispered. "*Shift...*" Vi stood and began to pace. Her mind was racing. Her gut was laying a new path before her. "This could work."

"What could work?" Taavin asked hesitantly.

"We have to go to the Twilight Kingdom to get the scythe. We also need to keep the crystal weapons in their places to ensure the birth of a new Champion." She looked to Taavin as she spoke.

"Yes, that's our top priority."

Not saving the world? Vi wanted to ask. She knew where his priorities lay and she'd indulge him right up until the moment she couldn't any longer—a moment Vi could now see on the distant horizon.

"We go to the Twilight Kingdom and collect the scythe. There, we have them use the powers of the shift to make a crown that looks like the crystals. Something real, tangible, not an illusion for Victor to see through."

Then, while they were there, Vi would use Fallor to get to Adela. They needed passage to Risen to get the flame and, ultimately, someone crazy enough to take them to the island of the elfin'ra.

"That... might work," Taavin relented.

"There's just the one small problem of the Twilight Kingdom being a sea away."

"I already planned for that." Vi looked to Deneya with a grin. "We now have enough old Solaris gold to buy a ship. All we need to do is collect it."

"Then we should do that," Deneya said with a nod.

"You look tired. Why don't you rest? Taavin and I can go and collect it." Vi grabbed two packs and handed Taavin two more.

"All right, I can tell when I'm not wanted. Go and have your alone time." Deneya was already nestling herself into bed.

"We'll be back soon," Vi said with a grin.

She and Taavin slipped out the door and into the dark town. There seemed to be fewer people about, likely because they were all clamoring somewhere else over Adela's treasure finally being found.

Vi opened her mouth, surprised when Taavin spoke first.

"I'm sorry."

"What?"

"I said, I'm sorry." Their eyes met. "The other night, I was harsh."

Vi gripped the strap of one of her packs tighter. "You're only trying to do the right thing."

"Yes, but doesn't excuse me when I act an ass."

"I snapped at you first," Vi said tenderly. "I'm sorry, too." Their shoulders brushed as they walked down a staircase that would lead to the beach by the cliffs.

"We're both trying to do what's right, and that's never an easy thing to do." He took her hand and Vi didn't hesitate to lace her fingers with his. The squeeze of his hand pushed forgiveness into her, a sentiment she tried to push back.

"There's something I want to ask you about," she said, pausing as their feet met the sand.

"Yes?"

"Jax, his life…" *and death*, she couldn't bring herself to say aloud. "Is it a stone in the river?" When he didn't immediately answer, she pressed, "Have there been worlds in which he died here and now?"

She almost told him not to say anything. She had her answer by the look on his face alone.

"I can't decide what his fate is," Taavin said, finally. "Some worlds he lives, and some worlds he dies. His life seems to be a variable, not a stone."

Memories flooded her, rushing like the seawater around their ankles as she started walking again, rounding the cliffside. Vi watched the little rocks being carried out by the tides, the larger ones stuck in place. "Why didn't you tell me?"

"I couldn't."

"That's not an excuse." The words could've been sharp and angry, but they weren't. She wasn't about to risk their restored peace. "You could've told me at any time. But you didn't want to because you didn't want to hurt me."

"Am I that transparent?" Taavin blinked into the morning's early light and Vi appreciated his profile. There might never be an hour of her life where the sight of all his sharp angles didn't fill her with a mixture of sorrow, joy, and longing.

"I know every corner of you, inside and out."

"I suppose if anyone would, it's you."

"Tell me about everyone else. Who does the goddess demand? Who can live? I won't fight Yargen's fate," she added hastily. "But if I can save someone, I will."

Taavin searched her face and sighed. "Regardless of the path we walk, Tiberus, Twintle Junior, Schnurr—"

"Schnurr?" Vi interjected.

"You met him, briefly." The words brought back a fleeting memory of a young boy in a war zone.

"He was with Fiera the night Mhashan fell—the young man with the moustache, who she directed to keep fighting at the break in the wall."

"And he becomes a leading member of the Knights of Jadar. He'll be one to watch as the years go on."

Vi groaned. "I should've killed all the Knights when I had the chance."

"They're a necessary counterweight. Without their presence, people wouldn't be driven to actions we need them to take."

"In any case…" Vi didn't want to speak about the Knights a moment longer. They made her blood boil. "Tiberus, Luke, Schnurr. Who else dies regardless?"

"Of the people you may be familiar with, Craig and Baldair."

She kept her face passive. Vi had never met her Uncle Baldair in her own world. He'd died years before her birth, before the war in the North had even ended. It was a wound on her father's soul deeper than she could comprehend. Though Vi had tried to, conjuring thoughts of Romulin passing until her heart couldn't bear it a moment longer and then multiplying that feeling by several hundred.

Baldair. His death was one she found herself longing to postpone.

"Very well." They were nearing the outlet of roaring water now littered with pieces of ancient Solaris gold. "The rest of them I still want to save, if I'm able."

She looked to Taavin and he held her attention. *Don't deny me this*, she wanted to beg. Saving the world was a large, unimaginable task.

Saving the people her heart still loved was a more reasonable goal.

"You know our purpose, right?"

"I do." She knew his. She knew hers. And Vi knew a moment would come when only one of their desires persisted.

"Then yes, I'll help you save them if you're able… and if it doesn't alter fate too dramatically," Taavin said. It almost sounded like agreement.

It had been six months since they arrived in the West.

The desert heat felt like the embrace of an old friend. The people, the smells, the food, all carried a surprising nostalgia for her. But she hadn't come here looking for an opportunity to reminisce. She'd come because the Crossroads was the one place they could turn pilfered, ancient, Solaris coins into usable Imperial gold on the black market.

They took every opportunity to exchange their coins. Even still, they sat on two plump bags of un-traded pirate gold and knew where more was, should they ever need it.

It was enough money to buy a wedge of property nestled within the busy market of the Crossroads—one with an iron gate for a door that Vi fashioned Fiera's roses onto, exactly like the property Vi had stolen the key to from the spice seller in Shaldan a world ago.

They had enough money to enjoy themselves from time to time. Much like tonight, when they had decided to visit the sparring pits at Taavin's suggestion. Vi found out why he'd made the out-of-character proposal the moment they arrived.

"He's grown up a lot," Taavin observed from her side, taking a sip from his flagon as his eyes remained on Baldair.

"Has he?" Vi wondered. She still saw very much the young man that had been in Oparium the year prior. Seeing him here with Jax and Erion had been a surprise. "He still looks like a foolish child."

"You speak like an old woman." Taavin grinned at her.

"I can't be old if I'm ageless." She grinned back at him then returned her attention to the men on the far side of the sparring ring. They carried on, jesting, betting on the fighters, drinking their brew, and remaining willfully ignorant to the battle that had begun to rage in the North—a battle Vi couldn't yet bring herself to see. "We should leave here, soon."

"I thought you wanted to change a bit more coin first."

"I don't want to saturate the market with old Solaris gold, especially not now that the prince is here. If he sees some, he may get suspicious. We have enough to get passage to Meru, and we already bought the shop." Vi rubbed the familiar key in her trouser pocket. She'd carried its otherworldly twin a long time ago.

"You should stay on this continent a little longer."

"Why?" Vi glanced at Taavin, suspecting what he'd say next would have something to do with why he was so insistent on coming out tonight.

"They're going to need you. Specifically, the prince and… her." Taavin motioned to the ring where two fighters entered.

The room went quiet for Vi. She could see the men and women still cheering on the fighters. The announcer called out the names of those about to spar. Swords rang out against scabbards as they were drawn.

But it was all a distant hum as her eyes fell on the adult Raylynn Westwind.

"I can't," Vi whispered, more to herself than anyone else.

"In the last world… she and the prince died in the coming weeks." Taavin's words were a dagger to her gut.

"I got her mother killed. I can't have anything to do with her." The words were like ash coating her mouth. *I got her mother killed and I left her body in a puddle of its own blood like the foolish child I was.*

"She doesn't know that and she could use your help."

Vi swallowed her fear and guilt. He was right. Raylynn didn't know what she had done—that her mother was just another in a long list of casualties in the fight for a new world.

"I thought you didn't want me to meddle too much?"

"I told you Raylynn's life was variable, didn't I? And you told me you wanted to save the people you could," Taavin said gently. After their tense moments in Oparium, the gesture was not lost on her, and Vi's heart warmed at his words. Taavin kept his eyes forward. Raylynn had begun to move. She was just like her mother—the sword was an extension of her body. "I have heard of these people through you, across so many lives. Seeing them now…"

"They're real," Vi finished for him. The crowd erupted at Raylynn's victory.

"Let's save them."

"When and where?"

"She'll take on Luke." Vi jerked her head to Taavin and he grinned at her. "She blames him for her mother's death and wants vengeance. She'll take the prince with her to get it. In your world, he died on the way to Twintle's manor. It's possible that Raylynn will also die rushing in to take on Twintle."

Vi brought up a map of the West in her mind, placing a pin where Twintle's manor was. "We have to head to Norin anyway. Helping keep them alive can be on the way."

"My thoughts exactly." Taavin laced his fingers with hers and brought her hand to his lips.

Vi gave him a determined nod.

They left at the same time as Baldair and his golden companions. The three men went after Raylynn, but Vi and Taavin headed toward their home. They filled Deneya in on their plans—she had just returned from trading a few more of their coins. The three packed their things and started off into the desert, toward the town of Yon.

It took Baldair and Raylynn nearly two weeks to arrive. Enough time that Vi and her company had bought temporary residence in a cramped apartment out back of a local metal worker's home. Enough time that Vi could begin to listen to the people in town, and figure out who was a Knight of Jadar, who was in their pockets, and who supported the Knights. By the time Raylynn arrived, Vi was wondering how the clever girl who had gifted her with the idea of making her own crystal weapons had grown into a foolhardy woman. She was walking into the lion's den willingly, challenging local combatants, winning handily, then strutting back to the inn where she and the prince were staying like she owned the town.

Vi was positioned by the window of their temporary abode. From there, she could see the inn. There was no glass, so she leaned against the wall to keep out of sight. Heavy footsteps approached—a familiar gait.

"Midsummer is almost finished being saddled. Prism is ready," Deneya said, walking over to sit with her. "Any changes?"

"No, all is quiet." Vi kept her eyes on the inn. Taavin had told them this was the town where Baldair died during Vi's original time. *But not tonight.*

They continued to stare out the window and, for a moment, Vi's eyes drifted to the dark-haired woman. Deneya was poised, quiet, and ready. There wasn't a trace of doubt or the edge of restlessness about her.

"How are you not bored of this yet?" Vi asked.

Deneya shrugged. "What else would I be doing? Living comfortably in Risen? Getting fat off the Queen's pension and taking my secrets of the Dark Isle with me to a faraway grave?"

"Maybe you'd be her personal guard?"

"That's what I was in your time, right? I wasn't an agent of the Order of Shadows?" Vi nodded. "I just don't see it." Deneya shrugged. "Me? A queen's personal guard? No."

"In a way, you're the crown princess of Solaris's royal guard." She grinned at Deneya and the woman rolled her eyes.

"I thought you weren't the crown princess?"

"You're right." Admitting as much had long since become easy. "I'm not. I'm just Yargen's Champion, much less prestigious," Vi said sarcastically and looked back to the inn and the quiet, dark night. "If you weren't doing this—if you could do anything—what would you want to do?"

"I could do *anything*?" she asked and Vi nodded. Deneya hummed thoughtfully. Her gaze was distant as she looked out the window. "Maybe head north to Dolarian, the land of the Draconi. I've heard that some of them can breathe fire and some can even fly. Though there is no greater lore than—"

Deneya was silenced as they both looked at the dark shadows crossing the ground below.

"It's time." Vi stood, hastily leaving their hut. Taavin straightened away from Midsummer and they shared a look that said it all. She swung up on Prism. "I'll meet you both after."

Prism sprang into action with the slightest touch. He was a good steed, just beginning to get on the other half of his prime. He'd have good years ahead of him yet—Vi was counting on it. She rode into the dark night as the inn glowed red from within, like the waking eyes of some primordial evil.

Glass shattered and two dark figures leapt from a high window. Vi gave the place a wide berth, swinging around the town's perimeter and flying over the dunes. She slowed Prism as she neared a side alley by the inn and jumped from the saddle.

With a thought, the fire that was now consuming the building was under her command. She could feel the inkling of magic fighting against her at the edge of her consciousness, but the Firebearer the Knights had employed was weak.

Stepping through a wall of fire and into the lower floor of the inn, Vi heard creaking from above, voices shouting. If they were shouting, they were alive. Acting on instinct, Vi sprinted upstairs and skidded to a halt. The fire parted, arcing around her, giving her a view of the man and woman.

"Baldair, Raylynn, come with me."

"Who—" Baldair began dumbly.

Raylynn grabbed his hand and yanked him forward. Vi trusted her to keep the man in tow as she descended the stairs, pushing away the fire. She led them out the way she came. Prism was there waiting, not bothered in the slightest by the rising flames.

"Take the horse." After years of riding him, she trusted the mount to keep them safe. "Take it and go. Do not seek out what has been lost," Vi cautioned. It was the best she could do. She couldn't outright say, *the crystal sword is long gone.* "Protect, instead, the weapon that has yet to be found. Do not seek the tomb. Do not let anyone seek the tomb."

"Do I know you?" Baldair took a step toward her. "Wait, aren't you… Nox?"

"This isn't the time," Vi scolded. Though she didn't step back or give up her ground. "My control will waver soon," she said with urgency, though she could've held the flames in position for a decade if she'd wanted to. "Go, go now!"

Baldair cursed and mounted Prism, but Raylynn continued to stare.

"Princess Fiera—"

"Go," Vi urged.

"Damn it, Raylynn, we have an opportunity and we need to take it. Let's get out of here!" Baldair shouted. But Raylynn was rooted to the spot, her eyes on Vi. "Raylynn."

The woman stepped to the prince, who helped her into the saddle. Vi watched the motion, already familiar and tender. She couldn't help but remember the slip of a girl who came to have her future told by a princess, and who yearned to serve the crown.

Raylynn had Vi's help then, just as she had Vi's help now, and didn't realize it in either instance. Vi smiled faintly and, while they were distracted, stepped into the burning building once more, allowing the fire to close behind her.

"Look, look there!" she heard a man shout outside, followed by a snap of the reins and the gallop of a horse.

"Zira, your daughter is safe for a little longer." Vi took in the burning inn around her. The moment of tenderness immolated on the flames.

17

"ARE YOU CERTAIN ABOUT just leaving it here?" Deneya asked as the waves off the coast of Meru crashed against her midsection.

"It's a mostly sheltered cove, we've anchored it at low tide, and no one comes this way." Vi listed off all the reasons she'd been repeating to herself for the past day while they decided what to do with the sailboat they'd bought in Norin. If Vi's plan worked out, they wouldn't need the small vessel again, anyway. "I don't want to go all the way to Toris and risk someone seeing it docked there for too long."

"But we risk coming back and not seeing it at all."

"Then we buy another boat."

"Oh, right, we'll just buy another boat, because money can solve all our problems. Perfect princess logic, that," Deneya muttered as she sloshed up the black sand beach to where Vi and Taavin were waiting. They carried two packs apiece and not much else. Deneya had the heaviest satchel of them all—the one completely filled with clanking gold coins.

While the gold of old Solaris had no meaning on Meru, gold was gold. If they needed to, they could smelt the coins into bars.

"I shudder to think of what your opinions of me would've been if we'd met earlier." Vi held out a hand, helping Deneya free her feet from the cloying sand of the tides.

"Everything happens in its own time, just as it's supposed to," Taavin said thoughtfully. It sounded like an echo of his bygone days as the Voice.

They started up the beach toward the lowest point of the sheer cliffs. There was no man-made path, which was why Vi had picked this particular location to anchor. No one seemed to come this way. But she could see a path up the rocks if they were careful.

It was noon by the time they reached the top. Deneya massaged her aching hands and rolled her shoulders while Vi and Taavin stood unbothered. Vi wanted to tell herself it was because the woman carried the heaviest satchel of all of them. But she knew it was more than that.

Vi wasn't tired now, just like she'd never grown weary on their crossing from the Dark Isle to Meru. It was the same reason she could pilot their vessel through the night and have enough energy come the dawn to adjust the rigging on their single sail.

With every step she took in this world, she was further from her own, and further from the mortal casing she used to know. Whether she wanted to or not, she was truly embracing her new body and purpose.

"The Twilight Forest isn't far." Vi pointed when Deneya had caught her breath. "Let's try to get there before nightfall."

"Heading for the Twilight Forest, intentionally." Deneya shook her head. "Never thought I'd see the day."

"Ulvarth hasn't yet begun his campaign against the morphi, right?" Vi looked to Taavin, who nodded once.

"Ulvarth doesn't begin making his moves for a few years yet, usually."

She turned back to Deneya. "But you still hate them?"

"*Hate* is too strong a word. Personally, I feel little toward the morphi, good or bad. But I know it's a tense subject for the Faithful, and Lumeria has made it clear that we don't want to give a reason for those tensions to boil over."

"Smart woman," Vi said under her breath.

They discussed the delicate politics of the Morphi and Draconi as they walked. Vi remembered what Deneya had said in Yon regarding the Draconi and noted the excited fascination in the woman's voice—rivaled only by the warm tones she used to speak about Queen Lumeria.

Perhaps, when all this was over, Vi could meet the Queen once more, but not as a tired girl. She'd meet the queen as… Vi's imagination abandoned her when she tried to picture herself beyond the fall of Raspian.

Perhaps she and Deneya and Taavin could continue adventuring, buying skiffs and sailing to the world's edges. They could go to the isle of Dolarian and see if there were truly fire-breathing, winged beasts or if it was all just lore. Vi tried to imagine herself sailing to the far reaches of the maps in her mind, which was somehow easier than picturing herself sitting comfortably on the Dark Isle.

No matter what, when it came to who she would become, her mind's eye was blurry.

Borrowed time, a voice seemed to whisper from somewhere within her.

Yes, I'm on borrowed time, Vi thought in reply, touching the watch around her neck. Her body was a gift from the goddess, one she'd eventually have to return for the world to be saved. The thought should panic her. Vi felt as calm as the tall, still trees of the forest. But the thorny thoughts snagged her like the underbrush as they pushed deeper into the Twilight Forest.

"How do the morphi feel about Lightspinning at this point in time?" Vi asked. Taavin looked to Deneya.

"What?" Deneya glanced between them. "I haven't been on Meru in a few decades. How am I supposed to know?"

"One way to find out. *Durroe watt ivin*." A ball of light appeared above Vi's open palm. It reminded her of the orbs she and Sehra would make when she was first learning her magic. Lifting her eyes from the illusion, Vi looked around the forest, waiting.

Deneya and Taavin both took a step closer. The three of them stood back-to-back, watching for any signs of movement. Collectively, they held their breaths until Vi dismissed the shining glyphs above her hand.

"I suppose they don't have as hard of a stance toward Lightspinning as they did in the world we left," Vi observed.

"Further proof that Ulvarth hasn't begun closing in on them," Taavin said bitterly.

"Let's keep going." Vi started off in no direction in particular. "We'll meet a Morphi sooner or later."

By late afternoon, their wandering intersected with the main road through the Twilight Forest and the three continued along it. There were no posted signs anywhere along the way, so they merely kept walking, hoping to be found. After about two more hours of wandering, they came to a bridge across a stream.

Vi paused, her hands on the worn stone, looking out over the water that flowed down and away toward the cliffs they'd climbed earlier.

"What is it?" Deneya asked.

"I wonder if it's the same stream we stayed near the last time we were here," Vi said thoughtfully, looking to Taavin.

"Perhaps, though I've had enough of that cave for several lifetimes." He grimaced. The man's mood only seemed to sour the longer they were on Meru. Vi couldn't blame him. This forest, this land, was a place of memories for them both—good and bad mixed together.

"Let's make camp soon," Vi suggested. "Get off the main road again and find somewhere that looks dry enough." She tilted her eyes skyward, peering through the break in the trees. "It looks like it'll be clear night, so we don't have to worry about rain."

They hiked for one more hour and then did as Vi suggested, breaking off the main road and finding a space between several trees where they could set up camp. Vi ignited a fire using *juth starys*, yet again, her Lightspinning didn't seem to summon the morphi. As night fell they split some of their hard baked bread.

"I'd love to get my hands on some more of the crackers Sarphos gave us," Vi said through her food.

"The ones he magicked to fill an empty stomach?" Taavin clarified and Vi nodded. "That'd be nice."

"Who's Sarphos?" Deneya asked. "And what's this about magic crackers?"

"Sarphos is a morphi we met the last time we were here." Vi chewed thoughtfully. "He was the younger brother of one of the people we're looking for now… though I have no idea if he'll be around yet." *It should feel stranger to think about someone not being born,* Vi thought to herself. But it had become quite normal. "He could use the magic of the shift to make a cracker that filled you up as if you'd eaten a meal. That power is one of the reasons why I think they could use the shift to make a fake crystal crown."

"I don't want any shift crackers." Deneya scrunched her nose. "But I would give my sword arm right about now though for some rovash."

"Rovash?" Vi asked as Taavin made a satisfied noise.

"I'd almost forgotten," he said wistfully. "I only got to eat it on high holy days." Taavin looked to her. "Rovash is a celebratory roast—giant spotted pheasant stuffed with dates, figs, and bread left over from the temples' holy celebrations."

"Cookeries would bake it slow over root vegetables." Deneya sighed wistfully. "If I'd known it'd be so long until I had it again, I would've bought a whole bird just for myself."

"You would've exploded," Taavin said with a small smile.

"Death by rovash would be an honor." Deneya grinned in return.

"Maybe we can all get some together… when this is all over," Vi said almost timidly, the thoughts from earlier still exercising their strong hold. Her companions fell quiet.

"What happens, when this is over?" Deneya asked delicately. None of them had ever discussed the topic aloud. It felt taboo. Like if they even uttered anything about the world being saved, it wouldn't come to pass. "You put Yargen back together with all her pieces like some divine puzzle and she beats Raspian into submission, heralding a new Age of Light. There's much rejoicing and a saved world … *Then* what happens?"

Vi looked to Taavin. He gave a tiny shrug. "Your guess is as good as ours. We've never made it that far before… never made it this far, even." He finished the last bite of his meal and looked at his hand, flexing his fingers. She wondered if he, too, was imagining the crystal skeleton within him that held his consciousness and gave him life.

"We should go to bed," Vi suggested abruptly. "Got a long day ahead tomorrow."

"Of what? More wandering?" Deneya said smartly, stretching out on the leaves they'd piled up as pallets.

"If that's what it takes."

"Would you like to sleep?" Taavin asked, touching her arm lightly and summoning her attention to him alone. "I can take first watch."

"No, you go ahead, I don't mind. You sleep less than the rest of us anyway." Vi smiled. He looked surprised, as if he hadn't realized she'd noticed. His expression softened a corner of her heart.

How could I not notice? she wanted to ask. She noticed, just as she noticed he ate less than the rest of them but could go the longest without tiring. She'd cataloged every little thing about him—from the way he ran his hands through his hair when he was deep in thought, to how he tapped his foot when he drank alcohol. She'd visually traced his figure like lines of a map so that she'd never forget how to get him back again if the world took him from her.

"All right, wake me if you feel tired."

"I will." Vi squeezed his hand and leaned in to plant a soft goodnight kiss on his mouth.

He settled down on his palette and held her gaze for a good while. They stared at each other through the firelight, as though communicating telepathically. Though Vi was left wondering what, exactly, he was thinking.

And when his eyes closed, she was left with nothing to do but peer into the dark void of the forest around them.

The night passed uneventfully. Vi sat with her back against a tree, scanning the woods. She didn't know how much time had passed, but eventually her eyelids began to feel heavy. They dipped closed, staying shut for a little longer each time.

A rustling sound came from behind her and Vi's eyes shot open.

She stood, whirling in place to find herself face to face with a spear pointed at her throat. Behind the blade were the steely gray eyes of a young girl with two golden buns behind each of her ears.

"State your business, Lightspinners," she demanded. Skeptical, forceful, though not outright brutal. This was not the same harshness that Arwin had greeted her with in Vi's world.

Deneya and Taavin were on their feet, but Vi held out a hand, both silencing them and stopping their movements. She leveled her eyes with the girl and gave her a smile.

"Hello, Arwin." Arwin's eyes went wide at Vi's use of her name. Then they narrowed as she thrust the spear forward threateningly. The girl opened her mouth to no doubt question, but Vi spoke over her. "Please take us to your father. We have business with King Noct."

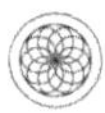

Vi was fairly certain that she and Noct were the only comfortable people in the throne room.

Arwin had been eying them sideways since they first met and she reluctantly agreed to take them to the Twilight Kingdom. Taavin was understandably uncomfortable in this place. Even if he knew this was a different Twilight Kingdom than the one they had last interacted with, it was hard to forget old conditioning. Deneya looked fascinated, but was very clearly aware that she was an outsider in this world of glittering twilight.

But Vi stood easily. She'd been here before, in this very room, standing in front of this very man. Though he'd admittedly looked somewhat older then. The beard had been thinner in her world. That must be what it was.

This time there were no children playing in the courtyard to consume his attention. He'd stood when they entered and regarded them as a monarch would. Then, he settled himself on the throne.

"It is not common for Lightspinners to come demanding me." He shifted. "Are you from the Queen?"

"No, we're not," Vi said, not so much as glancing at Deneya. The king didn't need to know there was a member of the Order of Shadows in his throne room. Deneya's business wasn't to spy on the Twilight Kingdom, anyway. "We've come from the Dark Isle."

"The Dark Isle?" Noct tilted his head to the side. "Two elfin and a human, all Lightspinners, from the *Dark Isle*?"

Vi had anticipated this skepticism. She'd encountered it before. But this time she knew exactly how to handle it.

"I am Yargen's Champion," Vi said confidently. "I have come from very far to collect that which is my birthright. I know that, deep within your palace, you hold a crystal scythe. It was bestowed on your family to keep safe until the Champion came seeking it."

"H-how?" Arwin stuttered, taking a step back.

"How, indeed." Noct smiled, his eyes shining. "How could you have come across that information?"

"I told you, I am the Champion." Vi put on the air of mystery she used when giving advice or fortune to those on the Dark Isle. Her voice was a deep whisper, her words shrouded in an air of knowing beyond that which mortal minds could comprehend. At least, that was how she hoped it sounded. "I have seen across time and space. I know Yargen's will and have heard her voice. I have witnessed the red lightning that heralds the end of days. Before this world is torn asunder, you must give me what I seek."

"All very impressive." Noct was unfazed. It'd take more than some lofty words to impress those on Meru, who were accustomed to more fantastical magics existing around them. "But your long-eared friends here could've known the truth from ages ago and told you."

"Elfin live long lives, but not that long," Taavin countered for her. "Give her the scythe and you will see that she speaks true."

Noct still looked unconvinced.

Vi chewed on the inside of her cheek, keeping her expression passive. In her time, the tears in the shift had been enough to convince Noct that she wielded a mighty power. If he didn't give her the scythe, what proof could she offer him of her abilities?

Luckily, the scythe wasn't her only mission here. There were other reasons Vi had sought out the Twilight Kingdom. One of them might just serve her now.

"Your highness, may we speak in private?"

"I will not leave your side with these strangers, Father," Arwin said firmly.

Noct was clearly intrigued by the request. "Approach me, and whisper what you have to say in my ear."

Vi ascended the dais and crossed to the throne. She leaned forward, cupping her lips around the king's ear. Arwin inched closer, her hands on her spear, ready to attack. Vi didn't point out how foolish the girl's protectiveness was. If Vi had wanted to kill Noct, he'd already be dead. Instead, she whispered.

"Your daughter Arwin favors a boy named Fallor—or will soon, if she does not already. But he will betray the trust of your family. He will gain and take the knowledge of your sacred shift to Adela. They might have already gotten to the boy. Keep us here and I will use my knowledge as Champion to protect your daughter and your throne."

Vi straightened away, Noct watching her carefully. She took two steps backward, bowed once more, and stepped off the dais to wait for his verdict.

The king stroked his beard, eyes settling on his daughter for a long moment.

"We shall go to the scythe now, and see if your words are true about your powers. If you are who you say, I will trust your other claims, and you and your companions will have rooms in the guest wing to stay in for as long as I see fit to host you," he said finally.

Vi bowed once more, a smile creeping onto her face as she did. Her fingertips nearly crackled with the phantom memory of the scythe in her hands.

18

N OCT LED THEM DOWN a series of halls and a familiar winding
stair into a council room that Vi knew all too well.

The walls were stone, with vertical tapestries running
from floor-to-ceiling depicting morphi champions standing victorious
in battles. Weapons hung between the tapestries, the low light of the
glowing stones above the center table gleaming off their polished
edges. Taavin inspected one of the hanging pieces.

"Is this the battle of Marthas?" he asked, breaking the silence with
genuine curiosity.

Noct paused, clearly startled, but a sincere smile spread across his
lips. "Why, yes it is."

"Marthas… when the elfin'ra finally surrendered?" Deneya had
joined Taavin at the wall.

"Just so."

"I didn't realize there were morphi there."

"Many don't." Noct chuckled, but the sound wasn't warm or
amused. It was sad. "Much of the morphi's contributions to and
alignment with the Kingdom of Meru has been expunged from

common memory."

The battle of Marthas, Vi silently repeated to herself. For a moment, her vision was hazed as what felt like memories played before her eyes. Memories Vi wasn't supposed to have but found bubbling to the surface all the same.

The elfin'ra gathered on the large island in the watery center of Meru's great lagoon. She could see the men and women surrounding them as if she'd stood there as well, the queen banishing them off to a distant isle and beseeching Yargen for the strength to seal them away. Vi felt her words as much as heard them—no, she didn't feel it, someone else within her did.

Help came in the form of the last Champion.

"That's Arnoch, isn't it?" Vi said faintly. The attention was now on her. "The warrior depicted," she clarified.

"It is." Noct's smile widened. "Impressive that you know your morphi history. Now, excuse me a moment." He stepped around the table and disappeared through the door in the back of the room. Arwin lingered, eyes on Vi and hands glued to her spear.

"How did you know that?" Deneya asked.

"Yes, *how*?" Taavin repeated, much less amused than Deneya.

"I read it in the Archives when I was there, long ago," Vi lied. She knew she hadn't read it. But she couldn't describe the imagery she'd seen. She didn't even know where it'd come from. Just laying eyes on the carefully stitched picture sparked something in her that wasn't entirely her own. Luckily, she didn't have to elaborate further. Noct returned with the scythe, tightly wrapped in familiar purple velvet.

Arwin looked between them, but unlike the last time, the girl wasn't bold enough to question her father.

The king placed the weapon on the table and undid the knots on the ropes holding the velvet closed. Even knowing what she was about to see, Vi's heart raced in anticipation. She was ready for the familiar shining crystal, glowing with the power of the gods. It wasn't until that moment that Vi realized she still carried the loss of the crown with her. She needed to feel a fresh surge of Yargen's essence in her veins.

Without hesitation, she reached out a hand to the blade.

The hazy light that surrounded the weapon drifted over her hand

and up her arm, before fading completely into her skin. The magic consumed her vision as though a tide of power was rising from within. Vi drew on it further, allowing herself to drown in this now familiar sensation.

The world came back into focus washed in darkness. She recognized the feeling of standing in another place and time. The future sight hadn't entirely been expected, but she welcomed it; Vi wasted no time in looking at her surroundings. She was on a cliff-side, a quaint town in the distance.

She squinted, looking at the town, specifically. *Mosant?* Her eyes fell on what was certainly the bell tower for the goddess's chapel there.

Vi turned her head to her right, where people stood. As usual, she couldn't hear what was being said. A group on horseback were mounted before a windmill. Vi watched as an old woman stepped out to greet them and was rewarded with a sword through her eye.

Vi's attention shifted to the vaguely familiar, mustachioed man holding the sword.

The world continued to oscillate in and out of focus. The next person to gain clarity was a young woman, hunched over in her saddle. The men were untying ropes around her and they hoisted her down. Her head was hung, but Vi didn't need to see her face. She knew that brown mass of unruly hair anywhere.

The Knights of Jadar had Vhalla Yarl in their clutches.

Vi tried to step forward. Moving through the vision was like trying to swim through a thick jelly. Yet she wanted to keep up with the men as they carried Vhalla into the open windmill. Shackles with embedded crystals were around her wrists and she put up no fight as she was thrown onto sacks of grain.

The door closed behind them, and ended what limited view Vi had been given.

No one said anything. But when Vi's consciousness returned to the Twilight Kingdom, just the breathing of her companions seemed loud.

"What did she do?" Arwin squeaked. Vi lowered her gaze to the pool of velvet on the table. A pile of obsidian shards and black dust was cradled in its luxe embrace. "She just touched it, and… now it's gone." Arwin inched closer to her father. The heel of her spear tapped on the floor with her shaking hand.

Vi lifted her eyes, looking to Noct, then to Taavin and Deneya. They all stared at her with wide eyes and soundless, slightly agape mouths. She curled and uncurled the fingers that had touched the scythe. The feelings there were muted, as if the appendage was no longer her own. However, pins and needles raced down from her elbow, and sensation returned as her head cleared.

"The power is within me now," Vi declared.

"How did she do that?" Arwin tugged on Noct's sleeve, looking up at him.

"Our mortal minds aren't meant to know how she did it, because she is the goddess's Champion," Noct said softly. "And we will now do everything we can to help her, because she is here to save us all from an impending age of darkness."

"Your help is required." Her voice didn't entirely feel her own. Vi's mind rocked back and forth with the tide of power that swirled in her. "I need you to make something for me, using the shift." Her eyes fell on Arwin.

"Me?" she squeaked.

"Yes."

"I…" The girl shifted her grip on her staff and took a more relaxed stance. "I will do whatever I can to assist you."

"Good. We shall begin after my companion makes a crown for us to work with. Now, if you'll excuse us, we are weary from our journey." Vi wasn't tired in the slightest, but she didn't want to be in the room a moment longer. She needed to sit down for a minute and try to get her racing mind under control.

"Yes, of course. Arwin, show them to their rooms in the guest tower."

Arwin nodded and led them with confidence. But Vi didn't miss her wary eyes looking back toward her now and then.

How cute and how fleeting she is.

"How did you do that?" Taavin grabbed her hand, jarring Vi from the thought. He slowed his steps, allowing them to fall behind so Deneya and Arwin didn't hear his whispers.

"I didn't do anything. It just… happened."

"That's exactly my point. You've always shifted the crystal's power willingly. It's never just happened, and you've never *absorbed it*."

"I've never worked with them to such an extent before. I understand their power and their will." *Their will…* The will of Yargen. Yes, that's what it was. Yargen was alive in each and every weapon, as she was in the Caverns, and the flame, and in Vi herself. All Vi had to do was listen. "It sought me out. It… lives in me."

"That shouldn't be possible."

"Why?" Vi asked him sincerely. "I am of Yargen's make, as are you." She held his hand tightly. "Can't you feel it?"

When they touched, magic darted back and forth between them. A connection deeper than the love that had traversed the ages spanned their physical forms. They were one and the same—each given physical shapes by the will of Yargen.

"I don't absorb power from the crystals." He pulled his hand away.

"But you could."

"I won't." Taavin looked forward.

"Why are you so unsettled?"

"Because I'm afraid."

"Of what?" Vi hadn't felt better in weeks. For the first time, she felt absolutely confident she could take on Raspian if she collected enough of Yargen's essence.

"Of not knowing what you're becoming." Taavin stopped walking, turning to her. Vi stopped as well and melted under the warmth of his viridian gaze.

"Taavin, I'm me." Vi took both of his hands in a firm but gentle grasp. "I've always been, and always will be."

He searched her face and opened his mouth after a moment's hesitation.

"Are you both coming?" Arwin called. She and Deneya had stopped ahead.

"Yes, of course!" Vi squeezed Taavin's hands. "Let's go."

The man remained rooted, staring at her for one more long breath. Finally, he nodded. Vi kept his hand clasped tightly in hers.

Part of her held on to the man who made her feel human, the man who was home.

The other part was governed by the essence of the goddess that was always just beneath her skin. Vi had to fight against uncomfortable urges all the way to their rooms. If she hadn't, she may have given into temptation and unraveled Taavin's magic to satiate the ravenous hunger waking in her—a hunger that needed to be fed with Yargen's essence alone.

"You want me to do… what?" Arwin asked, looking at the crown Vi had handed her.

"I need you to make it look like the scythe did."

"The shift can't make a crown into a scythe." Arwin's brow furrowed. They sat across a table from each other in a lounge that Vi had declared her own. After the incident of her absorbing the scythe's magic, no one seemed to question her much.

"No, not a scythe." Vi paused, thinking a moment. "Hold a moment."

She held out her hands and felt magic rush to her fingertips. Yargen's power pooled in her palms. Her stomach felt gutted by the mere notion of giving up the scythe's power. It had only been a part of her for a month while Deneya had worked to fashion a crown for them to work with, but it had felt like a lifetime.

Just like she had in the Caverns, Vi drew the power into a single location and condensed it down. However, unlike the Caverns, the well of power Vi leeched from was herself. As Yargen's magic collected in the air around her fingers, sparks of Vi's magic tethered it together. With a soft *pop,* a crystal appeared.

Reaching upward, Vi grabbed the stone and it writhed underneath her fingertips. Spikes of crystal grew from the "seed" of magic, then arced around and rose to points. Even though she had only seen the actual crystal crown from a glance, Vi knew its every detail, and she created an exact replica in crystal.

"I need you to make that crown—" Vi pointed to the one Deneya had made "—look like this one."

Arwin gawked at the crystal crown in Vi's fingers. The whites of her wide eyes nearly devoured the gray irises in the center. "How?" she said with a quivering lip. "How do you make something from nothing?"

"As Yargen wills," Vi said airily, smiling at the child. She set the crystal crown gently on the table. "Now, let's begin."

The girl studied the crown in her hands with a furrowed brow. Her magic shuddered, rose, and thrummed across the surface of the metal crown Deneya had crafted. Vi watched with new eyes. She saw the metal unravel and piece itself back together with every pulse of magic.

The shift was seeing the *between* of what something was, and what it could be. That had been how Arwin had explained it in her time. Or perhaps that was knowledge Vi was summoning from an otherworldly part of herself, just like the name of the morphi warrior who had helped fell the elfin'ra.

Arwin put the crown down on the table next to the one Vi had made. The metal had changed, becoming gnarled in places and smooth in others as it jutted like crystals. But it was still undeniably steel.

"It's not right," she said dejectedly.

"Try again," Vi encouraged.

"You should get one of my sisters to do it." Arwin slouched in her chair.

"I don't want one of your sisters to do it."

"Why?"

"Because I know you can." And because Vi wanted to endear herself to the girl. She wanted Arwin to trust her with her secrets, just as Arwin once had long ago. She wanted to be there the moment Arwin was ready to open up about any budding romance with Fallor, however long it took. "You will be stronger for it, and you want to be strong, don't you?"

"I do." Arwin ran her finger over the steel points of the crown. "But I don't even know how to use the royal shift yet."

"You will learn soon, I'm certain."

"Ruie says she's going to teach me soon!" Arwin covered her mouth suddenly. "I wasn't supposed to say that… you're not supposed to learn until you're fourteen."

"How old are you now?"

"Eleven… But I've been told I'm advanced in my magic."

"By who?"

Arwin paused, a blush overcoming her cheeks that instantly made her scowl. "No one."

"No one?"

"A stupid boy."

Ah, so Fallor was already present. No wonder Noct was ready to trust Vi.

"Well, he must be smart and not stupid, because I think you're advanced in your magic, too."

"You do?" Arwin slowly lifted her gaze to meet Vi's.

"I do. Which is why I want you to try again."

Arwin did as Vi bid. Time and again. That day, the next day, and in the coming weeks.

The girl worked tirelessly for three months as Vi watched silently.

She felt every pulse of magic, absorbing it into her as she had the power of the scythe. Cyphers of sorcery had been given to her in a tongue she couldn't read but somehow understood. Vi saw the glyphs behind her eyelids as she slept. She felt the knowledge they imparted to her in every action.

Day after day, that knowledge assured her of one thing: *You can do this.*

At first Vi thought the resounding confidence related to Arwin, and being patient enough to see the crown made. But day by day that theory waned. Her fingers began to itch as she watched Arwin work. Her magic reached out between Arwin's pulses. Vi learned the secrets of the shift not through direct teaching, but by watching one day after the next, until, finally…

"Do it again, but slower."

"What?" Arwin's head jerked up from the crown she held. It was the fourth one Deneya had made. The girl had succeeded in changing the crown from steel to a faint blue glass.

"Slower, this time," Vi said again.

"All right." Arwin was clearly uncertain, but she wrapped her fingers around the crown anyway. At the first pulse of magic, Vi reached across the table and wrapped her hands around Arwin's. "Wha—"

"Keep going," she said without taking her eyes off the crown.

Another pulse of magic.

The first pulse was always connecting with the item. The second was learning it, inside and out. Vi understood what Arwin was doing in the same way she'd come to understand the crystals.

When she manipulated Yargen's magic, she first collected the power, learning it. Then, she envisioned what she wanted to be made. The shift was taking the raw essence of something, unraveling it, and then tightening it back in a new shape.

The thought brought them to the third pulse—unraveling.

Vi watched with keen eyes as the crown unraveled between fast pulses of magic. They were too quick for normal eyes to see. But Vi's eyes weren't normal. They were goddess-given, forged by Yargen between worlds.

Fourth pulse—remaking.

She tightened her fingers over Arwin's and pushed her magic through the girl. Vi's brows knotted with focus. The blue glass hardened further and reshaped slightly. When they pulled their hands away, there was a nearly identical replica of the crown Vi had made in shape. All it lacked was the glow and swirl of magic crystals held.

"You just…" Arwin pushed her chair away from the table, but didn't seem to trust herself to stand. "You're a *human*. You can't use the shift."

"I am the Champion, and magic is magic," Vi said with unfounded confidence. "If it doesn't obliterate, it is of Yargen. And it's merely a matter of learning how to use a new set of powers."

Arwin bit her lip, clearly debating the accuracy of this. Vi couldn't blame her. She knew what Taavin had said about the morphi and how their power was viewed as deriving from Raspian.

Mortals and their misinformation. Vi's heart ached at the sentiment.

"Will you teach me?" Vi said.

"Teach you what?"

"Everything you know about the shift."

Arwin stared at her and gripped her seat with white knuckles. Vi feared if the girl let her chair go, she might topple over.

Despite her rigidity, Arwin managed a nod.

19

TIME PASSED EFFORTLESSLY.

Vi took her young tutor's lessons on the shift to heart. She studied Arwin's hand motions and listened intently to her words. But what the girl didn't say was the best teacher. Vi felt every pulse, every pull and tug on the threads of magic and life that made up each and every object within the world.

Taavin had said Yargen's magic was life. But it was so much more. Yargen's magic was existence itself. It was the world, cut from the chaos that Raspian sought to reap. Every mortal magic was a different way to understand and interact with the raw essence of life itself.

Her understanding helped Vi learn the shift—something she was certain she couldn't have done a world away, or even in this world, a few years ago. But that understanding didn't replace time, patience, and practice.

At first, she helped Arwin adjust the shift. Then, the girl began teaching Vi how to do it on her own. How to draw out the power and change an object from what it was to what it could be.

The weeks pulsed into months without Vi so much as realizing.

"How much longer do you think it will take?" Taavin asked her from where he sat on the couch in the center of the room. A common space was located between their room and Deneya's in the guest wing they occupied.

"Not much longer." Vi leaned against the arm of one of the chairs opposite. She'd only just returned from working with Arwin and could still feel the magic under her hands. "I'm nearly there."

"Good, we'll need to return to the Dark Isle."

"Not before Deneya has uncovered a link to Adela."

"We don't need Adela to get back." Vi heard the frown in his voice before she even turned to look at him. "We have a vessel."

"It's been a year. Do you really think it's still in the cove where we left it?" Vi asked with an arch of her eyebrows. Then, before he could speak, "Even if it is, do you think it'll be seaworthy?"

"I don't like the idea of working with Adela."

"I know you don't." Vi sighed, turning away. She grew more and more weary of this conversation. "But we'll need the strength and speed of her ship to get the flame… and to get to the isle of the elfin'ra."

"That's if—"

"It's happening at sunset," Deneya interrupted, barging in. "Sorry to interrupt, I know you both usually have your date this evening but—"

"But it's important." Vi straightened away from the chair. "Tell me what you've learned."

"Fallor will be meeting with an actual member of Adela's crew at sunset on the southwest ridge just outside of the forest."

Vi and Taavin shared a look. They'd been tracking Fallor's movements in secret. Messages had moved in and out of the city through merchants Fallor was working with as a page in the city guard. The *Stormfrost* had been spotted not far from Toris—confirmed through scouting done by Noct's eldest daughter.

"I'll go ahead and let you both know how it goes." Vi held up her right hand. She wore a silver ring on her middle finger that matched an identical one on Deneya's hand. The woman had given the token to Vi as a gift, imprinted with her communication mark should they ever be separated.

"You'll go alone?" Taavin was on his feet as well.

"There's no way I'll be able to get on the *Stormfrost* if all three of us go together. Adela needs to feel confident that she can overpower me."

"What if something goes wrong and she actually does overpower you?"

"She won't." Vi gave him an assured smile.

"You've seen Vi in the training grounds," Deneya said in her defense. "She can handle herself better than any of us… And has three times the strength," she mumbled the last part.

"This is Adela we're talking about." Taavin's face was as stormy as the sea he'd pulled her from all those years ago. Vi stepped over to him and grabbed his shoulder gently. "I do trust you, you know that, right? But I—"

"Worry," Vi finished for him with a small smile. "I worry for you too, more than you can know."

"Not to break up the moment, but if you're going to go, you should go now."

"I know." Vi gave a solemn nod to Deneya. "You two should pack up while I'm gone. We'll be leaving this place once I get Adela to agree to help us."

"Leaving?" Taavin repeated with surprise. "I thought you said you were *nearly there* with the crown. We can't leave until we have a replica."

"No, I just said I was nearly there. Nothing about the crown." She gave him a somewhat sheepish grin. "We have the replica. It's in the workshop."

"*What?*"

Deneya followed her into the hall. "If you've had the replica this whole time—"

"I haven't had it the whole time," Vi interjected. "Just for the past ten weeks or so."

"Fine. If you've had the replica for the past ten weeks," Deneya rephrased her words with frustration, "what have you been working on?"

"I'll show you later," Vi called over her shoulder with a grin. "Follow behind me and I'll see you both on the *Stormfrost*."

Down and out the estate, Vi moved quickly in the twilight. She knew Fallor's rounds, likely better than he knew them himself. She'd long since mapped out the young man's movements just like she had mapped out the whole city that was the Twilight Kingdom. Even when he thought he was wandering at random to lose any people who might be tracking him, he wandered in consistent circles.

When she found him, he was finishing up a conversation with a merchant. Vi couldn't hear what they said, but the merchant gave him a token and disappeared into the shadows of an alleyway.

Vi ignored the merchant, focusing only on Fallor as he walked up the quiet residential street. He headed right, and Vi followed in parallel through an alley. She twisted between rubbish bins and around opening doors to step back out onto the main street.

Fallor had pulled his hood. He was trying to lose himself among the crowd. But Vi followed twenty paces behind easily. He looked around nervously from time to time, and Vi would side step—always just beyond the edge of his periphery. He'd recognize her if he got a good look. Fallor had seen her and Arwin working together enough times.

So she lingered at the edge of the city, leaning in a doorway, watching as he walked up the rise to the gateway of the kingdom. The moment Fallor passed through the swirling, fog-like magic, Vi sprinted up behind him.

"Champion, would you—" Ruie attempted to say as she passed. The young woman was on guard duty for the night.

"No time." Vi gave her a short wave and plunged herself into the haze that surrounded the Twilight Kingdom.

She pushed magic out around her in a quick pulse. It cocooned and stabilized her in the between space. Another pulse of magic, and Vi felt her powers running like a bridge between the city where she had been, and the forest where she was headed. With a third pulse, Vi pushed herself along the pathway.

Reemerging in the real world outside of the Twilight Kingdom left her off-balance. Pinwheeling her arms, Vi grabbed onto a tree. It wasn't exactly a smooth landing, but it worked.

It worked.

A grin spread across her face as she sprinted through the trees. When the muscles of her legs began to grow tired, she felt a barely-perceptible shift. Yargen's magic was in her bones. It was her flesh. The essence of the goddess was woven within her just as the power of the scythe was.

The trees were a blur and Vi was hardly breathless. She focused solely on heading to the southwest ridge as Deneya described. Vi skidded to a stop before she lurched through the treeline just east of Toris. Pressing herself against one of the tall trees, she crouched low, the leaves of the forest floor settling around her.

Vi squinted into the setting sun, focusing on the woman and young man speaking at the crest of one of the rolling hills that cascaded down to the humble fishing town. The woman sat on a rock, talking as much with her hands as her mouth, though Vi couldn't make out the words. The sun glistened off the jewelry she wore, sparking in the light. Two large hoops pulled down her pointed ears. They were no doubt communication tokens, if the Adela of this world was anything like the Adela of Vi's. The woman removed an earring and passed it to Fallor.

Vi scanned the surrounding hills.

The lone woman was high up—visible for a wide distance. Others were watching her, they had to be. But wherever her fellow pirates were hiding, Vi couldn't see them.

Fallor talked with her for about an hour. At the end of their conversation, he tried to pass the token back to the pirate, but she refused with a sickeningly sweet smile. Anger flashed across Vi's chest, bouncing between her ribs, making her breath hot. But she promptly squelched the feeling. This wasn't her fight. She wasn't here to help him.

She was here to get to Adela.

Yet... Vi saw someone else in Fallor. A young Jayme, impressionable and filled with hurt that Adela would fan into rage.

Fallor took to the skies with a pulse of magic. The woman watched the eagle, ignorant that someone else was watching her. Vi slid up the tree in tandem.

The pirate wasn't a morphi, which meant she had to walk back to Adela. That meant there was a skiff somewhere nearby. Vi stepped from the trees and at the same time said, *"Loft dorh."*

Immobilize.

The glyph that sparked at the tip of her pointed finger was no longer the bright white-yellow it had been. Now it was tinted with blue on the edges, glowing nearly the same color as crystals. Vi felt a surge of magic at her left. She could almost hear the inhale of a man emerging from his hiding place.

"Juth mariy." An audible *crack* filled the air as she destroyed the Lightspinner's magic. There was one other pirate, at least. Vi began running toward the woman she had under her command.

She remembered holding Fallor with *loft dorh*. It had been a nearly impossible act. She'd keenly felt his every struggle against her magic tethers. But her grip now was so tight, the only thing Vi could feel was the woman's panicked heartbeat under her grip.

A pulse of magic shot across the field.

The first pirate was a Lightspinner. The other was a morphi. Adela was nothing if not prepared.

Vi stopped her forward momentum, bracing herself as the morphi's magic disruption washed over her. She focused on her glyphs. They wavered; the woman moved for a second as Vi's control flickered. The pirate collapsed with a cry, but was then held in stasis again as Vi's glyph sustained the shift.

Now, it was Vi's heart that was racing. Her left hand burned with power from the glyph. Her bones singed against her muscles. She could feel Yargen within her, seeking release, seeking to be whole again, as Vi drew on the goddess's essence.

"Get away from her!" a man shouted.

Vi didn't give him a chance to say anything else, levying another *"Juth mariy"* in reply. There was another pulse of magic, and Vi's glyphs nearly flickered out of existence. But they held enough for her to make it to the kneeling woman.

Ruthlessly, Vi grabbed the woman's hooped ear and jerked her face forward. *Loft dorh* faded. The woman was held in total shock of Vi standing over her. To the pirate's eyes, Vi was a human who wielded Lightspinning that couldn't be broken by the shift.

"*Narro hath*," Vi uttered, almost with a sinister note.

She felt the magic spring to life, her suspicions confirmed. All their waiting and watching had paid off. Vi had finally tracked down the elusive pirate Adela.

No, *more than that*, she had initiated a direct communication with her.

"Adela," Vi said sweetly, feeling the magic pull taut. "I have your crew. And while I know you don't care all that much for their lives, I will tell you that I have something much, much better. Something that will make you rich beyond compare. Something that will ensure your name is uttered in fear and wonder by every child for thousands of years to come.

"Let me on *Stormfrost* to parlay with you, and you'll know what it is."

Silence. Vi didn't even hear the wind moving over the grasses or the other pirates readying their next attacks as she waited.

"And who are you?" Adela's chilling voice was recognizable anywhere. Vi hated that it was as known to her as her own mother's.

"Yargen's Champion." Vi smirked. "The one who broke your magic in Oparium." Another pause. The other pirates stilled, some form of communication happening on the side. "Well? Don't test my patience, pirate queen."

"You intrigue me, Champion. Come aboard, if you dare."

Vi released the woman's face and her glyph vanished. The pirate collapsed at her feet, gasping for air and scrambling away. Vi looked down at her, magic surging from a font that would never run dry. It filled her to the point of being overwhelming.

"Take me to Adela, and you may live."

20

A SURREAL SENSE OF familiarity crept up on Vi as she stepped foot on the *Stormfrost* for a second time that felt like the hundredth. Much like the first time in her own world, the crew had gathered on the main deck. Adela was among them, identical to how Vi had first seen her, down to her icy cane.

Vi stood, motionless. The crew around her rigidly maintained their positions. They were the string of an invisible bow that Adela held in her frigid grip. One word, and they would lunge to strike clean through her heart.

Adela, for her part, wore a slightly amused smile. She stared at Vi and Vi at her. They waited each other out in the stillness, waited to see who gave first.

Vi knew it wouldn't be her. Time was one of the many things she had on her side. Time had made her *very* patient.

"You claim to be the one who broke my magic in Oparium." Adela's tone and look told Vi that she sincerely doubted that fact. "I thought the claim insanity. Perhaps just as much as your claim of being Yargen's Champion returned. Or maybe the real insanity is you willingly coming to the *Stormfrost* like a sheep to slaughter."

Adela smirked and the flash of blades being drawn caught Vi's eye. The crew looked at her like a prime cut of meat.

"I did not come here for slaughter," Vi said calmly. "I came to strike a deal with you."

"Yes, so you claim. Get to the striking, girl."

Vi was discovering one of the greatest annoyances of her current state was perpetually looking like she was eighteen. "Not among your crew."

"Any deal you strike with me can be done here and now," Adela insisted. Vi slowly shook her head. "Then I will let them kill you."

"It'd be a shame for me to raze everything you've built and kill every man and woman on this ship simply because you are stubborn."

"You think you can kill us?" a pirate broke rank and shouted.

"Do you doubt me?" Vi looked to the man and watched as he took a step backward. She turned her eyes back to Adela. "I will not speak among the rabble. This is your last chance. Parlay in private and have everything you desire. Or meet your end. I care not. The vortex continues with or without you."

Adela narrowed her eyes slightly. "Very well, come to my cabin."

The crew parted for their captain. Vi could feel their eyes gouging at her throat, making up for what their weapons could not do. But they made no motion against her. As long as Adela tolerated her, so would they.

Adela led her back to an entrance underneath the quarterdeck. It opened into a large cabin with windows lining the stern of the vessel. Ice stretched between beams of wood in place of glass, the world beyond blurred through the frost. A large desk was opposite a bed. Shelves lined the wall to her left, the books and scrolls held in by narrow rails. Two seats were positioned in front of the windows.

"Please, sit." Adela motioned to one of the leather chairs. "If it's not too cold for you." She smiled thinly.

"I'm not one you need to worry about." Dredging her spark to the surface, the air around Vi crackled, shimmering with heat. As she sat down, the thin layer of frost covering the leather evaporated into steam. She could feel Adela's magic pushing in against hers, trying to cover the chair once more. But Vi held the ice at bay with minimal effort, winning their first tug-of-war as Adela sat across form her.

"You're human, a Lightspinner, and you also know the elemental magics of the Dark Isle." Adela tapped her cane, punctuating each item. "You're like me."

"In some ways," Vi admitted. "I will not stop until I get what I want. I am not afraid to be ruthless. And I did grow up once, long ago, on the Dark Isle, just as you did."

"Is there elfin in your parentage as well?" Vi shook her head. "Pity, you'll be dead soon enough, then."

"I am timeless."

"Yes, this Champion business." Adela lifted her icy hand off her cane, waving it through the air as though the notion was nothing more than a fleeting thought. "Tell me what it is you want. And why I should let you leave my ship alive."

"What do you know of the crystal weapons of Yargen?" Vi asked, ignoring the opportunity to reiterate that there were only two options: Adela working with her, or everyone dying.

"Crystal weapons? Very little."

"I suspected as much, or you would've never left the crown of Solaris unprotected."

"It wasn't entirely unprotected," Adela said gruffly. "My magic was powerful."

"For one such as yourself, yes."

"Tell me about these crystal weapons," she demanded, tapping her cane on the ground.

"I'll tell you that these weapons are worth little to you and everything to me. If I do not get them, it will spell the end of the world." Vi looked out the windows. Adela—at least the Adela of her time—didn't care about the world ending. It was an intangible concept to a woman who only valued things she could put her hands on. "I need your help in getting them to where they need to go. Specifically, I need the *Stormfrost*."

"I am the pirate queen, not a ferryman at your beck and call."

"You are a mercenary by another name who will take jobs from the highest bidder regardless of who or what they are." Vi gave her a hard look. Surprisingly, Adela didn't look offended. She smiled wider, or perhaps it was a sneer. "I am the highest bidder."

"All right, put your gold where your mouth is, then. What is sailing on the *Stormfrost* worth to you?"

"I can give you access to the treasury of Solaris."

Adela threw her head back and laughed. "I *had* access to the treasury of Solaris when I wasn't even twenty-five. I took all I wanted and that treasure ended up being worth so little to me, I couldn't be bothered to go back for it. Do better." Vi had expected this reaction. But she couldn't be blamed for starting low in her negotiations.

"The Archives of Yargen." That got Adela sitting straighter. She wasn't laughing now. "I know pathways in and through them. I will give you access to those pathways."

"And get the Swords of Light away from the Archives?"

"You'd have to promise me more than the use of the *Stormfrost* to get me to do that." Vi wasn't even sure if she *could* do that. But she wanted Adela to think she could.

"What will the use of the *Stormfrost* entail?"

"I need you to deliver me to a few places, pick me up in a few others. Perhaps some comrades of mine as well. Nothing too difficult for the great pirate queen."

"That's a rather open-ended request. I have my own empire to run here on the seas. I need to know how much of my time you'll take to determine if what you're promising is worth it."

"I won't call on you more than five times in the span of the next ten years." In ten years, the Caverns would meet their end, one way or another; a new Vi would be born; and she would long know if her efforts to save the world had ultimately resulted in failure.

"Humans," Adela said, as though her own parentage wasn't part human. "Always thinking so narrow."

"I'm attempting to strike you a fair deal."

Adela hummed, looking out the windows at the sea drifting by. She caressed the top of her cane made of ice, smoothing away jagged shards as they grew around her fingers. Being part elfin explained her immense power, and her longevity.

"Access to the Archives of Yargen for five trips in the next ten years, whichever comes first," Adela summarized before bringing her bright blue eyes back to Vi. "You have your deal, Champion."

"One more thing."

"You are not accustomed to how negotiations work, are you?" Adela narrowed her eyes. "One puts everything on the table foremost."

"The boy, Fallor…" Her voice trailed off. The thought had vanished from between her fingers and Vi struggled to bring it back. Why had she brought up Fallor again?

Ah.

The memory of Arwin, soaking in the bath, staring at the ceiling, trapped in a bubble of pain and longing and what-ifs. The shade of Jayme on the boy. Fallor was nothing in relation to stopping the vortex, but she had made a promise to save the people she could, hadn't she?

"You are to cut ties with him."

"We have been working—"

"This isn't negotiable," Vi said firmly.

Adela pursed her lips. "Very well, we have other morphi we've been working on recruiting." Adela shrugged. "Or are they off-limits too?"

"Recruit away." Vi leaned back in the chair, folding her hands over her stomach and staring out at the ocean. Perhaps the Isle of Frost getting a shift was the stone in the river, and some other morphi would betray King Noct and his family. Perhaps she'd somehow made it worse. But for now Vi hoped that Arwin would have a few extra years of happiness. If she was lucky, regardless of what else came to pass in the world around her, she would have a hand to hold when the day was done.

She'd handle Jayme when her and Adela's deal was up. By then, she would have even more power. The pirate queen would agree to anything just to avoid angering her.

"Where will we be delivering you first?" Adela asked, still somewhat begrudgingly.

"First, we'll wait for my friends to join us. Then, to Norin."

"And you will tell me of the way into the Archives?"

"I will tell you how to get into the Archives once our deal has concluded and you have taken me to my fifth and final place."

"What assurance do I have until then?"

"I'm sure you'll think of some way to make my life miserable if I don't follow through." Adela smiled knowingly at that. Vi held out her hand, a plain, silver ring on her left middle finger. "*Narro hath.*" The connection sprang to life with the glyph hovering around the ring. "It's settled, come to the *Stormfrost*," she said, short and simple, before closing the connection.

"Who are your friends?"

"Curious, aren't you, for a woman who's all business?"

"Keep your secrets." Adela turned, looking out to sea. Vi couldn't tell if she was bothered or not.

"One of them is an elfin from Risen. The other is another elfin but from much farther away… where I'm from." *More or less.* Vi decided to answer Adela's question anyway. She was never going to be friendly with the pirate queen. But the more cordial they could become, the better. "May I ask you something?"

"You may ask." But Vi didn't miss that Adela made no guarantees about giving an answer.

"Why Solaris?"

"Pardon?" Adela swept her icy gaze back to Vi. It would've made her shiver, once.

"Why do you hate Solaris? You stole the crown jewels. You worked with the Knights of Jadar. You'll go out of your way to bring harm to Solaris, even offering discounts to people acting against the family."

"Was it you who killed my man in Norin years ago?"

"Yes." Vi would've expected Adela to be upset at that, but she only seemed amused.

"I was wondering when Janice informed me there was a Lightspinner…" Janice must've been the morphi that night. "I had bet it was one of Lumeria's men."

"You still haven't answered my question."

"Oh, yes, why do I hate Solaris?" Adela's wispy, white hair hovered like an aura at the slightest turn of her head when she looked to Vi. "Why do you think?"

"I think it's because Tiberus scorned you," Vi said boldly. "Because you loved him and he—"

Raspy laughter and wheezes cut her short.

"Because I *loved* Tiberus? That sod?" Adela shook her head several times. "No. Though he might have thought I did. His affections suited me, I'll be the first to admit. Tiberus was a means to an end for me to see if I could get the treasure."

"Then it's not about Solaris?"

"Why would it be?"

"Because…" Vi faltered. Her voice trailed off. Everything she'd known Adela to be. Everything the pirate queen had done.

"You thought this was all about a man?" Adela continued to get a chuckle out of Vi's shock. "No, girl. This is about me, and my power. Tiberus was a stepping stone, a test run, to see if I could become what I knew I was destined for.

"I want every so-called ruler on this earth to know that their dominion ends at the sea. I do not hate Solaris any more than I hate Lumeria, or any other ruler across the various kingdoms, empires, and republics of the earth." Vi chuckled softly. "You find my ambitions amusing?" Adela looked at her from the sides of her eyes.

"Not at all. What I find amusing is that you and I will do anything to get what we want. And you are the last person I ever expected to find kinship with." All the hatred Vi had felt for Adela was melting away like the ice on the chair around her. She didn't *like* the woman. But she was starting to *understand* her. Part of that transformed her disdain into ambivalence.

Adela fought to carve out her place in the world. What made her any different from anyone else?

TAAVIN AND DENEYA ARRIVED on the *Stormfrost* later that day, brought on the vessel by a skiff, and Adela showed them to their temporary quarters. Vi was reminded of the *Dawn Skipper*—two bunks, a table between them, and not much else.

"I don't want to say I doubted you but…"

"You doubted me." Vi grinned at Deneya. "I'm not offended. Adela's reaction was a coin flip."

"It was, and I'm relieved this worked out." Taavin crossed to the window, looking out at the sea that was now drifting past them as they moved toward the Dark Isle once more. "What did you have to promise her to get her to agree?"

"Nothing of consequence." Vi folded her arms and leaned against the closed door.

"Why do I get the feeling you're lying?" Deneya said uncertainly.

"Consequence is a matter of perspective."

"She's avoiding answering for a reason." Taavin faced Vi. "What were the terms of the deal?"

"We have ten years, or five trips on the *Stormfrost*, whichever comes first."

"Is ten years enough time?" Deneya asked.

"It all ends soon."

"That sounds ominous." Deneya sat heavily on a bunk.

"You still haven't told us what Adela expects in return," Taavin pressed.

"As for what I offered her… I offered a way into the Archives of Yargen."

"You *what?*" Taavin and Deneya said in unison.

"I had to give her something. But that was all I offered her."

"That's all, she says, as though handing the Archives to Adela isn't anything major," Deneya muttered.

"You didn't though." Taavin took a step toward her. "Did you?"

A smile curled Vi's lips. "All I promised her was a way in to the Archives. I didn't guarantee it'd be safe, and I didn't promise her a way out."

"You mean to ensnare her." Deneya was now grinning as well.

"I mean to prevent the world from ending. What the people of Risen do is up to them." Vi shrugged.

"I'll make sure the people of Risen are ready to protect the flame," Deneya proclaimed.

"The flame will be gone long before then." *And you'll be the one to take it*, Vi added mentally.

"If we take the flame from Risen, there's no more rebirths—no more turns of the vortex," Taavin said solemnly.

"As I said, it all ends eventually. It must."

He stared at her for a long moment. Vi could almost feel him reading her thoughts through her eyes. She tried to shield herself from it with an encasement of Yargen's magic around her.

"You have plans," he said finally.

"Of course I do."

"Care to share them?"

"When the time is right."

"You act like you don't trust us." Deneya rolled her eyes.

"I trust you both with my life."

"Then why didn't you tell us what you planned on offering Adela?" Deneya asked.

"Because it was inconsequential."

"What about your work with the shift?" Taavin's voice took on a hard edge. Even Deneya stilled as the atmosphere in the room became nearly suffocating. They'd found out. They must've heard from Ruie when word spread that she escaped through the shift surrounding the Twilight Kingdom without the help of a morphi.

"Is it true?" Deneya whispered. "Did you really go through the shift without the help of a morphi?"

Vi nodded.

"How?" Deneya shifted uncomfortably. "You shouldn't be able to… none of us can. Only morphi can master the shift."

"I'm not quite sure how," Vi finally admitted, staring down at her hands. "I got a feeling when working with Arwin. A feeling that led to an understanding."

"You can understand the shift."

"I can," Vi answered. But she didn't know if that was entirely the truth. Did *she* understand the shift? Or did the goddess within her, working through her mortal form? "Perhaps it's a boon. Now I will be able to make all the crystal weapon replicas so that the major events surrounding the crystal weapons remain unchanged."

She looked to Taavin as if she was the one giving a peace offering. If she could make crystal weapons, they could continue along his mission of ensuring the birth of a new Champion. Surely, he should be thrilled.

"Speaking of…" Deneya reached for her pack and produced the fake crystal crown she and Arwin had made. "We have it."

"We'll return south and find what Baldair did with the actual crown. Hopefully, it'll be an easy swap," Vi proclaimed. "We'll go by way of Norin so we can stop in the Crossroads and collect some gold from our hideaway." She looked to Taavin. He still regarded her with a thoughtful and somewhat wary gaze. "If my plans meet your approval as well?"

"The stones of fate in the river are unchanged. We're still heading toward the birth of a new Champion and protecting the future of this world in the process." His words were approving, but his body language said otherwise.

Vi reached out, taking his fingers and trying to smooth away the tension between them with her thumb on the back of his hand. A smile broke across her lips, one he reluctantly returned. Her fingers tightened. She had to hold onto him, for as long as possible, because holding him felt like holding the last remnants of the woman she'd once been.

Adela took them just south of Norin. They were taken ashore by rowboat and left without fanfare. In the distance, the *Stormfrost* was barely visible. By the time they reached Norin that evening, there were already whispers of the legendary pirate Adela being spotted.

They left the rumors behind and began the long trek to the Crossroads.

When they arrived a few days later, it was late, and the stars had been their only companions on the road for the final hour. Even the center of the Solaris Empire was relatively quiet.

"Glad to see it didn't burn down." Deneya looked up at the vacant storefront Vi had purchased years ago as she slid her key into the iron rose lock.

"It won't burn down," Taavin said confidently. "This place is going to play a pivotal role in the future of our world."

A deep rumbling distracted them. Vi and Taavin shared a look. Both turned to Deneya.

"Was that your stomach?" Vi asked with a laugh.

"It was a long walk today." Deneya rubbed her stomach. "Here, take my pack, I'm going to go find some food." Vi accepted the woman's pack and Taavin gave a nod. "I'll be back with sustenance soon."

Deneya headed off in the opposite direction as Vi and Taavin stepped into the darkness of the store. The shelves were perpetually vacant. Darkness clung to every corner. Vi crossed to the back of the room; there, hidden behind a curtain, was another doorway. This led to a narrow stairway and up into a cramped second-floor apartment.

Vi dropped her pack heavily and rolled her shoulders. Taavin's hands covered the sore spots, rubbing slowly. Vi sighed as he took a half step closer to her.

"You should take a hot bath."

"I should, and you should join me." She smirked into the darkness. "It's been a while since we've been alone."

"Now that sounds a delight," he whispered into her ear, lips brushing against tender skin. Warmth flooded her, from the top of her head to the bottom of her abdomen. "I'll draw the bath."

He stepped away and Vi caught his hand, then his gaze. Taavin locked his fingers with hers, pulling her hand to his face and kissing her knuckles thoughtfully. He straightened, a mischievous smile quirking his lips.

"Don't keep me waiting," Vi said softly, her voice gone deep with yearning.

"Never." Taavin stepped back, keeping his eyes locked with hers until the last moment he disappeared into the bathroom. He could have her yearning with just a look or a simple touch in an otherwise chaste location.

Being back on the Dark Isle, with him, made things feel simpler once more. At least for a little while, they could find moments to pretend he was a normal man, and she a normal woman. Their love could be uncomplicated.

As he rummaged in the bathroom, she set about sorting their things. The chest of gold coins from old Lyndum was right where they'd left it. They'd have to convert it once more into usable currency, restock supplies, and then head south. Vi closed the top of the chest and walked over to the lone window wedged between the buildings on either side of their narrow shop, as though their place was a weed that couldn't be contained.

She opened the window, allowing the room to air out with the cool desert breeze. Vi rested her hands on the sill, leaning out, savoring the sounds of revelry that hung on the crisp night. Laughter echoed up to her, drawing Vi's attention down to the street.

Two men clung to each other, swaying like willowy branches.

They were both clearly intoxicated; their dark hair was thrown every which way. She watched with a little smile as their steps mirrored that of a rolling tide, up and down and not quite stable.

Oh, to be that young and—

Vi clutched the windowsill.

"It can't be. It's too early," she whispered. Her eyes didn't lie. "Those idiots." Vi spun, racing through the room, not even bothering to change. Taavin had just emerged from the bathroom, naked to the waist, and the sight of him stopped her in her tracks. Vi let out a groan, resting a palm on his chest. "I need to make sure two drunks make their way home safely."

"What?" Taavin called after her as she started down the stairs.

"It's Aldrik and Jax. The Imperial army is here, *now*," Vi called back before dashing through the store and emerging out on the street beyond. She was only several paces behind the two men and closed the gap quickly. She could've stabbed them both between the ribs before they noticed her at their backs.

Vi rubbed her eyes, pressing to the point of pain and stars popping behind her lids. Then she pinched her cheeks till they were splotchy— though it might have been impossible to tell on her tan skin in the middle of the night. She began running, head down; her shoulder clipped the taller man and she stumbled, sprawling on the ground before them like a proper damsel.

Aldrik was nearly taken down with her. Jax held him up with the arm that was already around his waist. The booze slowed their reactions and they both reached to help her up on a delay.

"Aaaare—" a burp "—are you allrisht?" Aldrik tried to ask.

Clearly, this was not one of his prouder moments.

"I'm fine," she said curtly, batting their hands away and collecting herself off the ground. Vi stopped herself, blinking the tears she'd pressed into her eyes so they'd roll down her cheeks as she looked up at them. "My prince!" Vi bowed, bringing her forehead to the ground.

"Shhhh." He brought a finger to his lips. "I'm incognitooo. Haaving a night of fshun."

"Sorry, miss." Jax extended his hand and Vi ignored it, helping herself to her feet. He looked like he was barely managing to keep

Aldrik upright. Jax tilted his head so far he nearly fell over. "Do I know you?"

"I doubt it." Vi played with the short ends of her hair. She'd cropped it back to her ears before arriving on the Dark Isle. Long, short, long, short, her hair was the one thing that she could easily make sure was never the same between each meeting.

"I'm sure I do," he insisted.

"Forgive me for being blunt, but I think that's the alcohol speaking." Jax grinned wider at the remark and Vi smiled as well. "I'm a lowly one who wouldn't have the honor of meeting a prince or an illustrious member of the Golden Guard."

Aldrik burst out laughing. "She, she called you a *member*."

Vi had no idea why that was supposed to be funny. But Jax laughed along, snorting as he tried to regain control of himself.

"Well, now you have. Please do keep our appearance a secret? It's my fault the prince is out so late, and I don't want him or I to get in trouble."

If you wanted it to be a secret, you shouldn't be walking down the middle of the main street drunk, Vi nearly snapped. What she said instead was, "My lords, the Crossroads at night is not the safest of places. Perhaps I could have the honor of escorting you? I know these streets well, and I planned to enlist in the army come morning. I'm quite capable of being your temporary guard."

They had *not* planned on enlisting in the army come the morning. Their plan had been to head south, switch the crown, and *then* head North. But Vi didn't miss an opportunity when fate handed her one.

If she did this favor for them tonight, it was likely that they would keep her close at the front.

"Let her," Aldrik declared. "Secoond pretteh lady of the nighhht."

Second? Just what did that *mean?*

"Come on, then, walk with us back to the center of the Crossroads," Jax said lightly. The brief moment of recognition had passed and they began to walk. "Why do you want to join the army?"

"To serve the Empire." Vi sniffled, rubbing her eyes until a few more tears squeezed out.

"What'sh wrong?"

"I got in a fight with my parents about it," Vi said, looking at her feet. The sorrow in her voice at the mention of parents was genuine; it was compounded when she looked over at Aldrik. He had the bump in his nose now that she remembered her father having. His cheeks were gaunter than the last time she'd seen him. Deep bags clung underneath distant, harrowed eyes. "They don't want me to enlist. But I'm a woman grown. And well…"

"Yoooou ran away from hoome."

Vi nodded at Aldrik's slurred words.

"You should go back," Jax said firmly.

"Jax, don't lose-us sholdiers."

"You only get one family. Hold them close."

She'd been worried about the two men getting a dagger between the ribs by a cut-purse in the night. But it was Jax who caught her off guard, striking her breathless. Vi took a second to compose herself. Her family was, and would always be, a soft spot. She formed an answer befitting the seventeen-year-old girl she'd once been, and not the timeless traveler she now was.

"I do hold them close," she insisted. "But they have to understand I'm doing this for them. I'm fighting for them. So they can have a better life. They have to understand that this is *my* choice, not theirs."

"Yoooou're doing ah goodthing." Aldrik patted her on the shoulder and his hand stayed. He blinked into the brighter lights of the center of the Crossroads as they entered their aura. "Not like me. Not like someone who's done terrible things."

"That's enough for tonight. We're not far from your bed." Jax led them over to the Imperial lodging. Three, large, circular windows kept an eye on the square below. "Wait here just a moment, I'll be back," Jax said to her, giving her no time to reply before disappearing inside with Aldrik.

Vi sat on the stoop, elbows on her knees, staring at the other revelries happening at a bar across the square. Her mind was on Aldrik, on those haunted eyes— the ghosts of her actions haunting his nightmares. She clutched her hands so tightly together that her nails left crescent moons in her skin.

The door behind her opened again, startling her. Jax hopped down two steps, wobbled, and sat with a sigh.

"He'll be fine," he said.

"'Fine' is an interesting word choice for the hangover he'll be nursing." Vi glanced up at the second-floor window that she knew to be her father's room. "Does the prince drink to excess often?"

Jax's long silence was answer enough. When the "No" finally came, Vi knew it was a lie.

"Well, that's good, I suppose," she lied right back, pretending she didn't hear all his unspoken hesitations.

"And, for that reason, I appreciate your discretion about tonight's events."

"I don't really have any friends. So I've got no one to tell. Not that I would tell anyone. I'm looking to be in service to the crown and I know what's best for the crown isn't rumors of what the prince does during his downtime."

"He gets precious little of it."

"I'm sure," Vi murmured. "But he still has it better than he thinks." What Vi wouldn't give to be a "tortured" princess again.

"I wouldn't count on that."

"How so?"

Jax shrugged and Vi let that topic of conversation die. She didn't want to seem too eager for information on the prince.

"You said you wanted to enlist, right?"

"That's right."

"Come find me in the morning." Jax stood. "You can be under me, or Raylynn, depending on if you have magic or not."

Vi didn't have to force or fake her smile. She could enlist in the army and be near Aldrik. Moreover, she could fight along Jax and Raylynn. The idea of continuing to protect them both was appealing.

"Are you certain?"

"Yes, just remind me I was when the sun is up. Nights like this have a tendency to be forgotten." Jax laughed.

"I will."

"See you in the morning then—" Jax paused, holding out his hand.

"Gwen," Vi said, filling in the blank. "My name is Gwen."

"'Soldier Gwen' has a nice ring to it, don't you think?" Jax clasped her hand and they shook on both their second introduction and a deal.

"It does," she agreed. "Almost like it was fated to be."

22

VI, TAAVIN, AND DENEYA enlisted under Raylynn. Since Vi was the only person among them who could conjure her magic in the elemental ways of the Dark Isle, it was too much of a risk for them to try and join the sorcerer-warriors of the Black Legion.

Instead, they were foot soldiers—part of the nameless, faceless masses that exercised the will of the Emperor in his thirst for conquest.

Part of her thrived in the anonymity. It guarded her heart from seeing the Northern peoples she'd once considered friends and kin put to the sword. Being no one allowed her to move without raising attention or suspicion.

The other part of her clung to her identity. That was what motivated her to look after Jax and Raylynn, intervening on their behalf in more than one battle. Her small acts had no bearings on the outcome of the world's fate, but protecting them both honored memories of people she'd cared for.

"Thank you for today," Vi said to Deneya as she sat heavily around their campfire. The smell of burning bodies and ash was still thick on her from earlier in the day. "You really helped with Raylynn."

The very woman leaned against a tree some distance away, hair slicked to her neck with sweat, talking with Baldair. With every turn in the conversation, Baldair took a half-step closer. He never missed an opportunity to be by her side.

Their unspoken love was obvious to everyone but them.

"We'll have to leave her side, soon." Taavin didn't mince words. "Aldrik will sustain his injury soon."

"Yes, the one that brings him to Vhalla. Because nothing says 'fall for me' like being wounded and helpless," Deneya said dryly.

"You've been saying he'll sustain his injury 'soon' for months." Vi glanced at Taavin.

"Things aren't happening exactly when we expected."

"The world is changing. We're getting closer to the end of the vortex." Vi poked at their campfire with a stick, watching the flames dance.

"It's just variation," Taavin insisted. Vi shared a look with Deneya. The man wasn't going to admit they were on their final course until they were extinguishing the flame of Yargen. Vi had accepted that much.

Vi stood. "I'll be back. Off to the latrine."

"You know where to find us."

She always did. The campsites were mostly the same—only the terrain changed. The three of them set up their tents together, maintained their own campfire, and kept to themselves. The moment someone made a passing attempt to befriend them, Vi or Taavin would say or do something extremely off-putting.

They were the odd ones—odd, but effective. Too weird for anyone to want to spend much time with, too valuable to discharge.

"Do you think he's really going to do it?"

"Of course he won't. He's mourning, not suicidal. Well... I don't *think* he would."

Two men murmured by a campfire. Their backs were to her and neither seemed to realize Vi was there. She shifted her weight onto her back foot and floated her front foot forward before shifting her weight. The need for silence seemed suddenly paramount.

"You don't have me convinced... Listen, I'm worried. We should go after him. The attack today was hard on him."

"He was delivering a message. He'll be back within an hour and you'll feel foolish for this."

"What if I don't?" The man turned his head and Vi slid behind a tent, creeping around the back to remain out of sight and within earshot. He lowered his voice to a whisper. "What if I have every right to worry? It was his son in that village. There were no survivors and you heard the way he was talking. He had a whole plan on how he was going to get close to and attack Prince Al—"

"Stop that nonsense," the other man hissed. "You're going to get him killed for treason with that talk and there's no point to it."

"You don't know that. You didn't see his poisoned dagger. He was *serious*."

Vi pressed her eyes closed and took a breath. She started off in the opposite direction, away from the men, rounding back through camp in a different way than she came. She crouched down at Taavin's side, clasping his shoulder.

"That was fast."

"We have to go."

Taavin did one quick scan of her face. "What happened?"

"I overheard two men talking about someone going to attack Aldrik," Vi whispered.

"He's supposed to be wounded in battle. That's how it's always happened."

"I know what's *supposed* to happen, but that's not what's *actually* happening," Vi interrupted curtly. "Something changed."

"Too many somethings," Taavin murmured, glancing at the fire, as if he was the one who could find truth in flames.

"We need to move, *now*." Vi stood.

They both followed her into the woods. Aldrik's camp wasn't far—probably an hour by foot for a normal soldier. She wanted to cross the dense forest in thirty minutes. If anyone could do it, it was her.

Not looking to see if her companions could keep up, Vi began to run. The trees blurred around her and, seemingly in a blink, they emerged into the camp. Rising above the other tents was a large, square canvas structure.

She was so close.

Magic flared. The inside of the tent glowed orange.

They were too late.

Fate had sneaked past them. As Vi's eyes had been on Raylynn and Jax, thinking she had a bit more time to look after each of them before Aldrik required her attention, fate had made a mad dash for the prince.

Vi pushed past soldiers. Two guards positioned at the outside of the tent didn't even have a chance to stop her.

"What're you—" they tried to ask, but she ignored them, barging into Aldrik's tent.

A charred husk of a man was on the floor. The prince had his hand pressed against his side. He was on his knees, hair a mess, covering his face as he lifted his dark eyes to her. His jaw was clenched shut and he swayed.

"My prince, I'm here to help you." Vi rushed over. Aldrik slumped against her. His eyes were hazy. The man was an inferno to the touch. "*Halleth maph,*" Vi murmured. The prince was too far gone to hesitate using her Lightspinning.

"Don't heal him entirely," Taavin cautioned.

"But—"

"It's not what we expected, but this wound will be what takes him south."

"He can head south when he's not on the verge of death." Seeing Aldrik like this made Vi panic more than she would've wanted.

"Trust—" Taavin was interrupted by the two soldiers bursting in the tent behind them.

"The prince has been poisoned," Vi said hastily. She could feel the foreign substance attacking his body. "He dispatched the assailant, but he's wounded. He needs to return to Lyndum for healing."

The soldiers looked at the carnage, at the blood soaking her shirt.

"*Now!*" Vi barked, standing. Taavin took Aldrik's other side. "Fetch his horse and every other warstrider or hearty breed."

"Who are you to give orders?"

"I don't have time for your strutting and self-importance," Vi sneered, looking down at the man as she passed. "Your prince is dying. I am the woman trying to save him. That's all that matters."

The other soldier snapped into action, running from the tent and shouting, "Horses! Get Baston and five more mounts!"

As they emerged, six horses were trotting over, already saddled and ready to ride. War made people prepared to move at all times.

The soldiers helped Vi and Taavin hoist Aldrik into his saddle. They tied him to the saddle and packed healing herbs into his wound, bandaging it. Deneya was one of the women quickly stocking their mounts.

"I'll sneak off and head west," she whispered hastily. "I'll grab the crown from our place and meet you south."

"Thank you." Vi squeezed her hand.

"I'm ready to be out of here." Deneya followed Vi over to one of the other mounts. "You need to go. The prince doesn't look good," she said, louder.

"The Minister of Sorcery will be able to extract the poison from his blood," Vi declared to those assembled as she mounted one of the horses without permission.

"Who in the Mother's name do you think you are?" Some major Vi didn't recognize balked at her and Taavin as they saddled up. "Those are my—"

"There's no time!" Vi shouted and snapped her reins. As she passed the large, familiar black horse Aldrik was riding, she gave it a light smack on its rear.

The mount's dark eyes met hers and Vi could've sworn she saw recognition there. He might be called by another name now, but Vi would know Prism anywhere. The beast followed closely behind her.

Four soldiers, Taavin included, took up the rear as they began to race across the continent.

The North was a blur. The Waste even more so. The party stopped at the Crossroads, briefly, demanding fresh horses for the non-warstriders among them, food, and clean bandages for the prince. Two soldiers threw around the idea of staying and sending for Western healers, but Vi overruled that decision. Just when the debate grew heated, Aldrik gained enough clarity to side with her. She wasn't sure if it was Yargen helping her in that moment, but Vi said a quiet thank you to the goddess anyway as they set out once more.

Hooves thundering on the Great Imperial Way filled her ears. The noise was monotonous and deafening, and the only sound any of them could hear. When they left Shaldan, they had all been too panicked for small talk. Now, they were all too exhausted.

Sweat rolled down her neck, plastering her clothing to her skin underneath her armor. The heat of the desert made the appearance of the Southern treeline in the distance a welcome sight. She was even grateful for the storm clouds on the horizon. The idea of rain was a balm to her sun-beaten cheeks.

She was such a fool.

Rain pounded down around them nearly non-stop after they entered the forests. Tiny rivers ran around the horses' hooves and down the road. She went from constantly wiping sweat out of her eyes to blinking away rainwater.

A yell distracted her from her riding trance. Vi looked over her shoulder in a panic. A horse was down, its rider shouting curse words as his leg was pinned under it.

"You're not far." One of the other soldiers riding a standard mount pulled on his reins, rounding back to the other man. "You three go on ahead. Get the prince there. It's a miracle he's held on for this long," the woman shouted over the rain.

"You heard her, let's go!" Vi kicked her horse's heaving sides to force it up the steep incline toward the Capital.

Horns trumpeted off every wall. The sound echoed around them all the way to the palace. Vi followed the calls to a side wall where two large doors were opening.

Palace servants rushed to meet them. They went immediately for Aldrik, who nearly fell into their waiting arms the second he was untied. Vi dismounted and her knees bit into the stone of the Imperial Palace as she slipped and lost her footing.

"Soldiers, report!" A man rushed out to meet them. Vi blinked up at him and then, with the help of her horse, stood.

"The crown prince has been poisoned. Fetch the Minister of Sorcery. Have every cleric help him." It was more of a command than a report.

"We couldn't identify the poison, but the Imperial library will have the answer," Taavin interjected from her side. He looked as wobbly as she was. But his head was clear enough not to forget the most important part. "Have the library staff summoned to look up information on Northern poisons—poisons in general. Anything will help, just get every library apprentice on the task."

"With haste." Luckily, the guard on duty didn't seem to mind their barked orders, or at the very least he understood where they came from. "Marcus, help them inside. I'll go to the clerics."

"Sir!" Another soldier saluted and then guided them into the palace. The four of them entered through a side receiving room, shivering and soaked to the bone. Vi looked over her shoulder, staring at the door Aldrik was taken through. "I'll take your full report later. For now, let me find you food and some warm clothes."

"That'd be much appreciated," their companion said through chattering teeth.

"I'm going off to the toilet," Vi declared.

"Me too," Taavin said eagerly. Perhaps a little too eagerly. It had been a long ride, so Vi hoped his enthusiasm wasn't conspicuous.

As they left, their companion told Marcus about the soldiers they left behind on the road. Vi closed the door firmly behind her and started through a tunnel that connected to another large hallway. Voices could be heard behind several doors and Vi paused, looking to Taavin.

"What now?"

"We've done all we need to."

Vi leaned against the wall, scrutinizing him. "We went to war. We raced across the continent, keeping him alive—not healing him, to get back here and do… nothing."

"The magical Bond your parents form is a stone in the river."

"A Bond…" Vi murmured. Bonds were legendary things—two sorcerers whose lives were wholly intertwined in such a profound way that they could never do harm to one another. A Bond could even keep one sorcerer alive while the other was mortally wounded. "I suppose something that powerful *would* be a stone in the river."

"Even knowing it was a stone—or, *believing* it is—I was worried there. Things are changing and I admit to wondering if Aldrik could actually die."

"I don't like that thought." Vi pushed her soaking hair away from her face, slicking it back. "I'd always assumed Aldrik and Vhalla's lives were stones in the river."

"As have I," Taavin said hastily. "But uncharted territory has my nerves aflame."

Vi nodded, looking in the direction where commotion echoed in the hall. "Should we go oversee things?"

"I don't think we should risk it. He's here and the library staff has been summoned. It's best not to muddle fate further with our presence."

"Then our focus becomes finding and replacing the crown." Vi pushed off the wall and began to wander aimlessly away from the voices and commotion as she focused on their new task. Taavin followed her into narrow and narrower corridors. Her mind was leading her in a specific direction, some map or blueprint in the far recesses telling her where to go. Vi trusted her subconscious self.

"That will be work for the morning," Taavin said eventually.

"What do we do tonight?"

"Whatever we want." Taavin took a step closer to her, wrapping an arm around her waist. "You're a hard woman to get alone these days."

Laughter sprang forth, tired and airy. "All this was a long ploy to get me alone, Taavin?"

"I'll say it was worth it." Two strong arms closed around her. In one deft motion, Taavin hoisted her upward. Vi immediately sank into the cradle of his arms, resting her head against his shoulder limply.

"You seem happy," she murmured.

"No. Just relieved." He pressed his lips against her forehead. "Where are we headed?"

"I don't know," she murmured. "Somewhere quiet." Sure enough, they'd ended up in the bowels of the palace, deep enough that no sorcerers even maintained the candles or torches on the walls.

"I think you've achieved that." Taavin paused at an open doorway. A dust-covered bed stood stubbornly against time. "Does this look good to you?"

She hummed as she assessed their option. Vi murmured "*Kot sorre*" and pushed the dust from the bed with a glyph that also bunched the threadbare blanket. "Better."

"Good." Taavin carried her to the bed and laid her down. Vi caught his shirt as he pulled away. She used what strength she still had left in her to yank him forward. Taavin stumbled, catching himself with a hand on the pillow by her head. Dust filled her nose, nearly making her cough, but Vi suppressed it as his lips met hers.

She would not allow anything to break this kiss.

His fingertips smoothed over her cheek and, despite the exhaustion he must be feeling too, he kissed her hungrily. His tongue probed hers gently, eliciting a soft sigh from her. When he finally pulled away, he stayed close enough for their noses to touch.

"Thank you," Vi whispered. She wanted to get the words out before sleep claimed her. "Thank you for being here no matter what."

"There's nowhere else, no *time* else, I would ever want to be."

23

TAAVIN'S ARMS WERE TUCKED around her, enveloping her in a cocoon of warmth. Vi shifted in an attempt to nestle farther back into him. His body curled around her back and his breath tickled her ear lightly.

The halls were quiet. It was as if there wasn't another soul in the entire palace—as if this space they had found was out of time itself. She trailed her fingers along his forearm to his hand. Even in sleep, he laced his fingers with hers.

"Good morning," Taavin whispered in her ear, his voice husky and low. She closed her eyes to savor the sound.

"Good morning."

"How did you sleep?"

"Like the dead."

"I'm glad you came back to life for me, then." He chuckled and it reverberated through her own ribcage.

She twisted to face him. "I'd never not come back for you."

He leaned forward, nuzzling her nose with his, before planting a sweet kiss on her lips. It was too brief, and an embarrassing whimper escaped her as he pulled away. He let out another chuckle and leaned forward again to claim her mouth. His arms tightened, and they remained locked in this embrace as the minutes—it could've been hours, even—slipped away.

Taavin kissed her fiercely. He twisted, bringing his weight atop her. Vi sank further into the mattress.

Her world was him—his exploring hands, his hungry kisses, and his ragged breaths. He didn't have to say anything else. She knew. She could taste it on his mouth. She could feel it in the way his fingers caressed her.

The day slipped away from them. Dusk settled on their sweat-glistened skin as it winked through the narrow window that ran along the wall above the bed. A beam of gold elongated along their feet as they lay, entwined and breathless.

"It had been too long since we had a moment alone," Taavin murmured, kissing her forehead.

"Yes, well, we've been busy. War will do that," Vi said with a smile.

"I never thought I'd say this, but I miss the Twilight Kingdom."

Vi laughed. "It was peaceful there."

"When you weren't studying the shift in secret." His tone had a disapproving edge, but it was just playful enough to let her know the affront had long since been forgiven.

"Admit it, you're glad I did."

"It makes things convenient," he grumbled, and kissed her anyway.

"Speaking of the shift… Deneya will be here soon. We have to start looking for the crown."

"That's tomorrow's problem." He shifted atop her again. "Tonight, you're mine."

Tomorrow's problems promptly became today's.

Taavin went to hunt through the records in the Tower of Sorcerers for any mention of the crown being discovered. Vi navigated the depths of the castle and back up into the servants' quarters. There, she lifted three sets of uniforms from a supply closet while no one was looking, and took them back to the hideaway she and Taavin were using.

He was still gone, so Vi changed alone and returned through the hidden passageways and servants' halls to get to the royal quarters. Neither of the guards positioned on either side of the golden gate stopped her as she made her way quietly past them. Pitcher in hand and pale blue tabard over her shoulders, she looked like any of the other servants coming and going to attend the needs of royals.

A short hall after the gates opened up into a large atrium. Vi's feet slowed as she crossed the tiled floor. She came to a full stop, staring in awe. The fact that she was supposed to be a servant who had traversed these rooms countless times was lost for a long moment and she shamelessly gawked, taking in the sight.

A stained-glass dome with the sun at its apex washed the mosaic of the palace set into the floor in a myriad of colors. The dome contained the Dark Isle, Barrier Islands, and Meru off to the side.

Her eyes followed a golden staircase back down to the main floor. Two hallways stretched out on either side. Vi imagined Romulin running up and down these halls to let out energy. No… that was what *she* would've done, had she grown up here. Romulin no doubt spent a good portion of his time in his room, or a sitting area, quietly studying like the golden child he was.

Now having met Baldair, she could see what everyone had said about her brother inheriting some of his features and charm. But there was still a good deal of Aldrik and Vhalla in him as well. Romulin had been a healthy mix of the family—the best of them, in Vi's eyes.

Her eyes stung, watering suddenly.

Turning away from the atrium, Vi headed left down a long corridor lined with doors. She was drowning in emotions she wasn't expecting, and her body was trying to let them out through her eyes. Vi picked one of the doors at random and gave it a knock.

When no one answered, she cracked it open, murmuring a soft, "Excuse me?" The room was empty, likely reserved for esteemed guests or extended family. Most of the furniture was covered in drop-cloths, dust weighting them down.

She stepped back out of the room and moved on to the next. One by one, Vi crossed the doors in the hall, finding them all empty. Most were bedrooms, but there were handful of sitting rooms, offices, and a dining room interspersed throughout. Vi crossed back through the atrium, ignoring the staircase for the time being—as it surely led to the royal chambers—and headed down the other wing.

There were fewer doors here and they were spread wider apart. As Vi roamed down the hall, a cleric emerged from one near the end. His eyes met hers.

"Oh good, perfect, thank you." He quickly made his way to her, taking the pitcher from her hands.

"Yes, of course." Vi passed it to him. "The prince—is he all right?" she asked hastily.

"He is, thank the Mother." Vi didn't have to feign her sigh of relief. The Bond must've been formed. "It's been a miraculous recovery, a true blessing. Now, excuse me." The man immediately returned to the room from which he'd come.

That must be Aldrik's room. Vi turned to the door at her right. If the one to her left was Aldrik's, then…

Sure enough, she had found Prince Baldair's quarters. Vi stepped inside and locked the door behind her. The younger prince was still out at the front and wasn't due back for some time.

The main room was clearly set up for entertaining. A dining table was situated by the window, covered in a drab cloth. Between it and the door was a gaming area, complete with a billiards table and bar. The outlines of sofas and loveseats made up a sitting area.

Walking through the door at her right, Vi found the prince's bedroom. The four-poster bed was bare and the air was stale. The bedroom connected through a dressing room to a bathroom that had two doors, the second leading her back into the main room.

"Was this where you lived, Romulin?" Vi murmured, running her fingers lightly along the tabletop as she walked by the window. Had he been given this room as the younger son? Or had he taken what was currently Aldrik's room, since he'd been the royal child who was actually present?

Vi drew her attention inward, trying to imagine herself returning home to this room. She would've been happy enough, she supposed. At least, she thought the girl she had been would've found joy in this place.

This was not her world, and the emotions attaching her to the people and places in it became more and more like the tarp-covered furniture by the day—covered, unused, dusty.

"To work," Vi said, refocusing herself.

She started in the prince's bedroom, searching the most obvious places first. Vi crawled under the bed, feeling underneath the platform for any hidden compartments. She lifted the mattress, double-checking that there wasn't enough room for something like the crown to be hidden underneath.

Next, she checked behind the headboard and explored the mantel around the fireplace. She ran her fingers over the embellishments and carvings, pressing and pulling. Her fingers hooked on a small lever, hidden by a raised section of trim. She pulled, and there was a soft *click* to her right.

One of the built-in bookcases sighed as Vi pulled it away from the wall, revealing a narrow passageway that ran behind the bookcases to the chimney. It was certainly a hiding place for the prince—judging by the racy literature and sentimental tokens dutifully stored within.

But the crown wasn't there.

Vi placed everything back exactly as she found it and closed the hidden passage. She continued her sweep of the bedroom before moving on to the dressing room. All the while, Vi tapped the floor with the toe of her shoe, listening for fake boards.

Most of the prince's clothes had been packed away when he left for war, which made scouring the shelves easy. Vi found two other secret compartments built in false bottoms of the shelves. One had a lock of golden hair, a silver dagger, and a pile of notes. Vi promptly closed the compartment out of privacy, suspecting the hair to be Raylynn's.

The other compartment held a key, the outline of which was visible in the dust when she removed it. Vi flipped it over in search of markings that could offer a clue as to what it might unlock. The skeleton key was fairly large, but otherwise plain. The only embellishment was the Solaris seal stamped at the end.

Unhelpful.

Still, Vi pocketed the key and resumed her search. The key clearly hadn't been moved in some time, judging from the outline it left behind in the dust. It must unlock something important for him to hide it. She just hoped that "it" was more than a chest filled with scandalous tomes of daring women.

As she'd expected, the prince's royal apartment was filled with secret nooks in almost every room. Vi scoured the place from top to bottom, not stopping until she could be confident she'd explored every one. She found ten in total, including one servants' entry and passage that was void of any possible hiding spots.

The crown wasn't in any of these locations. Nor was anything that the key could unlock.

She was just placing the last of the fabric over the furniture when the ring around her finger grew warm. A glyph sizzled in her mind, begging for release. "*Narro hath,*" Vi murmured.

"Miss me?" Deneya's voice echoed to her from across the connection.

"Terribly."

"Then your agony will soon be over."

"How far are you?"

"I'm just about to start up the switchbacks now."

"Meet me in the Imperial Library." Vi paused, remembering what day and age she was in, now. Vhalla was present in the castle. Her chest tightened in a way that begged avoidance at all costs. "On second thought, the servant's entrance, the one not far from the water gardens."

"See you soon."

Vi released the glyph and did one last sweep of Baldair's room. Wherever the prince had hidden the crown, it wasn't here. Vi pursed her lips and left, heading down through the castle to meet Deneya.

The servant's entrance was busy at all times of day. Boards lined the main entry with schedules and memos. Someone was always coming or going, and no one paid Vi a second glance in her palace robes.

She perched herself on a bench just outside, watching the night fall as she waited. Soon enough, the silhouette of a woman cut against the watercolor sky as Deneya crested the hill.

"You're a sight for sore eyes." Vi stood.

"I'm marvelous, I know." Deneya smiled down at her. "It's good to see you, too."

"Let's find a place to board the horse. I doubt we'll get to use the palace stables again."

"Unfortunately." Deneya dismounted.

"I think I know a place."

"Lead the way." Deneya walked alongside Vi as she headed for an inn with a long row of stables that were usually unoccupied. "Any issues up here?"

"No, your end?"

"None."

Vi glanced at the pack the woman had over her shoulder, then to the saddlebags. "You have it?"

"Of course." Deneya patted her backpack and Vi could imagine the shimmering crown inside. "You find the real deal yet?"

"No, but we only just got here a few days before you."

"I know, that's why I thought you would've certainly found it by now." Deneya grinned.

"We need your help, clearly."

"Yes, you'd be lost without me," she proclaimed loftily.

"I did miss you." Vi nudged her shoulder against her friend's.

She snorted. "I doubt it. You've had a few days with Taavin all to yourself and judging from the glow around you, the alone time did you well."

Vi laughed and didn't even bother with a denial. "Yes, but now that you're back, it's nothing but work again. We must find the crown soon."

"What's the rush?"

"I'm not sure… a feeling?" Vi looked over her shoulder, feeling as if someone was following her. No one was there. The memory of the Tower—of Victor watching her movements without her realizing—was an unexpected companion in the castle. "I know Victor is usually the one to find it. And knowing what I know of him, once he finds it, he won't let it go."

"So we have to beat him to it," Deneya surmised. The statement brought Vi's thoughts to Baldair's empty room.

"Yes. But my fear is that we're already too late."

24

VI, TAAVIN, AND DENEYA BROKE the palace into segments in order to search for the crown.

Vi continued to search the royal quarters. Baldair might not have hidden it in his chambers, but he'd have access to every room in the Imperial wing of the palace. There were plenty more secret locations that were all potential hiding spots, and lots of locks for her to try the key on.

Deneya began looking through ledgers used by the palace guard. Vi supposed it was possible for Baldair to have entrusted the relic to his loyal soldiers. Though Deneya returned empty-handed day after day, which slowly squashed that theory.

Taavin remained assigned to the Tower of Sorcerers. He reported on overheard rumors, mostly from students; there were more tales of Vhalla's doings than anything relating to the crown. Whispers flew about how she had fallen from a tower rooftop and flown, how the crown prince was her personal tutor, and how Minister Victor wanted nothing more than to see her enrolled as the Tower's newest student.

Time whittled away Vi's patience. The crown began to haunt

her dreams. Night after night, she could imagine herself touching it, feeling the magic of Yargen seep into her. Day after day, she searched for that sensation, imagining feeling it on the briefest shift in the air.

Just when she was about to turn the whole castle upside down, fate and stones and rivers be damned, the military returned to the capital.

Vi, Taavin, and Deneya watched from the upper ramparts as palace staff and citizenry alike funneled into the Sunlit Stage, waiting for the military party to march up the mountain and make its grand arrival.

"They look so small and insignificant," Vi murmured.

"From this high up, everything looks small." Deneya leaned against the stone, looking down.

Vi wondered what the world looked like to the gods. Did they stand on walls higher than this? Walls that kept mortals from their divine domains? She could imagine Yargen staring down, and every mortal in the world being little more than grains of sand to be swept around by her hand.

"Here they come." Taavin pointed to the military party as it arrived. Cheers erupted for the Emperor and Baldair as they entered, a deafening roar that rolled across the whole mountainside.

"They certainly love him, don't they?"

"They do." Vi stared down at the speck that was Baldair. Somewhere in his mess of golden hair was the knowledge of what he'd done with the crystal crown.

"I feel bad for Aldrik… to be so hated when your brother is so loved," Deneya mused.

"His hardships prepare him for what's to come."

"That's grim."

Vi shrugged in reply.

"Now that the prince is back, does the plan change?" Taavin asked.

"We'll see." Vi stepped away from the stone railing and headed back inside the palace. "I'm going to see if I can steal a moment with Baldair."

"Why does she get all the fun?" Deneya asked Taavin.

"Because this is her destiny."

Vi came to a sudden stop. How she truly hated that word.

"What is it?" Deneya asked.

"I'm going to go this way. I'll meet you both back at our rooms later."

"Good luck." Taavin leaned forward, planting a warm kiss on her cheek before he followed Deneya in the opposite direction, down to their hideaway in the bowels of the palace.

Vi moved quickly through the servants' passages. She was one of many hustling to get from one place to the next. The return of half the royal family, even when expected, had turned the castle on its head.

Servants flowed in and out of the Imperial wing and Vi fell into step with them. By now, the guards had seen her come and go so many times that they hardly paid her any attention. Most of the people went up to the royal chambers at the top of the golden staircase. It was the one place Vi had yet to look because it was rarely unattended.

A war raged within her as she debated if she had time to head up there now. In the chaos, she might be able to poke around unnoticed. Ultimately, Vi went to the right for Baldair's rooms. She doubted he would've hid the crown up in his parents' chambers, unless he'd given it to his father. But if Tiberus Solaris had a crystal weapon, the whole world would know it.

However, on returning from a long trip, Baldair might immediately want to check the location of his prize. If she was lucky, he'd lead her right to it.

The servants were bustling in and out of the young prince's room, carrying trays of food and drink. Vi stepped off to the side, heading for the bedroom.

"Just where are you going?" a man asked.

"I'm checking the linens," Vi said.

"I was just in there, the bed is made."

"Did you check the towels?" The man nodded. "Extra sheets?"

"Why would the prince want extra sheets in his room?"

"Do you really need to ask that? This is Baldair we're talking about."

"Oh, Mother above." He muttered something else under his breath.

"Come on, I need your hands." A woman tugged on the servant's arm, successfully pulling him away from Vi.

As he left, Vi could hear him murmuring, "I haven't seen her around before…"

She disappeared into the bedroom, which was thankfully empty. Vi headed right back for the fireplace and pulled on the secret lever she'd found before. The bookcase opened with a soft *click* as the mechanism disengaged. Vi hurried over and stepped inside, closing it behind her. She listened through the wood as the commotion continued in the common area. Servants bustled about in the bedroom.

Then, silence.

Vi counted to fifty, then opened the hidden door slowly. On light feet, she stepped out and closed the shelf behind her. She'd learned every creaky board in this room from her investigations, and Vi made her way soundlessly into the dressing room, then into the bathroom. There wasn't another soul to witness her collecting towels into her arms.

She poised herself in front of the bathroom door that connected to the main room. The bundle of linens was shoved under one arm. Her other hand was on the doorknob.

Closing her eyes, Vi took a deep breath. Who would she be? Who did she need to be in this moment?

"Yargen, guide me," she whispered. It wasn't quite a prayer. More like… asking a friend for a favor.

The door to the main room opened, heralding male laughter, and Vi sprang into action. She pushed open the bathroom door at the same time as Baldair and two other young men entered through the main door. Her eyes met his.

"My prince!" Vi said, startled. She juggled the towels, allowing them to scatter to the floor. Baldair's laughter stopped and he regarded her with a confused and somewhat amused expression. Vi dropped to the floor, hastily gathering and folding the towels. "I'm so sorry. I was supposed to be gone, I know. But I realized the towels had not been properly refreshed for your arrival and I was terribly worried by the thought of you putting a musty towel to your face."

The words raced from her with an anxiousness Vi hadn't felt in some time. She couldn't place the source of the feeling. Her mind was a dark lake, smooth and glassy. Perhaps Yargen had heard her request and this was exactly what the prince needed to see and hear: a panicked young woman, unassuming, innocent, and ready to flatter him.

Two armor-clad feet appeared in her vision, followed by knees. Vi brought her gaze up to the prince who had knelt across from her, making a clumsy attempt at folding a towel.

"Forgive me, your highness," she murmured. "Not only have I ruined your return… but you are now doing a servant's work."

"There's nothing to forgive." He handed her the towel with a roguish smile. "Every time I return home, I hope a lovely woman is here to greet me. Really, I should be thanking you."

"You're truly incorrigible," a man Vi recognized as Craig muttered as he shut the door.

"I think what the prince is trying to say… is that you have nothing to worry about." The other man was at Vi's left, and passed her a much more carefully folded towel.

She paused, taken aback by the familiar face.

I know these eyes.

Daniel. Vi had seen him in the North, but only ever at a distance. This was the first time she'd been close enough to him to see Jayme in his features.

Her stomach twisted.

"Thank you," Vi murmured, collecting herself and the towel from Daniel's hands. She was here on a mission. Vi cleared her throat. "My prince, I understand if you need to report me to my superiors for not having everything prepared for your arrival."

"You don't really think I'm going to do that, do you?" He chuckled and stood.

Vi finished the last of her folds, standing as well. "I don't want to assume the will of a royal."

"I'm not my brother." Baldair shrugged. "Though, perhaps you could do me a favor?"

"Anything!"

"Help me out of this armor?" He knocked his breastplate.

"Really, Baldair? You're not here more than an hour and you're already trying to get some woman to undress you?" Craig said over a mouthful of food. He'd wasted no time in heading right for the spread laid out on the table.

"The task requires an extra set of hands," Baldair insisted.

"Mother forbid we're the ones to help you." Daniel chuckled, strolling over to the table as well.

"If you think I can help, then it'd be my honor." Vi smiled up at the prince.

"Then, follow me—"

"Wait," Craig interjected. She and Baldair turned. "Do… do I know you?"

"I don't know. Perhaps our paths have crossed in the palace," Vi said. "I've been here for a few years now," she lied deftly.

"Have you ever been a soldier?"

"I know the eyes of a soldier when I see one," Baldair proclaimed. He rested his thumb on her chin, knuckle underneath, and turned her face toward his. The prince made a show of studying her eyes. Vi supposed this would be the part when the young woman he flirted with would swoon. But she still floated in that glassy, dark lake of her mind. "These eyes are soft, tender. They haven't seen the trials of combat."

Vi smiled sweetly and batted her eyelashes, keeping her laughter at bay.

"I could've sworn I saw you in the North," Craig insisted, unrelenting. "I know your face from a battle."

She knew of the battle he referred to. It was in their first year—a night filled with fighting and fire, a night when Vi had helped Craig save Raylynn.

"My apologies, my lord." Vi kept her eyes down, the smile falling into an expression that resembled distress. "I really don't think—"

"Oh you've gone and upset her again. Don't mind him, Miss…"

"Ivy," Vi said hastily.

"Ivy, a lovely name."

"And possibly poisonous," Craig mumbled. Baldair shot him a glare.

"Follow me, Miss Ivy." Baldair led her into the bedroom.

"Yes, my prince."

"'Baldair' is fine." He stood in front of an armor stand, arms out.

"You'll have to tell me what to do, Baldair." Vi said the name as though it were a new pair of shoes—uncomfortable and not yet broken in. Her attempt seemed to delight him.

"Start with the sides, there are clasps there—yes, you found them."

Of course she did. Vi fought the urge to roll her eyes. It wasn't as if she'd seen every type of armor known to the continent. Vi diligently worked on getting the prince out of his armor, refraining from being too hasty or skilled but not allowing his instruction to carry on for too long. She didn't want to hamper their conversation.

"How is the front?" Vi asked as she continued to undo the buckles and clasps. "Will the war be over soon?"

"You didn't hear my father's declaration at the Sunlit Stage?"

"I was busy."

"Oh, right, well, we expect the North to fall soon."

"You don't sound happy about that." She helped hold the armor as he slid out of the main breastplate. Vi waited as the prince situated it on the armor stand.

"I'm happy the fighting will be over." Genuine conflict shone in his eyes. She realized this was the first time she'd ever had the chance to really talk with the man.

"You don't like war."

"What?" He roared with laughter as Vi helped him out of his chainmail. "I'm the creator of the Golden Guard, the most illustrious fighting force in all of Solaris. War isn't something I shy away from."

"I didn't say you did," she said thoughtfully. "I said you don't *like* it."

Baldair focused on the chainmail that pooled in his hands for a long moment. "Who *likes* it, really? Other than madmen." His voice was soft and somewhat distant, his expression oddly vulnerable.

"I agree with you." Vi knelt down to unfasten his greaves. "You're right. Who would say they liked war? War is awful and the longer it goes on, the uglier it becomes."

"You're not wrong."

"You know, I grew up in Oparium." Vi shifted the topic.

"You did?"

"Yes. When I was growing up, we didn't have many stories of

war, but we had plenty about pirates."

"I bet you did." He chuckled. Vi stood as he stepped out of his greaves.

"That summer… when you and Lord Jax and Lord Erion came to Oparium, that was what made me want to come to the castle." Baldair faced her. "My prince—"

"Baldair."

"Baldair," she repeated, glancing away as if still modest about using his name without title. "May I ask you something?"

"Anything, fair maiden."

"I heard a rumor you found the treasure. Is it true?"

Fear flooded his blue eyes. "I—"

"I'm sorry. Even if you had… I know, you can't say." Vi physically took a step back as she distanced herself from the topic. Baldair relaxed visibly. "I only thought of it now because of a story my grandmother told me when I was a girl."

"A story?"

"A tale of a vortex, of circles, of things repeating time after time— life and death, suffering and sacrifice, all hung in this vortex," her voice went soft and ominous. Baldair hung on every word. "She said there was one relic that could stop this vicious cycle of pain. It was the crown of the first Solaris king, bestowed on the true ruler of this land. That true king could command any loyalty, even loyalty from fate. He could bend destiny to his command."

His eyes widened slightly.

"Though, knowing granny… they were nothing more than stories from her softening mind." Vi shrugged and gave him a conspiratorial smile. "I merely thought, if such a power does exist… that you, a man of honor, would be the one I would want to wield it." She paused, allowing him to be enamored with her words for one more long moment. "If you did find it, then perhaps it's your destiny to use that power and save us all from war itself."

Baldair continued to stare at her before quickly plastering on a fake smile. "It's a wonderful story indeed. But I'm afraid you're right about it being nothing more than a story."

"No doubt. Now, is there anything else I can do for you?"

"No, thank you. My stomach insists on food in short order." He laughed lightly as they reentered the main room.

"We were getting worried." Craig's tone was the exact opposite of the sentiment.

"I gladly return him to you." Vi gave a bow.

"Gladly?" Baldair balked.

"Gladly." She winked and Craig and Daniel roared with laughter. "Excuse me, my lords."

Vi stepped out of the room and practically bounced down the hall. She'd put the crown in his mind, and Baldair would feel the need to go and check on it, if nothing else. But perhaps he'd also want to test if her words were true.

The prince was going to lead her to the crown. Now, all she had to do was—

She stopped in her tracks.

Victor crossed the main atrium, oblivious to her presence, and headed up to the Imperial quarters. Vi didn't know what business he had with the Emperor. But whatever it was, she could be certain of one thing: it wasn't good.

25

S HE WAS BEING IRRATIONAL.

There was no reason to think Victor's mere presence was a foul omen. Perhaps, when the Emperor returned, he summoned all the ministers one by one to give him updates on happenings in the palace. That seemed just as logical as the next thing.

Logical.

But not accurate.

In the years she'd traversed this world, across time and back, Vi had learned to trust her gut. More often than not, it was right. Sometimes, she had the wrong response—but the gut had the right sense.

Vi gripped the golden banister, staring up the staircase that led to the highest point of the palace. Without a second thought, she continued onward. Her brain tried to wander. The stubborn organ wanted to daydream about her parents living here and her being a girl, in this palace, rushing to meet them—all the trimmings of the happy childhood she never had.

Vi pushed away the thoughts and kept herself in the moment as she entered the Emperor's chambers behind another servant.

"Victor," Tiberus said from a nearby room. Vi followed the flow of servants and staff into an open antechamber, where the Emperor stood among weaponry and military fanfare. "You know I am very busy right now with the festival starting soon."

Victor's visit wasn't expected, then.

Vi kept her head angled away as she rounded the room to Tiberus. She held her breath as she accepted a piece of ornate plate from one of the servants undressing the Emperor, much as she had done for Baldair minutes ago. Tiberus didn't even so much as glance her way.

"I know, my lord." Victor's voice was deeper than she remembered it. He was still a boy in her mind. But the person before her now had the gaze of a man who'd set his sights on a prize. "But you told me to come to you with the results of my research on your future campaigns."

"Give that here," a woman hissed at her.

"Sorry," Vi mumbled.

Two blue eyes met hers. The woman tilted her head. "I don't know you."

"I'm new," Vi said hastily, turning away and going back for another piece of plate. She kept her focus on the conversation.

"You have found something useful?" Tiberus continued.

"Very useful. But tell me first, where is your eldest son now?" Victor said with a gleeful note. Vi was shocked he wasn't bouncing on his heels.

The Emperor turned to face the minister and arched a single brow. "Leave us," he commanded.

Servants filed out of the room with their heads down. Vi had no choice but to follow or be discovered. She trailed toward the end though, letting others go before her so she could listen as the Emperor continued to speak.

"Were it not for your manner, I would presume he would be making the necessary preparations for our court dinner for the start of the festival of the sun."

Vi rounded the corner as Victor said, "What do you know of the common girl named Vhalla Yarl?"

She barely resisted the urge to charge back. Pushing away the memories and daydreams of her own creation was one thing. Vi could keep herself focused. But hearing her mother's name on this man's tongue lit the spark in her like nothing had in years.

She's not your mother.

Vi knew that. She did. But the fire in her gut did not.

"Vhalla Yarl?" Tiberus repeated. "The name is not familiar. I usually make little effort to remember the names of the lowborn."

Vi continued to hover just outside the doorway. She folded her hands and kept her eyes forward. She was as still as a statue, even while the spark was an inferno within her.

"He has not sent one report to you about her? I'm sure it just slipped Aldrik's mind." Victor paused and Vi could almost imagine his wicked grin widening. "I am sure her name will be well known by you soon enough."

"Why?" Tiberus asked cautiously.

"Your son is with her now."

Why was Victor doing this? Vi kept her thoughts level. Was this to spite Aldrik out of a vendetta he'd long held against the prince for being the magical favorite? Or could it be more?

Victor knew by now that Vhalla was a Windwalker. Taavin's reports on the whisperings of the Tower had told Vi that much. All the sorcerers of the palace were abuzz with the presumed presence of a Windwalker.

If Victor was mentioning Vhalla to the Emperor, it could mean that he was trying to convince Tiberus to go hunting crystal weapons now that they had a Windwalker in their pocket. Victor was trying to make Tiberus the next Jadar, and convince him to use Windwalkers to get the crystals.

Vi had to switch the crown as soon as possible.

"Aldrik?" Surprise was apparent in Tiberus's voice. "Aldrik is not one to fraternize with—"

"Just what do you think you're doing?" The blue-eyed woman was back, grabbing her elbow and yanking Vi away from where she hovered in the doorway.

"I was waiting to see if the Emperor needed anything," Vi said, wrenching her arm away.

The woman's fingers snapped back around Vi's arm and she

yanked again. They were back in the main room. Several curses nearly flew off Vi's tongue. Cursing the woman was better than splitting her in half. "You were eavesdropping."

"I was not."

"Foul girl!" The woman was a blur as she slapped Vi. She blinked, dazed. Vi had taken worse strikes, but this one was utterly unexpected and caught her off-guard. "I know what it looks like when one of your ilk is eavesdropping. It's why I don't have the likes of you up here."

"The likes of me?" Vi rubbed her cheek. Clearly, this woman was the mother hen of the Imperial domain. She'd been lucky not to run into her sooner.

Her eyes raked over Vi. "Dirty shoes. Windswept hair. Basic robes. Tell me and tell me honestly, were you appointed up here today or is this some clever little attempt to see the Emperor and his family up close and personal?"

"I was appointed," Vi said. *As if anyone would be honest in this situation.*

"If you're lying, I will have the guards cut out your tongue and hang it with the laundry."

"The guards won't do that," Vi blurted before she could stop herself. The woman only seethed further.

"Tell me who appointed you and you won't have to find out what the guards will and won't do."

"I was appointed by—"

"She was appointed by me," Victor said from the entrance to the Emperor's personal armory. "She's attending me today, to assist me in getting ready for the Imperial events this evening."

"Minister." The woman stepped away from Vi and bowed her head. "I am compelled to regretfully inform you that I caught her listening in—"

"Surely you were mistaken," Victor interrupted in a tone as icy as his magic. "She is one of my most loyal servants in this palace." He approached her. "Isn't that right?"

"Yes, my lord," Vi ground out, bowing her head.

"Good, come along then." Victor started for the door and Vi was helpless to do anything other than follow. She kept a few steps behind him on the stairs. Magic sizzled on her fingers, on her tongue. Even though there was a good distance between them, she felt ensnared; she was looking for the most immediate escape. Victor startled her when he spoke. "They hate us."

She kept silent, which forced him to glance over his shoulder.

"They hate us, *sorcerers*, because they don't understand. And what they don't understand, they fear. And what they fear, they seek to snuff out of this world." She pursed her lips, letting him soliloquize to his heart's content. "But I'm not like them. I do not fear what I don't understand." He reached the bottom of the stairs and stopped, turning to face her. Vi looked down at him, remaining a few steps away. "I do not understand what you are. But I do not fear you."

"You should," Vi whispered ominously.

A smirk cracked his lips. "No… you're like me, just a few steps ahead on this journey, aren't you?"

"More than a few." Vi's chest tightened to the point of quivering. He saw her. Somehow, out of everyone, Victor had been the one to see right through her. He could see she wasn't like the rest. Until now, Taavin had been the only one to peer into the corners of her that no one else could see. Vi hated that Victor, of all people, would be the second to do so.

Let him see your sharp edges, a voice whispered to her. *Let him see you have achieved what he can only dream of—an evolution from the shell of humanity that holds him back.*

Vi's hand tightened around the banister.

"As far as I'm concerned, you work with me, or you are against me." He took a few steps back, giving her additional space. Vi didn't move. "The choice is yours."

At that moment, Baldair emerged from the side hall, nearly stumbling right into Victor. "*Oof*—Excuse me, Minister!"

"The excuse lies with me." Victor took a step to the side and Vi saw the mask of a kindly sage slip over his features with the deftness of an actor's well-practiced costume change. "I shouldn't get in the way of determined princes."

"I wasn't looking where I was going." Baldair shook his head and his gaze met Vi's. She held it. He backed away as though he were staring down a monster.

"Is everything all right, my prince?" Victor glanced between her and Baldair.

"Yes, of course!" Baldair chuckled. "Now, if you'll both excuse me… I have a bottle of wine I've been saving for something special and I think the festival celebrations will be just that occasion." He retreated quickly and Vi descended the last of the stairs with forced slowness, not wanting to look like she was ready to race after him, even if she was.

"Even the prince fears you on instinct," Victor said to her in whispered awe, so that none of the servants passing them would hear. "I'm right. You are the woman from all those years ago."

Vi glanced at him from the corners of her eyes. So many had written off her similarity to a young woman they'd once met to faulty memory. Just a bit of insistence, and her agelessness had thrown them off her trail. But not Victor.

"I know you are." He took a step forward. "I feel your magic. It is the same."

"You cannot comprehend what I am. My being was not made for a mind like yours." The words resonated from deep within and Vi followed their will on instinct.

"It's the crystals, isn't it? They gave you this power. They have made you ageless." He stepped forward, encroaching on her personal space and staring down at her. "What else do they enable you to do?"

"More than you could possibly know," Vi sneered up at him. She turned to leave.

"Help me find them. Work with me. I am not Egmun. I will be a willing student."

Vi froze, then slowly turned to face him once more. "I would see this world burn again before I worked with you," she whispered.

The man before her was nothing more than an extremely gifted sorcerer. He had a sordid history. He had experienced triumphs and pitfalls, most of which Vi didn't understand.

He was as flawed as any other human and just as capable of great and wonderful deeds.

Except in Vi's world, this man had murdered the people she called family. In Vi's world, he'd nearly cost her parents everything… just as he had in various ways across every other world, according to Taavin's recollections.

This man wasn't a stone in the river. He was a glacier, cold and unfeeling. That was how she would treat him.

"Then it is to be war between us," he whispered ominously and, for one brief second, Vi wondered if this moment had been an opportunity to guide him into more than the hateful man she had always heard him to be. Was it her insistence that he was wicked that pushed his wickedness over the edge?

"It has always been war." Vi put her back to him and strode out of the Imperial quarters. Her feet were hasty beneath her, but her head was held high. This wasn't a retreat. She was keeping two steps ahead of him.

Two became four.

Four became six.

She slipped into the back passages and began to run. Vi sprinted through the darkness, into the depths of the palace, keeping in a scream.

Though what she longed to scream about, she didn't quite know.

Vi slowed her feet and took a breath. She side-stepped behind a tapestry and emerged in a hall that led to the wine cellars. The soft clank of a lock disengaging in the distance caught her attention.

So, Baldair really was heading to the cellars.

"*Durroe watt radia,*" Vi breathed and felt invisibility slip over her as she moved forward. "*Durroe sallvas tempre.*" A glyph wrapped around her other wrist, masking the echo of her footsteps.

Light danced on the barreled ceiling ahead as Vi emerged into a large, underground wine cave. The walls on all sides, three floors down, were lined with casks. Most seemed new and well-tended. But farther down, the shelves became cluttered with cobwebs and caked in dust.

At the bottom floor, the barrels were locked in vaults. The wine was kept prisoner down here, most likely for its own safety. Some vintages had been exclusive to the Solaris family for generations. One bottle could be worth a fortune.

Baldair stood by a vault in the far corner. He held a torch in his hand and peered through the bars into the inky blackness.

"It's safe," he murmured. "No one has come for it."

Vi walked over, standing behind him, just far enough away that he wouldn't feel her breath on his shoulder. She followed the prince's gaze to the bottom left corner. The cask there looked like any of the others. Vi wouldn't have thought anything was different about it if not for the prince's sole focus on one, single barrel.

"And no one will use it," Baldair said firmly, walking away. The light of his torch retreated with him, enveloping her in darkness. Vi watched as that mote of flame danced all the way up along the walkways and out the entry high above.

"You're the wisest of them all," she whispered.

Baldair likely didn't even understand what the crown truly was. But he did understand that some powers were not meant for mortal hands. She pulled the iron key from her pocket and slotted it into the lock on the vault door.

It fit perfectly.

Vi extended her *sallvas* glyph to envelop the whole vault as she unlocked the door. Iron on iron squealed loudly as she swung open the bars. But Baldair was none the wiser, if he was even still close enough to hear at all.

She knocked on the barrels. Sure enough, the one in the lower corner sounded hollow. With a grunt and brute force, she pulled out the barrel. It was lighter than a wine cask should be and there was no sloshing liquid within. The top was nailed on clumsily, as if it had been removed once by an unskilled hand.

"*Juth calt.*" Glyphs flared around the nails, splintering the wood. Pale blue light washed over her face as Vi peered down into the barrel. Her pulse quickened; her breath hitched. She reached forward without hesitation, like reaching for a lover, a child, a part of herself that had been missing for eons.

Her fingers closed around the crown. The light brightened in intensity until the world went white.

She stood in a room beyond time. It was blindingly bright, yet she could see perfectly. Heat washed over her, but she was quickly cooled by unseen breezes.

A window was cut from the brightness. Vi looked through it, out onto the greatest map she'd ever seen. Hills and valleys rolled into plains and mountains. All kinds of people occupied these lands, making them their own. Cultivating them with the magic she'd bestowed on them.

She had bestowed magic?

Someone moved her head for her. The world around her changed as Vi's eyes looked in a different direction.

No, she wasn't looking through her own eyes. Because Vi saw herself enveloped in a bed of light opposite the body she occupied, staring back at her. Vi saw her body was hollow and fading. She had not been made for this world, and now she had no place in it.

This was the end.

Or, perhaps not.

"Time for time," a voice said, speaking with the force of every man, woman, and child on the earth below them.

"Time for time." The words echoed, but Vi didn't know who spoke them. Was it her? Or was it the body she was in?

She was suddenly falling. The vision slipped away as Vi reemerged into her physical form, where it lay on the cold floor of the Solaris wine cellar. She blinked several times, staring into the dim light her body was emitting.

Just like with the scythe, Yargen's essence had sought her out and she was helpless to try and refuse it. The magic seeped into her flesh, rejoining its other severed pieces and leaving only shards of obsidian behind. One by one, she would collect the last remnants of the goddess's power within her.

She would add up the pieces of Yargen until what the world had known as Vi was nothing more than that hollow, fading ghost.

Time for time.

"I know what I must do," she whispered to the living goddess within her. Vi would give her time on this earth for Yargen. The goddess demanded a body—in particular, the one Vi was merely borrowing.

She knew her true purpose now. Yargen had shown it to her. To fulfill it, she first had to peel herself off the floor. The next step was crushing the obsidian shards to dust under her boot. Then, she carefully put the barrel back where it was. Vi didn't suspect Baldair would return so soon after ensuring the crown was safe, but just in case he did, she didn't want him to be suspicious.

After that, it was merely a matter of planting the fake crown for Victor. "It's all going according to plan," Vi murmured. She knew Yargen could hear her. The goddess was watching and waiting in that ethereal prison for the moment she could be whole and present in the mortal realm once more. As Vi's presence faded in the world, Yargen's brightened. "We'll switch places, and you'll save this world."

Vi ascended the stairs and out of the wine cellar. As she walked, she fiddled with the watch around her neck. It had suddenly become heavy, constricting.

It felt more like a noose than a necklace.

"W E'RE LEAVING," VI ANNOUNCED as she entered the shared room she, Deneya, and Taavin had been using as their base of operations while in the palace.

"You found it." Taavin didn't mince words.

"I did." Vi looked at her palm. "The power is already in me."

"Where was it?" Deneya asked.

"Baldair hid it in a vault in the cellars." Vi held up the iron key. "That's what this was for."

"A miracle he kept it hidden and safe." Taavin sounded genuinely impressed. Vi was forced to agree.

"We're going to take the shifted crown and place it in a treasure vault or storeroom somewhere." Vi went to the back of the room, retrieving the fake crown from the sack where they kept it.

"Not return it to Baldair's hiding place?" Deneya asked.

"No, if we put it back in Baldair's hiding place, we risk Victor raising the prince's suspicions when he finally moves to take the fake crown. If Baldair has reason to think it's gone, he might raise the alarm and prompt everyone to look for the crown."

"Which would likely involve going to his father," Taavin murmured.

"Exactly." If the Emperor thought he had a crystal Weapon before the War in the North was over, it could change things dramatically. "Furthermore, the last thing we want is Victor to feel rushed to inspect the crown, or take it to the caverns when we're not ready, and risk him finding out its fake." No matter how good the shift looked and felt, Vi still feared Victor would somehow see right through it.

"So how do you propose we orchestrate Victor finding the fake crown without Baldair realizing his hiding spot was compromised?" Taavin stood from the chair he'd been sitting in. It was positioned opposite the sofa where Deneya sat, a now-forgotten carcivi board on the table between them.

"Before we leave, I'll sneak into Baldair's room and return the key to its previous hiding spot. Baldair has already checked on the crown once and believes it secure. If we don't give him a reason to, he shouldn't check again," Vi postulated. "Deneya, you take the crown and hide it in a vault somewhere. Falsify some records with the guard that will leave just enough of a trail for Victor to follow over the coming months. Let's not let him find it too quickly."

"You got it." Deneya stood and crossed to Vi, taking the crown from her.

"And I assume I'll give Victor his first breadcrumb?" Taavin asked.

"That was my thought as well."

"I approve of this plan," Taavin murmured. "It keeps things tidy. No need for Baldair to go making waves. And Victor stays on track with the crown."

"We're glad you approve. You know how important it is to both of us." Deneya shot him a playful look and Taavin rolled his eyes.

"I'll go take care of this." Deneya held up the bag with the crown. "And let you know what trail I can set up."

"Then tonight, I'll sneak into the Tower," Taavin said.

"And I'll sneak into Baldair's room at the same time." Vi remembered the servants' passage she discovered. With her glyphs, she could slip into his closet unheard and unseen. "We can start for the North tomorrow and get the axe."

"There's a stop we'll make first in the Crossroads."

"For what?" Vi asked, not able to spare her voice from exasperation at the idea of another delay.

"I'm going to let you two talk that over. Be back!" Deneya fled hastily.

"Vhalla will head there with the army, and that's where you must read her fortune. In doing so, she'll charge the watch with her essence and link it to us and Yargen. That's the key to ensuring the—"

"Birth of a new Champion," she finished for him. Vi stepped forward, looming over the chair in which he sat. "There won't be another Champion."

"Vi, let's not do this." He sighed.

"There won't be," she said softly. "I've seen it, Taavin. The crown showed me."

She could almost hear the echo of his heart racing. His eyes widened a fraction, their pupils dilating. The air around him thrummed with anxious energy. Her fingers twitched, begging to reach forward and take the power of the Caverns from within him.

Return it to me.

He stood suddenly and stepped away from her and the movement jarred Vi from the almost trance-like state she was in. Her hand was outstretched, as if she had been about to grab him. But Vi hadn't given her body permission to move. She snatched her hand back, holding it to her chest as if it were wounded.

"What have you seen?" he whispered.

"The end of it all." *It ends with me*, she wanted to say. She would be the last one standing, before she gave the goddess her remaining hours. "We are on the right path." Vi studied his face as conflict raged across it. "I expected you to be happy about this news."

"Hope is a fragile thing." Didn't she know it. "For all I want to believe we're on the right path… the stones in the river remain. Our duty remains."

"Seeing the birth of a new Champion is not your duty," Vi said sharply. "Saving this world is."

"Part of saving it is ensuring it doesn't end," he retorted. "We finish things here and head West to the Crossroads. From there, we'll rejoin the Imperial army and swap the axe."

Taavin started for the door, but Vi remained in place. She wished she could make him understand, wished things were still simple, as simple as they had ever been, between them. But something held her back... only for a moment.

Vi broke free of whatever tethers were holding her, raced after him, and wrapped her arms around his waist. She clutched him tightly, her cheek on his back. Taavin's warmth seeped into her and thawed the icy indifference that had been trying to encase her.

He felt like him, and she like her.

Yargen's magic was quiet.

"There's a point when we won't be able to run from it anymore," she whispered.

"I know."

"Do you?"

"I do."

All they had ever had was borrowed time. Eventually the choice would have to be made to risk everything, and that choice was nearly upon them. The moment she held the axe, there would be no going back. The flame of Yargen would be extinguished. Its magic would be used to restore Yargen in Vi, and its ashes used to summon Raspian.

"Then we'll follow along until the axe," Vi said, sparing him the agony of spelling it out bluntly.

His hand covered hers. "Thank you."

She nodded and closed her eyes. For a little longer, they could enjoy these fleeting moments of peace; they could enjoy each other.

Because if what Vi saw truly came to pass... neither of them was long for this world.

It took the army a few months to finally arrive in the Crossroads. The military arrived carried on the back of desperation, a sandstorm on their heels.

Tales of Vhalla Yarl were whispered on every tongue in the

days following. People spoke of her bravery, of the power of the Windwalker, of her running into the storm head-first and saving them all. Vi was certain there were embellishments here and there; much like the rumors Taavin heard in the Tower of Sorcerers, every story was more fantastic than the last.

But there was also truth there.

Vhalla Yarl had performed a feat that had endeared and indebted thousands to her.

Then, one morning, out of nowhere, Vi woke up from a tortured dream feeling filled with purpose. She slipped out of bed, well before Taavin or Deneya rose, and silently dressed. Her two companions didn't so much as stir as she donned the traditional robes of a Western future seer.

She traversed down the stairs and silently began to get the shop in order, placing things just so on instinct. Her hands moved like a puppet's, obliging silent commands she'd been ignoring since absorbing the crown. An hour had passed when she realized she wasn't alone. Vi didn't know how long it had been, but Taavin stood at the foot of the stairs that led up to their apartment.

"What is it?" The man was shirtless, his broad chest and sculpted abdomen on display. Vi knew it well. Her fingers had run over those carved muscles countless times since the day she'd made them. Seeing him sparked yearning. It sparked emotions in her that wouldn't serve her well today. So she looked away.

"It's today."

"What is?"

"Vhalla Yarl will come to me today."

"How do you know?" He approached.

"I just do." Vi shook her head, staring at the door that led to the main market of the Crossroads. It seemed so long ago that they'd purchased this place and she'd sculpted roses in honor of Fiera.

The sentimentality made her weary.

"Then today it is," he said without a trace of doubt, slipping his fingers into hers. Vi faced him.

"I need to do this alone," she whispered.

"You've never operated the shop alone."

"I know."

"What will you do about the illusions for your eyes? How will she believe you're peering into the future without them to make your eyes glow red?"

"I'm not sure." Vi shook her head, trying to shake off the creeping, crawling hands working their way up her spine. They'd grab hold of her mind and who knew when they would give it back. Her fingers tightened around his, holding onto Taavin like a tether. "Please, trust me," she whispered.

"I do." He cupped her cheek thoughtfully, bringing her eyes to his. "Immeasurably and completely."

"Thank you." She leaned forward, kissing his lips gently. "You and Deneya wait upstairs. I'll come up when I'm finished."

He nodded, his nose rubbing against hers. But he didn't step away. "Is everything all right?"

"What?"

"You haven't been the same since we left Solarin… Is everything all right?"

"I've been fine." She rubbed his arm reassuringly. At least, she hoped that's the impression she gave.

"Don't lie to me." He pulled away, staring down at her. "I see you."

"You always have." Vi looked back to the door. The market was setting up for the day. "I'll be better once we have the final crystal weapon in hand."

"Do you really think that?" he murmured under his breath.

"What?" Vi wasn't sure she heard correctly.

"Nothing, it's nothing." Taavin smiled. "Good luck today." He finally retreated.

Vi returned her attention to her preparations. She opened the shop for the day by unlocking the iron gate and pushing it aside.

"One more thing," Vi murmured. She unhooked the chain from around her neck and slowly placed it into a box on one of the shelves. How Vhalla was supposed to see it, of all things, Vi didn't know.

But this was how it was meant to be. Of that, she was certain.

There was nothing more to do but wait.

"Let's look in here," a man's voice said in the afternoon near her doorway. The sound shot electricity up her spine and she stood straighter, pausing her pacing to look.

The curtain to the shop lifted and Vhalla appeared, followed by Daniel. Vi watched as the brown-haired woman entered the room, running her fingers over the cases at its center.

"*Irashi*, welcome." The western tongue put her into character, and Vi sauntered over to Vhalla and Daniel. She leaned against the cases containing all manner of objects gathered for future telling. "Welcome to the finest curiosity shop in all the land. And what can I help you with today?"

"I think we're just looking." Vhalla stepped back, as though Vi was about to bite her.

"No one is 'just looking.' All desire." Vi folded her arms. "Tell me, what is yours?"

"Sorry to disappoint. Let's go, I'm hungry." Vhalla grabbed Daniel's arm, steering him to the door.

"There is not one curiosity you have, Vhalla Yarl?" She stopped short at Vi's use of her name. Daniel stepped forward, holding out an arm, as if to guard her. Vi smiled thinly at the unnecessary protection. "I know your winds will not tell you what the flames will tell me."

"How do you know my name?" Vhalla whispered.

"I can know many things, and tell more, if you wish it. The fire burns away all lies." She spoke on instinct, giving herself to the sensation that had roused her from sleep and had guided her all day.

"You're a sorcerer."

"I am a Firebearer." Vi nodded.

"What's your name?" Vhalla found some bravery, pushing away Daniel's arm and stepping forward.

"I've had many names. I could give you one, or I could let you choose a name for yourself. Then it will be something we alone can share."

"Tell me the name you would like me to call you. Invented or otherwise."

"Vi," she said simply, after little debate. If anyone in this world was to know her true name, it would be Vhalla Yarl. "Would you like me to read your curiosities?"

"Read our curiosities?" Daniel chimed in.

"I am a Firebearer. I am one with the flames, and with my eyes I can see into the future. You come to me with curiosities, *questions*, in your heart, and I will give you the answers."

"I'll do it," Vhalla said suddenly. It brought a smile to Vi's lips though the smile didn't feel quite like hers. This wasn't her joy. This was the contentedness of the goddess within her.

"You must pick four things: three to burn, one to hold." She motioned around the room.

"Are you sure this is a good idea?" Daniel whispered into Vhalla's ear.

"It'll be fine. Why not live a little? I am here, and somehow she knew my name," Vhalla replied as she scanned the items available to her.

The first thing Vhalla chose was a silver plume from a jar of quills.

The next item Vhalla chose was a bunch of wheat, followed by a handful of rose petals.

But the most important thing was the last thing—something to hold.

Vhalla lifted a chain from a box and Vi let out her breath slowly as not to be an audible sigh of relief. The woman had selected the silver watch Vi had worn through time, and the one that would ensure the birth of a new Champion.

Time for time.

"This… this is what I will hold." Vhalla crossed back to her.

"An interesting spread. Come." Vi took the goods to burn and led Vhalla to the back room where a fire burned in a pit on the floor. "Are you certain you wish an observer?" Vi looked pointedly at Daniel who had followed them. "I will read the futures as I see them."

"I suppose… if you don't mind?" Vhalla said to Daniel.

"I'll wait right out here." Daniel got the hint, and slipped back out the heavy curtain and into the main shop.

With that settled, Vi knelt before the flames. She raked her hands through the coals and Vi began by making a few soot marks on Vhalla's cheeks and brow. She hesitated for just a moment, staring into the brown eyes of her mother.

No, this wasn't her mother. *Focus. Don't get lost in old memories.* She didn't want to feel anything toward this woman.

In that moment, Vi didn't want to feel anything at all. She gave herself fully over to the guiding hand of Yargen.

"Vhalla Yarl, blessed bird of the East. The one who can soar without wings. The first chick to fly the cage. The first to return to our land." She leaned back and began to throw the items into the flames. With each one, she poured her magic into the fire to make it roar.

The flames danced from white to orange, to a crimson so deep it was nearly black. The color changing was new, and Vi had no idea what it meant. She leaned forward on instinct, dipping her face into the flames.

"The present burns away, leaving the future to rise from its ashes." Vi reached down, grabbed a fistful of ash, and threw it into the air. "You will march to victory, and it will be won upon your silver wings." *Go to war, Vhalla, and win.* "But the winds of change you will set free will also shatter the tender hope on which you fly." *Victor will rise to power, and nearly everything you thought you loved will be threatened.* "You will lose your dark sentry." *Only to see him rise again as an Emperor.*

Vhalla clutched the watch with white knuckles as she spoke. Vi could almost see the girl trembling.

"Two paths will lie before you: night and day," Vi continued. "Go west by night. Fade into the comforting obscurity of a shroud of darkness. You will find a familiar happiness there, if you can ignore yearnings for the sun."

Go west? Why go west? She wanted to ask. But her mouth was not her own. Panic rose. Vi wanted to claw at her throat, but her hands weren't her own.

"The other road will burn away your falsehoods by the light of dawn. You will own your wants for all to see. But take caution, for the fire that will expose you will give birth to an even greater power that will consume the land itself.

"And now, for payment."

"Ah, right." Vhalla put down her sack, her hands still trembling as she fished for gold.

"I do not want coin."

"What do you want then?"

"That watch." Vi's hand pointed to the one Vhalla had been holding. The one that had been carried from another world, marked by Yargen, and was now imbued with Vhalla's energy.

"This one? All right, of course."

Vhalla passed it over, and as she did, Vi felt a shock of magic shoot up her arm. It was the same feeling as when she touched a crystal. Her watch had always been an item of fate, but its purpose had shifted. The token now waited for the moment it would be returned.

"Our current business has concluded." Vi stood. Vhalla slipped into her shoes, all but running toward Daniel. Vi watched as they left, adding ominously, "Heed my words, Vhalla Yarl," before the young woman disappeared onto the street beyond.

She collapsed with a gasp, clinging to the door frame to keep upright. Her body had been held by puppet strings as she'd acted out the motions at the commands of another.

"This was what you always wanted, isn't it? A puppet in mortal form?" Vi rasped, feeling sensation return to her limbs. Her skin tingled in response, as if to say a delighted *yes*. She pushed herself off the ground, standing as tall as she could, but knowing just how small she was. She'd seen it, from Yargen's view: the world was little more than a speck. "You'll have it. But not for a little longer. Give me a little longer." Vi's attention drifted to the stairs.

Inside her mind, began a persistent background percussion.

Tick... tock...

The countdown ran not to the end of the world. But to the end of her.

S ORICIUM WAS A DESOLATE wasteland compared to Vi's memories of the thriving capital of the North.

They arrived with the military as soldiers once more. The Imperial forces had been split after an assassination attempt on Vhalla's life failed. Baldair, Aldrik, and the Emperor all took a different path to Soricium, in yet another variation from the worlds Taavin knew. Unfortunately, Vhalla traveled with the Emperor. And since Vi, Deneya, and Taavin were under Baldair, they had a long march without eyes on Vhalla or Aldrik.

Vhalla was the first to arrive in the Northern capital. Alone. Something had gone wrong involving the prince along the way. Vi heard stories of Vhalla's heroism, and much like in the Crossroads following the sandstorm, each one was more impossible than the last.

There was no one they could ask for the exact details. So Vi, Taavin, and Deneya spent their days agonizing, holding their breath, and waiting. Surely, Vhalla and Aldrik couldn't die. At least, she wanted to believe that. But if the goal was to change things, then she had to become comfortable with *anything* changing. These people didn't mean anything to her, not really.

Yet, as the days passed, Vi realized she didn't want to imagine a world without Vhalla or Aldrik. They were not her parents, but much like Jax, they wore the faces of the people she loved. She wanted to save this world for them, even if they were nothing to her.

Or rather, she was nothing to them.

When she finally did see Aldrik and Vhalla, together again, in the flesh, Vi felt ten stone lighter.

"I knew they'd be fine," Deneya said as she followed Vi up to the top of the ridge that surrounded the basin that contained Soricium. They went to the axe together, Taavin catching some of the few hours of sleep he needed back in their tent.

"You did not." Vi glanced over her shoulder. No matter how many times Vi came up here, the sight still jarred her. The Empire had burned and cut down every tree of the forest, save for the most sacred, which remained safe behind the walls of the fortress.

"I did," she insisted. "Yargen is looking out for the girl."

Vi snorted. Yargen was too busy clawing at Vi's ribcage and skull, seeking control over her body, to focus on Vhalla Yarl. "Either way, I'm glad."

"Is the tomb far?" Deneya asked, changing the conversation.

"No, it's just beyond the top of the ridge." Vi led Deneya into the forest, following a familiar path. This was a new world, but her feet still knew the way.

"Seems like such an obvious place for the axe to be."

"Only because we know what to look for. The North is filled with ruins like this. The Empire doesn't know what's important and what isn't."

Deneya folded her hands and placed them behind her head, strolling. Ahead, the towering stones of familiar ruins loomed. Vi's feet slowed.

"It was night the last time I came here, too." The ruins looked almost identical to how they did in her memory. "It was the first time I saw the end of the world."

"Let's hope this time is more cheerful." Deneya clasped her shoulder. "We're only here for a look, right?"

"For now." Though Vi was already bracing herself for the first time her fingers closed around the axe. Each of the crystal weapons showed her a vision more vivid and important than the last. "The entrance is this way."

She led Deneya to the far back side of the ruins. Unlike when she had last been here, when obsidian had lined the opening, there were now live crystals with jagged points barring entry. In her time, her mother had taken the axe, and the crystals had died. It was the very act Vi and Deneya were working to circumvent.

Resting her hand on one of the crystals, Vi reached out into the network of magic and affirmed that the crystals stemmed from a single source. The axe was within, still safe and sound. The stones crackled and shrank to her will. Exercising control of them was becoming all too easy.

"After you." Vi motioned down the path.

"Oh, why thank you, fair lady." Deneya gave a bow with a flourish that made Vi bark with laughter.

"But of course, oh noble knight." Vi held out her hand as if she was escorting Deneya to a ball. With a snicker, Deneya took it and they dusted off the nobility neither of them needed any longer, parading forward.

Deneya's laughter faded as they reached the circular center of the ruins. Crystals lined the walls, pulsing faintly with magic. Moonlight streamed through an oculus in the roof, casting an eerie ring around the axe embedded in a crystal-covered pedestal.

"This is it, then."

"It is." Vi gazed at the axe, as though it were about to grow a mouth and begin speaking to her. If it could, the secrets it could tell. Judging by the power that hung in the air, the axe hadn't been moved since it was originally placed here by the daughter of the Champion. It was one of the few places on the Dark Isle where the crystals hadn't ever been touched. "This is a place of great purpose," she whispered.

"It makes me feel uncomfortable."

"Does it?" Vi tore her eyes away to look at Deneya.

"Yes… as though everything here is on a delay. Or that we've stepped into another world."

"Perhaps we have…" Vi trailed off. Her attention was on the axe once more. Her presence was already empowering the weapon, imbuing the air between her and it with divine energy. She thought of the otherworldly place Yargen waited.

"Then all the more reason for me to get this over with as quickly as possible." Deneya stepped forward. Vi matched the movement and the woman held out a hand. "Don't worry, I won't touch it. Just taking some measurements."

Vi eased away, folding her arms to keep them from lashing out. She'd lunge for Deneya to keep her from the axe.

Turning, Vi put her back to the weapon as Deneya began to measure the handle and blade. Some part of her couldn't bear to see another person so close to the crystal weapon.

Nervous energy rose within her and Vi began to pace. This wouldn't take too long. Deneya didn't need much. She needed to make an axe that was *relatively* close in shape and size, not perfectly identical. Vi would use the shift to handle the rest. They would leave soon.

What was taking so long?

She lapped the tunnel once more and froze as she reached its mouth. Soft voices echoed to her.

"Has anyone ever gone in?" That was undeniably Vhalla Yarl's voice. She was here. Yargen above, why was she here?

"In? No," a masculine voice responded, one Vi recognized but couldn't quite place. It wasn't Aldrik. Which then begged the question: *Why was Vhalla here in the middle of the night with a man who wasn't Aldrik?*

Too many questions, not enough time for answers. "*Durroe watt ivin.*" An illusion fell like a curtain over the opening. Just in case they somehow saw through it, Vi blocked the entry, crystals growing with a wave of her hand.

"What the—"

Vi clamped her hand over Deneya's mouth. "They're here," Vi whispered.

"Who?" Deneya said just as softly when Vi released her face.

"Vhalla Yarl and someone else."

"Taavin said she wasn't coming until the end of the war."

"Taavin was wrong." Vi cursed under her breath. "I've illusioned the only opening… they should leave." Her eyes drifted to the crystal axe. She should've just taken it and been done with this place.

They waited in breathless silence. *Let them leave*, Vi willed. She didn't know what it would mean if Vhalla somehow got the axe now.

She'd listened to stories of nearly a hundred worlds from Taavin's memories, and in none of them did Vhalla Yarl get the axe before the war was over.

"Wait, what are you doing?" Vhalla's male companion asked.

"We have to go in through the top," Vhalla responded.

Deneya cursed under her breath and turned to Vi. *Now what?* she mouthed as Vhalla and the man continued discussing the impossibilities of the climb.

"*Durroe watt ivin*," Vi said and felt an illusion slip over her shoulders.

"Lovely makeover. You'll be so mysterious you'll scare her away." Deneya spilled her sarcastic words hastily.

"That's the hope," Vi replied back in all seriousness. "We don't want her taking the axe until we've had a chance to replace it with the fake." She had no interest in repeating her mistake in letting others take the crown.

"So you're going to scare her away." Comprehension lit up Deneya's face brighter than the soft light of the crystals.

"Try to. Help me?"

"Always."

Soft panting stole their attention. "*Durroe watt radia*," she and Deneya both whispered in unison, a moment before Vhalla leaned over the opening above and let out a soft gasp as she beheld the contents of the cavern within.

Don't do it, Vi pleaded silently as she watched the woman inch toward the edge.

Her plea went ignored, as Vhalla stepped off into the empty air. Magic flared up around the young woman with the unique signature Vi recognized from her own mother. She fell gracefully to a large crystal, until her foot slipped and she whacked her head.

Vi bit back a groan. Out of everything Vhalla Yarl faced, Vi would rebel against fate and all the gods that wrote it, if Vhalla died from a clumsy slip and fall and *that* was what ended the world, somehow.

But Vhalla, thankfully, didn't die from a tumble onto a rogue crystal. She stood, walking through the room in awe, touching the tips of crystals along the way. Vi watched as they responded to her magic, tilting her head slightly. The pulses of power were similar to Vi's own early experimentations with crystals.

Vhalla's eyes were on the blade, as she approached with shuffled steps. She inspected it, closed her eyes, and took a deep breath. As if sensing Vi's watchful gaze, she looked over her shoulder, and then back to the weapon. Vi could see Vhalla's uncertainty and chose to capitalize on it. Dropping her illusion, Vi heard the softest of whispers from Deneya at her side.

As Vhalla's finger met the crystal of the blade, the whole room lit up.

Deneya's illusion of light faded into feathers cascading to the floor. The woman always had a flair for theatrics. Vi had known that since Egmun and Aldrik in the Crystal Caverns, and prayed it helped them once more.

"Leave it," she said, loud enough for Vhalla to hear.

Vhalla looked in her direction, eyes wide, like those of a prey animal.

"Leave the blade; do not take Achel from its tomb." Vi used the old name for the weapon, given by the Northerners. It was the name she'd known from stories told around campfires growing up. Vi rested her hand on the crystals behind her, allowing them to create an opening back out to the forest beyond. She'd long since let go of her illusion over the entrance. "Heed my warning and leave. Do not touch the magic of the Gods, Vhalla Yarl."

"Who are you?"

"I've had many names," Vi gave her standard response as an illusion slipped over her, washing her in light.

Deneya grabbed her wrist, and they both were enveloped by Deneya's other glyph, which rendered them invisible once more. Vi shared a worried look with her friend. They both returned their attention to Vhalla Yarl, waiting to see what fate held.

The whole affair must've overwhelmed the young woman, for she was on her knees, gasping for air. Or perhaps the magic of the crystals was too much for her, after all. Vi felt energized by them, but even she could recognize that the air was thick with their power in this ancient place. Vhalla stood and went for the axe. For one brief, glorious second, she hesitated and turned to the opening Vi had created.

But Vhalla didn't move as Vi had hoped. Instead, she gripped the handle of the axe and freed it with a tug.

Vi covered her mouth to conceal a groan. The noise was part frustration and part the uneasy sensation of all the magic that had seeped out of the axe over the centuries returning eagerly to its origin. The crystals around them went dark as the blade briefly shone brighter. Without magic to support them, the stones began to crack and shatter.

Vhalla Yarl sprinted past them, axe in hand, into the dark night as dormant crystals fell.

Deneya held her arms over Vi's head, shielding her from the rain of glass-like stone. She watched as Vhalla sprinted by them, axe in hand. Vi nearly lashed out to tackle the woman for the weapon.

When the stones were done falling, Vi went to the opening and looked around. There was no sign of Vhalla or her companion.

"Now what?" Deneya said gravely, emerging to stand at Vi's side.

"I'm not sure exactly," Vi said thoughtfully. "But this means we can't rely on anything from here on to be as we expect. We're done playing by Taavin's rules."

28

"Think about this," Taavin pleaded as Vi stormed out of their tent. Deneya gladly stayed behind to pack their things. She clearly wanted nothing to do with the heated debate between Vi and Taavin over their next steps. "It makes a lot more sense to try to get into the fortress after the war is over, when they're negotiating the terms of surrender."

"*If* Tiberus negotiates those," Vi retorted.

"He negotiated for the West and that was after a ten-year siege. There was much more bad blood then to prevent such talks."

"He had brides to pick from, and he was a different man then."

"Fine, you're not wrong," Taavin mumbled.

"No, I'm not." Vi spun, fighting to keep her voice down so she didn't draw attention to them. "Who's to say he won't torch the fortress and all its sacred trees like he torched the rest of the North?"

"Are you doing this because you think it's the right thing, or is it personal?"

"This has nothing to do with me!"

"It has everything to do with you. Ever since you first stepped foot on this world, you've been trying to circumvent what must be done. You've been pushing against me."

"Maybe because you need to be pushed."

"I'm not doing this. This is against every plan—"

"Forget the plans, Taavin. Vhalla was there tonight. *She has the axe.*" Even though it wasn't the first time she'd told him, Taavin still looked shell-shocked by the words. "We don't know what will happen next. We have to act. And, yes, the only thing that's important to *me* is getting that axe and seeing Raspian defeated by Yargen, whatever that takes." She had to force the final words out. "But I know this matters to you. And out of love and respect for you—"

"For me? Not the world?" he blurted the interruption.

"Yes, for *you*, you frustrating man." Vi grabbed his hand, squeezing tightly. "I'm trying to honor your wishes because I love you. This is your one chance for me to continue setting up the life of a new Champion. Either we go to Sehra tonight and leave this place after, or we leave now and forget the next Champion entirely."

"You infuriating woman," he growled, taking a step closer to her. Taavin wrapped his arm around her waist, yanking her to him. "You have always made me act against my better sense. No matter the time, place, or world."

"I'm not sorry," she murmured with half a grin before his mouth crushed hers.

He kissed her like they were hidden away and not standing in the open among the moonlit tents of the Solaris army. He kissed her like it was their last chance to hold one another. She guessed every kiss from here on would be just the same.

"I know you're not," he muttered hot and low over her lips. "Thank you."

"You're welcome," she whispered in reply, eyes darting from his mouth to his eyes. Vi didn't dare tell him that there were one or two things he might tempt her with to prevent them from leaving tonight. She could already taste desperation on him for every moment they had left.

"Now, what's your plan to get in?" Taavin took a step away,

though their hands were still interlocked.

"I'll need you to illusion us both—make us invisible in the darkness, or nearly so."

He pulled her down behind a nearby tent. Taavin looked around, then said, "*Durroe watt radia.*" They stood, moving once more past the tents, this time with a glyph of invisibility swirling around them. "What next?"

"I'm going to hope that Yargen already gave me something I can use." Vi looked up at the large stone wall that encased the fortress. "She gave me a word for making and removing barriers, and this wall was made by Groundbreakers, which are a fracture of her magic."

"All right, I see your logic. But if this doesn't work?"

"Then we force our way in with *juth calt.*" Vi shrugged. "It'll be louder and more chaotic. But we're invisible, so we'll slip in through the fray."

"Tactful."

"We're in 'making this up as we go' territory, remember?"

"Unfortunately." He sighed, though a grin pulled at his lips. If Vi didn't know better, she'd daresay he was enjoying this. Going off script was the slightest bit thrilling—if they ignored the fate of the world that hung in the balance.

They walked through the darkness toward a back section of the Imperial army where soldier's tents were fewer and siege weapons were in greater numbers. It meant there were less people here to take notice of them.

In the darkness, she and Taavin approached the wall. Vi ran her palm along the smooth stone. Normal workmen and tools couldn't create something this perfect. It was a wall fashioned entirely with magic.

Closing her eyes, Vi sent small pulses of her own power through the wall. She tried to understand it, much like she would a crystal. She stood there for several long minutes, breathing and feeling.

"*Rohko,*" she whispered, imagining the barrier that was the earthen wall peeling back like a curtain. There was a soft groan and the sound of stone grating on stone. Vi opened her eyes, shocked to find an opening, much like she imagined. "Let's go, quickly!"

Archers patrolled the walls, so Vi had no doubt one of them would soon notice the break in defense. They rushed across a narrow flat area, void of anything, to a secondary inner wall. Vi repeated the process, "*Rohko*," and the wall opened for them, easier than the last.

She said a mental thanks to Yargen and pulled Taavin through. They emerged on the other side of one of the great trees of Soricium. Vi looked up. She never thought she'd be so glad to see the familiar branches. After spending years trying to concoct ways to escape from under these boughs, seeing them above her made her eyes prickle with tears.

"We should keep going," Taavin reminded her softly.

"You're right." Vi shook the nostalgia from her eyes and pressed on into the fortress.

She knew the pathways and stairs like old friends. Not much had changed between this world and her own. Perhaps Soricium was one eternal constant, built hundreds of years before rebuilding a world in rewound time even became a thought to Yargen. This one place stood, and would always stand. Or so she hoped.

Still, the Emperor torching it all still seemed a too-viable possibility.

They crossed a bridge and Vi paused. She stared down over the rope rail to the masses huddled below. Everyone who was able had retreated into the fortress before they erected the walls and the Empire closed in. Half the city was cramped together, living in squalor. But they lived.

Vi gripped the rail.

"If we truly succeed in seeing this world continue on… No more war for this continent," Vi whispered into the cool night air, speaking more to Yargen than Taavin. "Too much has been lost on this earth already."

Taavin didn't reply. He merely stood as witness to her quiet, idealistic vow, waiting until she was ready to proceed forward once more.

Up and up they spun on staircases, crossed bridges, and ascended into the heights of the canopy. Vi remembered the quarters Sehra had occupied before her mother died and she became Chieftain. They were the same quarters Ellene occupied after. She paused on the landing, raising a finger.

"That's where my rooms were," she whispered into Taavin's ear so she didn't alert the guard that patrolled the bridge between where they were and Vi's old chambers.

"I've never seen it before." His breath was hot on her ear as he whispered in reply. "I can imagine you here."

"Can you?"

"After all the stories you've told me, yes."

There was no time for further conversation, however pleasant the reprieve. Without hesitation, Vi allowed herself into Sehra's room.

She moved through the archways of woven branches into a side hall that connected to a balcony. That balcony flowed into a room that only had three walls. Curtains of flowers gave privacy to the room's occupant and reminded Vi distinctly of the Twilight Kingdom.

There, sitting upright on the bed, green eyes shining in the dim light, was Sehra. Vi released Taavin's hand and stepped out from the glyph. From Sehra's point of view, she appeared from thin air, and the girl's expression showed the fact.

"I'm not here to hurt you," Vi said in the old tongue of the North. The accents were familiar to her, no power of Yargen needed.

"Who are you?" she asked, sliding to the edge of her bed.

"A friend." Vi pushed vines of bell-shaped flowers aside, stepping into the girl's space. Sehra would be about thirteen at this point, she guessed. But even youthful, Sehra had the same intensity she'd keep all her life. Vi dropped to a knee to seem less threatening. "I will not hurt you."

"You're of Mhashan?"

"I'm of Yargen."

Sehra stood, crossing purposefully over to Vi. Her every movement carried regal poise beyond her years.

"You know of Yargen?"

Vi held out her hand and whispered, *"Durroe."* Just like all those years ago, a miniature glowing orb appeared in her palm. But this time, even without the clarification words, the orb was sharp. It was a perfect ball of light, hovering.

Sehra lifted her hand; the moment she was about to touch the shimmering illusion, Vi released her magic and grabbed the girl's fingers lightly. She covered Sehra's hand with her other hand. The girl regarded her warily, but did not pull away.

"I've traveled from where your fate leads. From very far, indeed…" Vi searched the familiar face. It was Sehra, all right, merely twenty or so years younger than Vi remembered. "I've come because there is something you must do."

"For Yargen?" she asked. Vi nodded. "What must I do?"

She wished everyone else would be as easy as Sehra, who knew enough of the old magics, even at this point, that a small display was all the proof she needed. All that, combined with the knowledge that Sehra in Vi's time had been instructed by a traveler, led Vi to determine the most direct path was the best one in this instance.

Manipulation and suggestion hadn't really gone well for her tonight, anyway.

"Soricium will fall," Vi said apologetically. The words hurt to tell the girl. But her war-weary eyes were unfaltering in their attention. "When it does, you must see that your mother demands to negotiate the terms of surrender." Sehra nodded, continuing to listen intently. Vi braced herself for what had to come next. "When Mhashan fell, the Emperor engaged Princess Fiera—"

"You wish me to betroth myself to the Empire's dark prince?" Shock and disgust leaked into Sehra's voice.

"Fate is often most cruel when we hope it to be fair." Vi took a deep breath. She was toeing the line of saying too much, and she knew it. At least Sehra had come up with the idea of an engagement on her own. "You will return home a free woman. You will have two daughters… One of your own blood, and one of your enemy's. Yet both will have the power of Yargen."

"A Solaris will have the power of Yargen?" she whispered.

"You must nurture this power. When the time is right, take the eldest child. For her life, for yours, and for the lives of your people."

"You have made clear the will of Yargen."

"Good." Vi stood, releasing the girl's hand. She wanted to embrace Sehra tightly and tell her that everything would be all right.

Vi might have, if a commotion wasn't rising outside on the walkways and bridges. The smacking of sprinting feet could be heard. Someone banged on Sehra's door.

"Sehra?" Za called through the door. Vi smiled knowingly. That relationship didn't exist beyond protector and protected. Sehra was yet a child, after all. The door opened. "There's been a tunnel discovered in the walls."

"Good luck," Vi whispered to the girl. She reached her hand back and felt Taavin's warm palm close around hers. The glyph surrounded them both once more, and Vi disappeared from existence as Za rounded the entrance of the room.

"Are you all right?"

"I am, Za," Sehra said firmly, still looking at where Vi stood. "I need you to take me to my mother."

"It's not safe."

"It is. There is no one unwelcome in the fortress." The girl turned to her guard, looking twice her age as she commanded, "Now, we go to the chieftain. There are things I need to discuss with her."

Za gave a bow and led the girl from the room.

"Why go to her, and not her mother?" Taavin asked when they were alone.

"I wanted the relationship with her in case our paths ever cross again. She'll be the one in the South. And the Sehra of my world said a traveler instructed her about what to do. I didn't have a sense that I needed to obscure things."

"A sense…" Taavin rounded to look her in the eye. "You said you had a sense in the Crossroads as well."

"I did."

"That sense might be the will of Yargen, flowing through you."

"Who knows." Vi looked out over the branches at the Imperial camp beyond so he didn't see the truth on her face. "Let's go."

"Just where are we going?" he asked, though he was already following her.

"The axe will be too guarded here. We'll meet them back at the Crossroads and take it from her then—before it makes its way south and into Victor's hands."

Vi's fingers twitched. *Soon.* So very soon the last of the crystal weapons would be in her possession.

29

"I AM SO TIRED OF trekking across this continent!" Deneya moaned from her bedroll.

"Keep it down." Despite herself, Vi chuckled. She very much shared Deneya's sentiment. "There might still be Northerners in these woods."

"After two nights ago? I doubt it."

Two nights ago… Those had been the final hours of Shaldan. They'd heard the fighting in the distance, echoing eerily through the towering trees. Vi could almost feel the earth weeping for the deaths of its children as she'd lain staring up at the canopy with wide eyes.

"I wonder what happened." Vi glanced in the direction of Soricium. "*How* it happened, rather."

"One war looks much like the next," Taavin said solemnly.

"You're right. At least we didn't have to be there for this one." Vi stared at the fire she kept burning magically between them. Part of her willed Yargen to give her some kind of sign in the flames that they were on the right path. The other part of her was afraid of what she might see. "We should get going for the day. We want to make it out ahead of the army."

"It'll take them weeks to move a mass of that size," Deneya said with a yawn. "We can get a few more hours of shut-eye."

"We've slept late enough."

"Lies."

"Don't you want a bed?" Taavin tried to reason with her.

Deneya just rolled onto her side, gathering more leaves under her head. "Look at this pillow, so lavish. Don't be jealous."

"Deneya—"

"Deneya is sleeping." She snored loudly for emphasis and Vi couldn't resist laughing. It felt good to laugh. So good that guilt made an attempt to follow it as if to ask how dare she be even remotely happy right now. But Vi shut out the negative emotion.

There was always someone hurting in the world. Someone was suffering every moment of every day. Sometimes, that person was her.

Vi wouldn't feel guilty for brief moments of joy.

"Shame that we'll have to leave Deneya behind." Vi extinguished the hovering fire with a thought and began rolling her own bedroll. "She was such a good companion."

"Indeed. Certainly did a few things along the way," Taavin said, packing up as well.

"What were they, again?" Vi asked Taavin with a grin.

"You know, I can't recall."

"They must've not been very important, then."

"Perhaps it's not a shame we'll have to leave her behind after all."

"All right, I'm up." Deneya sat. "And before either of you gets smug, it's only because you're both that terrible at teasing. I couldn't stand to listen a moment longer."

Taavin laughed and the sound was a recharge to Vi's system. Between the tense moments of guiding fate and holding the world together with straining threads, there were still traces of normalcy— moments of pretend. These, more than anything, were the moments that kept her human.

She vowed to cling to them until her last breath.

Traveling so light, it took them only a moment to pack up their basic camp. Vi led the way through the forest. She knew these trees from years spent underneath them. The thought they might have been in different locations than her world never even crossed her mind.

Even if the trees were different, she knew how to read secret signposts made by Northern scouts, hidden from Imperial eyes.

The sun hung high overhead when Deneya stretched out a hand. "Stop."

"What is it?" Vi asked.

"I hear it too." Taavin nodded at Deneya.

"Hear what?" Their long ears were picking up something Vi couldn't.

"A horse, in the distance," he said.

"Northern?" Deneya asked.

"No, they'd be riding noru," Vi said.

"This is definitely a horse."

"Are there many?"

"Just the one, I think." Deneya looked to Taavin. He hummed in agreement with her assessment. Deneya faced Vi. "What do you want to do?"

"Let's wait and see who it is."

They crouched behind the massive trunk of a tree, hidden by shrubs and branches. Soon enough, Vi heard the clops of hooves through the forest. The rider wasn't going particularly fast.

A messenger? Vi wondered.

Her eyes widened when the horse came into view, a rider slumped over in the saddle, barely keeping herself upright. Twigs and leaves stuck out of brown hair Vi would recognize anywhere.

"What is she doing here?" Deneya hissed.

"Don't ask me." Taavin panicked at the sight of yet another thing going off-plan.

It fell to Vi to act.

"*Durroe watt ivin,*" she hissed, stepping from underneath the branches and into an illusion. Her eyes were blue, skin paler, hair lighter. She looked as generic as any other Southern soldier as she called out, "Vhalla Yarl?"

Vhalla straightened instantly in her saddle, looking over her shoulder. She gripped the reins of the horse tightly. Her wide eyes darted between Vi and the path ahead, clearly ready to bolt.

"Did they send you after me?" Vhalla asked warily.

"Send me after you? Who's 'they'?"

"Who are you?"

Vi put her hands in her pockets and sighed. She glanced sideways, slowly bringing her eyes back to Vhalla. For good measure, she chewed on her lower lip, dragging out the obvious uncertainty.

"Mother, I can't lie to the Windwalker… Who am I? I'm nothing more than a coward." Vi chuckled tiredly, slipping further into the character she was inventing on the spot. "I should ask if they sent *you* after *me*."

"Why would I…?"

"I'm a deserter," Vi said plainly. "Got too scared of the idea of that last great battle and fled. We all did."

A shadow crossed over Vhalla's face. "We?"

Vi motioned to Taavin and Deneya. They emerged from their hiding places with their ears hidden underneath illusioned chunks of hair.

"We just want to go home and see our families again."

For a brief second, a look of disgust flashed in Vhalla's eyes, but it faded before it could gain momentum. The woman looked back at Soricium and sighed heavily.

"I suppose I can't blame you. I'm barely shy of being a deserter myself."

"The Windwalker, you'd never—"

"Don't tell me what I'd never do," she nearly shouted. Vhalla's lower lip quivered and it was then Vi noticed her bloodshot eyes.

Sehra lived.

That was the only explanation for Vhalla's presence. Aldrik had been betrothed to the chieftain's daughter, as planned, and Vhalla couldn't handle it.

"You have no idea what I've done," Vhalla continued.

Vi raised her hands as if to show she was unarmed in both weapon and word. This was not the mother she knew. This was a war-weary and fragile young woman, pushed past the point of breaking.

"Sorry."

"No, I'm sorry." Vhalla shook her head. "I should go."

"Where are you going?" Vi asked.

"I… I'm not sure." She sniffled and wiped her nose with the back of her hand. "I was thinking of the Crossroads. Seems like a good place to disappear."

Go west by night. Vi's own words echoed back to her. Had Vhalla left in the night, striking out for the West when all seemed lost, when she needed comfort?

Vi had let Yargen lead her in the Crossroads when she was speaking with Vhalla. Had Yargen foreseen this meeting? There was no other way for Vi to interpret the situation. Yargen had hand-delivered the woman before her.

And Vi wasn't about to let her go.

"Then, the way I see it, we're headed in the same direction and none of us wants to be found. Why not travel together?" Vhalla was clearly uncertain, so Vi added, "It'll be safer for all of us to travel in a larger group."

"I don't want anyone to know where I am."

"Who are we going to tell?" Vi motioned around her. "The army isn't here, and a bunch of deserters certainly aren't going back to report in."

Vhalla fumbled with the reins and then dismounted with a sigh. "All right. I need to walk the horse for a bit anyway so he can catch his breath. We can go together for at least a little."

"What made you depart so quickly?" Vi asked casually, taking a few wide steps to walk alongside Vhalla. Deneya and Taavin hung back. The young woman shot her a venomous glare. "Sorry!" Vi held up her hands. "I didn't mean—"

"I know." Vhalla sighed, her hands going up to the watch around her neck.

The pocket watch-turned-necklace was almost identical in size and shape to Vi's. But where the cover of Vi's watch was mirror smooth, Vhalla's watch had a sun split in half by a wing. It was a symbol Vi didn't recognize. But if she was forced to guess, she'd surmise

Aldrik had made it for Vhalla—assuming the Aldrik of this world kept similar hobbies to her father.

Vi might not recognize the jewelry, but she did recognize the motion. *Like mother, like daughter*, she thought with a somewhat bitter note.

"I know you didn't mean to upset me," Vhalla continued. "I left because…" she trailed off, and just when Vi had given up on the woman speaking again, she continued, "because I found out something that made a part of me feel as though it were dying."

"Dying?"

"It's hard to explain." Vhalla smiled weakly. "My heart exists beyond myself. My life is not wholly my own. And the parts of me that were in another's hands were crushed in an iron grip."

The cryptic words told Vi two things. The first was that she had been correct in her assumption about Sehra's engagement. The second was a little less clear, but Vi was certain Vhalla was referencing the magical Bond forged between her and Aldrik all those months ago.

She wasn't surprised to see the young woman dancing around the topic. Bonds were rare and precious things. Knowledge of them could be used against the sorcerers who formed them.

"I think I understand," Vi said delicately.

"You do?"

"Maybe?" Vi gave Vhalla an encouraging smile. If Vi hadn't been there the night Aldrik returned south, if she didn't have fate's full picture, then she likely wouldn't have grasped all the layers to what Vhalla was trying to say. "At the very least… I have some idea of what it feels like to have a vulnerable part of yourself existing outside your skin."

Vi didn't know if it was her or Yargen who felt the sentiment more keenly. Despite herself, her eyes drifted to Taavin.

Vhalla's intention to walk with them "a little" melted into the rest of the day. Vi didn't dare point out that Vhalla was now setting up camp with them.

"Are you sure you want to stay with our motley crew?" Deneya asked.

"Don't scare her away," Vi scolded with a laugh, and a quick glance at her friend to say she wasn't entirely joking.

"It's funny," Vhalla murmured, focused on her bedroll. "I thought I wanted to be alone. But it turns out, it's nice to have some company."

"We're honored to hear it. Traveling with the illustrious Windwalker—"

"Can you…" Vhalla trailed off, straightening away and looking out into the dark forest. "Can you not do that?"

"Do what?" Vi was honestly confused.

"That 'illustrious Windwalker' bit. I'm not illustrious. I'm not… I'm not anything, right now."

Vi opened and closed her mouth, struggling to find words. The self-deprecating statements had been ongoing throughout the day, peppered through their conversations. One side of her wanted to smack and shake the woman, shout at her that this wasn't Vhalla Yarl at all. The Vhalla Vi had known was proud, and strong, and self-assured, but gentle to boot. She was everything a daughter aspired to be.

This Vhalla was meek and soft-spoken, oozing out between the cracks of a thin-shelled, tough exterior. This Vhalla believed every horrible thing she said about herself and more. They were the words of a young woman trying to find her place in the world and doubting at every turn.

For all her words frustrated Vi, they also softened a part of her heart to the point of aching.

"You're wrong." Taavin was the one to speak. Vhalla was clearly surprised that the man whom had been silent for most of their journey today spoke. "I won't even apologize for saying it plainly. You're wrong, Vhalla Yarl."

"What do you—"

"Know? What do I know?" He arched his eyebrows at her and chuckled with a small shake of his head. "When it comes to matters of importance, I know a fair bit." Taavin picked up a stick, poking at Vi's fire before throwing it in. "I come from a—uh—faraway town." That was certainly one way to describe Risen. "In this town, there's much lore surrounding fate, destiny, and the red lines of the Mother that link us all.

"Our stories teach that everyone on this earth has a purpose and a role to play. Their choices guide them to key moments in this grand, shared story. Even—no—especially you."

Vhalla continued to stare at him, eyes shining in the firelight. She sat, settling herself in her bedroll. "I can't, or won't, argue with your stories. I'll see you all in the morning." Clutching her pack to her chest, she rolled over and pretended to go to sleep.

Deneya slapped Taavin's shoulder. "You jerk, you upset her," she scolded with a whisper.

"I was just trying to help!"

Vi ignored their conversation, staring at Vhalla. Whatever she felt for the woman, Vhalla was on her own journey, just as Vi was on hers. She couldn't lose sight of what she must do.

Right now, her eyes settled on the strap of the bag Vhalla was holding. She was never without that pack, always keeping it close and clutching it whenever one of them drew near. Her heart began to race, and with every beat, Vi heard a resounding *yes*.

The axe was in that bag. Vhalla had taken it with her. All Vi had to do now was wait for the opportunity to take it from the lone, unguarded Windwalker.

They traveled together, all the way to the Crossroads.

There wasn't much time for plotting or planning on the road out of fear that Vhalla would overhear. But Vi assumed her companions were aware of the situation. She hadn't been patient when she'd made her move to take the crown. She would be patient now and move slowly and methodically.

"It's good to be in civilization again," Deneya said with a stretch. "I want to bathe for days."

"Me too," Vi said, glancing at Vhalla. She'd grown quiet as they'd neared the city. "I suppose this is where we all part ways. No questions asked, just like you wanted."

"And your secret is safe with us," Taavin chimed in. "No one will hear you're in the Crossroads from any of us."

"If I even stay here," Vhalla said quickly, a little too forced. She was definitely planning on staying here, at least for a little. "Thank you all for the company. The journey somehow seemed faster with you all." Vhalla reached up and took her second pack from where it was strapped to the saddle. "You can have the horse."

"Are you sure?" Vi asked.

She nodded. "I stole it after the last battle." Deneya roared with laughter that cracked a grin on Vhalla's face. "So I recommend changing the leathers from military issue, at least."

"We will." Vi took the reins. "Thank you for this gift."

"Take care, all of you." Vhalla waved and headed down a side alley.

"Follow her," Vi said with a glance at Taavin.

"Meet back at our shop?"

She nodded. The man stepped away and ducked behind a rubbish pile. She could see a ripple in the air when he emerged from his hiding place, now invisible. Vi only caught the faint distortion because she knew what to look for.

"Deneya, you still have the measurements for the axe?"

"I do."

"I need you to make or procure one as soon as possible for me to shift."

"On it."

Deneya departed as well and Vi went back to their shop alone. She tied the horse in the back alley, setting out water. Then, she brought their supplies to the apartment upstairs. It was evening when her friends returned.

"She's sleeping in an alley with one eye open," Taavin reported.

"We can make that sleep heavier with *loft not*." Vi held out a hand for the axe Deneya was holding. The woman passed it over.

Holding out the weapon, Vi encased it in a pulse of magic. It had been a long time since she had used the shift, and the magic felt rusty. On her third try, she finally got the weapon perfected into something she was convinced could fool Vhalla.

"It's unnerving watching a non-morphi do that," Deneya murmured.

"Don't worry, it's the last weapon—you won't have to see me use the shift again."

"I wouldn't say I was worried…"

"Taavin, lead us to her." Vi remained focused. Her fingers itched with yearning for the crystal weapon. She was close to it, terribly close. The axe was the final piece that would make everything fall into place.

Cloaked with *durroe*, they proceeded through the Crossroads as unseen specters. Her heart raced with every twist of the back alleys and maze-like streets. Behind every turn could be Vhalla and the axe. Any moment could be the last when she felt this insatiable yearning, this intolerable incompleteness.

Taavin came to a full stop.

"She's not here."

"Where is she?"

"I don't know." He dropped hands with Vi and Deneya. The illusion vanished from around them and Taavin frantically searched the empty alleyway. "She was here. I saw her fall asleep."

If Vi had been in Vhalla's shoes, she'd have kept moving. She'd sleep in spurts and always look over her shoulder. She wouldn't linger in the same place for longer than she had to, and she would change her appearance at the first opportunity.

Even after all this time, it still seemed she was her mother's daughter. Yet Vi had failed spectacularly at using that to her advantage.

With a grunt of rage, Vi spun, punching the wall of the building next to her. A singe mark was left behind from the crackle of flame around her fist, but her skin wasn't split. There wasn't even a bruise.

Taavin and Deneya regarded her with expressions she didn't recognize and didn't bother trying to decipher.

"We'll find her. Whatever it takes, we'll find her," Vi swore. The axe was in this city, and she'd be damned if she was going to let it slip through her fingers.

30

VHALLA HAD BEEN RIGHT to head to the Crossroads. It was arguably the largest city in Solaris, sprawling in all directions. It was also one of the densest and boasted a diverse population.

If there was anywhere the Windwalker could slip away, it was here.

The days bled into each other. Day after day they split up and searched, looking high and low. The hunt for Vhalla was like running on a track. Vi was exhausting herself and getting nowhere.

She wasn't sure how she could know every inch of the Crossroads and not be able to find one woman. But Vhalla Yarl clearly didn't want to be found. So she remained hidden.

"What's the plan for tomorrow?" Taavin asked, looking at the various maps Vi had purchased that were currently spread out across one of the tables in their shop. Vi had continued operating the curiosity shop in the hope that, for some reason, Vhalla would come back.

She hadn't.

"We're chasing a hare in a forest," Deneya murmured, staring at the red, blue, and green ink that marked different areas they had each explored. "This is pointless."

"We have to find the axe." Vi cracked her knuckles, folding and unfolding her hands to try to alleviate some of the restless energy that perpetually lived within her.

"I know that." Deneya folded her arms, leaning away from the table. "But I'm saying how we're approaching this is pointless."

"What do you mean?" Taavin asked.

"If you hunt a hare in the woods, you don't chase it all about. It'll outrun you, hide in holes you can't reach into, run to places you didn't know were there because it knows the woods better than you."

"Vhalla doesn't know the Crossroads better than I do." No one on the continent had a firmer grasp of all the maps of the world, Vi was certain.

"Clearly, she does."

"Fine, then how do you catch a hare in the woods?"

"Two ways." Deneya held up her fingers. "One, you use a fox—a beast that knows the woods as well as the hare."

"Fresh out of foxes."

"Vi, she's trying to be helpful," Taavin said with a sigh, running a hand through his hair. Deneya ignored them both.

"Two, you set a snare." Vi pursed her lips but remained silent, motioning for the woman to continue. "I think we have a snare coming our way in the form of the Imperial army. If Vhalla Yarl is here, she'll be drawn out by them—by the presence of Aldrik."

"Or go further underground. You heard her on the journey here, she was well and truly done with the prince."

"But she's not. She never is," Taavin said. "I think Deneya is right. This could be what draws Vhalla from her hiding place."

"I propose," Deneya continued. She pointed to the center of the map, at the heart of the Crossroads. "We have two of us right in the thick of it all between now and when the Imperial army arrives."

"You want to watch over the hotel where the Imperials usually stay," Vi realized.

"Yes. If she's going to try to see Aldrik, he'll be there. And she might try to sneak in beforehand."

Vi tapped her fingers on the table and then turned to Taavin. "You have any other ideas?"

"I wish I did… but all of this is new. I don't have a single past world to leverage." Discomfort flooded the words. He clearly hated that he didn't know what was coming next and Vi couldn't blame him. He was the one who'd always known what was happening.

Now, he was starting to have to play things by ear.

"All right, we'll take turns on who stays in the center square. The other one of us will patrol the city."

"What if she comes back here?" Deneya asked.

"One of us should keep an eye on the shop," Taavin said. "Both of Vhalla's visits to the shop are stones in the river. The second time is when the birth of a new Champion is cemented and the watch is given… While it doesn't usually happen until after the Caverns are destroyed, things are changing and we can't be too careful."

"I agree." Vi chose the path of least resistance. Even though Vhalla was still operating on the future Vi had told her when she was last here, there was a possibility she'd come back sooner.

Anything was possible.

Vhalla not coming back to the shop at all wasn't something they could entirely rule out. More and more of the world was changing, and that meant Vi had to come to terms with the idea of a world without a Vi Solaris.

"It's crowded today," Taavin murmured from Vi's side. He wore the face of a Westerner. Vi was illusioned as well; they weren't taking any chances with Vhalla recognizing them.

"It is… Excuse me, sir." She tapped the shoulder of a kindly looking gentleman at her side. "Do you know if there's some kind of event happening today?"

"You haven't heard? Lord Ophain is coming ahead of the Imperial Army," the man said. "He's holding audiences for the public. I recommend you get in line if you'd like a word with him. I think it'll be hours before you'll get in, even if you line up now."

"Thank you for the advice." He nodded at her and left. She then spoke only to Taavin. "You should get in line."

"What?"

"Get inside that hotel and take a look around. Make sure she hasn't been hiding among the staff this whole time."

"I think the staff would recognize her, given her acclaim…"

"One would hope, but we well know how people only see what they want to." Vi squeezed his hand. "Come back tonight and report on whatever you've found."

"All right." He moved to leave, but Vi held fast.

She pulled him close, giving him a gentle kiss. "Thank you for all your help."

"It's my duty." Taavin smiled and gave a wink. "And my honor to follow you to the ends of the earth."

"Let's hope it's not the end," Vi called after him. She watched him leave with a small smile, one that slowly fell as she turned away. When he was at her side, the world was good and everything would be all right.

When he left, the world was cold. The only thing that gave her warmth was the flame of her purpose, the driving force of why she was even on this earth at all—to summon Yargen once more.

"Soon," she murmured to the goddess.

Soon. The word resonated within her, as though in reply.

Vi began to make rounds as the square filled. More and more people lined up, ready to seek an audience with Lord Ophain. Vi scanned each of them, looking for a pair of brown eyes she'd recognize anywhere.

When the Lord of the West arrived, the crowd erupted in cheers and fanfare. Vi kept her eyes off the man atop his warstrider and his military detail. She looked among the people, her eyes landing on a lone woman sitting atop a pedestal bearing a lamppost.

The woman wasn't cheering with the rest of them. She observed the world around her with brown eyes that had serious intent. Vhalla was smart enough to wear a scarf to hide her hair, but it didn't throw off Vi.

She made a wide loop, moving unseen through the crowd. Vi made it a point not to stare for too long, lest Vhalla sense her presence. Finally, she perched herself on a stoop high up enough that she had an unobstructed view of Vhalla's back.

The sun drifted lazily though the sky and Vhalla moved herself into a shaded nook. Vi remained as still as a statue. The woman didn't even so much as glance her way.

When the afternoon heat had scared away most of the people, a man emerged from the hotel, tapping his cane. He spoke in a booming voice that echoed across the square.

"Lord Ophain has taken to rest out the midday heat. Audiences will resume in the evening. Do not hold the line, we will form a new system upon your return."

Vi scanned for Taavin in the dispersing remnants of the crowd, but she couldn't distinguish him from any other Westerner. His illusion was too perfect and she hadn't bothered to study it carefully.

Vhalla moved, and thoughts of Taavin vanished. She went for the hotel and entered after a brief discussion with the man holding the cane. Vi shifted her weight from foot to foot to alleviate some of her energy. She hoped Taavin was in that hotel.

All she could do from where she stood was be patient, and wait.

The doors of the hotel opened shortly after Vhalla had gone in and Vi straightened from the wall she'd been leaning on. But it wasn't Vhalla who departed. It was a man with a thick mustache wearing a band of red crimson around his bicep. There was a symbol on the band drawn in black. From Vi's distance, she couldn't make out the details of the symbol, but she knew what it was.

A phoenix holding a sword in its talons—the symbol of the Knights of Jadar.

She scowled at the man from afar as he moved through the square. He consumed her attention with a familiarity she couldn't place. How did she know him? *Did* she know him? Or was this eerie sense of recognition merely the ghost of a memory from a past life?

Vi tore her eyes away, bringing them back to the hotel. The Knights of Jadar weren't her quarry right now. Vhalla was, and she couldn't miss the moment the young woman departed.

After another hour, a woman emerged from the hotel wearing the same headscarf as Vhalla. She kept her head down, and Vi couldn't see her face, but she followed anyway. Either this was Vhalla... or Vhalla had switched the scarf with a decoy and, in that case, Vi hoped

Taavin had been inside to keep eyes on the real Vhalla Yarl.

Keeping her illusion wrapped tightly around her fingers, Vi followed a few dozen paces behind the woman. Tucked into a side street was a narrow bookstore. Vhalla went inside and Vi took her time strolling by. She saw Vhalla—for now she was sure it was her—retreat upstairs through the window.

Vi stepped into an alley where she could still see the building. At the very top, near the roof, was another tiny window. Vi held her breath, waiting.

A soft blue light subtly illuminated the ceiling of the top-floor room.

"Found you," Vi whispered.

She began to run.

Vi sprinted through the Crossroads and made record time back to their shop. If she hadn't known better, she would've guessed she'd flown rather than ran. Taking the stairs two at a time, Vi raced upward to their apartment, grabbing the satchel their fake axe was stored in.

She didn't bother to wait for Taavin or Deneya—she sprinted back to Vhalla's apartment. Her heart beat in her throat, making it hard to breathe. Otherwise, despite all the running, she was hardly winded.

The shop was dark. The woman she'd seen behind the desk was gone.

Vi rounded the building, looking for a back door. There was none.

"*Durroe sallvas tempre*," Vi whispered, approaching the door. She glanced in through the windows, looking for signs of life. When confirmed all was quiet, Vi tried the handle.

Locked.

Vi let out a cry of frustration. She wanted to bang the door down. She wanted to storm in and grab the axe by force if that's what it took.

But she took a breath and stepped away, releasing her magic.

Vhalla had made a temporary home here. She felt safe. Vi knew where she was, knew she had the axe. All she had to wait for now was an opportunity to take it. The last thing she wanted to do was risk raising Vhalla's suspicions, sending her on the move again.

Still, Vi stood frozen, staring up at the window. She imagined the feeling of the axe in her hands. Her eyes fluttered closed as the phantom swell of power overtook her.

"Soon," Vi whispered again.

Soon, that same voice replied in agreement. Louder, this time, than the first.

31

THEY WATCHED VHALLA IN shifts over the next few days. One of them always had eyes on the modest bookstore. Sometimes, Vhalla worked behind the shop counter. Sometimes she wandered. But the other woman—the one Vi had presumed to be the actual shop owner—never left the building.

Someone was always there. And Vi didn't dare risk entering while they were.

When she wasn't watching the store, she tried to sleep. But that was an ever-elusive thing. Whenever she tried to still her mind, her thoughts went instantly to the axe. As if she could search for it even in dreams.

"You're still awake," Taavin said with surprise as he appeared at the top of the stairs.

"I am."

"I thought you were trying to nap."

"I was."

"Going well?" He made a soft *hmm* noise.

"Clearly." Vi tore her eyes away from the ceiling to look at him. Just the sight of the man nearly moved her to tears. "Hold me, please?" she whispered softly.

Taavin didn't hesitate. He set down the food he'd gone to procure, not even bothering to put it away on their shelves, and laid down next to her. He scooped her into his arms. Vi twisted so her cheek was on his chest. Her eyes fluttered closed and she gave a soft sigh.

This was the reason she could keep breathing. Her sanity was held together by his arms.

"I'm so frustrated and exhausted," she admitted with a sigh. "I'm exhausted of hunting—of this gnawing, needy feeling I can't shake." He was silent and let her speak, his arms tightening slightly. "All I want to do is move. And yet all I want to do is stop. Stop it all. Stop this relentless march of time toward an end that I both want and don't want.

"I can't explain it. But I'm being torn apart from the inside out." Vi pressed her eyes shut and pushed her face further into his chest, as if she could fall into him and away from the world.

"I know," he whispered, kissing the top of her head. "I know."

"You can't."

"I do."

"How?"

"I see you, Vi." His arms tightened around her as though he was trying to meld them like clay into one being. "Sometimes, what I see frightens me, or I don't understand it, or both. But I still see you. No matter how much time passes or what duties are piled on you. I see you."

"At least someone does." She smiled weakly.

"I always will."

"It's always been you."

"Vi," he spoke tenderly, his voice deep with emotion. Vi listened to it resonating through his chest. "When this is over—"

"Don't," she whispered.

"When this is over," he continued. "I hope I'm with you, in some form."

"I…" Her voice cracked, and Vi couldn't find words. Luckily,

Deneya saved her.

The ring around her middle finger grew hot and Vi bolted upright. Taavin's arms fell from her and the mantle of duty replaced them. The moment of weakness had passed; Vi almost felt foolish for having it at all.

"*Narro hath.* Deneya, what is it?"

"They left, both of them. Bring the false axe." Deneya's voice echoed in her mind. "I'm going to follow to see where they go."

Vi stood. "We have to leave."

"What is it?" Taavin asked as she released the glyph.

"The shop is unattended."

Taavin was on his feet as well. Vi grabbed the satchel with the shifted axe and they were off. Taavin, luckily, could keep up with her as she sprinted through the Crossroads.

"*Durroe sallvas tempre,*" Vi said as she skidded to a halt. A glyph surrounded her hand.

"*Durroe watt radia.*" Taavin grabbed her fingers, making them both invisible.

"*Juth calt.*" Vi wasted no time exploding the inner mechanisms of the door lock. The storekeeper would never figure out how exactly all the pins broke at once.

Inside, Vi dashed up the stairs. In the upstairs apartment, her eyes landed on a ladder that led up to an attic moments before her hands landed on it and she scrambled upward.

The axe wasn't there.

She knew it before she began searching. But Vi searched anyway. She tore through the contents of the room and turned over the bed. Taavin helped, but they were done quickly.

"It's not here." He gave sound to her thoughts.

Vi cursed. "*Narro hath.*" A swirl of magic appeared around the ring she wore. "Deneya, it's not here. She must have it."

"I know."

"What?"

"I was just about to contact you. There's trouble on this end. We're in an alley behind a restaurant due west of the shop. She has the axe and is threatening some unfriendly looking men with it."

"Don't move, we're on our way." Vi released the glyph and jumped down the ladder. Taavin followed without question, even though he hadn't heard the other half of the conversation. What was Vhalla thinking, showing the axe like that?

Foolish woman.

Foolish mortal!

Vi headed west and found the restaurant. Just as she was rounding the side, she saw a man bolt out from a nearby alley. A sense of familiarity overtook her. Who was he? She'd seen him before.

A shout cut through her thoughts. "The Windwalker—the Empire's monster—has returned to wage war upon the West!"

Men and women emerged from restaurants, parlors and homes. They paused in the street, listening to what the shouting man had to say. "Look down there and find your brethren lying in pools of their own blood. Faces ripped open as only she can do."

Vi moved toward where the man was pointing, but Taavin pulled her back.

"Don't. She's going to be on the run. Chasing won't help now."

"We can get the axe," she seethed at him.

"It's true!" a new voice called. "Th-there's three! They're dead!"

Whispers and glances multiplied around them.

"Go find her! Give her to the Knights. We're the only ones who have ever been able to tame her kind. Clearly Solaris cannot be trusted."

"The Knights of Jadar." The mere words were poison to everything good in her life. "I should've known this all comes back to them."

"They're framing her for murder," Taavin grumbled.

"Not framing," Deneya said. She'd joined them. "Vhalla really did murder those people. But they didn't look like they gave her much choice."

Vi stared at the alleyway quickly flooding with people. Taavin was right. A manhunt was on and Vhalla would slip between all of their fingers once more.

As much as she wanted to rage and punch the wall at her side, she fought to keep a level head and refused to let her spark get the better of her. The Knights wanted Vhalla. The Knights knew she had a crystal weapon. They would no doubt try to unlock the Caverns to rebuild old Mhashan. That was all they ever wanted.

"By Yargen's light," Vi whispered. "That's it."

"What is?" Deneya took a step back as Vi spun to face her and Taavin. Vi's arms wrapped around their shoulders, pulling them close; she kept her voice low.

"I know where they're going. I know what's going to happen."

"How?" Taavin asked skeptically.

"I had a vision, when I touched the scythe."

"And you didn't tell us?" he balked.

"It didn't seem relevant at the time. Listen—*listen*—it was Vhalla. She was tied to a horse and was in Mosant. There were men with her, Knights of Jadar."

"How do you know it was the Knights?" Deneya asked.

"Let's talk as we walk." Vi's mind was moving too fast for her feet to be still. She began heading back to their shop. "I know it was the Knights, because I saw one of them here, when Ophain arrived. He had a mustache and an armband with the Knights' sigil. I didn't make the connection until just now."

"If you're talking about the fellow with the magnificently ridiculous mustache, he left the restaurant with Vhalla tonight," Deneya said eagerly.

"I know, I saw him too. He's going to capture Vhalla. I don't know how, but he will, and he's going to bring her to the windmill on the mountainside of Mosant, no doubt on the way to the Crystal Caverns."

"A mustached man... Knight of Jadar... Schnurr!" Taavin's murmurings evolved into a single excited name.

"Yes!" Vi could see it now. Schnurr had been under Fiera's command years ago during the fall of Norin. The man she'd seen in the square had been a much older Schnurr.

"His death is inevitable, in all worlds," Taavin said. It was an echo of a conversation they'd had on the beach in Oparium, something she should've paid much closer attention to. "I wasn't even thinking of tracking his movements because he usually meets his end during one of the battles in the North."

"So he's never captured Vhalla before?" Deneya asked.

"No," Taavin said gravely. "Perhaps I was wrong about Schnurr, and his life is variable."

Vi had no desire to see Schnurr's life left to the hands of fate. Not when she wanted to wring the neck of every Knight of Jadar personally. But her focus was the axe, not the Knights or the man who seemed to be their current general in the gap Twintle left.

"We'll go to Mosant." They arrived at the shop and Vi hustled inside. "Taavin and I will."

"What am I doing?" Deneya asked as Vi rummaged through her bags.

She pulled out a small box and opened it. A hoop earring was inside—her communication token with Adela. "I'm going to call the *Stormfrost* to Norin. You're going to Risen."

"Vi, you can't mean—" Taavin started.

"This is it," she interrupted firmly. "This is the moment, Taavin. This is what we've been working toward, what every Vi and Taavin has worked toward for the past ninety-three turns of the vortex. We're not following Yargen's red lines of fate anymore. We're drawing them ourselves."

"And what if we get it wrong?" he challenged, though his protest wasn't as strong as Vi had once remembered.

"Then this ends. One way or another, this ends." Vi looked to Deneya. The woman had been a steadfast and loyal companion. "What do you think?"

"I get a say?" Deneya arched her eyebrows.

"You've been with us through all of this… I think it's only fair."

"I never much liked the idea of being the ninety-third version of myself. I like the idea of the world being trapped in a futile loop even less." Deneya grabbed her traveling pack from the corner of the room with determined movements. "I'd rather see the world end than be chained to the wheel of fate."

Vi looked to Taavin.

His eyes were fraught with frantic hopelessness. Vi crossed to him, wrapping her arms around his waist. She held him in an effort to bring comfort to him, as he had brought it to her.

"It's all right," she whispered, placing her forehead on his and looking him in the eye. Deneya packed, giving them some privacy with her back to them. "We can do this."

"If she goes to Risen, if she extinguishes the flame… that's it."

"I know."

"There's no more lingering essence of Yargen to restart the world. The last of her autonomous consciousness will be lost."

"I know." Vi sighed softly. "Everything ends eventually."

He pressed his eyes closed and held his breath. Vi braced herself with him. They would take these final steps together, holding and helping each other along the way.

"All right." Taavin opened his eyes and stepped away. "Deneya, when you go to Risen, you'll need to get to the Voice…"

Their conversation faded away as Vi sprinted downstairs and began to saddle the horse Vhalla had given them. Deneya would extinguish the flame and bring its ashes to her. Vi would extract the magic from within them just as she would extract the magic from the axe, and the remaining power in the Crystal Caverns.

After that, the only piece of Yargen's essence that was left was—

Her hands hovered midmotion, forgetting what she had just been doing. She let out a small whimper as if she'd been punched in the gut.

Taavin.

The only other remaining piece would be Taavin. Vi pressed her eyes closed and breathed for a moment, working to calm her swelling emotions.

Everything ends eventually.

Luckily, she wouldn't be far behind him. She would rejoin with the goddess, too, in a way. Vi remembered her fading corporeal form from her other vision. After Taavin was gone, all that would remain was Yargen, and the dark god she was destined to battle.

<h1 style="text-align:center">32</h1>

Vi rode in front, Taavin tucked in close behind her, as they made their way through the Crossroads. He clung to her as she navigated the narrow roads to the Great Imperial Way that would take them south. Vi didn't know when the Knights would capture Vhalla, but she suspected they hadn't in the two hours it had taken to see Deneya off.

Even still, Vi rode hard. Hard enough that Taavin had to remind her to ease up. They would surely arrive in Mosant before the Knights so long as they didn't kill the only horse they had.

They traveled by moonlight at night, and covered their heads during the day to keep safe from the oppressive sun. When the icy winds of the great Southern pines overtook the landscape, Vi knew they were close. The moment they entered the pine forest, Vi guided them down a hunter's trail.

By dawn, they arrived, their breath turning into clouds that caught the morning's first light.

"Look, there." Vi raised a hand, pointing to a windmill high on an upper ridge of Mosant. "If they're coming from the deep Waste rather than the main road, they should be able to navigate up the other side of that ridge without townsfolk ever seeing them."

"Is it the same one from your vision?"

"I think so, but there's one way to find out. Come, we'll go through the forest and keep out of sight."

Her plan made their pathway up the ridge much slower. At a certain point, Vi made the decision to tie off the horse in a circle of trees. There were ample shrubs holding on to their brilliantly colored leaves to conceal the mount. Continuing on foot, they scaled the mountainside, higher and higher until they could see the path that led to the windmill.

Vi stared at it, examining the door, the cracks in the worn stone; she took stock of every last detail and compared it to her memory of the vision. When she was satisfied, she finally said, "It's the same," and breathed a sigh of relief.

"So Vhalla will come here, then."

"She'll be *taken* here."

"Assuming we're not too late."

"I don't think we are." Vi scanned the ground for signs of a struggle. "They killed a woman in my vision in front of the steps. Even if they removed the body, there would be blood."

"And there hasn't been rain to wash any bloodstains away." Taavin ran a hand through his hair. He wore an uncertain expression. "So we're either *very* late, or slightly early."

"I'm confident in the latter. We had a head start on them."

Vi sat down in the brush, situating herself against a tree where she could see the front door through the leaves. Taavin crouched down next to her. After the first hour, he shifted to lean against the tree as well. By the time night fell, he was sitting with his side flush against hers.

"They might not be coming tonight," he murmured. The first spoken words in hours startled her.

"You're likely right."

"Want me to make camp down the hill, with the horse?"

"You can, if you want. I'd like to stay here and keep an eye out. It was night in my vision, so who knows when they might arrive."

"All right." Taavin stood, brushing himself off.

Vi listened to him go. She tipped her head back against the tree. The night was still and the evening birds were singing. Even when the world was nearing its possible end, the birds still sang as if nothing was wrong. Footsteps approached, and Vi turned to see Taavin there, holding their blankets.

"I thought you were going to make camp?"

"I am making camp." Taavin sat right next to her and threw the blanket over both their legs. He leaned forward, tucking it in on the sides. "You didn't really think I was going to leave you here alone in the cold, did you?"

"Maybe I did." Vi gave him a tired grin. After riding through the night, she was exhausted.

"I should be offended by that."

She laughed airily and rested her temple on his shoulder. Taavin gave her a light kiss on the crown of her head. He stretched an arm behind her with the corner of the second blanket in hand. Soon enough, she was bundled against him.

"Do you want to rest?" Vi murmured, already feeling sleep overtake her.

"No, I'll take first watch."

"All right." She yawned. "Wake me if you see the Knights."

"I will," he promised.

Vi slept surprisingly well that night. The next morning, she and Taavin watched the windmill's sole occupant—an elderly woman—make her way into town. She did not so much as glance in their direction as she passed the thick brush concealing them.

The woman being alive meant for certain they'd made it before the Knights, which helped Vi sleep even sounder the second night. It was still possible that things had changed so much between her vision and now that they wouldn't bring Vhalla here. Vi mentally gave them two more days before they would split up; he would wait here and she would head off to the Crystal Caverns.

Even if the world had changed since her vision and Knights didn't come to the windmill, she knew they would end up there. They always did. In every world, the crystal weapons sought to be returned to the

Caverns.

Vi was dozing when the thunder of hooves startled her. She straightened and listened carefully.

"I hear it too," Taavin whispered as he hastily folded their blankets.

Sure enough, a group rode up. Vi recognized Schnurr at its head. Vhalla was tied to a horse in the center, looking even worse than she had in Vi's vision with heavy shackles, inlaid with crystals, around her wrists. Vi balled her hands into a fist and gritted her teeth. She wasn't sure which made her angrier: the fact that the Knights of Jadar were a perpetual thorn in her side, or what they had done to Vhalla.

She and Taavin remained crouched low, holding their breath, and watched what unfolded through breaks in the brush.

The elderly woman they'd seen before came out to greet the travelers on her doorstep. She couldn't get out a word before Schnurr skewered her through the eye with his sword. Vi didn't even wince as he cast the woman aside. Her corpse landed in an identical position to the vision Vi had seen.

"It's the same," she whispered as quietly as possible into Taavin's ear.

"Good."

She didn't know if she'd call this "good" but it was at least playing out just as Yargen had showed her. The Knights of Jadar untied Vhalla from the saddle and carried her in. Vi watched for a second time as the woman was thrown unceremoniously onto bags of grain. The group followed her inside and the door closed behind them.

"What now?" Taavin whispered.

"I… don't know," Vi admitted. "This is everything I saw."

Taavin pursed his lips, clearly thinking over their options. "Well, we know they're going to take her to the Crystal Caverns."

"Yes, and we can't let them do that."

"Do you want to free her, then?" he asked. "We're not playing by the rules anymore, right? We don't care if we change fate. This is it."

Vi struggled to find words. "Who are you, and what have you done with my Taavin?"

"I will always be your Taavin." He gripped her hand.

"Let's wait and observe," Vi declared. "We'll move when an

opening presents itself."

"You've always been good at seeing opportunities."

She gave him a weary smile and brought her attention back to the windmill.

Night fell. The movement in the windmill settled and Vi assumed everyone had lain down to rest. She wondered how much closer she'd let them get to the Crystal Caverns. She'd killed Knights there before; she could gladly do it again. Perhaps she'd ambush them when they left. The creative and delicious possibilities for destroying them were endless.

"What was that?" Taavin whispered in the still night.

"I didn't hear anything."

"Listen," he hissed and cupped his hand around his ear, leaning toward the windmill.

Vi did the same motion and closed her eyes, focusing. Sure enough, there were dull thuds coming from within the windmill.

"Wind scum!" someone shouted.

"*Durroe watt radia*," Vi said as she bolted from the brush, dashing over to one of the windows. She was barely tall enough to see inside, even if she jumped. But she bounced like a fool to get glimpses of the fight raging within.

Vhalla, still cuffed, was managing to hold her own against the Knights. She was fumbling with a key, trying desperately to remove the cuffs.

Vi jumped again.

The tides of the skirmish had changed. The Knights were advancing. One held the crystal weapon. Vi's heart raced even faster.

"Kill the wind bitch!" a man shouted. The other raised the axe.

She could let Vhalla die. If they weren't working toward the birth of a new Champion any longer, Vhalla wasn't technically needed. She could let them fight it out, kill whoever was left, and take the axe. No one would know what happened to it. If she let Vhalla and the Knights die here and now, everyone who knew about the axe's whereabouts would be dead. In one fell swoop, every loose end would be tied. It'd be clean. No one would come hunting for Vi and she'd finally, *finally* have the axe.

Vi pushed the thoughts away in horror.

No, that wasn't clean in the slightest. That wasn't right, or just. There was still no magic from Vhalla. The woman wasn't fighting back with the ferocity Vi knew she possessed.

Vi had to intervene.

She threw out her hand and cast a ball of flame toward the door. The wood caught instantly and the flames darted within, as if her magic was seeking out the axe itself.

"Vi, that's enough!" Taavin hissed from their hiding place. Her eyes were on the dancing flames eagerly consuming her magic and growing in size. She imagined those sacks of wheat they'd thrown Vhalla onto; it would burn just like the wheat Vi had thrown into the fire in the curiosity shop. "Stop, or you'll kill Vhalla too!"

She withdrew, both in person and in magic. Vi retreated into the bushes, lowering the flames just as Vhalla emerged, sprinting down the front steps of the windmill.

The young woman looked around frantically. "Aldrik?" she called.

Your prince didn't come for you. But from a world away, Vi had. She didn't know if she'd saved Vhalla, or risked killing her with her improvisation. Yargen only knew the truth.

Vhalla wasted no time mounting a horse. She still had the axe, stashed away now in a saddlebag. Vi continued to stare, eyes glinting in the firelight, wondering if saving her and burning the Knights had been the right decision... or if it had somehow cost them their world for a final time.

As if sensing her piercing gaze, Vhalla glanced over her shoulder in their direction as Taavin gripped her ankle and whispered, "*Durroe watt radia.*" Vi hadn't even realized her glyph had fallen when she'd started the fire.

If Vhalla saw anything, it was only for a moment, before Vi vanished from existence and remained the unseen hand of the Solaris Empire.

33

VHALLA RODE INTO MOSANT. Vi emerged from the brush, watching her descend the ridge. Men and women, up at this late hour, greeted her.

"What now?" Taavin asked. She hadn't even heard him come up to her side.

"She'll be too well-attended for us to take the axe here."

"Why not just grab it?"

"Because if we grabbed it by force, Vhalla would fight us. Knowing her, she'd do so to the death. I don't know if she fully understands what she has or not… but given how carefully she's kept it secret, I think she has some idea." Vi had employed similar logic when she'd decided not to take the crown.

"If we're committing to this being the end of the vortex, then we don't need her anymore." His thoughts had run parallel to hers, and Vi hated it.

I need her, a voice all Vi's own shouted from within. "I don't want to kill her," Vi admitted.

"You could've fooled me with that fire."

"I know. It was impulsive."

"Your impulses have always been as wild as your flames."

One side was her, the other was Yargen. Success or failure seemed to depend on if she was the one in control or not. *Had Yargen been the one in control of that fire?*

"I don't *want* to act impulsively," Vi murmured, dismissing the notion with a shake of her head. She had to move forward. "The least impulsive thing to do would be remove ourselves for a while and stop chasing after the axe. We know where it will ultimately end up and we can wait for it to arrive."

"The Caverns."

"Exactly. No matter how much has changed… I know Victor. The only time he'll relent in his search for the power of the crystals is when he's dead," Vi said bitterly, her eyes still on Vhalla below. "Let's allow fate to bring the axe to us."

People were beginning to stream out of their homes. Vi noticed more and more turning in their direction. The windmill still burned.

"It's time to go." She retreated away from the ridge and Taavin followed her. They hiked down to their horse and rode through the familiar forest, back to the cabin that still stood at the foot of the Crystal Caverns.

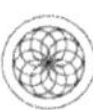

The grip of winter was undeniable. It wouldn't be long until the first snowfall of the season blanketed the entire mountainside. Vi sat at the entrance to the Crystal Caverns with Taavin, waiting as they had every day for weeks.

"What if they're not coming?" she was finally forced to wonder aloud.

"They always—" He stopped himself short, realizing that referencing what had "always" happened was now unhelpful. "Maybe things have changed too much and Victor won't go after the axe. We could go to them and see what's been happening? There may be an opportunity to take it at the palace." Vi chewed over this idea. "We'll take the main path toward Solarin. There's no way we'll miss them on the way."

"If we leave now, we'll make it just after nightfall." Vi stood and extended her hand to Taavin. "One last time to Solarin?"

He took her hand and Vi helped him up.

Sure enough, they made it to the palace in the early evening. Their gold was starting to run dry, but at least they had enough to board the horse. Vi and Taavin slipped into the palace—an act that was now second nature—and headed for the Tower of Sorcerers.

The Tower was quiet. Vi and Taavin moved unseen. She'd been planning to head to Victor's office first—at least, until she saw a haggard man stumbling into the Tower library.

"Where are you going?" Taavin hissed as she tugged him in that direction.

"It's Aldrik."

"So?"

"Wherever Aldrik is, Vhalla usually isn't far behind. She was the last one to have the axe, so it makes sense to check with her first."

Taavin relented, and followed her into the library.

The crown prince swayed, rubbing his eyes and shaking his head. He looked drunk, but Vi couldn't tell for sure. He began rummaging through the shelves, picking up a book and dropping it heavily on a table before reaching for the next.

Just what had transpired here while they were waiting for the axe? Was the prince's state some indication of foul play?

As if guided by fate, Vhalla appeared in the doorway. The young woman watched the man for a while, before announcing her presence with a soft, "My prince."

"What—when did you get here?"

"Aldrik, what's wrong?"

"Baldair. He's sick, Vhalla."

Vi watched the exchange. A rush of heat went to her head and her stomach churned, as though she was the one who was sick. She'd overlooked the first rule Taavin had taught her in these past weeks of waiting: Yargen always demanded her due. Even in changed worlds. The ink on the pages of some people's destiny was long dried.

"It's serious, isn't it?"

"It started as a cold, aches, chills. It's autumn fever."

The two continued speaking, but Vi tuned out the majority of the conversation. She should feel grateful, she presumed. In her world, Baldair died the first time he headed to war. He'd been barely eighteen. She'd prevented that; now, he was twenty-two. She'd bought him three years. It hardly seemed like much of anything at all, but to the people who loved him…

She could see the pain on Aldrik's and Vhalla's faces as they spoke of a man they so clearly loved. *Family.* She remembered what it felt like to lose that.

The two left the library and it was only then that Vi realized her ears had been full of ringing that was just now beginning to fade.

"Are they going to see him?" she whispered.

"Yes," Taavin replied from her side.

"He's going to die."

"I think so."

Vi released her glyph.

"Where are you going?" Taavin was on his feet as well, appearing out of thin air.

"I don't know yet." Vi looked to him, holding out her hand. "Come with me?"

He took her waiting palm and that was all the affirmation she needed. This man was going to follow her to the ends of the earth, but asking him to follow her into the room of a dying man felt like too much.

Vi wandered the palace. Her feet felt the weight of every Vi before her. The ghost of every Solaris was over her shoulders, looking down at her, wondering how—with all the powers she possessed—she could not stop such misfortune from befalling them.

Vi ignored them. She had done her best. Every version of herself had done her best. That much was all Vi could believe.

She walked to the entrance of the royal quarters. Vi could almost smell the sick in the air from where she stood, hidden behind a corner so the guards didn't see.

"What do you want to do?" Taavin asked in a whisper.

"I want…" She shook her head, sending the notion that had been creeping across her mind scattering like rats. "I want to get away from here. There's nothing… there's nothing for me if I stay."

They retreated into the depths of the castle and slept in their old hideaway. But nightmares of Baldair and Raylynn filled her mind. They haunted her all throughout the next day, and those thoughts brought Vi back to the entrance of the royal quarters. Taavin had agreed to wait for her in the Tower library at her request.

She needed to do this alone.

Vi disguised herself as a cleric to pass by the guards. Then, she waited outside the prince's door. She stood in the hallway till her feet ached, unable to bring herself to enter, doubting every movement until now.

Just when she was about to turn away, Aldrik bolted from Baldair's room. Vi quickly stepped down the hall and uttered *durroe* so he wouldn't see her suspiciously lingering. When Aldrik returned, it was with a cleric. Vhalla Yarl was escorted out next; she was covered in blood that wasn't her own. Aldrik brought her through a door across the hall and Vi seized the opportunity.

She relaxed the glyph around her fingers. With the clothing of a cleric, she boldly stepped inside Prince Baldair's chambers. Clerical supplies filled the once-happy room like tiny tombstones.

"Just one of you?" a man said. Vi recognized him by his attire as a head cleric.

"I think more are coming," Vi said, hoping she wasn't wrong. She had no idea what she was doing, but it was too late to back out now.

"Good, we need the hands. Now, bring me those rags."

Vi grabbed a pile of rags that had been set on a low table by the door. She carried them though a side door and into the prince's bedroom. Here, the stench of illness was so thick that Vi was surprised she couldn't see it in the air.

The golden prince was coated in blood, doubled over and coughing.

"Don't just stand there, girl. Put them down and hold this," the man said sharply, motioning to the bucket in his hands.

Vi placed the rags at the foot of the bed and did as she was told. The head cleric left the room immediately and Vi could hear him clanking around the clerical supplies as Baldair heaved monumental coughs, blood and spittle coming up with each one. When he seemed to find a reprieve, Vi reached for a rag to gently wipe his face.

His cerulean eyes were half-hidden behind heavy lids. But he seemed to gain a moment of focus when he looked at her.

"Hello," she whispered.

"He—" He was coughing again, and Vi held up the bucket once more to catch everything that came out.

The door to the main room opened and closed. Discussions flew through the air and among the hasty words, Vi gathered the head cleric's name was Julus.

"I'd like a salve and potion there, suppressants, mostly— something with mint and valerian," Julus commanded.

"Understood, sir."

"You two get rid of these bloody rags."

"What can I do?" Aldrik asked.

"Just stay back, my prince. You'll only risk contamination."

"He's my brother—"

"Let us handle this."

Vi lingered in the room, somehow retaining her job as the blood collector and mouth wiper through the night. She watched as they poured potions down his throat that the prince instantly coughed up. Vi was there to catch everything in the bucket—exchanging it for a fresh one when it was full of fluid and soiled rags. The clerics were relentless, determined to find something that would stick on Baldair's sweat-slick skin or stay in his stomach.

Aldrik paced in the main room. Now and then he would come in carrying something Julus ordered, only to be sent away again. Vi watched him drift in and out and an idea crossed her mind.

There was something the crown prince could do.

"I'll exchange this one myself," Vi murmured, standing with her bucket. Another cleric instantly filled in the gap she left behind. Vi wandered out to the main room. There were definitely fewer clerics as the night dragged on, and it made the lone man dressed in black stand out all the more.

Vi set the bucket down in a corner. She wiped her sweaty palms on her thighs and approached.

"My prince," Vi said quietly.

He nearly jumped at the sound of someone addressing him. "What?" Aldrik said curtly, staring down the bridge of his crooked nose.

"I'd like to request something of you."

"*You* would like to request something of *me*?" He arched his eyebrows.

"Yes."

He sighed dramatically and looked back out the window. Vi would've interpreted it as dismissal if not for his sharp, "Well, what is it?"

"Do you know where to find Raylynn?"

"I don't concern myself with my brother's concubines."

"She's the best swordswoman in the world, far from a concubine," Vi said and allowed her tone to communicate she didn't appreciate his word choice.

"Yes I know where she is." Aldrik sneered at her. But Vi remained passive in the face of his gruff exterior. That confused him all the more.

"Please bring her."

"Who do you think you are, commanding me?"

"You want to help, don't you?" Vi snapped back. She gave him an intense stare that she usually reserved for people she was threatening. Aldrik straightened away, as if she'd slapped him. More likely, he had seen his own expression used against him. "Get her."

Vi walked away, satisfied when she heard his retreating footsteps.

She continued to help the clerics. As Baldair finally seemed to settle, they left the room one by one to get some sleep. Soon, she was one of three, and there was still no sign of Aldrik.

"One of you should stay. I want him monitored around the clock," Julus commanded. "I'll be of no use unless I get some rest, and the Emperor will want a full report in the morning."

"I can watch him until dawn," Vi volunteered before anyone else could.

"Fine, you do it." Julus yawned. "You, go to the Tower and get Waterrunners from Victor, or a Groundbreaker. We're going to need all the hands we can get. This won't be pretty tomorrow."

"Yes, of course."

There were more orders, but Vi didn't hear them as they left the room, leaving her by herself. She wasn't alone for long. Within the first hour, Aldrik appeared with a worried-looking Raylynn.

"Thank you, my prince," Vi said as she rushed over to them.

"How is he?" Raylynn asked.

"Dozing," Vi replied. Baldair was in a hazy, half-drugged sleep. Not the ideal condition for the conversation she wanted to have. But she had to work with what fate gave her. "He'll have clerics with him around the clock from now on."

"That's a relief." Genuine kindness crossed Aldrik's features. It was the first time she saw a glimpse of her father in the otherwise harsh man.

"Now, Raylynn, there's something I wish to discuss with you. My prince, you should get some rest."

"First you think to order me, now you'd dismiss me?"

"Are you not tired?" Vi arched her eyebrows in a mirror of what he'd done to her earlier. It gave him the same pause as her earlier look. Vi could've sworn she saw recognition somewhere in his assessment of her. Even if his conscious mind wouldn't admit it, Vi wanted to believe that somehow, he knew who she was. "Keep up your strength. Consider it cleric's orders."

His eyes darted between Vi and Raylynn before he turned away, muttering gruffly, and closed the door behind him.

"And who are you?" Raylynn folded her arms over her chest.

"A cleric."

"No, you're not," she said, starting for Baldair's room. "No cleric orders Aldrik around like that. Besides, I know your face."

Raylynn delivered the statement so calmly, without even turning, that Vi stopped dead in her tracks. She stared at the woman's back, waiting for her to turn around with a smug grin. But she never did. That truth was delivered plainly and Raylynn moved immediately to Baldair's bedside.

Vi followed slowly behind and looked at the scene she had orchestrated. Baldair lay in bed, drifting in and out of consciousness. His eyes fluttered open as Raylynn reached for his hands.

"I'm here," she whispered. "It's me."

It had always been her at his side. Vi had seen it from a distance. She'd heard whispers from the soldiers. The man known as the "Playboy Prince" had found his singular golden woman long ago.

"Ray…"

"Don't speak, you idiot," she scolded lightly, running her fingertips over his forehead. Baldair's eyes drifted, but before they could close, they landed on Vi. Focus overtook him once more. "Yes, she's here, too."

"Who… are you?"

Vi was in two places at once. But this wasn't the sensation of the unique visions crystal weapons gave her. This was brought on by memory. She was in a different room, standing before a different bed, occupied by someone who would've been a family member in a different world, who was destined for death.

She was honest then, and she would be honest now. She'd come here not for fate, after all. But for herself. For the love of family that transcended time and space.

"I'm the one who did this to you."

"*What?*" Raylynn seethed, turning sharply.

"I'm the one who pulled the strings of fate to bring you here, to this moment, Baldair. The flame of your life was supposed to be extinguished years ago." Vi dragged her feet over tiredly, pulling up a chair that had been cast aside so the clerics could have room to work. "I'm the one who tried to keep you alive." She looked from Baldair to Raylynn. "And I got you to help me do it without you realizing it." She thought back to reading Raylynn's future as Fiera. Raylynn had dutifully defended a golden crown, just as Vi had hoped.

"I don't—" Baldair wheezed and Vi braced herself for another coughing fit. But the cleric's medicine held and he finished, "understand."

"I know." Vi smiled tiredly. "It's hard to explain. I don't entirely understand some days myself… even still."

"You were the one who saved us that night in the West," Raylynn said. Vi nodded. "It wasn't the princess."

"Fiera is dead. I was there when she died."

"Impossible. You'd have to be at least thirty—forty, even. You don't look a day past eighteen."

"I've been eighteen a long time." Vi sighed heavily. Her body would be the one thing she would be ready to give back to the goddess when the time came. She'd mourn the loss of her mind and its thoughts—its memories—but her corporeal form was tired of feeling very old and very young all at once. "I've come from a world away, on a mission to save this one."

Baldair looked at her in a fevered haze. Vi would be shocked if he remembered any of this come morning. But Raylynn's expression was completely believing. The woman had her mother's eyes and intuition.

"You brought us here for a reason, to tell us the flame of Baldair's life will be extinguished?"

"Yes."

"Why?"

"I don't fully know myself." Vi shook her head. "Perhaps because I felt I owed this to you after meddling in your lives for so long."

"Nox?" Baldair whispered.

"That is one of my names, yes." Vi smiled tenderly at him. "I wanted you to know that I'm sorry. If I could save you, Baldair… Raylynn, if I could've saved your mother, or Fiera, I would have. It wasn't for lack of trying. But the goddess will have her due and—"

"Enough," Raylynn said faintly. She gave Vi a tired smile. "I'm not afraid of death, Nox. And I'm not afraid of giving myself to the Mother."

Vi focused on Raylynn. "Baldair will not survive this. In some ways, that might be a blessing. If the future remains unchanged—" which was a bigger "if" than any of them could know "—there is a storm coming that will claim the lives of many in this city. Even if I saved Baldair now, I'm certain he would be taken then. Fate would catch up with him in more brutal ways each time his life was stolen from it. But if *you* were to leave—"

"No."

"But you could—"

"I will stay by his side to the end." Raylynn met Baldair's gaze. The prince's ocean-blue eyes were filled with tears. *"On my terms,"* she added.

But what Vi heard was, *I love you.*

"If you stay here much longer, you might not survive." Vi didn't know how she could make the woman understand that while Baldair's life would come to an end regardless, hers wasn't conscripted by fate.

"Death comes for us all."

The expression knocked the wind from Vi. She remembered Taavin's words and how ready he was to give himself over to fate. Before her were two people who had accepted much the same.

"It was fun while it lasted," Baldair said to the woman gently caressing him.

"It was," Raylynn agreed.

Vi stood wordlessly, excusing herself from the room. She gave the lovers space until dawn, waiting in the main room of the royal apartment. A new cleric arrived shortly after and Raylynn left with Vi.

They departed the Imperial wing of the palace together, stopping at an intersection in the servants' halls. Raylynn paused, and Vi stood silently beside her.

"Thank you," Raylynn said finally.

"You have nothing to thank me for." *Not yet, at least.*

A tired smile crossed her lips. "Then why do I have the distinct feeling I have quite a lot to thank you for?" Vi's lips parted. Raylynn held out her hand. "So, thank you."

"You're welcome," she managed to squeak out. Vi's fingers closed around hers and they clasped palms tightly.

With that, the golden-haired swordswoman departed in the opposite direction, as though this was the moment their fates diverged. Vi watched her go. Vi *let* her go.

Silent tears streamed down her face and fell to the floor in heavy drops. Vi fled to a quiet room where she could mourn alone. She wept for all the hardship and hurt, for everyone she'd lost all over again, and for the family she'd never known.

34

VI STAGGERED BACK TO the Tower library. She impressed herself that she managed to change into black robes lifted from a storeroom along the way. Sure enough, Taavin was there, waiting on a window seat, reading, and looking as if he didn't have a care in the world.

"You were gone quite a while." He closed his book slowly. Dawn was breaking over his shoulder.

"Prince Baldair is dead."

Taavin observed her, saying nothing. He didn't even move. Vi wondered if he was judging her for what she confessed to the prince and Raylynn. She wouldn't be surprised if somehow he knew what had transpired.

"Is he?"

"Yes." Vi closed the distance and determinedly wedged herself between Taavin and the window. His arm wrapped around her. His embrace was the one thing that could keep her together. "Well, I don't think he's dead yet, but he will be very soon."

Taavin was quiet for a long moment. Vi met his eyes in the

reflection of the window. "Will we be searching for the axe today?"

"I don't think so. The death of the youngest prince will be the catalyst. All of this is going to come to an end very soon."

"You think so?"

Vi nodded. "If Vhalla has the axe, I think she might seek out the Caverns on her own to try to find some cure for him, or a way to cheat death."

"Ah, cheating death—you get it from your mother."

"Not funny," Vi said deadpan.

"Forgive me." He kissed her neck lightly and Vi wriggled closer to him.

"Let's just… wait here for a while and see what happens? I'm tired, and just want to exist quietly for a while."

"Certainly."

At some point, she fell asleep in his arms. Around her, the day began like any other. Guards showed up for work, servants cleaned the halls, and the Tower initiates went in and out of their library, looking oddly at the anonymous couple in the corner.

Once more, time drifted around them and they remained untouched. Vi didn't feel the turning of the hours. She didn't feel hunger gnawing at her or exhaustion pricking her eyes. Taavin's arms were stasis. They were the strength she needed to stand when the moment came.

And it came in the form of two familiar voices.

"… if there's one thing Elecia would hate more, it would be being someone else's puppet."

Aldrik and Vhalla sprinted by the library opening. The man was half dragging her, leaving Vhalla to take two steps for every one of his long strides. Without needing to be asked, Taavin stood and extended his hand to Vi.

"What will your father…" Vhalla's voice faded away as they continued racing up the tower.

"Shall we?" Taavin asked, almost thoughtfully.

"Fate won't let us linger much longer. *Durroe watt radia.*"

Taavin echoed her and they sprinted behind the prince and the Windwalker. Vi and Taavin passed the Minister's office in time to see the lone uppermost door in the Tower closing.

"I gave him that key," Vi whispered.

"What?"

"Years ago… that was the room I was in when I first came to the Tower. Aldrik was just a boy. The night I left, I gave him the key."

Taavin was silent for a long moment. Then, he whispered with fragile optimism, "Perhaps this is all how it was meant to be. Perhaps this really is the time we will succeed."

"Let's hope."

Aldrik stepped out into the hall once more and began to stride down and away. Vi heard the click of the lock engage behind him. He was trying to protect Vhalla from his father? Had she overheard their conversation correctly?

"Let's get a head start. They'll go to the Caverns tonight. I know they will."

They left the palace and rode out of the city. Vi set their course, heading down the Great Imperial Way, not taking the expected shortcut to the Caverns.

"It had to snow," Vi grumbled. She doubted *kot sorre* would work in snow as well as it had in the sands of the Waste. She imagined strange-looking snow banks at the ends of ditches where her glyphs pushed through the powder.

"I suspected that's why you were swinging wide."

"We should have time. We'll go to the cabin first and leave the horse there. We'll continue on foot. It'll be less noticeable than the horse's tracks." She prayed there was enough time for all of it.

But Yargen looked over them. She and Taavin made it to the cabin in record time. They started the hike to the entrance of the Caverns, Vi walking ahead with Taavin stepping in the footprints she left behind. Then they repeated *"kot sorre"* over and over. Their glyphs grazed the top of the powder, pushing and piling it to cover their tracks.

Just as they reached the cliff in front of the entrance to the Caverns, two horses could be seen in the distance.

"You think that's them?" Taavin whispered.

"Who else would it be?" Vi looked to Taavin. "Listen, if this goes wrong—"

"It won't."

"If it does… I'm sorry, for risking it all."

"Don't apologize." Taavin reached up, tucking a stray strand of hair behind her ear. "All you've done, you did for our world. Yargen could not ask for a better Champion."

Vi swallowed all the emotions he inspired by just looking at her. She still had so much she wanted to say to him, and time was running out. But there was no opportunity now and she had to focus on what was to come next. "We're going to need all the chants we can get in there."

"I have an idea."

"What?"

"Follow me." Taavin led her into the Caverns, the stones glimmering under their feet. The world seemed to hold its breath. Almost all of Yargen's power was now condensed in this one place, split across her, Taavin, and the Caverns themselves. "It's a word Yargen told me long ago… but I could never make it work right in Risen. Perhaps it was meant for here and now."

"What are you talking about?"

Taavin gripped a nearby crystal and uttered, "*Chronot.*" The entire cavern flared, a rune sinking into every crystal that lined the walls. It made them all glow with fractured portions of the glyph, power illuminating every corner. Time itself seemed to hold its breath in the presence of the magic.

"Slow," she whispered.

"What?" He seemed incredulous at the translation.

"*Chronot*, to slow…"

"Yes, it makes glyphs cling longer. You should be able to cast two to four at a time but… how did you know that?"

"I heard it, in the word."

"That's not possible," he whispered.

"But I did."

"Only Yargen—" The sound of hooves silenced him. "*Durroe watt radia. Durroe sallvas tempre.*" Taavin chanted first and Vi followed. She tapped a crystal lightly, willing the Caverns to darken to their dormant state.

"There! There's his horse," Victor shouted, though his voice was different—deeper in some ways and pitched in others.

"We have to hurry!"

"Carefully!"

The mounts kicked up a confetti of ice and snow as they skidded to a stop on the ridge beyond. Vhalla was astride one. But Vi blinked at the man on the other. Aldrik?

No… Magic coated the man so thickly that Vi wondered how Vhalla couldn't feel it. Victor was using an illusion of Aldrik to get Vhalla to the Caverns. Which was clever, she'd grant him that. Perhaps he doubted Vhalla would give him the axe otherwise.

It also explained why he was doing his best impersonation of Aldrik's voice.

"We need to go. We're close now," Victor said with Aldrik's voice as he dismounted.

"Right…" Vhalla regarded the massive entrance to the Caverns warily. Vi suspected the woman's expression was identical to her own when she'd first laid eyes on the place. Even if Vhalla couldn't sense Victor's illusion, she could pick up on the gravity of this ominous space.

Something caught Victor's eye. He turned toward the valley. "We need to go!"

Vhalla worked to keep up with Victor, plunging herself into the darkness of the Caverns. Vi took a steadying breath as she laid eyes on the axe. She didn't know the details of what was about to happen. But she knew that, one way or another, the power would finally be hers.

Victor placed a crystal in the Caverns, much as Egmun had, and the space illuminated once more. Blue and white light washed over them and magic cascaded down from the ceiling like stardust.

"There's no time," Victor muttered.

As the two continued forward through the first archway, Vi released Taavin's hand and he quickly used *durroe* to conceal them both in sound and sight again. She could no longer tell where he was, and in the Caverns, it was nearly impossible to make out his magical signature from any other crystal. Vi pressed forward, listening in on the conversation that was continuing before her.

"…we missed Victor along the way," Vhalla said as Vi approached the archway that led into the antechamber. She was just in time to see Victor grab her. "Aldrik, your hands are cold. Let me go." Victor laughed at her rising panic. The sound pricked uncomfortable goosebumps into Vi's flesh. "Let me go!"

"No, I don't think so, my little Windwalker." Victor had dropped his poor attempt at Aldrik's voice. "Do you know how long I've bided my time? Waiting, *waiting*! Everything has been going according to plan, and you will not take this from me now."

My plan, Victor. I've been the one who was waiting, Vi thought darkly as she watched him shed his illusion. Victor had tricks up his sleeve she wasn't expecting, however. He produced a crystal from his pocket, slammed it into the base of Vhalla's neck, and coated it with ice to keep it there. Vi scowled, her spark tickling her fingertips. Victor had clearly taken it upon himself to do some additional crystal research.

She combated the urge to protect Vhalla.

Vi's focus was on the doors that Victor brought Vhalla toward by force. A new barrier was there, albeit a clumsy one. Vi had wondered what exactly happened to "end" the War of the Crystal Caverns. She always suspected that people merely stopped going there, thus, no more monsters. But judging from the traces of Aldrik's magic in the new barrier over the doors, the man had inherited some of his mother's intuition when it came to the crystals.

Victor lodged an insult at Vhalla and threw her against the doors.

"*Rhoko.*" Vi held out a hand to help the barrier fall.

She watched as blinding magic wrapped around Vhalla, tightening across her. Vi could feel an aspect of the woman's power knotting with the crystals. Victor was using the young woman as a catalyst, trying to unlock the door himself.

If Vi released her glyph now and destroyed the barrier, Vhalla's magic would be wrapped in with it. There was no time to separate the two; they were intertwined. Vi panicked. Severing the magic could result in Vhalla losing her power.

Your mother found the strength to overcome overwhelming odds and be reunited with her power, thanks to this.

Fritz's words appeared in Vi's mind, as if ushered there by Yargen herself. He'd written them on the letter attached to the watch he'd gifted her. Vhalla had lost her magic in her time, too.

Have faith, Vi commanded herself. Everything was on a course for success. If she didn't believe that, she couldn't complete this task.

Closing her hand into a fist, Vi yanked her arm back. The thick barrier of crystals on the door shattered.

"*Kot sorre,*" Taavin whispered from somewhere nearby. The doors swung open, giving Victor access to the heart of the Caverns.

The man rambled madness to Vhalla as he carried her within, throwing her down like a rag doll. Ice coated the Windwalker, keeping her in place. Vi blinked, swaying, but kept her footing. Destroying the barrier had left her momentarily stunned.

"What is he doing?" Taavin whispered at her side.

Vi watched as he laid crystals around Vhalla's prone form. *What was he doing?* Vi worked to get her mind moving again after the burst of energy.

"Don't lump me in with the incompetent fools who are so hungry for power that they are blinded by it," Victor boasted to Vhalla. "I am of a far greater stock." He believed that because of Vi. "Egmun thought he could take this power, but he didn't have *you.*"

It clicked for Vi, then, and she wanted to scream. She'd been so focused on driving the momentum to get the weapons to the Caverns that she hadn't thought about how old actions would echo in the future. Around and around the world spun, mistakes made and made again.

"He was Egmun's student. He knew the same things as the former Minister… he's going to use her as a sacrifice." She kept her voice a whisper.

Taavin's hand clasped over her shoulder and he was visible to her once more. The touch barely registered through the numbness that tingled over her flesh like dark magic. "*What?*"

"I will kill you," Vhalla swore through chattering teeth.

"Will you? I would certainly love to see that."

"I will. *I promise.*"

"That would be impressive, as this place will soon become your tomb." The Minister affirmed Vi's suspicions.

"Are you going to let her die?" Taavin asked. His eyes were filled with genuine uncertainty.

"I don't want to." But Vi couldn't promise she wouldn't.

Vi stepped forward, out of Taavin's grasp. He disappeared from sight. Trusting her invisibility to remain in place thanks to *chronot*, Vi strode forward into the living core of the Crystal Caverns. She ignored the raving lunatic and prone woman as she walked around the edge of the room. The only reason she could ignore them was because she could feel the dark god underneath her feet, waking.

She'd given Raspian a taste of freedom for the War of the Crystal Caverns, and now he knew his time had come.

"I fear, my dear, that you must die without ever seeing my new world order," Victor was saying. "But know that your death will build a society that favors sorcerers for eons to come."

Vi positioned her stance wide, connecting her magic with the crystals around her as Victor wielded the axe. She was ready to make the transference. It would shatter the axe before it could wound Vhalla. That was how this would end, Vi decided.

But right as Victor was about to deal his final blow, a tall shadow appeared in the distant entryway, barely visible through the archways and doors.

"Aldrik!" Vhalla screamed.

"Vhalla!"

Mother above! Vi nearly shouted.

"It seems you shall be the first Solaris to die by my hand!" Victor said with glee.

Oh, Yargen, this was becoming a mess. Fire and ice battled as Aldrik and Victor levied their magic against each other. Chaos took over the Caverns and Victor finally put a temporary pause to it when he blocked the prince's progress with a wall of ice in the doorway.

"*Rhoko,*" Vi whispered, hating herself for using the word. But she had to regain some control and contain the situation. Her magic flowed through the crystals on either side of the door, strengthening Victor's barrier of ice. Aldrik slammed into it, *hard,* and winced. He banged his fists against the frozen wall, bloodying them. No fire or rage was going to break through her barrier.

Vi's chest ached as she watched the frantic prince staring at Vhalla. Her hand pulsed with the magic that was keeping them apart. This suffering and the deaths that would follow would mean something when she ultimately succeeded. That was the only thing she could cling to.

Za and Sehra were in the Caverns now, too. Vi was grateful they came and escaped the Capital, until one of the warrior's arrows managed to pierce her barrier with a flash of light. Sehra was using her limited Lightspinning to try and get through.

The chaos had distracted her from Vhalla and Victor. Somehow, Vhalla had freed herself and the two were now struggling over the axe. It had only seemed a second, but it had been long enough. Victor snatched the axe and had it over his head.

A scream rose in Vi's throat and was stopped short as Victor swung the axe down, carving through Vhalla from shoulder to sternum. Vi saw glyphs appear where the crystals met her flesh. She recognized the shapes as *halleth*. Taavin was working to ensure Vhalla survived this so Vi could focus on what she was meant to do.

The axe shone brighter, as though the magic within was trying to explode outward. Vi reached toward it with her mind and closed her magic grip around Yargen's power, pulling it from the blade. The bright light of future sight tried to overtake her. *Not now, not yet*, Vi begged.

She kept herself grounded in the present by grabbing for the power that surrounded her. If she kept absorbing Yargen's magic, she could keep the visions at bay. The crystals in the room flared brightly. The axe turned to obsidian, falling from Victor's grasp.

Kneeling down, Vi pressed her palms into the floor and closed her eyes, remembering the word she'd seen glowing in this place years ago. "*Suladin.*"

Magic lifted off the stones and flooded her senses. Victor was still shouting. Attacks were being levied against him. Vi's world was a hazy blend of light and magic. She saw the intricacies of the barrier that had been crafted to seal Raspian and, for the first time, began to understand them.

She pulled at the edges of the glyph, trying to uproot it from where it was anchored. *"Juth calt. Juth mariy,"* Vi whispered over and over, focusing on the cornerstones that kept Yargen's power in place.

The world tilted, and a streak of red lightning shot across her skull. Raspian could sense that the cage holding him was weakening. He fought to be released once more.

The power surging through her made Vi dizzy. It swelled her veins to the point of pain. Everything within her hurt, and then was healed instantly by Yargen's magic. Her mind was overwhelmed.

Tilting her gaze up, she tried to focus on the real world as the edges of her vision became hazy.

Victor reached down and picked up a crystal. He used it to channel power, not even realizing what he was reaching toward. The eyes of the dark god flashed in Victor's briefly.

No!

Aldrik was there now. The barrier she'd made must've been destroyed when she'd focused on gaining the power of the Caverns.

Vi couldn't tell if everything was happening incredibly slow, or very fast. Time had gone sideways. She was losing the battle to keep her mind in the present.

Aldrik scooped up Vhalla, fleeing with her as the Caverns began to break beneath them. Victor followed close behind.

The crystals around her exploded as the last of Yargen's essence was absorbed into her and Raspian was freed. The burst shattered the doors to the barrier room. The ground cracked beneath Vi, while rocks jutted up around her. Victor didn't even turn to look over his shoulder. He was so focused on tracking down his prey that he was ignorant to the true work being done.

Raspian's essence roared forth. It sought out the man who had gained just a taste. Just as Vi was a channel for Yargen, Victor had become the first channel for Raspian. He would taint the world with the dark god's magic, not even realizing the power he had.

Vi's vision grew tunneled. The power was about to overwhelm her. She couldn't fight it any longer.

The last thing she heard was a man's scream, before the world went white.

35

T HE BLINDING WHITE OF the vision faded with the crackle of
power. She moved, casting another beam into the darkness that
engulfed her. She was shooting blind, her target evading every
attack.

Spinning, she searched the desolate wasteland for any sign
of Raspian. Vi moved across the ashen stone and rubble of a great
civilization that had been reduced to dust. Her feet hardly hit the
ground; her body no longer felt like her own.

Lightning cracked behind her. She spun on instinct, readying an
attack. A plume of smoke rose from a dark spot on the ground where
lightning had struck the earth, but there was nothing else.

A growl at her ear was the only warning she got before rows of
razor-sharp teeth sank into her shoulder. Two clawed hands wrapped
around her. They dug into her abdomen, flaying her alive. Lightning
sparked through her, rising within her until she was limp and lifeless.

Then, darkness.

The vision slipped away like a veil.

Vi cracked her eyes open. They were crusted with sleep, or perhaps it was blood and sweat, given how much everything hurt. She raised a palm to her temple, feeling a tender spot where her head must've met a bit of jagged stone when she collapsed. Vi let out a groan and sat.

A fire crackled happily in the hearth next to her. Snow fell outside the window, piling high. She looked to the bed across from her—it was perfectly made. Deneya always tidied up her bed before leaving for the day.

Massaging her temples, Vi closed her eyes. That had been the most horrible dream. Red lightning sparked behind her lids and they shot open once more.

It wasn't a dream. She could already feel Raspian's essence on the earth like oil on water.

The door opened and her attention went to the man in its frame. Given his tired and worried eyes, she wasn't the only one who could sense Raspian's renewed presence.

"How do you feel?" Taavin asked, crossing over to her bed and sitting on its edge at her side.

"Fine." The aches were already dissipating and she didn't need him worrying about her. She needed information. "What happened after I passed out?"

"They made it out alive. I kept Vhalla stable for as long as I could—not healing her so much that it would raise questions."

"But enough to keep her alive," Vi finished for him. She looked to the window once more. "That was unnecessary."

"What?" He took her hand. "Didn't you—"

"It doesn't matter. Raspian is free. Though some of his magic went into Victor."

"I could sense it," Taavin said with a cautious note. As though he was suddenly wary of her. "He headed toward the Capital."

"Expected. Blood will run in the streets of Solarin." The words were passive; though she physically spoke them, she didn't feel them. She was a mouthpiece of sorts, it seemed. Perhaps she was in shock. The dream—no, vision—she'd had was fresh in her memory. That was the only thing her mind could focus on. "It's time to go to Salvidia." Taavin stood, pacing. "You're uneasy," she observed.

He looked at her with that same wary gaze. Vi couldn't recall if she'd ever seen it from him before. He finally stopped, his back to her.

"I know that we've committed to this being it, the final time," he said delicately.

"Yes, in me is now the essence of Yargen that was in the Crystal Caverns and three crystal weapons. All that remains is to collect the remaining essence from the ashes, and the final crystal weapon in you."

His back straightened. Taavin was taut and stiff as he slowly turned to face her. Hurt shone in his eyes.

Had she said something wrong?

He'd already known this truth.

"I know," Taavin said softly. "But Victor has a trace of Raspian's power… would it not be better to see him ended? In case Raspian's essence was inadvertently split, as Yargen's was?"

Vi thought about this a moment and then shook her head. "No, if he had the actual essence of Raspian, he'd be dead. His body is not made for such things. He has a fracture of the dark god's magic… much like a crystal shaving. It's a bit of magic, but not the essence itself."

"Better to be safe?"

"I'm confident." Vi swung her feet over the side of the bed.

"I know," Taavin said hastily, crossing over to her. "I know we've already given up on ensuring the birth of a new Champion. But lingering here for a few more weeks—that's all—and giving the watch to Vhalla couldn't hurt, could it?"

"Why do you seek to delay the inevitable?" Vi was reminded that even though she'd blessed him with an immortal body, he still very much had a mortal mind.

"A little bit of assurance that somehow, maybe, if this doesn't work… there's hope."

"I am the hope of this world."

Taavin knelt before her. "Then, if not for the world, what about to ensure there is a new Vi born? Not for the world but for… somehow, for us. A new Taavin will be born, and then—"

"I don't care about the birth of a new Vi." He recoiled as though she'd slapped him. But Vi had spoken plainly, calmly, and without emotion.

"Vi, stop this," he whispered. Taavin shook his head and brought his shining green eyes back to hers. "If not for you, or me, or us, then for Vhalla. She lost her magic in the Caverns. If you don't return the watch to her, she'll have no chance of getting it back once more. Victor will surely kill her."

"Vhalla's death matters not to me."

"How can you say that?" He blinked up at her. "A day ago you were seeking to save her *and* the world."

"Those were sentimentalities of a narrow mind."

"What are you saying?" Taavin stood and, instead of pulling away, leaned forward and wrapped his arms tightly around her. Vi stiffened under his touch. Something in her was fighting to escape. A war for her heart and mind threatened to tear her apart. "This isn't you," he whispered in her ear. "Sentimentality, love—these aren't narrow-minded. These are the greatest gifts we have in this world. The only things that make this world worth saving."

Vi felt a snap inside her, and she could move again. Her hands were her own. Warmth flooded her and Vi reached for the man it poured from. She wanted to drown in it, in him.

Tightening her arms around him, pulling him onto the bed with her, Vi whispered, "All right."

"Yes?"

"We'll give the watch to Vhalla. But not for anyone to be born and not even for her magic." She managed to say the words before that cool and detached feeling overtook her once more.

"For what, then?" he whispered.

Vi pulled away, just enough to look him in the eye. "For you, Taavin. For a few more stolen moments with you."

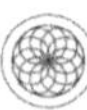

Victor's influence spread. With even a sliver of Raspian's power at his disposal, the man wrought turmoil across the continent. It seemed to follow behind them as Vi and Taavin made their way to the Crossroads one final time.

But they made it without issue, and Vi had never been more

relieved to see their quiet shop and second-floor abode still standing, waiting for them.

"I was half worried it wouldn't be here," she said as she dismounted in the back alley and tied their horse to a post.

"The West always holds out against Victor. At least for a while."

"Just like they held out against the Empire. It's a stubborn land."

"Ah, so stubbornness is in your blood."

"What little blood I have left."

"Don't speak like that, please," he said as he followed her inside.

"I'm sorry." Vi drifted up the stairs, setting her pack and saddlebags down heavily.

Two arms closed tightly around her. They stood in the center of the room, Taavin at her back, clutching her tightly. He buried his face into her shoulder, kissing her neck lightly.

"Don't be sorry," he whispered. "Just be with me."

"Because you'll be gone soon," she breathed. His grip tightened further but he didn't say anything. The silence was unbearable. "I know I've chosen this. But I'm not ready, Taavin. I'm not ready to lose you."

"You never will be."

She twisted, keeping his arms around her. Vi grabbed his face with both her hands, smoothing her fingertips up the cheekbones and browline that she knew so well she could carve it from memory. "If I let you go now, I'll be alone," she barely managed to say around the lump in her throat. She closed her eyes, keeping the distinct prickle of tears safely behind her lids. "I can't do this alone."

Taavin leaned forward, kissing her gently. It was another postponement of the inevitable, but Vi gave into it. The less she had to think about what the next days would hold, the better. For all she knew, this was the last time she could lose herself in the weight of Taavin's body over hers.

He took a step, forcing her to take one backwards. They shuffled to the bed. Taavin's hands slid up her sides, pulling the loose tunic she wore with them. Vi raised her arms over her head, allowing him to undress her.

Her back on the bed, Vi beckoned him atop her. She trailed her fingers down the expanse of his skin and then back up to his face. The man was magic—magic in his bones, magic in the way he moved. This was what she wanted to give herself to, forever. Every shift of their bodies was fire and life, the last brilliant burst before their own flames would be extinguished.

If they were meant to burn, then they burned together.

"In another world," he breathed heavily, pressing his forehead against hers. "I would've married you."

Vi laughed, then responded, equally breathy, "The crown princess of Solaris and the Voice of Yargen… Do you think it would've worked?"

"Of course." He nipped at her earlobe and then kissed down her neck to her collarbone. "It would've united two continents. Our union would've shocked and changed the world."

Fantasizing about such a thing was pain and delight in equal measure. Vi closed her eyes and imagined it as his fingers laced with hers. She imagined she made love to a husband. She imagined their union was one the world could know about—that their lives were their own.

The daydreams continued as he lay next to her, Vi's head on his chest. She traced the lines of his muscles, drawing different ways to connect them as though they were glyphs yet to be discovered. Taavin kissed her forehead from time to time. His own fingers moved lazily on her bare back.

Dawn had come and she was ready to spend the day with him. She was ready to have eternity with him, but all they had was a few short hours before nightfall. As the day continued its relentless march, Vi finally pulled herself from the bed. She sat with her back to Taavin, the watch heavy around her throat.

"It's time. I feel it." Just as she'd felt it the last time Vhalla had come to the curiosity shop.

Taavin stood, moving before her. He hadn't bothered dressing; Vi savored every inch of his glorious frame.

"I'll be the one to return my consciousness." He held out his hand. "All you need to do is give me the watch."

Vi lifted her hands to her neck, slowly unfastening the clasp.

The token was heavy with the weight of destiny. She held it over his waiting palm, her hand trembling.

In the end, he didn't make her do anything. Taavin closed his fingers around the watch, taking it gently from her. Vi looked up at him, silently begging him not to do this.

There was no other choice. This was the end for them. She'd known it was coming all along, and yet she still spent every minute breaking inside.

"If you succeed and the world isn't rebuilt again. If you somehow make it on the other side alive… See this watch still finds its way to the next Taavin." His emerald eyes met hers. "Give him his memories." Taavin cupped her cheek, his fingers in her hair at the nape of her neck. "Let all of me return to you, Vi."

"I will," she lied—the most beautiful lie of her life. She'd seen Yargen's vision. Time for time. The goddess would have her body and return to this world. Taavin's collective memories, everything that made him Taavin, would be locked in a watch, and Vi would be lost forever as a castaway from a bygone world. "I love you, Taavin."

"And I love you, Vi Solaris. I always have, and I always will. My life was never complete until the moment you returned to it. You gave me meaning. You gave me my past and my future." He bent over and claimed her mouth hungrily. She grabbed his shoulders, digging her fingertips into his soft skin. When he pulled away, Vi let out a soft whimper, one he ignored. "It's time."

She stood, watching as he stepped back. Taavin held the watch, his lips murmuring fast and low. The only words she could make out were "*Narro hath loreth,*" to imprint a communication mark.

There were a thousand words she wanted to say. A thousand more times she wanted to tell him she loved him. She was the ninety-third Vi to let him go, but this time hurt more than any of the others. She didn't need to look into the past to know that.

She had held him, loved him, in an impossible time and place. The light of Taavin's glyphs began to consume him. They covered his entire form. His eyes opened and, one last time, they met hers.

Then, his gaze became unfocused. His pupils dilated. He fell to the ground, the watch clattering across the floor.

Vi dragged herself over to him. The world spun as she knelt over the body he had occupied. She touched his arm, trailed her fingers to his shoulder, gently rocking him.

"Taavin," she whispered, staring at his wide, soulless eyes. "Taavin." Vi choked on his name and doubled over.

She sobbed.

Tears flowed freely, her shoulders shaking. She gasped for air. The only pain she'd ever known that came close to this was the knowledge that her world was gone. That everyone she'd loved had been undone with a goddess's broad stroke.

But this.

This.

He was gone, and she would never see him again. This was the end of their love story. This was the last moment she had with him and she hadn't found the words to tell him how much he meant to her. She had decades with him and had never found those perfect words to encapsulate it all. She needed at least another hundred years and then some.

"Taavin, please." A high-pitched wail escaped her. She didn't care if half the Crossroads heard it. Let the world hear her agony. "Please don't go," Vi begged futilely. "Don't take your warmth, your love—it was all I had left." The begging was catharsis. She pleaded with the cruel gods whose game she was trapped in. And yet, without those same gods, she would've never met him worlds ago.

Vi buried her face into his shoulder, weeping until the tears no longer came. She expelled the last of her humanity, the last of her feeling, through her eyes. This was their curse, after all.

They had never been made for happy endings.

Finally, when the sun hung low in the sky, Vi peeled herself away from him. With one hand on his shoulder, she whispered, "*Juth mariy.* Come undone."

His skin began to glow. Pure light peeled off his body like ashes cast from an invisible fire. The magic she had made that held him together unraveled all too easily. Beneath it all was the crystal she had taken from the Caverns. It was the essence of Yargen that had lived in the Sword of Jadar, the Caverns, and the scythe.

She allowed that power to flow into her, as if she could steal some of the last of his essence. After getting a taste of it, Vi couldn't help absorbing it hungrily. It dulled some senses and heightened others. Yargen's power was a balm to her pain and she invited it into her.

All she was missing was the Flame of Yargen.

She was nearly complete.

Blinking, Vi saw the world with new eyes. Everything seemed to have a vibration to it, a faint outline of magic that she had never seen before. In everything was both light and darkness, woven together and held in perfect balance. She looked down at her hands and saw the power of Yargen shining over top them. Tiny glyphs of words she was certain she would've never understood before had meaning.

The language of the gods was becoming known to her. With two of the three parts of Yargen within her, there was no Lightspinning she couldn't do.

Taavin's body had been reduced to obsidian dust. There wasn't even a lock of his hair for her to keep as a memento. Vi reached for the pocket watch. It was all she had left of him, and now she had to give it away.

She dressed slowly in the same robes she wore the last time she met Vhalla in this place. It no longer felt like a costume she donned to play at fate.

Downstairs, Vi destroyed the few remaining objects on the shop's shelves with *juth*. It was an empty catharsis, and did little to make her feel better. Finally, she pulled back the curtain and lit a single candle.

Memories danced like shadow puppets in the flame of ninety-two other moments when a Vi had stood ready to perform this task. Each was a vision she shouldn't have. Each carried an instruction for what must be done, but Vi didn't want to expend the effort to understand what was being asked of her.

She didn't want to think—Mother above, she barely wanted to breathe. Everything was too confusing and wholly too much. Taavin was gone, there was little reason left for Vi to remain in the world as she was. Her time was up. She was ready to submit to Yargen.

"I don't want to do this," Vi whispered into the darkness. Her hand was still clutched around the watch. It had been Taavin's final wish to see it given to Vhalla to ensure the birth of a new Champion. She wanted to honor that, but… "I don't have the strength to give him away."

Then don't, a voice whispered from within. *Let me. I know what must be done, and you have given me enough strength to do it.*

Yargen's words were as clear as her presence. Vi could imagine the goddess standing behind her, hands on Vi's shoulders, ready to swap places. Vi closed her eyes and let out a soft sigh.

"Thank you," she murmured. "I leave it to you."

Her physical eyes opened once more. But all Vi continued to see was darkness. Tonight was the beginning of the end as Vi relinquished her body to Yargen's will.

When she came to, hours later, the watch was gone. Vi could only assume that it had been given to Vhalla, but her mind was blank on the details. Try as she might, Vi couldn't quite grasp why the watch had been so important in the first place.

Every time she reached for the explanation she knew existed, the words evaporated like morning dew.

CONSCIOUSNESS HAD FADED IN and out over the past few weeks. She would go to sleep somewhere, and wake up somewhere else. Her movements were sometimes jerky and sometimes fluid. Vi could feel the goddess settling in, as gracefully as trying to squeeze into a too-tight pair of trousers. Except, the trousers were her skin.

But mortal bodies and mortal minds were surprisingly flexible things… or at least, they could be when prodded enough. The transition wasn't easy, but Vi's awareness slowly returned with consistency, and she started to remember more hours than she forgot. For as much as Yargen wanted to be fully in control, they were still missing a piece of the goddess's essence. Thus, for now, the goddess had to continue to work with Vi, making her will known with whispers or outright commands.

Vi stood at the top of the palace, watching the battle for the future of the Dark Isle unfold. How she'd made it back to Solarin and sneaked past Victor's barriers in the city was unknown to her. Aldrik and Vhalla had ridden into the city with an army from the West, North, and East. Vi didn't move from her spot the entire first day of the battle. The second day of fighting dawned and Vi saw the tides of war already shifting in their favor.

It wouldn't be long now.

She twisted the watch that bore the sun and wing around her neck, staring out the window. This was not her watch. The watch Vi had carried had been smooth and unblemished. That watch had carried something important to her…

… something…

What it was eluded her now.

She'd last seen the watch she now wore on Vhalla's neck, when they were leaving the North after the end of the war. How it had jumped from Vhalla's person to hers was a mystery lost in the darkness of that last, long night in the Crossroads. It was a mystery Vi didn't try to remember. Yargen assured her it was better not to think about it. And, frankly, it seemed so insignificant in the face of all the horrible things she'd seen and let transpire over the years.

Day by day, her emotions became more muted. Perhaps it was survival, since she was now sharing a palace with the mortal lunatic, Victor, who was becoming more and more twisted by the powers his body was not meant to house. Raspian was chewing up Victor alive, savoring each bite of the mortal man.

Or perhaps she was unfazed by the horrors, and the human part of her had left entirely with Taavin. All that remained was the Champion, a vessel waiting to become the goddess.

Taavin. The name had her eyes fluttering closed as she allowed the memory of his hands to touch her all over. It was because of him that she was still here.

She'd told him she would see Victor ended before heading to Salvidia. She would look after Vhalla Yarl. Had it been a vow to him or herself? Had it been a vow at all?

Vi couldn't remember anymore. It didn't really matter. She was here, now, and Victor would be dead soon. A few days more in the grand plan didn't make much of a difference.

Reaching into her pocket, Vi retrieved an earring and uttered, *"Narro hath."*

The connection stretched out into the ether. Vi watched the circling rune as she waited in silence. There was a long pause before Adela's voice was heard reverberating toward her, as if the woman stood on the other side of a long cave.

"I was beginning to think you'd died."

"I am beyond death."

A noise somewhere between a chuckle of amusement and a sigh reverberated through to her. "Always the odd one… I assume this is the moment where you call on me?"

"Yes. You will go to Risen and collect Deneya—my companion that you dropped there about a year ago. She'll be waiting to meet your men to the south of the city. Then you will come to Oparium, where I will meet your men in the Cock and Crow. Finally, we will head to Salvidia so that I might put an end to this vortex."

"Fine, fine." Adela dismissed matters of the world's fate with a yawn. "This will use up your remaining trips. You won't have a way to get back from Salvidia."

"That's acceptable."

"Is it? I hear the elfin'ra are thrilled for fresh meat since their barrier fell. Can't imagine what they'd do to the Champion of—"

"That's for me to worry about, not you," Vi interrupted.

"Very well." Adela made a clear effort to sound both tired and bored of the situation. "I will head to Risen and then meet you in Oparium."

Vi dropped the communication glyph and the connection fizzled. She returned the hoop to her pocket and brought her attention back to the fighting far below. Howling wind slammed against the castle's main entry, battering the heavy doors. Vhalla was there, assaulting it with her gusts.

"*Rhoko*," Vi murmured and watched the crystals Victor had caked the doors with shatter. "You'll need your strength, Vhalla Yarl. Save it for the real battle."

As the army poured into the castle, Vi descended to meet it.

On her path through the various hallways, she unlocked every door that was barred. With waves of her hands, she sent Victor's imitation crystals scattering, though more were likely to grow. Raspian's power radiated from Victor's body, condensing in the halls he frequented.

They looked like Yargen's magic to the naked eye, since they were also godly power given form. But Vi could feel how wrong these stones were. They would soon all be destroyed when the man himself perished, then Raspian would need a new mortal vessel—one that would allow him to face her.

Vi continued to walk calmly as the sounds of war filled the air. She descended to the cleric's old rooms, mostly abandoned now, and donned some clerical garb. Vi put a cloth over her face and knotted her hair simply at the top of her head. Then, she set out to find the clerical portion of the army, adopting her new identity.

Running full tilt to the stables, Vi searched for signs of healers. She saw a few arriving at the end of the vanguard, led by a woman with dark spiral curls—Elecia.

"My lady!" Vi ran over to her. "There's a wing of the castle that I think would be perfect for triage," Vi blurted before Elecia could say anything. She kept her voice frantic, as though she was panicked and not deathly calm. "I can show you—it's a hall not far from here."

"Show me," Elecia demanded. "You five, take the men you think we can save and follow us."

Vi escorted them through the castle to a central dining area that had originally been for servants and staff. It connected up through a stair to the old clerical wing. She looked to Elecia. "Will this do?"

"Well enough. I know where we are. Go and make yourself useful by directing other clerics and wounded here." Elecia spoke to the five who had carried wounded soldiers with them. "Lay them out here, the worst on those tables. We'll overflow to the garden down the hall if we need to."

Vi went to leave, but something stopped her. It wasn't a whisper of the goddess, but words from the young woman she'd once been. *If* she was successful, and the world didn't end… This was the last moment she had to adjust anything in the Solaris Empire.

These final hours were her last chance to right any wrongs.

"Elecia." A sliver of the girl she'd once been returned with the memories of the sting of a betrayal most cruel.

"What?" she said sharply, turning.

"Wounds of the mind can be more damaging and harder to heal than those of the flesh," Vi said. "The man with the sword of wheat lives. Tell the remaining members of his golden brethren to seek him out. They will do what must be done."

Daniel is alive, Vi wanted to say. *Look after him.* But she couldn't. It was hard to speak straight now. Her mouth—her entire body—wasn't really her own anymore, and every action was a negotiation.

"All right…" Elecia said uncertainly and confusion alight in her eyes.

"Excuse me," Vi gave a bow and spun on her heel, leaving before the woman could question her.

She didn't head back down to collect other wounded men and women still lying on the streets of the city, as Elecia had instructed. Instead, she strolled out to a garden and positioned herself hidden among the shrubbery, where she could watch a birdcage greenhouse.

This is a place of fate.

Aldrik appeared, frantic, Vhalla dying in his arms. There was no sign of Victor. He was defeated then.

She'd been right: the magic he'd siphoned from Raspian was little more than a taste. If it had been anything of substance, Vhalla and Aldrik wouldn't have been able to end him. She could already feel the dark god's magic leaving this place like a heavy fog lifting. It dissipated into the ether between the worlds of men and gods, to search for its next host.

Aldrik ran out and then returned with Elecia. But the curly haired woman soon darted from the greenhouse, shouting, "I'm going to try to find Sehra!"

The instinct was right. Out of everyone, Sehra was the only one with enough magic to heal Vhalla. But the girl was not versed enough—not powerful enough—to cure the wounds Vhalla had.

Durroe watt ivin. The words echoed from within. She didn't need to speak them aloud anymore. She was as much the words as the words were her. The glyphs bent to her will, rising to the surface, and giving her Sehra's face.

She stepped forward and drifted down the path before entering the greenhouse.

The first thing she noticed was the smell of roses, potent and bright, warm and oddly familiar.

Where did we smell these before?

Ah, yes.

These were Fiera's roses. Just one inhale took her all the way back to the early days on this world. But that had been a different Vi then, a less *evolved* one. A Vi who had wants and fears—all things she was now able to set aside.

"Sehra," Aldrik pleaded with tears in his eyes. "Save her please, your magic, can it—"

"I understand." Vi's eyes rested on Vhalla. Their last meeting in that long, dark night had been so contentious and painful. Those were emotions she hardly felt now, looking at the girl. Crackles of red lightning illuminated the air around Vhalla, visible only to Vi's new eyes. Her magic had been cast out of balance. *Raspian was a wicked entity, indeed.* Kneeling next to her, Vi spoke gently, "You did well. The crystals' magic is diminishing. They were never meant to be used as they were, manipulated for man's greed. They weren't left with that intent."

"What?" Aldrik asked.

"You saw them. They turn brittle and shatter under their own weight. They will be gone by dawn." *And I will take the magic of the divine off this land for good.* If Vi had one wish left, it was to see that nothing of Raspian, or Yargen, ever returned to the Dark Isle.

"Princess, we need to act quickly," Aldrik urged. "She's dying."

"I know." Vi's attention remained solely on Vhalla. "Vhalla Yarl, after all that you have been through, do you still want to be upon this earth?"

"How can you ask that? Of course I do."

"*Of course,*" Vi repeated. Fate still had plans for Vhalla, after all. Plans that Vi's yet mortal consciousness couldn't fully grasp. "Very well. I will grant you the power of Yargen one more time. I will change this fate set before you."

Her body moved and both of Vi's hands were on Vhalla's cheeks. She felt a small smile cross her lips. Was this what happiness and contentment felt like? She couldn't remember.

Halleth.

The word flowed through her. There weren't any modifiers, any need for clarification—simply, heal. With a tender touch, Vi guided every frayed and out-of-place thread of magic within her body back into its rightful spot. She mended wounds. She sought to return Vhalla to the state she was in before this darkness had settled on the land.

Satisfied, Vi pulled her hands away and stood. She swayed slightly, looking at Vhalla and Aldrik for what she knew was the last time. These people she'd watched over for years. Now, she would leave them to live out their days as they were meant to do.

"Are you all right?" Aldrik asked her.

"I am, but time is short. I'm no longer meant for this world." She had a dark god to settle the score with.

"Sehra, we can seek out another cleric."

"No need." Vi paused at the door. "You did well, but things are only beginning. The vortex still spins." And the only one who could end it was her.

"Sehra!" Vhalla jumped to her feet.

"If that is the name you choose." Vi gave her one last smile and slipped out the door, walking away from the lives of Vhalla and Aldrik one final time.

37

SEA MIST SPRAYED HER face as Vi sat serenely in the rowboat that carried her far out around the corners of the cliffs of Oparium. Her hands were folded neatly in her lap, feet tucked under her. She swayed with the rolling of the ocean, never off-balance, always expecting the next wave that would jostle the little vessel.

The pirates who were escorting her, however, had less luck. They were tossed back and forth in the gray seas. A storm brewed on the horizon; Vi searched it for red lightning.

The *Stormfrost* stood anchored in a wide-mouthed cove. The mist that peeled off of it in sheets acted as a natural camouflage, mostly obscuring the vessel in fog. But there wasn't much travel in these waters yet. Victor had died a mere day ago, and significant rebuilding had to happen before anyone was trading in the seas around the Dark Isle.

The pirates gave her wary glances from time to time, more when they hooked up the rigging. The natural magics surrounding their bodies, the ones Vi was learning made up every living thing, vibrated with apprehension. She made them anxious, which amused her.

At least, she thought it was amusing to her.

One of the men reluctantly offered her his hand to help her on deck and Vi accepted it. He went rigid at her touch and then massaged his palm when her fingertips left it. A smile quirked her lips. Yes, these mortal anxieties were, indeed, amusing, much like she imagined a mother would be amused by their child fretting over a rip in the dress of a beloved doll.

"I was beginning to wonder when you would come," Adela griped, tapping over to her with her cane in hand.

"Everything in its own time. No sooner. No later."

"Yes, well…" For the first time, even Adela seemed off-put by her. "Your friend is below. I trust you remember the cabin."

"Thank you," Vi said and gave a nod.

She descended belowdecks as Adela shouted, "Raise the anchor! Let's get out of this backwater place!"

A woman emerged from a cabin door. Her bright blue eyes met Vi's and they were flooded with relief. Deneya threw her arms around Vi's shoulders. Vi slowly lifted her arms and gently patted the woman's back as she believed a friend would.

"It has been forever."

"Not that long."

"Okay, you're right, it's been about a year." Deneya laughed, pulling away. Her face suddenly became somber. She scanned the otherwise empty hall. "Where's Taavin?"

"His consciousness returned to the watch. Why? I do not know. It was his will I believe. The watch is within Vhalla's possession and the essence of Yargen that his body was constructed from is within me now."

"Okay… that was a lot." Deneya clasped her shoulder, giving her a light shake. "I'm not ashamed to admit that I only followed half of that. And that's okay but, Vi, what really happened?"

"I have told you what has happened."

"No, I mean, with you."

"I have told you what has happened," Vi repeated, slightly more curt. She couldn't blame the mortal for not fully understanding, but it would be tiring to say the same explanation over and over.

"No, you're…" Deneya trailed off again. Confusion furrowed her brow. "You're different now."

"I know."

"It's all the crystal magic, isn't it?"

"Yes."

Deneya stared at her expectantly. Vi suspected she was waiting for her to explain further. But Vi didn't make even a remote effort to do so. It was clearly too much for Deneya to understand.

"How are you holding up?" Deneya asked delicately.

"I'm fine. Do you have it?" Vi shifted the topic of conversation.

"What? Oh. Yes."

"Show me."

Deneya led Vi back into the cabin. It was the same as last time—two bunks on either side of a small window. Beneath the window was a table and on the table was a golden box.

Vi opened it and, with her new eyes, saw the glyphs of a thousand divine words swirling around every speck of ash.

"When they find out the flame is gone, they'll likely kill the Voice for it," Deneya said gravely.

"She served her duty to this world." Vi hoped the words would cheer Deneya, though they didn't look like they did. "She was meant to die." Still, no change in her expression. Vi sighed. "You see, because she died, I will be able to become—"

"I understand what you're saying," Deneya interrupted. "What I don't understand is how you can say it that way."

"What way?" She'd merely been stating fact.

"As if someone's death means nothing." Deneya approached her. "When I last saw you… you negotiated with a pirate for a single boy's life who was nothing more to you than a friend's lover—a friend from another world, even. You enlisted in the army just to save the daughter of a woman you'd once called 'friend.' You fought fate to save a man whom you, in fact, had no relationship with, because he shared the same face as the man who'd raised you." Her purple-ringed eyes searched Vi's. "What happened to that woman?"

"She's gone," Vi said, lightly touching Deneya's forearm. "But it's all right, because I am here now. I will protect this world."

"I don't know who *you* are. And I don't even know if I want you here." Deneya shook her head and stepped away. "What Champion sees the lives of those they're sworn to protect as forfeit? What world is worth protecting if everyone in it is just a piece on some game board for higher powers?" Deneya waited for a response, but Vi kept her mouth closed. She could see the woman didn't really want to hear anything she had to say. With a sigh, Deneya opened the door. "If you need me, I'll be on deck."

Deneya was in pain. The idea of people dying still hurt her. Vi looked to the ashes for solace. Deneya couldn't see the lines of magic that connected everything and everyone to keep the world in balance, like Vi could. She didn't know how life continued on within those unseen connections.

She was oblivious to the meaning in everything.

That was all right. A slight smile crossed her lips. Mortals could be like that, couldn't they? And their shortsightedness made them endearing.

She sat on the lower bunk that did not look like it had been slept in. She took the open box, placed it in her lap, and remained transfixed on its contents.

"But you understand, don't you?" Vi whispered.

I do.

"You will help me see that all these deaths have meaning? That there is no pointless suffering… even if they cannot see how their pain has a hand in fate?"

I will.

"Thank you." Vi beamed from ear to ear. "Is now the time?"

Not yet. Enjoy your final hours on this earth.

"When it happens, will it hurt?"

No, it will not hurt. When it happens, you will not feel anything.

"Good," Vi murmured. She closed her eyes, thinking of the most logical path to Salvidia. It would take them at least five days to get there. That was a lot of time to sit with a goddess. "I would like to ask you something."

You would like to ask me a great many things.

"True." She chuckled faintly. Laughter felt weird now. Even

breathing felt strange, as though it was an unnecessary task her body insisted on doing. Yet, when she tried to stop, her lungs burned until her mouth gave in. "Tell me of the world beyond Salvidia? Tell me what lies beyond the seas, beyond the large continent to the southwest of Meru?"

You wish to know of the whole world.

"Yes." Vi closed her eyes, remembering the vision Yargen had given her of the room high above the world. The place where everything was seen and known.

You will know it, child.

"When?"

When we reach the final stop on your journey, I will give you the opportunity to know everything.

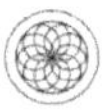

Vi stood on the deck of the vessel as they approached the isle of the elfin'ra. It was a barren place, with stone structures cutting up the horizon like pretend mountains. Somewhere, in the center of it all, were those ritualistic ruins that had stood for centuries. The same ruins Vi had seen in one of her early visions.

In that vision, there had been a body wrapped in a bag. A blood-offering had summoned Raspian in the failed future she'd been born into. Taavin had explained to her then that there were three ways to summon Raspian—the blood of the Voice, the blood of the Champion, or the ashes of the flame.

In this world, Vi came willingly. They would not need her blood because the ashes of the Flame of Yargen would be freely given to summon the dark god.

"I'm not asking my crew to get any closer," Adela grumbled at her side. "I hope you're a strong swimmer."

"Give me a rowboat, that's all I require."

"Fine, then our deal is done."

"There are terms that persist." Vi faced the pirate queen. "The boy Fallor."

"Yes, I understand, I'll never touch him." Adela looked forward. "Now stop staring at me with those creepy eyes."

Adela feared her now, too. The fear that vibrated at her edges was different than the others. Adela still denied being afraid to herself. The pirate had stopped allowing fear to enter her mind long, long ago. So the fear was suppressed and muted. But it *was* fear, nonetheless.

Adela demanded a rowboat be readied. Vi followed close behind.

"Here's your rowboat." The pirate queen motioned to the vessel. "Now I've done all you asked. Tell me of these passageways into the Archives."

Vi looked at Deneya. In her hands was the box holding the ashes of the Flame of Yargen. Just from the way she held herself, she stuck out in the group of pirates. She could never fit in here, and Adela would take her far from Risen if Vi didn't do something.

Perhaps Deneya had been wrong, and there was just enough humanity within her to save an old friend. Vi silently thanked Yargen for making her wait to absorb the last part of the goddess's essence.

"Deneya will show you the passages. Take her back to Risen."

"I'm coming with you," Deneya said, stepping forward.

"No. This is not a place for mortals," Vi said softly. "Go back with them to Risen, and show them what you know of the Archives." Vi suspected Deneya had learned much when she'd gone to procure the Flame.

Deneya searched her face and Vi tried to silently encourage her agreement. This was the only way she would get back to Risen. Vi was out of negotiated trips.

What Deneya did once there was up to her. She could try to flee. Or she could tell them about a passage into the Archives, only to have an ambush waiting.

"All right." It seemed Deneya was smart enough to figure those things out. She stepped forward, awkwardly hovering before Vi. "Be careful saving the world, I guess."

Vi nodded her head. "All will be light."

With the box in hand, Vi sat on the railing of the *Stormfrost* and swung her legs into the rowboat with ease.

"Lower me," Vi commanded, and the pirates followed her orders. As soon as the rowboat met the water, Vi glanced at each of the ropes holding it. With *juth calt*, she destroyed each one. Then, she envisioned the glyph for *kot sorre* in the water behind her. She pushed it forward and the skiff moved over the waves toward the isle of the elfin'ra.

A group of men and women had collected on the beach. They'd likely been drawn over by the sight of the *Stormfrost* in the distance. In Vi's world, this meeting might have been the moment Adela crawled into bed with the elfin'ra. Perhaps even in this world, the pirate queen would've allied herself had it not been for Vi sending Adela away.

The skiff beached itself and Vi released her mental hold on the glyph. The elfin'ra surrounded her in a semicircle. They whispered under their breaths, but none made any motion to attack. They all watched as Vi stood and stepped onto the sand and surf of an island that had been surrounded by an impenetrable barrier for thousands of years.

Finally, a man stepped forward. Vi recognized him from her vision and assumed him to be some sort of high priest of Raspian.

"Who are you?" he asked.

"I am here to meet with your lord," she said to him. "I have brought you the ashes of the Flame of Yargen so that you may summon him. And so that we might once and for all bring an end to the vortex."

38

THE HIGH PRIEST LED her down a beach path that quickly became gravely as it meandered between boulders and then buildings. The isle on the whole was smaller than Vi had expected. Yet she wasn't surprised by its size. No, *she* was surprised; but the goddess who was taking over her mind and body was not.

"Why would Yargen come to us?" the high priest asked casually. He was merely curious, not disbelieving.

"Because this world is held in balance by him and—" Vi almost said *me* "—Yargen. Due to the actions of man, it has been thrown dangerously out of order. I have been working to correct it for thousands of years."

"*You?*" The man looked her up and down with his red eyes. "You are her Champion?"

"I am." There were murmurs at the admission behind her.

"Tell me why I shouldn't slay you here and now and use your blood to summon my lord?" The man grinned wickedly at her. "That way he might usher in a new age of darkness without the burden of Yargen's strongest warrior."

"Because you cannot kill me," Vi said lightly. Part of her was amused at the idea of them trying, though Vi couldn't tell if that was her own feeling or the goddess's. "And because I bring you the ashes willingly."

"I say we kill her now," a woman shouted behind her.

A man clearly agreed because he lunged for her. Vi turned her head and thought, *juth calt*. He seized and fell to the ground. Another woman screamed and rushed over to him, shaking him as a trickle of blood came out of his pasty lips.

"Foolish," the priest sighed, as if the man's death was little more than a frustrating inconvenience. Vi sympathized with the sentiment. "Please, no more of that," he said to the group behind them. All of the others nodded in unison. "Our lord will need your blood fresh for his glorious return. To waste your life is to go against his will."

They crossed into a desolate city square. More people were beginning to follow them as they marched through the cobblestone streets. The elfin'ra on the whole were an emaciated people with hungry eyes.

"Why do you worship Raspian?"

"I'm surprised you would ask." The man glanced at her.

"I admit to being curious."

"Very well… On Meru, there were once temples for both Raspian and Yargen. But after her last victory that ushered in this age of light, Yargen cast Raspian's temple out to sea on a lone island." Vi wondered where that isle might be. Perhaps it was Salvidia. "Unlike all the other times they had done battle, this past time she sealed him off in an unnatural way and ruled that none should worship him."

"There were those who worshiped him before?" Vi tried to imagine a time when worshipers of Yargen and Raspian lived side-by-side. Thanks to the goddess, she had hazy visions of such a thing occurring on ancient Meru.

"Oh yes. What is light without the darkness? Or darkness without the light? I do not revere Yargen." He scrunched his nose in a scowl, accentuating the point. "But I understand her role. I merely choose to relish the darkness. I choose the chaos his beast makes in our world. We all choose this because we believe that in nothingness exists true equality."

Equality through the destruction of all things… Vi certainly didn't agree with the notion. But as the Champion of Yargen, she wasn't supposed to. Perhaps, as he said, all she was meant to do was understand it.

They ascended an endless flight of stairs to a ridge. On the other side, a pathway sloped toward the sea. It ended on a plateau where a lone altar stood. Vi glanced behind her at the red-eyed men and women who had followed them to this point.

All these people were willing sacrifices for Raspian.

She wanted to tell them that their lives still meant something. But in their eyes, their greatest purpose was the one they stood ready to fulfill. She could see it in each one of them, how they walked with relaxed faces, as though in a trance. The closer they got to the altar, the more the elfin'ra moved as one unit, breathing together, marching together.

The moon was high as Vi crossed the threshold of the stones that surrounded the altar. At the center was the relief carving of a dragon, curling around on itself to form a perfect circle. A line had been drawn through the middle and cleaved the whole image in two, off-setting the halves. The image was meant to represent Raspian's dragon breaking free of its lunar prison, ready to reap chaos on the world.

All those assembled moved around the symbol. They formed a second row, then a third. When everyone was in position, five complete circles of elfin'ra stood shoulder to shoulder around the altar.

The head priest positioned himself at the center of the circles, before the altar.

"Bring me the ashes," he commanded.

Vi opened the box. This was the moment she let go of herself. Yargen had made her body with the intention of its eventual return to the goddess. Fulfilling that intention wouldn't hurt. Yargen had told her that much.

Bringing the box to her face, Vi tilted her head down and inhaled deeply. The ashes filled her nose, mouth, and eyes. The magic they contained blinded her and burned her from within, singeing every corner of her body. But there was no pain. She felt only warmth, like sinking deeply into a familiar bed, the blankets layered so high, she never wanted to escape.

Her inner organs seared away. Underneath the once-tender flesh was crystal, and more crystal. Just as she had been in Taavin, the crystal was alive in her. It had always been.

Yargen? she thought. Vi's existence was more inward than outward now.

I am here with you. I am *you.*

Vi coughed and a waterfall of ash cascaded from her mouth and back into the box. Slowly, the world came back into focus. She could see and hear, but her body was fully in Yargen's control. She thought she'd been ready to fully relinquish control, but being a mere observer in her own skin rattled a corner of Vi's consciousness that she thought had been long smothered.

"Summon him for me." Vi felt her mouth form the words, but she did not feel herself say them. Her arms stretched outward, carrying the box forward. Her arms were awash in light, every color swirled atop them, settling into her skin before shifting again. Judging from the reactions on the elfin'ras' faces, this was not her vision alone. This was her new body—the body of a goddess returned.

Together, Vi thought frantically.

A subtle hum was her reply.

I want to take this final step together. I can help you.

How? Yargen demanded. Vi could feel the rest of the unspoken question. How could a mortal help a divine being?

You have fought him as yourself, time and again. He knows you, Vi insisted. *He does not know me. Let me help you end this.*

Eternity drifted through her mind as the goddess debated her proposition. *Very well, mortal. So it shall be.*

The sensation of her body returned to her with tingling waves of magic. In her mind, she stood side-by-side with Yargen. It was not the same control as before; Yargen was not forfeiting out of necessity because her essence was not complete. Yargen was *allowing* Vi this final act.

"Scatter the ashes on his mark, and we shall begin," the priest boomed.

The elfin'ra parted so Vi could enter the symbol. She did as instructed, scattering the ashes all around her. She stepped back out of the symbol, discarded the box, and watched as the elfin'ra closed back the circles again, all looking to their high priest.

The head priest raised his arm and drew a dagger from his belt. He sliced himself from forearm to palm. He held his wound over a stone chute that directed his blood into the carving of the split dragon below. The crimson river flowed unnaturally fast down the carved channels, filling in the outlines. As soon as the symbol was drawn in blood, it began to glow a bright red.

He began chanting, words fast and low that Vi barely recognized. She understood them though Yargen's ears as the language of the gods, but trying to comprehend them with even a fraction of a mortal mind was impossible, so she didn't try. She was beginning to learn the limitations of her shared space—what she could and couldn't control, how much Yargen would let her understand and do.

The men and women of the circles raised their arms, joining their voices with their leader's. The chanting grew louder and louder; some were wailing the words by the end. They threw their heads back in what looked like ecstasy, eyes rolling back.

Dark, ominous clouds rolled in overhead. The wind picked up around them, swirling to this spot, as though there were a void before her, sucking in the air. Vi widened her stance, bracing herself. Even in a place of darkness, her magic connected with the earth. She felt Yargen's powers grounding her, connecting with the land beneath her feet.

The head priest descended from the dais with a purposeful stride. His face was red from shouting, and his eyes glowed a brilliant vermilion. He stared at her issuing a silent challenge; Vi readied herself, allowing ripples of magic to pulsate from her form.

When the man reached the center of the circled zealots, everything reached a crescendo in a bolt of blood-red lightning.

It struck the man, sparking off and sending the other men and women around him flying back. Their bodies, dead, littered the ground. Magic arced through the air like the rebirth of a cosmos, all condensing on a glowing figure rising from where the leader of this dark ritual had once stood.

A roar cut through the ringing in Vi's ears as the man tilted his head back and let out a primordial cry. He should be dead; the lightning had struck him square in the chest. Instead he wore the red light as a second skin, seeming to grow in size before Vi's eyes.

She'd seen all this before. Perhaps that was why she was so calm. She'd seen it in her vision of her failed future, and Yargen had seen it countless times. This was how it always began: a battle to determine which god would rule the next cycle of the world.

The man's jaw elongated with his screams. She watched as it jutted painfully outward. Vi heard the crunching of bones and witnessed new growth to make room for rows of razor-sharp teeth. His skin became hard and leathery as it stretched across plated armor underneath. His face became even more sunken and skull-like. His hair floated around him, swirling with the magic tempest he was birthed within. His eyes rolled back completely, exposing whites that seemed to glow faintly.

Lightning continued to strike around them. The electricity burnt away each of the bodies, as if rabidly consuming what scraps were left of the mortal essence that had brought both divine beings back into the world. Raspian continued to grow, remaking the mortal form that was given to him into something he found suitable.

Then, all at once, the wind died, the lightning ceased, and the world was still.

She didn't have to look around to know that time and space had shifted. Reality distorted around the weight of the gods. The landscape had become even more barren, every building crumbling to dust. The horizon had all but vanished. Over Raspian's right shoulder, the moon hung, cracked and bleeding, about to give birth to a wyvern that was ready to consume the world whole.

This suspended reality, outside of time, was a temporary battleground for them. It was the place the opposing gods could exist simultaneously: not quite the mortal realm and not quite the land of the divine. They could decide the victor here—who would return to the real world and rule, and who would be trapped in this liminal space until the next great battle.

Vi didn't dare take her eyes off the dark god. She watched him warily. At any moment, he would attack, and their final battle would begin. The memory of her final vision, following the destruction of the Crystal Caverns, cut through all of Yargen's influences and stood out in her memory.

The vision, that's why you need me! Vi tried to communicate hastily with the goddess.

Vision? What vision? Vi didn't have a chance to respond as Raspian raised a hand, pointing a clawed finger at her. Lightning punctuated his every movement. He opened his mouth and sound filled her mind.

"You *finally* meet me once more, Yargen."

"It's time," Yargen said through Vi's mouth, using the language of the divine. Vi felt her lips make the sounds and understood the meaning of the words, but she couldn't have repeated them if she tried. "Go willingly into your darkness. Meet me once more in a thousand years."

"After you trapped me in that pit? No, perhaps you should feel what it's like to be contained and smothered with no natural way out."

He lifted his hand and Vi felt the magic collecting there. Yargen acted before she could.

She moved, tilting to the side, her hand swinging back. A spear of light trailed the line of her fingertips through the air. Her hand closed around it. She flung it forward.

The spear crashed against Raspian without so much as stunning him. He lifted his hand and a crack of lightning shot into the sky above. It arced through the clouds and came down as a hailstorm of bolts.

Vi dodged each one quickly. She retreated, gaining distance. Each attack carved static electricity through the air, giving her a split second to react before a bolt of red lightning scarred the earth where she had been standing.

Raspian lowered his hand and lumbered forward. He swung his other hand upward to cleave the land beneath her feet. Her body was sent tumbling back, head over heels. She dug her hands into the earth, seeking purchase. Just when she found her footing, a large rock fell atop her back and Vi cried out in pain.

She might be sharing her mind, but Vi felt every blow as though it was solely her own to bear.

"What a weak mortal form you chose this time," Raspian said with his booming voice. "You have committed yourself to one girl, Yargen, when I have had generations of devotees ready to bleed for me. I took the essence of hundreds. What can one mortal do for you?"

We have to get on the offensive, Vi urged the goddess within her. *He's larger and slower. We can out-maneuver him.*

She lifted her head and brought her hands under her shoulders, pushing upward with a grunt and finding her feet. With a strength no mortal should possess, she dislodged the boulder. Her focus returned to the dark god just in time to see Raspian swinging a clawed hand down toward her.

Vi's instincts kicked in. "*Mysst xieh!*" The words escaped her, even if they no longer needed to be said. She reached across her abdomen. *Mysst soto larrk*, Yargen's voice echoed in her mind as her magic wove a sword into existence. Fingers around the hilt, Vi drew it as if from a sheathe and slashed it across Raspian's lower stomach.

Light flashed off the sword like steel on flint. There wasn't so much as a scratch left behind on his gut. Raspian swung up with his other arm, reaching for her face. Vi bent backwards.

Wildly off balance, she flailed. Yargen's instincts kicked in. Her right foot swung out, her left bent as she tipped backwards, and she allowed herself to fall. A word Vi didn't understand echoed across her mind. She plunged into the earth as though it were a pool of water. The once-hard stone vanished into puffs of light.

Suddenly, she was falling through the sky.

Vi twisted mid-air and looked at the ground beneath her, desperately trying to keep up with the goddess. Raspian spun in place, looking for her. His thunderous steps shook the ground.

A spear of light was back in her hands. Wielding it in both, Vi was ready to use all the momentum of her fall to sink into his shoulder, but a bolt of lightning shot her down from the sky.

Smoking and spinning off-course, she shoved the spear into the ground before her body met the hard earth. She spun around the weapon before it vanished. When Vi landed on the ground, she broke into a run. Raspian had turned to meet her.

Vi stole back control of her body from Yargen. She bounced backward at the last moment, flipping through the air. She'd never done such acrobatics in her life, but being divine had its perks. Yargen seemed to know Vi's intentions at the same time, if not before, they crossed Vi's mind.

When she landed she reared back. *Misst soto gotha.* A bow appeared in her hands and Vi released three arrows at once. As they flew toward Raspian, she threw out a hand, allowing her spark to run rampant. It was a hybrid of her Firebearer magic and *juth starys.*

Fire erupted around Raspian's feet and he let out a roar as one of her arrows sank into a soft spot between the bony plates that protected his body.

So he can be wounded, Vi thought.

Not easily, Yargen replied.

Raspian recovered faster than Vi expected. He raised his arm in a straight line and the earth mirrored his motion. Clay grew like a Groundbreaker's wall. The hand Vi had thrown out in the attack was enveloped in slime. Vi tugged and tugged, but the red earth hardened before she could free herself.

The dark god approached. She could feel static building in the air. Vi readied an attack when her free arm moved without her permission.

Mysst soto laark. The glyphs for the words appeared around her hand as it closed on a sword. In one motion, without any hesitation, her body moved and sliced off its own arm.

Vi screamed, though mostly in her own mind. No blood poured from the wound. It hardly hurt more than any other blow she'd taken, but the shock of cutting off her own arm made her dizzy.

Yargen was in control. She sprinted away from Raspian, pouring power into the severed stub of her arm. Crystals emerged, taking the shape of a new elbow, forearm, and hand. By the time her fingers closed in a fist, the appendage looked as normal as the last.

A wave of red magic erupted behind her. Vi looked over her shoulder, watching it crash over every rock and ledge. There was no way she could outrun it.

Spinning in place, she crossed her arms before her, kneeling. *Mysst xieh rohko hoolo.* The words combined in a way Vi had never expected, but with Yargen's full power surging in her veins, a cocoon of light surrounded her just before the rush of Raspian's power overtook her.

Sharp snaps, like whips against the outside of her barrier, filled her ears. Vi kept her eyes closed, breathing and focusing on nothing more than putting power into her shield. She felt it beginning to crack, worn thin under the assault. Lightning reached in, searching for her like flailing tentacles before fizzling out.

As soon as it faded she bounced upward, pushing the barrier out from her in a blinding flash of light. Raspian roared in frustration, holding his eyes. Vi moved for him. *Mysst sut.* This time, an axe was in her hands.

Wielding it two-handed, she leapt and swung it against the side of his face. Raspian recovered, turned, and opened his mouth. He caught her weapon between his teeth, clamping down and shattering it.

Vi tumbled with her remaining momentum, thrown over to his side. Raspian lunged for her. The weight of worlds threatened to smother her as the god was atop her. He grabbed her shoulder with his claws, pressing her into the ground.

We need to move! Fall in the sky! Vi thought loudly, willing her body to sink into the earth and appear elsewhere.

Too soon.

"*Loft dorh!*" Vi shouted as Raspian swung a claw for her face. He froze, tipping forward, off-balance. Vi scrambled out from underneath him, his claws ripping her shoulder.

On her feet again, Vi spun as Raspian regained control of himself. *Chronot!* Vi thought. It had been Taavin's word. But Taavin had gained the word from the goddess who was now within her, and the magic blessedly worked.

Vi's glyph remained steady on Raspian, fading slowly. *Thank you, Taavin.* She spared a brief thought for the man she loved and the moment she did, her heart beat faster. She felt her breath. She tasted the metallic tang of panic in her mouth. She felt human and *alive*.

Summoning an axe to her hands again, Vi swung it overhead at the nape of Raspian's neck. It stuck, sinking deep into his skin. Magic, not blood, oozed around it, releasing into the air as a dark and rusty haze.

Raspian's features softened. He became clay-like and was absorbed into the earth before Vi's eyes. She spun, searching frantically for him.

Thrusting her arm into the air, a bolt of power shot upward, reflecting off the swiftly cracking moon. In this distorted reality of the gods, it seemed like everything was connected in odd ways. The sky was closer. The ground was malleable. The stars were gone unless they decided to put them there.

Her magic illuminated the barren earth. Light rained down as droplets that seared the ground like acid. A roar echoed across the sky as Raspian emerged from below with an eruption of lightning and lava.

Kot sorre. Vi pushed the lava back with a glyph in each hand, holding it at bay. She locked eyes with the god who was trudging over to her as the molten earth cooled. The sky was still filled with fading light and she could see every gnarled element of his nightmarish form.

Durroe watt ivin. Nine illusions fanned out from her, surrounding Raspian. Vi ran to the right. The other illusions danced around her, darting in and out, trading places. She was the living version of a street urchin's card game—find the queen. Raspian was twisting, trying to keep track of her.

Vi lifted a hand, firing a bolt of pure light at him. Every other illusion repeated the same motion. Raspian swung at one, his claws sinking through it. The mirrored version of her dissipated on the wind as her magic struck him in the back. She danced again, struck again.

"Enough games!" Raspian snarled. He tilted his head back and roared at the sky. Vi didn't have time to react before lightning rained down all around her, one bolt striking her square in the chest. She felt it arc between her ribs. Her body seized as she fell to the ground, wheezing.

Blinking into the void above her, Vi gasped for air.

Keep moving.

She didn't know if it was her voice or Yargen's that commanded it, but Vi struggled to her feet. Her whole body continued to seize and tremble as the lightning created a cage over top of her, pinning her to the ground.

A clawed hand closed around her neck. The red magic sank back into Raspian's arm as he hoisted her into the air. He held her aloft as she gripped at his forearm, gasping for breath.

"An age of darkness will rule this land once more." His terrible voice echoed in her mind as his lifeless eyes locked with hers. Every nightmare too horrible to be remembered come dawn lived in those eyes. "A thousand years of destruction. A thousand years when the land is razed and the earth is reset."

Vi pressed her eyes closed, blocking him out. Aldrik, Vhalla, Taavin, Romulin, Jax, a new Vi—everyone she'd loved in the world she'd been born into still lived in this world. Even if they were not the same people she once knew, even if they never knew her as she was now, they were living, breathing people who deserved a future.

"They deserve a future," she wheezed, opening her eyes. Eyes trained on his shoulder, she snarled a defiant, *"Juth calt!"*

The taut skin stretched over the unnatural armored plates of his body exploded with shards of bone. Raspian roared and his arm went limp at his side. He dropped her and Vi scrambled away, gasping for air.

Halleth, halleth, halleth. Heal me, Yargen, she begged. The light within her flashed brightly atop her skin like a protective coating. She felt the interior damage from Raspian's lightning mend. She felt the tissues in her throat reconnect.

But as she ran, the ground went soft beneath her. She was suddenly up to her waist in murky water. The light above her was going dark. Blood spilled from the fractured moon, flooding the land. Vi tilted her gaze upward and saw an eye open in one of the larger cracks.

She felt like she had been holding her own against the dark god. But the longer the fight dragged on, the more control he was gaining over this temporary bubble they fought in. Soon, she would be drowning in his essence. His beast of chaos would be free of its cage and carry him back to the real world. She would be trapped here forever.

The water was rising. Vi worried that she would soon drown underneath its currents.

Raspian walked atop the water, crossing to her with ease. Vi continued to wade through. She glanced over her shoulder, panicked.

How do I kill him?

You cannot kill him. If our power is whole, neither of us can die.

Then what do I do? Vi frantically asked the goddess within her. *He's gaining the upper hand!*

We must seal him away.

We, not *you*. They were in this together. She had worked for decades toward this moment, to recollect the goddess. And even though she had lost everyone along the way, Yargen still stood by her.

Vi looked down at the water before her. *Mysst xieh.* A glyph appeared and Vi jumped onto it. *Mysst xieh.* Another glyph. She jumped from spinning magic to spinning magic atop the water, racing away from Raspian. She crossed the deepening channel created by the breaking moon toward the bank on the other side.

Her feet on solid ground again, Vi looked back to Raspian, but he was gone. She found high ground and held out both her hands. *Uncose*—Taavin's word for "expose truth." Light flashed across the land, the river of blood evaporated, and Raspian was visible once more.

Vi raced down, bounding across the stones. *Kot sidee!* She pushed a glyph onto him, forcing him to brace himself. *Mysst soto tonc.* A spear appeared in her hand, and she threw it at his head. He grabbed it but in doing so didn't notice how she closed the gap in one giant leap, a sword in hand. Vi plunged it into his gut with a mighty scream.

Darkness exploded from the wound. She released the weapon, watching the magic unravel and the sword disappear as it sank into him. Raspian's glowing, dead eyes fixated on her as darkness sprayed like noxious gas from his body. It filled the air around her, threatening to suffocate her.

Soon, the world was blotted out entirely and the faint glow of magic that coated her body was the only light she could see by. Even the sky had vanished.

Vi spun, looking for any sign of him. She raised a hand, firing a beam of light into the darkness, and then another. She was shooting blind.

Uncose, she tried again. The light flashed out along the earth, but it did nothing for the darkness in the air. Vi moved over the desolate wasteland, climbing over rubble and buildings and what must be the remnants of the lives Raspian's loyal followers had made. Her feet stopped in the center of the glyph of the dragon, split in two. Vi spun in place, still searching.

Lightning cracked behind her, sparking a surreal sense of familiarity. She was in two places at once. She had seen this before.

The vision.

She turned, looking to the lightning on instinct. A plume of smoke rose from the dark spot on the ground, but there was nothing.

She heard the inhale. He was behind her. This was the moment of her vision, a truth that she had seen but that eluded Yargen. This was why she was meant to be in this battle. Vi only had time for one choice, one decision, one word, before his claws and teeth overcame her.

Wein.

Glyphs shot out from her midsection. One rose to the crown of her head and the other sank to her feet. A thick coating stretched over her skin, turning it to stone. A protective barrier, identical to the one Deneya had used that fateful night in the Caverns, now covered her.

Raspian was dedicated to his attack. His teeth and claws struck her barrier, bouncing off harmlessly. Vi spun, no longer turning away from the face of darkness itself. His gigantic arms were outstretched, ready to crush her.

Grasping both sides of his face, her brow furrowed, Vi snarled aloud, "*Suladin dupot chronot hoolo.*"

Suladin—seal him and lock him away once more for a millennium.

Dupot—enhance this power and make it stronger than ever before.

Chronot—slow its natural weakening over time.

Hoolo—stabilize and elongate.

Half of the words were hers and half were Taavin's. They had come from the goddess, but she and Taavin had made them their own. She heard him within her, across time and space, his voice echoing inside her.

The glyphs that surrounded them condensed into crystal. It started at Raspian's feet and began to creep up his body. He roared, swinging for her. Vi released his face, leaving crystal handprints embedded in his flesh, and stepped out of reach.

Her mouth began to move. The language of the gods spilled from her tongue almost like a song. The words were light and airy; they boomed power and whispered twisting glyphs into existence. Despite Raspian's struggles, the crystals continued to grow up his body, caging him.

With a final roar, Raspian promised he would one day return—as he always did.

Then, silence.

Stillness.

The crystals grew toward the moon. They would patch the cracks and smooth over the edges of chaos that nearly escaped into the world she loved.

Yargen's chant hastened, faster and faster. Vi felt power siphoning from her body like someone was pulling an invisible rope from her navel. Light flickered around her, growing ever stronger, fading, then brightening once more as the goddess's essence was drawn out to power the crystals.

This was how the Crystal Caverns had been formed, Vi realized. History was repeating itself. Yargen would split herself again. A new cavern would be made to entomb Raspian, hidden on a new land. And when that tomb was inevitably breached, Yargen would be too weak to fight him.

"Yargen," Vi whispered aloud. Her voice was her own—quivering, tired, scared, and human. "Do not split yourself again. The world needs you whole. Stop this vortex."

Silence within her was the goddess's response. Vi hoped she wasn't too late. She swallowed hard.

"Take me. Take my life. Seal him with all of my magic. Buy time for this world with the time left in me."

Are you certain?

Vi closed her eyes, a tired smile crossing her lips. One final time, the memories of all those she loved flooded her. She thought of the faces of every person she adored—those lost in her world who had lived on in her memories. After this, they would be gone for good.

And she would be gone, too.

"Do it," Vi said with conviction. "This is my destiny. This is what you brought me all this way for. The world still needs you."

Another few seconds of stillness before light exploded out from her. Vi watched as the raw essence of Yargen peeled away from her body. She couldn't stare directly at the goddess; Yargen was too blinding and too incomprehensible in this form. Vi squeezed her eyes shut.

Flames seared her from the inside out as her spark was set free one final time. Every layer of skin boiled off of her bones. Her tongue crisped and her hair singed. She unraveled in the reverse of how Yargen had made her. Cycle after cycle of becoming condensed into this singular moment of release, lifetimes in the making.

And Vi gave herself over to the brilliant void of nothingness.

40

Tick…

… Tock

Tick…
… Tock

Tick… Tock.

Tick. Tock.

Tick-tock.

Something ticked softly in the distance. A sound she shouldn't be able to hear—because she shouldn't have ears, at least not working ones.

She was dead. She'd died.

Hadn't she?

Who was she, anyway?

"Vi Solaris."

Ah, *yes*, that was her name. Or rather, it had been one of her names. She'd had so many of them. *Vi Solaris*—it was a good name. She'd thought that before, hadn't she? Yes, certainly. That name had meant something to her… something important.

"Vi Solaris, it is time to wake up."

It wasn't so much *waking* in the way Vi had once understood it. More like going from a state of stasis to a state of awareness. The light around her was blinding. She could see every color blending together into a brilliance far greater than what mortal eyes were meant to see.

She was a spirit—an idea of life. She was a slice of consciousness in the primordial void, drifting for who knew how long.

I know this place.

"Yes," a familiar voice said. Every man, woman, and child in the world was speaking all at once through the voice.

I shouldn't be here.

"No, this is not a place for you."

Her back settled on something solid. She had been drifting like a leaf through space and had finally settled somewhere soft. Vi blinked, which was odd, because she didn't really have eyelids in this state. Or maybe she did have eyelids? She blinked again. Yes, there were definitely eyelids of some kind.

Around her, a room came into focus. Marble columns supported a ceiling so high she couldn't see it. A bed of plush feathers and clouds surrounded her. A woman with long, black hair stood by a wide window that overlooked the whole world. Vi found herself inhabiting the vision she'd seen after absorbing the crown, but this time from a different vantage.

A familiar face of angular cheeks and sharp eyes regarded her. A silver necklace hung around the woman's neck. The chain was weighted down by a vaguely familiar silver pocket watch that had a sun and wing on its surface.

Ah, that was where the ticking was coming from.

"You look like Fiera this time." Vi smiled, though the expression felt weak and tired.

"Do I?"

Vi remembered the last time that she had been in a similar space with the goddess, a place where eternity stretched on forever. How painful it had been before, to lay eyes on Yargen's raw form. She was grateful now that Yargen took the shape of something—someone— easier to comprehend.

Before.

What had happened before?

"The battle with Raspian," Yargen reminded her gently.

Yes, that was it. The pieces clarified and slotted back into place, one after the other.

"I died," Vi whispered. She sat up. A body was attached to her essence now, though Vi had the distinct feeling that what she perceived as a body was merely another aspect of Yargen's magic. It was another way her mind tried to comprehend an impossible place and situation.

"In a way."

"Death seems fairly black and white."

"I have carved earth from nothingness. I have breathed life into creations of crystal. For me, very little is black and white." Yargen crossed over and sat on the edge of the bed. "Yes, you gave the raw essence of life itself—such a powerful thing—and the body that housed it back to me, so that Raspian could be sealed. But consciousness does little to seal away dark gods."

"You took my body and life essence, but not my mind."

"Just so."

"Was what I gave… enough?"

"Yes." Yargen smiled with Fiera's lips. It was as tender and warm as the real princess's.

"Then the world…"

"The world you helped shape will be safe from Raspian for another thousand or two thousand years, perhaps more if we're lucky. Things were not rebuilt, this time." The smile became slightly coy and her eyes a little sad. "Eventually, he will break free of that containment. Or mortals will somehow find a way to set him free, whether they know what they're doing or not. Though I have made sure he is well hidden, this time."

"I see." Vi smoothed her hand over the foggy blanket atop her, watching glittering starlight dance underneath her fingers.

"Do not despair." Yargen rested her hand on hers gently. Magic and life shot through her. Vi inhaled sharply. Feelings were starting to return. Vi felt like laughing and weeping, singing and screaming, all at once. "That is simply the order of things. When he returns, I will be ready."

"You are not fractured, then?"

"Do I look fractured to you?"

"I've been told my eyes can lie to me around the divine, so I've stopped trusting them in moments like these."

Yargen chuckled at that. The sound was pure delight and as sweet as bells. "You have been an amusing one to watch, all these revolutions of the vortex."

"It's really all over then…" Vi looked out the window. She saw nothing but a bright blue sky, clear and filled with light. She brought her attention back to Yargen. "So why am I still here?"

"That is something I have debated for many mortal years now."

"Years?"

"For me, it has only been a moment." Yargen stood once more, looking down at her with Fiera's fiery eyes. "I have been thinking while I harbored your consciousness, keeping it safe from the passage of time. What is a just reward for a Champion who has served me so faithfully across the ages? Then, it occurred to me…

"Do you wish to return to that world?"

"What?" Vi whispered. Something jolted in her chest. It felt like a heartbeat, the first of what could be many.

"You enabled me to return the watch to Vhalla Yarl, and a Vi Solaris was born into the world you have saved. This new Vi's body is as you know it, though the world is slightly different than you remember. Your actions did cause ripples of change these past eighteen years. However, if it would please you, I could return your mind to that form."

Vi considered this, trying to wrap her head around it. "What would happen to the new Vi's consciousness? Would she know what's happened?"

"No, she wouldn't. You and she are mirrors; it would be a seamless merger of your awareness. Though there might be some memories and feelings from your separate childhoods that would get confused from time to time—memories you won't be sure which one of you made."

"Would it feel like two people at once?" Vi had that sensation before with Yargen. She wasn't keen to have it again.

"No. You would have one mind. One, final Vi Solaris."

"Would I feel like me?"

"Mortal feelings are elusive to me."

Vi looked around the room, considering this offer. She would be returned to the body of the ninety-fourth Vi Solaris, born into the world she'd saved. It would be a chance to live in a time that was not ending. And, if Yargen was to be believed, it wouldn't result in pain or confusion for the girl who was currently walking in that skin.

"What's the alternative?" Vi dared to ask.

"I would fully join you with my essence. You would live forever as an aspect of me. You would know every corner of this world and whatever comes next in a way a mortal never could, just as I promised."

"Are my parents and brother alive in this new world?" Yargen had mentioned ripples of change caused by her actions. Just because there had been a Vhalla and Aldrik when she'd left the Dark Isle didn't mean they still lived now.

"They are."

Relief made her dizzy and a sound somewhere between laughter and a sob escaped her. There were changes, but the people she held dearest were still there. She could still have a life with them—the life she'd been robbed of. "Tell me one more thing: is there a new Taavin?"

"Yes."

"Then I wish to return," Vi said gingerly, a smile working its way onto her lips. "I would rather live one life with them than an eternity without." Vi paused, then added hastily, "No offense, your magnificence."

Yargen laughed in delight once more. She crossed over to the bed and leaned forward. "I didn't expect you to choose differently."

Vi stared at the watch around the goddess's neck, realizing where it had come from. It was the timepiece Yargen had traded with Vhalla during that long, dark night. That meant the watch with Taavin's essence was still out there.

"Time for time," Vi whispered.

Yargen lifted her hand, touching the watch with a smile. "When Aldrik gave this to Vhalla, he bestowed on her his minutes, his hours, his days. I think he would be very pleased to know he was really giving them to you."

A thousand questions danced on her tongue but she remained in stunned silence as Yargen leaned forward. The visage of Fiera melted away to pure light. The goddess placed a single, tender kiss on Vi's forehead.

The air was sucked from Vi's lungs as she fell backward and descended from the realm of the divine one final time.

The room vanished into a misty light. Wind sped around her. Her eyes dipped closed and—

Vi woke with a gasp. She jolted forward, covers thrown from her shoulders and pooling around her waist. The smell of fresh wood, sap, and the damp tang of morning filled her nose. It was a familiar, nostalgic scent—one she hadn't smelled in a long time.

She looked around in the darkness. The walls were smoothed and polished. Overhead was a gnarled ceiling of decorative roots and branches that spilled down, weaving into the four corners of her bed. Across from the foot of the bed was a dresser, adorned with carefully painted portraits in gilded frames.

Turning, Vi peered at the candle on her bedside table. Her breath hitched as she lifted a hand.

The candle lit on command.

Vi threw off the familiar covers, standing. She grabbed at the sleeping gown she wore, feeling the cotton. She rushed over to the corner of the room. There, a pile of supplies was neatly stacked in the corner between the dresser and the window. A quiver she knew so very well hung on its peg, bow attached. She ran her fingertips over the fletchings of the arrows and the Solaris sigil emblazoned in the quiver's leather.

This was her room. Everything was just as she remembered it: the clothes she'd laid out for her birthday hunt, the candle she'd struggled to light. That meant she had woken at the dawn of her seventeenth birthday once more.

That also meant—

Vi sprinted from the bedroom. Her heart was racing faster than her feet. Every emotion was competing for dominance within her. Yargen's hold over her body and mind had been so slow that Vi hadn't realized for how long her emotions had been muted. It seemed like it'd been forever since she'd truly felt anything.

A strangled noise of hope and fear escaped her mouth as she rushed into the main living space of the quarters. The couches were in a slightly different spot than she remembered. Or… were they?

Yargen said time had continued along while her consciousness had been in stasis. There were changes and variations from the world she'd come from. Vi shook her head, turning to the door that led to her personal study. Only one thing mattered right now.

She yanked on it so hard that it slammed into the wall as Vi rushed into the room. Every map was where she remembered. The table where she'd drawn them was as much of a mess as she'd last left it.

Five presents were stacked atop the drafting table, neatly piled and out of place in the room.

"Don't let this have changed," she pleaded. *Let Fritz's gift be a stone in the river.*

Vi pushed aside four of the gifts and reached for a small parcel wrapped in black silk. It was feather-light and a had a black envelope slid under a black ribbon. Vi's fingers trembled as she ripped open the seal on the letter—the Broken Moon of the Tower of Sorcerers. The symbol of the Tower was something she needed to change the instant she got back to the palace. She couldn't look at it now without seeing Raspian's followers.

But Sorcerers and the sorting of symbols could wait. Vi hurriedly skimmed the letter that began with, *"Dear Vi"* and ended with, *"Your friend who cannot wait to meet and teach you, Fritznangle Chareem, Minister of Sorcery."* She didn't need to read every word. She knew what it said.

Unwrapping the silken scarf, Vi found a silver pocket watch. She smoothed her fingers over its tarnished face. Her hands clutched it so tightly that her fingernails dug into her palms and her knuckles were white.

Vi dropped to her knees, tears flowing down her cheeks. Every emotion rushed through her at once. It made her tongue thick and her words awkward.

"Narro haath," she dared to whisper.

Light sparked around her clenched hands. It formed the shape of a familiar glyph, one she understood better than ever. Magic raced across the ether, connecting her with the man whose communication mark had been imprinted long ago on this most precious token.

Silence.

And then, a familiar voice.

"What… Who—"

Vi covered her mouth, tears still falling in rivers down her cheeks. A new dawn broke through her window. With all the strength she could muster, Vi managed to say, "Hello, Taavin."

Vi stood on the bow of the greatest vessel ever constructed for the Imperial Armada. She had spent her last month in the North drawing out ideas for the plans, based off the *Stormfrost* and what she had seen in Meru's fleet.

Of course, an actual shipwright in Solarin had to go through all of her drawings and turn them into usable blueprints. That process had taken nearly four months of convincing him that, yes, there were ways to build ships in the manner she'd drawn. He merely needed to expand his way of thinking and broaden what he considered "possible." Leveraging her family's relationship with Erion Le'Dan had ultimately helped expedite the process.

The construction had taken just over a year in a dry dock to the north of Norin.

It had been two agonizingly slow years until she'd christened the ship and they'd set sail. All of the patience she'd learned seemed to have been a casualty of her battle with Raspian. But in the end, the time it took to build was a good thing. There were other matters that had to fall into place.

Diplomacy took time, especially between two continents that had been closed off to each other for centuries.

"Is that it?" Ellene bounced from foot to foot. Vi had expected more of a fight from Sehra when she'd proposed that Ellene come along on this first diplomatic trip. But the moment Vi pointed out that this was the perfect opportunity for Ellene to spend some time studying Lightspinning in the land that invented it, Sehra instantly agreed.

"Yes. Careful, or you'll fall over the railing."

"I will not. I'm not that clumsy."

"You certainly are," Jayme said dryly. She leaned against the railing to Vi's left. Her back was to the land that had just come in sight.

"I am not!"

Jayme shot Vi a knowing grin that seemed to say *It's just too easy to rile her, isn't it?*

In the seventeen years Vi's consciousness had floated in Yargen's primordial stasis, the world had continued. But things were different in this world—different, and in so many ways, better.

There was no Adela terrorizing the seas of the Shattered Isles. After thieving from the Archives, the pirate queen decided to make herself scarce. Which also meant that Jayme was never recruited to act against Vi.

Because of what Vi had mentioned to Elecia, Daniel's existence was discovered much sooner. Elecia had told Jax, who went East immediately after the end of the war, and multiple times after. He found Daniel and, while he respected the man's wishes to remain mostly anonymous, he sent word to Aldrik and Vhalla. The royals had kept Daniel's life private and the man well taken care of.

So while Vi could still sense Jayme had mixed feelings about certain things, especially when it came to the crown's conquest and Mad King Victor, she didn't see the precursors of betrayal in the woman's eyes.

"I'm really glad you're both here with me," Vi said tenderly.

"Oh goodness, here she goes again." Ellene rolled her eyes. "You're not going to get all sappy on us for the next hour, are you? You've been terrible ever since you turned seventeen."

"No, I haven't!" She laughed, knowing well her friend was correct. Emotions were lovely and Vi had enjoyed feeling them again over the past two years. Perhaps a little too much, at times. "I'm just glad we could make this voyage together."

"I'm excited to see what the Crescent Continent holds." Jayme finally looked over her shoulder at the strip of land growing in size in the distance.

Footsteps approached from behind them. "I think that goes for all of us."

Jax and Elecia joined them at the bow. Elecia was dressed in finery that befit the Lady of the West. But Vi was still growing accustomed to seeing Jax in formal ceremonial garb.

She had memories of their wedding. Or rather, the Vi who had grown up in this world had those memories. The ceremony had taken place in the Cathedral of the Mother in Norin, and what Vi could picture was a breathtaking affair.

Elecia had grown impatient with Jax about five years ago. He was always stalling their relationship for "no reason." First it was heading to the East. Next it was setting up a new Golden Guard in the South. Then it was accepting a position to watch over Vi in the North when the first appointee—a man Vi had been too young to remember—retired.

In a way, Vi had now lived the best of both worlds. Her first childhood was full of memories in which she'd grown up with Jax as her surrogate father. But she also had memories of him finally chasing after his happily ever after. Now, she got to see him standing hand-in-hand with the woman he'd loved in every world.

Fortunately, while she could parse the memories apart, nothing was confusing or painful. It didn't feel as though she was competing with someone else for headspace. Yargen had been blessedly correct in that respect. And, as far as she could tell, the people she loved were none the wiser that her consciousness had undergone a transformation.

Vi turned her attention back to Risen.

The world spun, seasons changed, and people changed, but the one constant remained: love—the love of friends and family, the love that bound people together through the ages.

That was the love she now sought.

"You should go below and get ready, Vi," Elecia said thoughtfully. "We'll be dropping anchor before you know it."

"You're right. Excuse me."

Her cabin was one of the largest on the vessel. It was positioned in the back, with grand windows overlooking the sea. In many ways, it reminded her of Adela's cabin. Vi smiled to herself every time she entered, wondering what the pirate queen would think if she knew she'd inspired the flagship of Admiral Crown Princess Vi Solaris's budding armada.

The clothing she'd requested was neatly laid out: a fitted pair of leggings with a white split tunic that bore the Solaris crest. A wide belt attached a ceremonial sword to her hip. Everything was carefully embroidered in gold thread, reminiscent of a coat she knew so well she could draw it from memory.

On top of the tunic was a simple envelope. Vi lifted it, flipping it over. She'd said goodbye to her family when she left—that had been the hardest part, especially after getting to live nearly three years with them in Solarin while all the logistics for her voyage were being worked out.

The Senate was still adamant that it was too risky to have both heirs running all over the world and putting themselves in harm's way. But Vi got the impression Romulin would be all right staying in Solarin and working with Andru, the son of the head of Senate, and Minister Fritz.

Before she left, Vi had tasked them with brainstorming and ironing out some details for her next big idea. It was still in its infancy, but in a few years' time, if all went according to plan, Solaris and the Kingdoms of Meru would be reunited. And that called for a celebration to shake the ages.

Vi would oversee the diplomatic elements of treaties and alliances. Romulin, Andru, and Fritz would run with her wild ideas of lavish parties, friendly sorcerer competitions, and other ways to share knowledge and culture. She couldn't wait to see what would ultimately come to pass.

Her parents didn't come on the voyage because they refused to be separated. Not because they couldn't be; they simply didn't want to be. Vi didn't argue with that reasoning. She knew better than most what they'd gone through to be together now.

On the back of the envelope was a golden seal bearing the sun. She slid her finger underneath to break it, then slid out the letter and sat on the bed to read it.

Our dearest daughter,

We asked Elecia to give you this on your arrival to the Crescent Continent for one final reminder of home before you step off onto a new land for the first time.

Vi cracked a smile at the first line. It would be her first time… in this body.

We will of course remind you that these negotiations could open trade that would change our Empire and the lives of our people for the better. But we know you already understand this. After all, you were the one who somehow managed to open discussions with a closed off land that we, and our forefathers, had long since written off.

You will conduct yourself with grace and poise, of that we're certain. You've grown into a young woman wise beyond her years. We are so proud, and have every faith in you.

But the most important thing we wished to remind you of is that this is an opportunity for a grand adventure. This is the start of your journey. This is the moment you begin to write your story.

Go and explore. Seek adventure. Seek the world we have always seen you dreaming of.

When you are ready to return, your throne will be here waiting. We, and your brother, will be here waiting with all our love. But don't worry for us. We'll be fine.

For the first time, she could believe it. Solaris had a bright future ahead of it.

Our love goes with you. We cannot wait to hear all the stories you will have to tell when you return… Whenever that might be.

Your parents

Vi brought the letter to her lips and kissed it gently. "I love you too, mother, father," she whispered against the parchment. She could almost detect the faint scent of her mother's perfume, mixing with the smoke that always seemed to coat her father's clothes.

She read the letter twice more before setting it aside and beginning to dress. It felt like permission. It felt as though, somehow, her parents understood. One story had ended, but thanks to Yargen, she had a new one just beginning. Vi couldn't stop beaming from ear to ear, and she bounded back on deck in time to see the details of Risen coming into focus.

They anchored as close as possible to the port—close enough that Vi could see the ceremonial delegation that lined the docks, ready to receive them. Her heart raced as she took her position in the front of the rowboat that would take her ashore.

Elecia and Jax were behind her. Ellene and Jayme were behind them in a separate vessel. Vi worried the silver ring in the shape of a phoenix that she wore on the middle finger of her right hand. It was not Fiera's exact ring, but her father had commissioned it from old schematics found in the Le'Dan archives as a gift for her eighteenth birthday.

The rowboats pulled up to a low dock and Lumeria's guard was ready to receive them. Men offered her assistance, bowing their heads as they helped her out of the small boat. Somehow, Vi managed to disembark without stumbling, and she said a quiet thanks to the sun above.

Lumeria stood down the dock, hidden behind her veil and flowing fabrics. A line of honor guards stood on either side, creating a walkway for Vi. She approached stiffly and bowed low.

"Your highness, Queen Lumeria, it is an honor to meet you."

"It is," she replied in her whispering tones. "Or should I say, meet again? Which would you prefer?"

Vi straightened in shock. She had told Deneya years ago that she could share the truth with Lumeria in her reports, but… she hadn't been expecting Lumeria to actually *believe* the stories. Jax and Elecia arrived at that moment. She was prevented from questioning as they bowed.

"Your highness, I present Lady Elecia of the West and her husband, Lord Jax."

"Welcome to Meru, Lady Elecia and Lord Jax."

Vi turned to the next two. "This is Lady Ellene of the North—she is blessed with Lightspinning—and her honor guard, Jayme." Vi had changed Jayme's post before they set sail.

Even though things were better in this world, Vi still thought it was healthier for her and Jayme if the woman reported to Ellene. Besides, Vi didn't know where her travels would take her, and Jayme needed to remain on the same continent as her father as much as possible.

"Welcome." Lumeria raised her voice slightly, and said, "See that the dignitaries and their guards are shown to the palace."

Soldiers stepped forward, each one appointed to a different person. Vi watched as they paired up with her friends and family. There was not a single trace of foul play, which was a welcome change from the last time she'd stepped foot in Risen.

"I am to be your escort."

She met a familiar pair of blue eyes. "Deneya," Vi said with a sigh of relief, and threw her arms around the woman.

"This is a nice change from the last time I saw you on the *Stormfrost*. It's good to see you again," Deneya whispered as she held Vi in a crushing embrace. She pulled away abruptly and looked Vi up and down with narrowed eyes. "It really is *you* this time, isn't it?"

"Yes, it is. I'm goddess-free."

"Good. I mean, not good. Yargen don't smite me, I just like my friend. Now, Vi, follow me." Deneya stopped her rambling and started after the rest of the procession.

"I'm glad nothing horrible befell you for… you know." Vi stopped herself before she could say "stealing the Flame of Yargen."

"I'm just glad I made it back in time." Deneya and Vi had lost their communication token when Vi's body had been destroyed. Without it, they'd only been able to exchange a few letters, in which they didn't dare write too much. So there were still large gaps Vi was ready to have filled in between now and when they'd parted ways on the *Stormfrost* twenty years ago.

"In time for what?"

"To make sure my Queen knew of Lord Ulvarth's treachery." Deneya shook her head sadly in the face of Vi's shock. "Stealing the

Flame of Yargen and framing the last Voice."

"Then the Voice survived?" she asked hopefully.

"Unfortunately, the woman had already been put to death."

Vi winced. She felt every bit of guilt and sorrow she should've felt on the *Stormfrost*.

"Tell me, at least, that Ulvarth faced the same fate."

"That's the greatest crime of them all. He's been stalling trials and leveraging favors from friends in high places to spare his neck from the executioner's block." Deneya scowled. "Lumeria is fed up and, for now, has locked him up and thrown away the key. Hopefully being away from public eye will cool his influence, and she can revisit the matter in the future."

"Good to know that justice for the wicked being elusive isn't exclusive to Solaris." Vi had spent the past few years entrenching herself in Solarin's politics. Some of the records she'd read—like a sham trial involving her own mother—made her skin crawl.

"Indeed." Deneya paused. "Are you all right with a detour?"

"If we have time?" Vi glanced back to Lumeria.

"She made sure we have time for this." Deneya stepped off into a side alley and Vi followed. It was right before the public crowds began to thicken, ready to watch and welcome the first dignitaries from the Dark Isle in centuries.

Deneya led her down the narrow alley to the back of building that lined the port. They climbed several flights of rusted stairs toward the top floor. Deneya stepped up to the door, opened it with a flourish, ushered Vi inside, and closed it behind her.

Inside was a simple room—a meeting space for traders, perhaps, judging by the tables and chairs. A row of windows overlooked the port and Vi could see her own vessel in the distance. The sun glistened off the sea, casting everything in a warm glow. Including the man who stood, framed by light.

Vi moved forward in a trance. She held her breath until he turned to face her, then exhaled his name like a prayer. "*Taavin.*"

"Vi Solaris." He still regarded her warily. It was the physical embodiment of the verbal distance he'd kept in all of their communications through the watch she now wore.

She approached slowly, as though he were an animal that might spook. "It's good to see you."

"Yes, well. I only agreed to this meeting because you said you had something for me." He was as stiff as Vi remembered him being the first few times they'd met. The memories brought a nostalgic smile to her lips, and that only seemed to frustrate him more.

Just as there had been a Vi born into this world, so there was a Taavin. But like all the other ninety-three Taavins, he lacked his memories.

Reaching up to her neck, Vi undid the chain there. She held out the silver pocket watch to him. Taavin accepted it with both hands, running his fingers over it.

"This… is what has my mark."

"Yes." Vi motioned to one of the sofas. "Let's sit?" He followed her, still fascinated by the watch.

"You said when we were in person, you would tell me how you got this."

"It will be easier to show you." She paused, hesitating. The crescent-shaped scar was missing on his face, and his hair was shorter than she remembered, but everything else about the man was the same. Should she force him to endure the memories of his past selves? Was it cruel to bestow that on him once more?

Give him his memories. Let me return to you, Vi.

"Show me… how?"

"I'd like to give you a choice," she said softly. "It will be a lot to take all at once. It might hurt. And once I give you this knowledge, I can never take it back."

He chuckled deeply. "I'm not afraid of whatever magic you have."

"Then you wish to know?"

"I did not help you come all this way to stop now."

Vi closed her eyes and took a deep breath. She opened them with purpose, looked him right in the eye, and said, "*Thrumsana.*"

Glyphs appeared from the watch in his hands—layers and layers of them. They swirled around him, filling the room with symbols that Vi could still understand even though Yargen was long gone from her body and mind. In every shining symbol, she saw an entire turn of the vortex written in the language of the gods. She saw joy and sorrow, victory and defeat—she saw herself and Taavin in every one.

Taavin dropped the watch and clutched his head. He trembled, groaning. Vi reached for him.

"It'll be all right." She wrapped her arms tightly around his shoulders. "It'll be over soon."

His shakes became violent but Vi only held him tighter. The magic began to shine brighter. Taavin's ragged gasps grew longer and longer. The watch had fallen to the floor and it now glowed white-hot from the endless release of magic. Vi clutched the man in her arms, watching as the watch cracked, released an exhale of fire like a dying breath, and then disintegrated to dark ash.

The magic faded and the room returned to normal. Taavin pushed her away roughly, staggering to the windows. He placed both hands on the panes and continued to inhale and exhale loudly.

Vi stood, waiting for his verdict. Would he truly remember her? Would he still be the Taavin she knew?

Would he hate her for the pain she'd forced him to endure one final time?

She dared to approach him. He still didn't turn. "Taavin?" she whispered, hoping and pleading at the same time.

He spun in place, looking at her with shining emerald eyes. Vi saw recognition. *He knew her.*

A surprised, strangled noise escaped her as something like a laugh of relief. Taavin moved for her and Vi stood in joyful shock. *This should be impossible.*

And yet, those were his arms wrapped around her. His hand on her face, in her hair. His lips pressed to hers—him kissing her as though they were still saying goodbye. Vi's fingers knotted in his clothes, tugging him closer still. She deepened the kiss, as if to remind him that this was *hello.*

The world wasn't ending any longer, though it still contained its share of problems. Light and darkness, chaos and order—everything was precariously balanced. Vi knew better than most that every action was what kept them—all of them—from slipping into despair.

A kiss couldn't change any of that. A kiss wouldn't ensure the happiness of Meru and the Solaris Empire, and all the people within for years to come. A kiss wouldn't be the end of the brutal dance of light and darkness.

But if one kiss could, this kiss would be it.

... Not ready to say good bye to Vi and Taavin?

Flip the page...

Get a BONUS SCENE!

Want more Vi and Taavin?

Want a sneak peek of where the Air Awakens world will head in the next novel set in this universe?

Head to my website and subscribe to my newsletter to get a BONUS SCENE that takes place 2 years after the Epilogue:

http://elisekova.com/vortex-bonus-scene

ABOUT THE AUTHOR

ELISE KOVA has always had a profound love of fantastical worlds. Somehow, she managed to focus on the real world long enough to graduate with a Master's in Business Administration before crawling back under her favorite writing blanket to conceptualize her next magic system. She currently lives in St. Petersburg, Florida, and when she is not writing can be found playing video games, watching anime, or talking with readers on social media.

She invites readers to get first looks, giveaways, and more by subscribing to her newsletter at: http://elisekova.com/subscribe

Visit her on the web at:
http://elisekova.com/
https://twitter.com/EliseKova
https://www.facebook.com/AuthorEliseKova/
https://www.instagram.com/elise.kova/
See all of Elise's titles on her Amazon page:
http://author.to/EliseKova

Enjoy Vi's Story?
See where it all began by reading Vhalla's tale...

THE AIR AWAKENS SERIES

A library apprentice... A sorcerer princes... And an unbreakable magic bond. The rare elemental magic that lies in Vhalla Yarl will not only change the Empire's future, but the heart of its Crown Prince. Perfect for readers who want magic and romance!

Series complete!

"I read the full series in a just two days. The worlds was thrilling and the characters endearing... Recommend for fans of Sarah J. Maas and high fantasy"
- Kristen, 5 Star Amazon Review

ACKNOWLEDGEMENTS

My Readers — I want to start by acknowledging all of you. Without you, there would be no story, no books, and no world of Air Awakens. Some of you were with me from the start and have seen this world evolve and grow. Or, you may have just joined me with Vortex Chronicles. However long you've been reading my work, thank you. This book, this world, is truly for each and every one of you and it wouldn't have happened without you with me every step of the way.

The Man — From late, sleepless nights, to early starts, you're with me every step of the way. Without your support both professionally and personally I wouldn't be where I am now. Thank you for all the hours you spent with me, talking through story ideas, listening to me as I struggled to find the best narrative path forward, and helping me with your insights. Thank you for pulling me off the kitchen floor when I was down, or pulling me away from my computer when I couldn't take anymore. You are truly my muse and my light.

Rebecca — I asked you to push me, and you delivered. I will never be able to express appropriate gratitude for your patience and help throughout this series. This story evolved so much thanks to you. You challenged me to be better and work harder. I greatly appreciate everything you did to help make this story what it is.

Michelle — You are an incredible friend and colleague in this crazy author career. I appreciate your insights. I love your candor. And I am so inspired by you. Thank you for talking me out of the initial terrible ending I had for this series and pushing me to make something much, much better.(I hope you enjoyed what I decided on!)

Kate — Thank you for your help and support throughout this series. You came in at the eleventh hour and turned things around with a speed I didn't think possible. I appreciate everything you've done for me.

Danielle — You have seen every high and low, good day and bad with this series, and you stuck with me through all of it. I could not have asked for, or dreamed of, a better friend in the publishing world. Thank you for all your cheer-leading, insight, and support along the way.

The Noble Order of Female Fantasy Authors — Ladies, you have become a cornerstone of my day to day survival. You are each unique, incredibly talented, and profoundly supportive. Thank you so much for talking me through the good times and bad, for being there to sprint with, and for being the best friends one could hope for.

Mary and Sarah — I know this manuscript changed a lot from the one you beta read for me. Please know, in part, it was due to your feedback! Thank you for helping me make my work better. I really appreciated all of your insights.

Amanda — From arranging swaps, to general support, you are always there. I don't know how you do it all AND remain such a beautiful soul, but here we are. Thank you for everything. I truly appreciate all you do for me both personally and professionally.

Lux — You're such a lovely person; it has been my supreme delight to sprint with you throughout this series. I hope we can motivate and inspire each other for years to come. I am honored to call you friend.

Devin, Mia, and Veronica — Thank you all for your continued support of me, my work, and my career. Over the past year you have all helped look for ways for me to get my work out into the world. Hopefully, we can do the same with Vortex Chronicles and many more books in the years to come.

The Tower Guard — Last, but certainly not least... To all of my Tower Guard members, you are so essential for me to keep continuing on as an author. Knowing you are in my corner, having you all to laugh and cry with, has really made this career such a profound experience. Thank you for all you've done in helping me get my books out into the world. Here's to the next one!